BORDER COUNTRY

LIBRARY OF WALES

Raymond Williams was born in the Welsh border village of Pandy in 1921. He was educated at Abergavenny Grammar School and at Trinity College, Cambridge and he served in the Second World War as a Captain in the 21st Anti-Tank Regiment, Royal Artillery. After the war he began an influential career in education with the Extra Mural Department at Oxford University. His life-long concern with the interface between social development and cultural process marked him out as one of the most perceptive and influential intellectual figures of his generation.

He returned to Cambridge as a Lecturer in 1961 and was appointed its first Professor of Drama in 1974. His best-known publications include *Culture and Society* (1958), *The Long Revolution* (1961), *The Country and the City* (1973), *Keywords* (1976) and *Marxism and Literature* (1977).

Raymond Williams was an acclaimed cultural critic and commentator but he considered all of his writing, including fiction, to be connected. *Border Country* (1960) was the first of a trilogy of novels with a predominantly Welsh theme or setting, and his engagement with Wales continued in the political thriller *The Volunteers* (1978), *Loyalties* (1985) and the massive two-volume *People of the Black Mountains* (1988-90). He died in 1988.

BORDER COUNTRY

RAYMOND WILLIAMS

PARTHIAN
LIBRARY OF WALES

Parthian, Cardigan SA43 1ED
www.parthianbooks.com
The Library of Wales is a Welsh Government initiative which highlights and
celebrates Wales' literary heritage in the English language.
Published with the financial support of the Welsh Books Council.
www.thelibraryofwales.com
Series Editor: Dai Smith
First published in 1960
© Raymond Williams 1960
Library of Wales edition published 2006
Reprinted 2024
Foreword © Dai Smith 2005
ISBN: 9 781902 638812
Cover design by Marc Jennings
Cover image: *Little Train* (1948), by Charles Burton
Typeset by Elaine Sharples
Printed by 4edge limited

LIBRARY OF WALES

FOREWORD

I first read *Border Country* when it appeared as a Penguin paperback in 1964. Its author was familiar to me for his pathbreaking critical studies *Culture and Society* (1958) and *The Long Revolution* (1961), but an undergraduate from the Rhondda at Oxford did not buy hardback novels, and I had only been made aware of the existence of Raymond Williams' 1960 novel from biographical blurbs. I shelled out my five shillings and took it home. For me it crackled with the excitement of a discovery I had somehow known all along. I did not stop reading until, some time the next day, it was finished, and I have never stopped re-reading that original copy since. The hook for me was the instantly recognisable emotional and intellectual journey of a working-class boy who goes away from his shaping community. By the 1960s this had become a familiar pattern, one to be repeated for generations, but it was an experience originating directly, as occurred in Raymond Williams' own life, from that first limited grammar-school exodus of the 1930s. This is still usually told as a story about successful individuals gratefully climbing ladders. Not so here – instead, with a subtlety of touch matched by an integrity of vision, the novel does what no history fully can do and little fiction has achieved: it shows the inescapable intertwining of individuals' lives and social conditions in the fluidity of lived experience that we all share. Although you can approach *Border Country* in more than one way, the final route out will always be the same, for, as Matthew Price reflects at the end of the book's odyssey: 'The distance is measured, and that is what matters. By measuring the distance, we come home.'

Border Country is a deceptive novel. It grips us immediately with its story of one man running and never stopping, but from the first page it also asks the reader to think deeply about how we conceive our general history as a society. The style of *Border Country* is pared down, almost entirely pruned of similes and metaphors, and quietly serves its straightforward tale, but the novel is also clearly and defiantly proud to be so plain. It is patently a novel about Welsh people set in Wales, and it deals centrally with the myth and reality of the 1926 General Strike, as it was felt through Welsh history and in individual lives. Yet it is geographically marginal to those thunderous struggles in the coalfield, and its Welsh character is more locally rooted than nationally defined. On publication in 1960, this novel, which had been worked on since the late 1940s and was completed in 1958, seemed to some to be, in its dogged realism, past its time, but in its global relevance today it is more contemporary than ever.

The novel is set in motion, from its very first sentence, with Matthew Price running for a bus in London. He is a university lecturer who is working on population movements in the industrialising valleys of South Wales in the nineteenth century. He is dissatisfied with the scholarly techniques he has learned to measure this human displacement and renewed settlement. The results have 'the solidity and precision of ice cubes, while a given temperature is maintained.' In actual life no such precision is possible. So what exactly is being measured? It is the overall picture, without which no change can be measured, but after which the real nature of existence has been lost: 'The man on the bus, the man in the street, but I am Price from Glynmawr,' Matthew muses to himself.

Raymond Williams from Pandy spent his lifetime working out how not to betray that individual essence whilst at the same time understanding its wider and connected cultural being. I believe he showed the way best in his fiction, where the journey is undertaken not in order to go back – for that is never possible – but in order to see how social renewal can occur as growth in human terms. *Border Country* is, therefore, concerned with both Space and Time as the twinned defining attributes of human communities.

The time-shifts move us from Matthew's return – by train and car – to be with his dying father, Harry Price, railway signalman, to Harry's own coming to Glynmawr with his young bride, Ellen, to work in the 1920s. It is the General Strike of 1926 that brings one form of self-definition to a head. In a number of brilliantly poised passages of dialogue, Raymond Williams takes his variously committed railway workers through the gradations of political commitment and self-sacrifice which weighted their act of solidarity with the locked-out miners with such profound social significance. Its meaning resonated as late as 1984, when the last industrial reference back to 1926 was made. And possibly, if we understand such support in terms of irreducible human values rather than political flotsam, it retains such meaning even beyond its particular time. Certainly that is how Williams would have us see it. His insistence is that it is only by contemplating how individual destiny interplays with wider forces, always experienced spatially, that we can makes sense of life in the human chronology of Price from Glynmawr. The alternative, and profoundly so, is submission to non-sense.

The novel's most plangent tone is, in counterpoint then, a lyrical one. 'I know this country,' the writer informs us in the prefatory note to its first printing and we can easily see that he loved it too. Not as a landscape for tourist consumption but as a land made over and over, often with intense struggle between social classes as much as against nature, to create human habitation fit for the potential of always changing communities:

Once they were up on the road, Harry and Ellen could look out over the valley and the village in which they had come to live...

The narrow road wound through the valley. The railway, leaving the cutting at the station, ran out north on an embankment, roughly parallel with the road but a quarter of a mile distant. Between road and railway, in its curving course, ran the Honddu, the black water. On the east of the road ran the grassed embankment of the old tramroad, with a few overgrown stone quarries near its line. The directions coincided, and Harry, as he walked, seemed to relax and settle. Walking the road in the October evening, they felt on their faces their own country: the huddled farmhouses, with their dirty yards; the dogs under the weed-growing walls; the cattle-marked crossing from the sloping field under the orchard; the long fields, in the line of the valley, where the cattle pastured; the turned red earth of the small, thickly-hedged ploughland; the brooks, alder-lined, curving and meeting; the bracken-heaped tussocky fields up the mountain, where the sheep were scattered under the wood-shaded barns; the occasional white wall, direct towards the sun, standing out where its windows caught the light across the valley; the high black line of the mountains, and the ring of the sheep wall.

The patch of eight houses lay ahead: set so that looking to the north and west the spurs of the mountains lay open in the distance. Harry stopped, put down the leather box, and looked around. 'All right, last bit,' he said after resting, and they went on to the houses.

Within its frame, then, of Time and Space, we share in and comprehend human endeavour and human growth and human loss. There is not a false or sentimental note anywhere in this book. Nothing is romanticised and nobody is idealised. We are never allowed to see what is local in action as being somehow limited in reach or implication. Raymond Williams fully understood that his country on the border was only different in its specific shapes, so that at someone else's border, in the changing particularities of other histories of migration and settlement and struggle, the narrative, personal and general, continued.

I believe that *Border Country* is one of the most moving and accomplished novels of the twentieth century, written anywhere by anyone. In Wales, the fact that it was written by Williams from Pandy is an occasion for small, extra celebration. More importantly, in its new Library of Wales format, it deserves to go out more widely than ever into the world, so that by being measured it can properly come home to us again.

Dai Smith

BORDER COUNTRY

PART ONE

CHAPTER ONE

1

As he ran for the bus he was glad: not only because he was going home, after a difficult day, but mainly because the run in itself was pleasant, as a break from the contained indifference that was still his dominant feeling of London. The conductress, a West Indian, smiled as he jumped to the platform, and he said, 'Good evening,' and was answered, with an easiness that had almost been lost. You don't speak to people in London, he remembered; in fact you don't speak to people anywhere in England; there is plenty of time for that sort of thing on the appointed occasions – in an office, in a seminar, at a party. He went upstairs, still half smiling, and was glad there had been no time to buy an evening paper; there was plenty to look at, in the bus and in the streets.

Matthew Price had been eight years a university lecturer, in economic history. He knew of nothing he more wanted to be, though his anxiety about his work had become marked. He was generally considered a good lecturer, but his research, which had started so well, had made little real progress over the last three years. It might be simply the usual fading, which he had watched in others, but it presented itself differently to his own mind. It is a problem of measurement, of the means of measurement, he had come to tell himself. But the reality which this phrase offered to interpret was, he could see, more disturbing. He was working on population movements into the Welsh mining valleys in the middle decades of the nineteenth century. But I have moved myself, he objected, and what is it really that I must measure? The techniques I have learned have the solidity and precision of ice-cubes, while a given temperature is maintained. But it is a temperature I can't really maintain; the door of the box keeps flying open. It's hardly a population movement from Glynmawr to London, but it's a change of substance, as it must also have been for them, when they left their villages. And the ways of measuring this are not only outside my discipline. They are somewhere else altogether, that I can feel but not handle, touch but not grasp. To the nearest hundred, or to any usable percentage, my single figure is indifferent, but it is not only a relevant figure: without it, the change can't be measured at all. The man on the bus, the man in the street, but I am Price from Glynmawr, and here, understandably, that means very little. You get it through Gwenton. Yes, they say the gateway of Wales. Yes, border country.

It was a long bus-ride out, and it was dark when he got off: town dark. The lamps had been lit among the bare trees, and shone down into the little front gardens. There were trees and gardens all along this street. When, soon after their marriage, Matthew and Susan had seen this street, they had felt they could settle in it. It was suburban, whatever that might mean, but this was little enough to pay for trees and a garden. Theirs was the end house: grey, single-fronted, with a wide bay window. At the gate stood a laburnum, as he had learned to call it except when it was in flower, when it was a golden chain again. On the gate had been a panel announcing 'Laburnum House', but this had been burned. Collecting the names of houses had been one of their earliest pastimes, before they married. Susan, the daughter of a Cumberland teacher, had been one of Matthew's first students. They had married two months after her graduation. While she was still his student, they had walked, endlessly, around a London still strange to them both. Their direction, always, was from a large street into a smaller, until they were virtually lost and had to ask their way back. They had found this street on one of these walks, and since they had settled in it a new line of shops and a new junior school had been built nearby. Their two boys had been born and would grow up here, and would think of it as home.

As Matthew pushed open the door, there was a shouted protest. Harry, just inside the door, was jumping to tap back a limp red balloon, which had to float between the door and the stairs as goals. He missed it as the door opened suddenly, and the balloon floated down under Matthew's feet.

'Anyway, that's not a goal, that's interference,' Harry shouted.

'You were missing it, anyway,' Jack shouted back furiously, his hair loose over his eyes.

'Half-time,' Matthew said, punting the balloon away and closing the door. 'Anyway, where's Susan?'

'Getting tea. Anyway it's no good, all its wind's going.'

Matthew walked through to the kitchen, first stumbling on a heap of marbles and cursing. Susan opened the kitchen door and there was a further scuffle as Rex, the collie pup from Glynmawr, tore out and jumped up at Matthew. The telephone rang.

'Not again,' Matthew said. 'They time the bastard for when I get home.'

'Say no anyway. We don't want a drink with anybody, we don't want coffee, we can cook our own supper.'

'They can't hear you, Susan. And I'm not answering it.'

'All right.'

He took off his coat in the kitchen, and closed the door, but the ringing went on.

'Are you sure it's not work?'

'That would be important, of course. Some tidy little committee.'

'It sounds as if they're serious,' Susan said, as the ringing continued.

'These social types always are.'

They looked at each other, anxiously, seeking reassurance. The boys opened the door and Jack asked, 'Are you ever going to answer that thing?'

'All right,' Matthew said, and went quickly out. He picked up the receiver and said, impatiently, 'Price.' Susan had followed him, and was watching his face as he listened. There was a sudden tightening to attention, and he glanced up at her.

'Yes who is that exactly?... I see... When?... Yes... Yes, thank you.'

He was pushing the receiver tightly into his face, as if he could not understand what was being said. When the call ended, he got up and stared at Susan, saying nothing. She watched him, intently, while the boys shouted as they ran past.

'Tell me, love.'

'My father.'

'An accident?'

'No, some kind of stroke. It was a bad line. They can talk endlessly but they couldn't make it clear.'

'They want you to come?'

'Yes.'

'Could you get through tonight?'

'I don't know. I simply don't know.'

'I'll pack your things. You ring inquiries. You must get as far as you can.'

Matthew nodded, but moved away from the phone. The dog was barking as the boys played with it in the passage.

'All right,' Matthew said, standing quite still.

'Ring inquiries,' Susan said, facing him.

'All right.'

They looked at each other for a moment, as the boys and the dog rushed past them; then each turned to what had to be done.

'He's a proper collie,' Jack shouted, 'only of course he's got to be trained.'

'We know that,' Harry said.

2

Abruptly the rhythm changed, as the wheels crossed the bridge. Matthew got up, and took his case from the rack. As he steadied the case, he looked at the rail-map, with its familiar network of arteries, held in the shape of Wales, and to the east the lines running out and elongating, into England. The shape of Wales: pig-headed Wales you say to remember to draw it. And no returns.

The usual photographs were at the sides of the map. On the far side was the abbey, that he had always known: the ruined abbey at Trawsfynydd that had not changed in his lifetime. On the near side was the front at Tenby. A railing horizon, in the wide paleness of sky and sea; then, making the picture, two girls smiling under cloche hats, and an Austin drawn up beyond them, the nose of its radiator in the air. Like the compartment, the photographs were more than thirty years old: nearly his own age. Damp had got in at the corners, irregularly staining the prints.

The wheels slowed, and the train passed under the gaunt footbridge and drew up at the platform, past the line of yellow lamps. A scurry of rain hit the misted glass. He jerked at the window strap, and reached out to open the door. No one else got out. He stood alone on the dark platform, looking around. Starting as late as he had, there had been no useful stop after Gwenton; he would have to walk the five miles north to Glynmawr.

The light rain swept his face, and he moved away, quickly, under the wooden awning of the station building, glancing up at the fretwork pattern of its edge. The engine whistled. The guard was already back in his window. As the train pulled out, for its next thirty miles, Matthew turned up his collar and re-lit his pipe. He waved, briefly, to the guard as he passed.

Down first into the town: that was half a mile of the walk. For here was the station, by the asylum: both on the outskirts, where the Victorians thought they belonged. The wind was blowing from the dark wall of the mountains, rattling a hanging sign.

As he walked to the gate, a porter came out of the lamp-room, and held out his hand. Matthew gave him his ticket, looking past him at the gaslight of the lamp-room, and the red wall of its fire. He smiled, and the porter looked at him strangely. Then they separated, Matthew returning the good night. You come as a stranger: accept that.

As he walked down the station approach, a car drove towards him, raking him with its headlights, in which the rain drifted. The driver blew his horn, but Matthew ignored it. He walked on, steadily, turning his face from the wind. So much of the memory of this country was a memory of walking: walking alone, with the wind ripping at him; alone it seemed always, in memory, though not in fact. The car was turning behind him, but he took no notice. Then farther down it overtook him, and drew in close to the pavement.

'Where you off to then?' a voice called from the car.

'Glynmawr,' he answered, abruptly.

'Glynmawr? Where's that then?'

'About five miles north.'

As soon as he had answered, he walked on. He was set, now, on the walk. He wanted to come back like this: slowly, with obvious difficulty, making up his own mind.

'You'll get wet, you know, Will,' the voice said suddenly. Matthew stopped, and swung round, arrested by the name. Always, when he had lived here, he had been Will, though his registered name was Matthew, and he had used this invariably since he had gone away.

'I'm sorry. Who is that?' he asked, walking back to the car.

'Come on, mun, get in.'

'Oh, I see,' Matthew said, and walked round through the headlights and opened the door. Morgan Rosser sat behind the wheel, heavily coated, his bare grey head stiff and poised, looking forward.

'I'm sorry,' Matthew said. 'I should have recognized your voice. Only sometimes we only recognize when we're expecting it.'

'You thought we'd leave you to walk then?' Morgan said, looking across at him.

'I expected to walk. Nobody knew the time of my train.'

'I've got timetables. Get in, Will. Don't stand in the wet.'

Matthew hesitated, and got into the car. Morgan leaned across him, heavily, and pulled the door shut.

'Your Mam rung me,' he said, settling again in his seat. 'She said Mrs Hybart rung you a quarter past five, you said you'd get the first train.'

'Well, thank you, anyway. I didn't expect it.'

Morgan did not answer, but with a hard movement sent the car forward. Matthew jerked back, then steadied himself. It is like that, this country; it takes you over as soon as you set foot in it. Yet I was sent for to come at once.

Rain had made the glass in front of him opaque. He looked down, then across through the fan of the driver's wiper. They turned out of the approach, then down the long road into the town. Nothing moved along it, except the bare trees in the wind. Again, in the town, the narrow main street was deserted, as they turned past the Town Hall to the market, and then up the long pitch to Glynmawr. He stared out at the empty town. It was years since he had sat beside Morgan Rosser in the car, along this same road. The last time had been before he first went away.

'How are you then, Will?'

'Not bad, thanks. And you?'

'This is bad though.'

'Yes.'

'He's been too good a man, Will.'

Matthew turned and looked at him. The good-looking face was set and calm, under the thick grey hair. The eyes looked forward, at the narrow road.

'Maybe.'

'It's what we ought to have known, Will. The strength, yes, and that's what he showed. But now this, always.'

'We'll see,' Matthew said, and Morgan glanced at him, and then back at the road.

They sat in silence until they were into Glynmawr, with its intermittent groups of houses and the fields between them. In the headlights, along the road, every feature came up in its remembered place. By the school the road had been widened, and the corner was less dangerous. The headlights beamed along the banked hedges, and cut quick swathes through the gateways to the fields.

'Anyway, it's good to see you again, Will. Even if you did think we'd leave you to walk.'

'Aye, only then after all you were late, see,' Matthew said, quickly. He felt the older man stiffen, and then the relief. 'Fifteen seconds,

11

mun. At most. And then you come out of them gates with your head down, so I nearly run you over. Even then I had to stop and ask you the way to Glynmawr.'

'Well I told you, accurate.'

'Aye, near enough.'

'And the rain, see. Wouldn't you keep your head down?'

'Aye, I suppose.'

It was easy at last, and enough had been re-established. They relaxed as the car slowed and the headlights shone back from the headstones at the first chapel, above the river. The car turned into the lane, and now the trees were arched overhead, and it was suddenly darker, the lights of the car isolated. Matthew stared out at the wet red earth of the banks, as the car rolled and slipped on the rutted pitch. Then the pitch flattened, the houses came up into view, and at once they were among them.

'Should remember this house, anyhow,' Morgan said, as he stopped the car.

'You're coming in?'

'You go on, Will. I'll come after. I've got you here.'

'All right,' Matthew said, and opened the gate to the house.

3

He walked round to go in by the back door. But the door was opened before he reached it, and his mother stood waiting just inside the kitchen. He leaned forward, and quickly kissed her cheek.

'You got here then, Will.'

'Yes, and the lift.'

'I been listening for the car. I knew Morgan would do it. He's very good.'

They moved together into the kitchen, and as Matthew put down his bag Morgan came in behind them, closing the door.

'You'll be hungry, Will.'

Matthew had turned away, and was taking off his coat. He hung it on the line of pegs beside the door, where the working coats hung. The pegs were laden, and he had to push at the other coats to hang up his own.

'And you, Morgan, you'll have something.'

'No, no, girl, I haven't come for a meal.'

'It's all ready, look.'

There was a dark home-cured ham on the table, and cut bread and butter and a bottle of wheat wine.

'Only first...' Matthew said, and hesitated, watching his mother's face. It was too like an ordinary home-coming, with his father at work. It needed an effort to think of him lying upstairs.

'Well, yes, you'll want to see him. Only leave it a bit, Will. He's sleeping heavy.'

Matthew looked past her, across the kitchen. As a rule they needed to put very little into words, but now with nothing said he felt himself hardening. Some things at least must take precedence.

'Has there been any change?'

'No, Will, I don't think so. You'll have to see. Look, sit down, the both of you. Sit down at the table.'

'I won't stay,' Morgan said, but sat on the edge of the hard chair between the table and the sink. Matthew, still standing, felt suddenly awkward. He seemed too big to be standing there, close to his mother.

'He's sleeping, is he? Shall I go up and look?'

'No, I'll go up. In a minute. It's the injection, Will, he's very heavy.'

'What injection?'

'Morphia, isn't it? The doctor's been twice.'

'What doctor?'

'Evans, he's a nice chap. He's taken over from Powell.'

'What did he say?'

'He said coronary.'

'Thrombosis,' Morgan said. 'It's the blood to the heart.'

'I want to know how it happened,' Matthew said. His voice seemed loud and sharp in the hushed room.

'Sit down and eat then,' Ellen said.

'Aye, come on, Will,' Morgan said quickly. 'Too good to go wasting.'

'You have some then, Morgan,' Ellen invited.

'No, no, girl. She'll be keeping mine for me at home.'

'It's cold, it'll wait,' Matthew said. 'I'll eat when I've seen him.'

He saw the others watching him, and sat in the arm-chair, away from the table. His mother stayed, standing in the centre of her kitchen.

'Well? Tell me.'

Ellen moved to the table, and poured wine from the tall green bottle into the two glasses. She set one in front of Morgan, and handed the other to Matthew, who took it and put it straight down on the dresser.

'You won't have eaten since dinner, Will.'

'It's all right.'

'Tell Will how it happened,' Morgan said.

'Yes, Will, I was going to say,' Ellen apologized, turning to her son. Looking up at her, he saw the sudden pain in her face.

'It was in the box. This morning, about ten past eight.'

He watched her, hearing in her voice that she had said this often already; that the account had already been given to several others.

'But the first was last night, and he didn't say.'

'How?'

'He was in the end garden. He had fifty savoys he wanted in before dark. He had the pain then, but he tried to finish the planting. Then it got worse, and he came back in here. It was just dusk, I hadn't put on the light. He sat where you're sitting, but he didn't say. He told me today he was glad it was dark, so I couldn't see his face.'

'Yes.'

'I could hear from his voice there was pain, though he hardly answered. He said leave the light off, the dark rested him. He sat there for more than an hour. I thought it was tired. Only after, when I touched his forehead, I felt the sweat. I put down my hand to his hand, and he was catching the chair.'

'But then?'

'You know what he is, Will. He said it was nothing. I said he was sweating. He said it was nothing and would go.'

'An hour?'

'I hadn't touched him, Will. Not till then. And the worst was over. When I put on the light he got up.'

Matthew looked away, along the line of the dresser.

'Did he look bad?' Morgan asked.

'Yes, Morgan, he was grey. He got up and walked straight up to bed, said he'd leave supper. We both went and lay down. I said must he go to work. He said yes, of course, there was nothing to prevent him. If I'd known, of course.'

'You're not to blame your Mam,' Morgan said, sharply. 'You come now, and she says herself if she'd known. I've argued with Harry since before you was born. There's nothing anybody can do.'

Matthew hesitated, looking away from the dresser.

'I know. I hadn't thought of blaming.'

'If he'd only have said,' Ellen cried. 'He told me today it was like a fist gripping him, gripping deep, he said, where he didn't know that he was. But he sat in the dark. Then this morning he got up half-past five, and dressed in the dark. I said how was he and he said better, the pain had gone. I heard him go off on his bike. Then at quarter to nine he was back here.'

'Who brought him?'

'Well, Jones the stationmaster found him. He'd just cleared a train and he shouted across to Jones. When Jones got up there, he was lying on his back by the fire. Jones thought he'd gone.'

'I see.'

'He was grey then, grey like stone, and the sweat was terrible. Jones got a coat under his head and called down to Phillips the ganger. They thought perhaps call a doctor there, but Phillips said carry him home. Phillips and Elwyn got him out to Phillips's car, and brought him.'

'Elwyn?'

'Yes. You remember Elwyn.'

15

'Of course.'

'If he'd not have gone,' Ellen said. 'I can see that now.'

'But it's no use thinking all that,' Morgan said, sharply. He was still sitting on the edge of the hard chair between the table and the sink; filling the space in his heavy black overcoat; the face square and ruddy, under the thick curling grey hair.

'It's thinking from now,' he said, still looking at Matthew.

'Of course,' Matthew agreed, and walked across the kitchen to his overcoat. He took his pipe from a pocket, and with his knife began poking the dead ash into his palm. He still faced the coats, with their smell of work.

'Will, you look now like Harry, standing there by the door,' Morgan said. Matthew closed his knife, and blew down the empty pipe.

'Do I?'

'You get more like him,' Ellen said. 'Powell thought it was him the last time you was here, and he saw you across the field.'

Matthew went to the fireplace, and threw down the ash in his hand.

'Can I see him now, then?'

Ellen was standing very still, on the same spot. He could see more clearly now, in her face, the fear of the day. She had been colouring her hair, so that it was almost the yellow he remembered. The skin was pale, under the fine red lines on the cheeks. The eyes and the mouth seemed to have shrunk.

'All right, I'll go up first then.'

'And I'll get along,' Morgan said. He stood as he spoke, and then lifted his glass and drank down the wine.

'Thanks again for the lift, Morgan.'

'I'll be out again,' Morgan said, moving to the door. Ellen hesitated, and smiled. As he closed the door, she walked down the passage to the stairs. Matthew followed her, a few steps behind, and stopped on the landing while she went into the bedroom. He heard her voice, very low, and a sudden deep voice, that he could not make into words. Ellen came out, and beckoned to him.

'Only stay two or three minutes, Will,' she whispered. He nodded, and walked quietly into the room.

4

The back bedroom, which Harry and Ellen always used, was small and crowded. There was only a narrow space to move round the bed to the single small window. The head of the bed was behind the opening door. Matthew stopped, in the warm drug-heavy air, and looked down.

The head on the pillow was much older than he had looked for: ten years older, at least, than when he had seen his father in the summer. The eyes were closed, in the flushed, drawn face.

'Will.'

'Yes.'

Harry opened his eyes and drew his right arm from under the covers. He leaned up a little from the pillow, and Matthew bent over him, taking the extended hand. The hand was pale, delicate, beautifully formed. The skin was very soft as he touched it, but the grip was hard.

'This is no way, Will, to be welcoming you home.'

'Well, I'm glad to come, and I know I'm welcome.'

'Of course you are.'

The voice was deep and rough, very slow with effort. The effort merged, in the son's mind, with memories of irritated correction. Always, in this voice, there was more than could easily be said, in any feeling.

'Stay with me, Will. But I shan't talk.'

'I'll stay.'

He moved and sat on the edge of the bed. As he looked down, at the hurt strength of the face, he seemed to feel the pressure on his own face, as if a cast were being taken. He could hardly breathe, while the long effort lasted, but then he turned, sharply, and looked away into the room.

The heavy mahogany wardrobe filled almost the whole space left by the bed. From the lampholder in front of it a length of flex drooped across the room to the headrail, where it was knotted and led into a switch. The flex was of two kinds, joined above the bed with what looked like the pink adhesive cover of a bandage. In the far corner of the room was a cupboarded water-tank, piped to the back- boiler in the room below.

He looked back at his father, who was not sleeping, but, with his eyes closed, fighting for strength. He knew that it was necessary to sit still and not talk, at the very moment when the pain and the danger were releasing feeling and concentrating it, so that his whole mind seemed a long dialogue with his father – a dialogue of anxiety and allegiance, of deep separation and deep love. Nothing could stop this dialogue, nothing else seemed important, yet here, with the pale hand lying by his own hand, with the face no longer an image but there, anxiously watched, the command to silence was absolute, while the dialogue raced.

He turned away, and again looked round the room. On the walls hung pictures of his grandparents: placed, in each case, so that the eyes seemed to be watching the bed. The pictures were relatively unfamiliar, for he had rarely been in this room where his parents slept. The women he looked at quickly, in their high black dresses, with the brooches at their throats. Ellen's mother, very like Ellen now, but easy and smiling, without strain. Harry's mother – but there, for a moment, the heart stopped. The hard, strong, deeply-lined face; features coarse, almost animal in their rough casting; yet deeply composed, by the smiling mouth, into a gentleness that was part of the strength and the suffering. She had died too soon for Matthew to know her. She seemed, now, very far away.

The men were nearer, inevitably. Will Lewis, Ellen's father, whom Matthew had never known though for years he had carried his name. A sharp, dark, inquisitive face, this hill-farmer turned miller; intelligent or cunning from alternative sides of the bargain. The eyes confident, extroverted without disturbance. Beside him, Jack Price, at sixty: the Jack Price his grandson remembered. Here again was complexity. The mediocre photograph had the life of a fine portrait. At first it was only his son's head on the pillow, the strong, rough features partly hidden by the moustache and the line of beard fringing the jaw. Jack Price, labourer, very formal in the stiff, high collar and the smooth, unworn lapels and waistcoat. Then the eyes, colourless in the hazy enlargement, but not his son's eyes, clouded, unfocused; eyes still with the devil in them, the spurt of feeling and gaiety. Remembering their living excitement, Matthew stared back, feeling their world. But the light in the bedroom was yellow and poor, and his own eyes watered with strain and had to be closed.

Silence settled in the crowded room, and then, across the valley, a train whistled. Harry looked up. Matthew turned at the movement but Harry was puzzled; he did not seem to know where he was. They could hear the train now, on the down line: a goods, labouring at the gradient. The heavy regular beat, beyond their range, seemed alone in the world in the silent valley.

'I keep going off,' Harry said. 'But I listen for the trains.'

'You need the sleep.'

'I'm used to the trains, Will. Don't worry.'

'All right.'

'How was your journey, Will?'

'Very good. I was surprised really.'

Harry looked at the alarm clock on the mantelpiece. He stared at it for some time, as if disbelieving it.

'That would be what then, the five-eight Paddington?'

'Yes, I just caught it.'

'It was awkward for you, Will. Having to leave your work.'

'No, now, it's all right.'

'It was awkward,' Harry repeated, and the voice, for a moment, held the remembered irritation and impatience. Matthew smiled, and saw the immediate response and lightening in the heavy eyes.

'In any case,' Harry said, looking away, 'I want you to know I appreciate you coming. You're a good son. I want you to realize...'

He stopped, and the colour rushed up into his face. Cold with alarm, Matthew leaned forward. His legs were stiff where they had been crossed as he sat on the bed. He felt the numbness as he moved, watching the eyes close.

'It's all right, it's the pain again.'

'Do you want anything?'

'No. It'll be...'

Matthew watched the effort in the face, and felt its counterpart in his own stiff tension, in the taut, anxious nerves round his mouth and eyes. There was a sound at the door, and Ellen came in.

'Mam,' Harry said, his voice very deep, hardly more than a breath.

'Yes, it's all right,' Ellen said, and leaned over him. Matthew stood for a moment with his eyes closed, then walked out of the bedroom. As he walked downstairs to the kitchen, he felt the past moving with him: this life, this house, the trains through the valley.

CHAPTER TWO

1

The four train ran north through the brakes and the green meadows under the Holy Mountain, and passed the up distant signal of Glynmawr. The worn black engine, with its name *Clytha Court* on the grimed, brass-lettered arc, laboured at the long bank. Above and behind it, its white plume flared and spread, then climbed and thinned until at a height the wind from the mountain plucked and scattered it into the grey felt overhang that, hiding the sun, moved slowly west to the farther mountains. On this October afternoon the train was late: four twenty-three at Glynmawr would be four twenty-seven, but by country time it would still be the four.

At the outer home signal, where the hedge was glatted to a worn path across the fields to the old road, the bank flattened, and the busy rhythm was broken. The four slackened and slowed to Glynmawr station, and drew down to stop with a heavy sigh of steam just short of the sleeper-paved crossing. The platforms at Glynmawr were not set opposite each other.

'Why it was, see, they knew you was odd, and they built according.'

'No, no, mun, it's the lie of the ground.'

'Or the boss of the railway was cross-eyed, they built this one in his honour.'

'No, no, it's the lie of the ground.'

To the up platform a zigzag path led down from the road and the bridge. At the bottom of the path the porter waited. Ted Wood from Aldgate had married and come back with a Welsh girl in service, but

21

he couldn't say where she came from; only the 'more, more' echoed along the carriages as they drew to a halt. Three children from the County School jumped from a compartment and raced around him and up a short cut to midway in the zigzag path, while he made no move but shouted that this would be the last time. One other door opened, and a young couple in their middle twenties got out. They put down their luggage, a suitcase and a leather box, and then the man got in again and brought out a corded wooden box and a paper parcel and a frail. The girl was anxious that he seemed to take so long, though he moved quickly, not even glancing along the platform. When he was out again, she closed the door but still he turned and tried the handle. Then he stood back and, glancing along the platform to the engine, gave the right away. The guard, farther back, had not yet appeared at his window.

The *Clytha Court* whistled, and spitting steam again drew slowly out. The porter, who had not yet moved, stared towards the guard's window. He had taken out a large blue check handkerchief and was carefully blowing his nose. 'Hoiup,' came the shout suddenly, and the guard's peaked, laughing face jumped into view. With a flick like a stone for ducks and drakes, he threw a heavy leather bag, and two large envelopes joined by a rubber band, straight at the porter's chest. Wood could not get his hands down in time and the leather bag hit him as he held the big handkerchief. By the time Wood could shout, the guard was being carried away down the platform, past the standing couple and their luggage. He was head and shoulders at his window now, laughing and leaning out. He called to the couple as he went by:

'Tell him stop blowing his nose on signal rags.'

'What?'

'Stop blowing his nose on signal rags.'

But the words were carried away on the wind, and the smoke came back now out of the cutting, and the carriages were curving away to the north. The words had been heard – it was not that – but this was not talk for an answer; the shout was enough.

The couple picked up their luggage, and walked along the platform.

'You see that?' Wood said, waiting for them. 'Mad they all are down here like that, mad as hatters.'

'Having a game on,' the girl said, smiling.

'Some flipping game. Throwing bags.'

'He's from Newport,' the man said, but not as an explanation.

'Let him go back there,' said the porter angrily, and winked. 'I'll have him.'

They stood together, and the porter looked at the luggage. The girl looked at her husband, waiting for him to speak.

'Mr Rees about then?'

'Stationmaster? You want him?'

'I'm the new signalman.'

'I thought perhaps you was.'

There was a pause, and the luggage was put down.

'We got to find lodgings, we got nowhere fixed,' the girl said anxiously.

Ted Wood took off his cap, and rubbed carefully at his fine, glossy hair. He was quite tall, and the pale face was bonily handsome. He looked at the girl, more frankly than she was used to. Her eyes were a very light blue; the long hair, escaping from the blue hat, was sandy yellow. Her husband stood very close to her, heavy in his black cap and long black overcoat. The face under the cap was very strong, with prominent cheekbones and a broad, heavy jaw. Under the big nose the mouth was wide, with ugly, irregular teeth. The solidity of the face and body made the extreme smallness of the hands and feet sudden and surprising. But the dominant impression was the curious stillness of the features, and the distance and withdrawal in the very deep blue eyes. He looked up now, slowly, and Wood turned with an easy excitement, as the stationmaster came towards them from his office under the bridge. Tom Rees was very tall, with thick egg-yellow over the brushed peak of his cap, his moustaches waxed to points that accentuated the long thinness of the face.

'Here he is,' Wood said.

'Price? Mr Price?'

23

'Aye. Mr Rees is it?'

'Glad to meet you, my boy, certainly. And Mrs Price?'

'How do you do, Mr Rees?'

'They said your good man was married, when they sent me his bit of paper. If I'd known you were coming with him today...'

'We've got to get lodgings. Harry should have written.'

'Lodgings is no trouble. We'll fix you up.'

'Thank you.'

The stationmaster looked again at his new signalman. He had heard well of him, and the first impression was good, but there was something there that disturbed and slowed.

'Now let's see, what time's it get dark?' he said briskly, with a quick touch at the gummed pricks of his moustache. He was, after all, the stationmaster, and Price his new signalman and really no more than a lad. Decisions must be made, even against that withdrawn heaviness.

'Six, half past.'

'You're on early turn in the morning, so this evening sometime you've got to be here, learn the box.'

'I'm ready now.'

'Aye, aye, of course, but the lodgings, boy, the lodgings, got to see to that before dark.'

'Don't worry, Harry, I can find it,' the girl said quickly.

'We'll go up the box,' Tom Rees said. 'Only before we go...' He looked back along the platform, making sure the four of them were alone. The porter, behind his back, winked at Price. 'One of your mates, Harry,' Tom Rees said, 'Morgan Rosser, a young chap about your own age. Come from Pontypool, his father was a ticket collector.'

The girl looked along the platform and under the bridge to the box. Its bricks were grey, and its light-brown paint had begun to peel in the sun. She could see a figure standing there, near the barred window above the line. The sun broke through for a moment, and glinted along the rails, away south under the face and rockfall of the Holy Mountain and the copse of birches above the high, black siding.

'It's a tragic thing with Morgan Rosser,' Tom Rees said. 'His young wife, Mary, died the end of August, giving birth to his little girl.'

The girl nodded, but said nothing, staring at the black figure in the box.

'He has a decent house, you see, down the far end,' Tom Rees went on, 'and he has an old woman, a housekeeper, and the little girl, nine weeks.' Harry also was staring down the platform at the box, but his eyes were fixed and dark, as if staring anywhere.

'It would be good for him and good for you,' Tom Rees said, 'if it was there you went to lodge.'

'Shall I ask him?' Harry said, roughly.

'We'll all three go up,' Tom Rees said, frowning. 'Only you see how it is. With it so recent.'

Ellen turned and looked at her husband. He met her eyes and at once looked away.

'I'll put the luggage in the office.'

'Don't worry about that, mate,' Wood said quickly. 'I shan't pinch it.'

'I'll just put it in,' Harry repeated, and gathered up the suitcase and the two boxes. He walked on down the platform and Ellen followed, beside the tall stationmaster. The porter took the frail from her, and walked a few paces behind. While Harry put the luggage in the office, Tom Rees and Ellen went up the steps to the box. They were opening the second of the two doors at the top as Harry followed them up. He had to wait as they moved in from the door. In the space between the doors was a low shelf, with three red fire buckets. One was filled with sand, one with clear water, and the one in the middle had blue soapy water in it, and a big piece of yellow soap and a little hand brush on the shelf beside it. Tom Rees moved, and Harry could see Morgan Rosser. He was smiling and shaking hands with Ellen.

'Here he is then,' Tom Rees said. 'Harry Price, Morgan Rosser.'

Harry went up the step and across the box. They shook hands, and Morgan, though the smaller man, had the tighter grip. Tom Rees had prepared them for a man in mourning, but Morgan was easy, alert, confident. His face was small, with neat, regular features. The brown eyes were bright, the lips under the small black moustache full and red. The hair, a deep black, was tightly curled all over the crown, and came very low beside the small ears.

'Glad to meet you, Harry. Of course I knew you were coming.'

'Aye,' Harry nodded, looking slowly around the box.

'Now, Morgan, it's like this,' Tom Rees said formally. 'Harry and his wife want lodgings. I wondered, as the first chance, whether they might come to you?'

'Well,' Morgan said, smiling and rubbing at his chin, 'the rooms are there.'

'Harry should have written before,' Ellen said, anxiously. With the two new men she was trying very hard to be easy and sociable.

'There's me, my little daughter, and Mrs Lucas my housekeeper,' Morgan said. 'And you can have the one front bedroom, and the room under it, and the meals Ma Lucas will see to.'

'It sounds very nice,' Ellen said. 'Is it much?'

Morgan laughed. 'Look, no secrets in public, my dear. I know your husband's money, because it's my money. You go and see if you like it. Harry and I'll fix the rest.'

'We're very grateful,' Ellen said, and smiled.

Morgan smiled back, and winked quite openly. Beside him, Harry was staring up at the yellowed diagram of the box's signalling circuit. It had been hung so high on the wall that his head was sharply bent back.

'Well, there you are you see, it's all settled,' Tom Rees said, looking happily around. 'Now you and Harry get down and get your things in. Harry can come back about half past seven, all right?'

Harry nodded.

'Far, is it?'

'Two mile.'

'Just under,' Morgan said. 'You just follow the road, Harry, past the school and to where the river comes alongside the road. There's the Baptist chapel on your left and the Methodist the other side. Then up the lane see, beside the Methodist and there's the whole patch. Mine's the third on the right, the farthest.'

'We'll find it,' Ellen said, pleased that everything was so easy. Harry looked away and spoke as he moved to the door.

'Right, then. It's all clear. Thank you.'

Ellen turned and followed him, taking leave of the others.

'And Harry, get Ma Lucas to get a meal mind,' Morgan called.

'Thank you,' Ellen said, and followed her husband down the steps. Ted Wood was standing by the door of the office, waiting for them.

'Want a hand with it, Harry?'

'No, no, I can manage. Two loads, I'm coming up again.'

He took up the suitcase and the leather box, and Ellen took the parcel and the frail.

'Going to Rosser's?' Wood asked.

'Yes,' Ellen said.

'He tell you how to get there?'

'Oh, yes.'

'That's all right then. Wherever you go down this place, it's the same. Cross the grass, past the muckheap, over two mountains, and it's the sixth chapel on the left.'

'Go on,' Ellen laughed, 'it's not bad as that.'

'You mark my words,' Wood began, but Harry was already some way down the platform, and turning for the zigzag path. He looked round now, and Ellen, smiling goodbye, hurried to follow him. Wood watched as they made their way up to the road: the girl's bright hair and easy walk, the colour of her hat and coat, and beside her the stiff figure in black, his arms bent outwards with his load, his face set above the quick, steady walk.

'That's one way of running a railway,' Wood said as they disappeared. He took out his big handkerchief, and folded it carefully before he lifted it to his face.

2

Once they were up on the road, Harry and Ellen could look out over the valley and the village in which they had come to live. To the east stood the Holy Mountain, the blue peak with the sudden rockfall on its western scarp. From the mountain to the north ran a ridge of high ground, and along it the grey Marcher castles. To the west, enclosing the valley, ran the Black Mountains: mile after mile of bracken and whin and heather, of black marsh and green springy turf, of rowan and stunted thorn and myrtle and bog-cotton, roamed by the mountain sheep and the wild ponies. Between the black ridges of Darren and Brynllwyd cut the narrow valley of Trawsfynydd, where the ruined abbey lay below the outcrop of rock marked by the great isolated boulder of the Kestrel. Fields climbed unevenly into the mountains, and far up on the black ridges stood isolated white farmhouses and grey barns.

Within its sheltering mountains, the Glynmawr valley lay broad and green. To a stranger Glynmawr would seem not a village, but just thinly populated farming country. Along the road where Harry and Ellen walked there were no lines of houses, no sudden centres of life. There were a few isolated houses by the roadside, and occasionally, under trees, a group or patch of five or six. Then lanes opened from the road, to east and west, making their way to other small groups, at varying distances. To the east, under the wooded ridge, lay Cefn, Penydre, Trefedw, Campstone. To the west, under the wall of the mountains, stood Glynnant, Cwmhonddu, The Pandy, The Bridge, Panteg. The village was the valley, the whole valley, these scattered groups brought together in a name.

To Harry and Ellen, this was not strange country. Harry had been born in Llangattock, only seven miles north-west, and Ellen in Peterstone, three miles farther north. A river runs between Llangattock and Peterstone, and that is the border with England. Across the river, in Peterstone, the folk speak with the slow, rich, Herefordshire tongue, that could still be heard in Ellen. On this side of the river is the quick Welsh accent, less sharp, less edged, than in the mining valleys which lie beyond the Black Mountains, to the south and west, but clear and distinct – a frontier crossed in the breath. In 1919, a year before coming to Glynmawr, Harry and Ellen had been married in Peterstone church. They had known each other as children, and were engaged when Harry came home from France with a bullet through his wrist. He had gone back, and later been gassed, so that one lung was permanently damaged and he could not smoke. After the wedding he had gone back to the railway, where before the war he had been a boy porter. He had become a porter-signalman and been moved from station to station in the mining valleys, Ellen moving with him in lodgings. Now, with the signalman's job in Glynmawr, there was a chance to settle, to move nearer home. As they walked, carrying their things, they were facing the northern ridge beyond which their own villages lay.

The narrow road wound through the valley. The railway, leaving the cutting at the station, ran out north on an embankment, roughly parallel with the road but a quarter of a mile distant. Between road and railway, in its curving course, ran the Honddu, the black water. On the east of the road ran the grassed embankment of the old tramroad, with a few overgrown stone quarries near its line. The directions coincided, and Harry, as he walked, seemed to relax and settle. Walking the road in the October evening, they felt on their faces their own country: the huddled farmhouses, with their dirty yards; the dogs under the weed-growing walls; the cattle-marked crossing from the sloping field under the orchard; the long fields, in the line of the valley, where the cattle pastured; the turned red earth of the small, thickly-hedged ploughland; the brooks, alder-lined, curving and meeting; the bracken-heaped tussocky fields up the mountain, where the sheep were scattered under the wood-shaded barns; the occasional white wall, direct towards the sun, standing out where its windows caught the light across the valley; the high black line of the mountains, and the ring of the sheep-wall.

At the end, past the grey school and the master's cottage, they could hear the river as it came towards the road, and soon they could see it, fast-flowing and stone-strewn below them, and there ahead was the first chapel, alder-shaded, and beyond it the other chapel, larger and better-built, its graveyard tidier. The lane ran up steeply from the road, and from its high banks the trees arched over. They turned up the lane and climbed steadily. Then round a long curve the pitch eased away, and the tree line opened. The patch of eight houses lay ahead: set so that looking to the north and west the spurs of the mountains lay open in the distance. Harry stopped, put down the leather box, and looked round. 'All right, last bit,' he said after resting, and they walked on to the houses.

At a cottage an old man sat by his low door. A collie sat at his feet, but came slowly out to Ellen and Harry as they approached, its tired, bloodshot eyes barely heeding them.

'There, boy,' Ellen said, reaching down.

The old man was watching them, but with a tired stillness.

'Which is Mr. Rosser's?' Ellen asked.

'Up,' the old man pointed. 'Last one.'

Harry walked on without checking, though he had nodded to the old man. His fingers felt cut from the cord of the box-handle, and he could feel the strain of the weight under his shoulders. He went straight on and through the side-gate to the back door of Rosser's house. 'You knock,' he said to Ellen, and she went past him and rapped with her knuckles on the bare wooden door. At first there was no answer, and she put down the frail and tapped at the nearest window. A voice called back, and in a moment the door was opened. Mrs Lucas, very short, thick-bodied, with arms under her rolled-up sleeves heavier than a normal man's, looked up at them, busily wiping her hands on a worn white towel.

'Yes?'

The voice was deep and hard, but polite enough.

Ellen introduced herself, and explained. Mrs Lucas, watching her, became visibly more pleased.

'It's what we need and I shall be glad of it. Come in the both of you.'

Ellen followed her, and Harry brought in the case, the box and the frail. Mrs Lucas led them in, talking as if she had always known them.

30

'Only I'm sorry I didn't answer the door, didn't hear it till you tapped the window. Only I'm bottling, got pears till I don't want to see another pear. Only the little girl, see, come and see her, she's lovely, like her poor mam, you never knew her, Mary Watkins Pendarren. Put those things anywhere, Mr Price. I'll clear all this up later. Only I'll show you the room.'

Ellen turned, and caught Harry's look. He smiled suddenly, almost laughing, and as she followed Mrs Lucas away to the stairs, looked round the kitchen, across at the baby in its high cradle near the fire, and took off his cap and coat. He sat on the nearest chair, reached with his foot for the pear basket, and helped himself to a pear so yellow and soft that his fingers mushed in it as he held. He began to eat the pear, looking around, pleased. The baby gave a cry and then was quiet. The women, stepping heavily upstairs, talked but he could hear no words. He sat back, letting out his breath, and rested, easy. Across the valley a train whistled, running north from Glynmawr.

3

Harry and Ellen were used to lodgings, but settling into this house was particularly easy. The formal arrangement was with Morgan – Harry paid him four shillings a week – but in practice they seemed to be Mrs Lucas's lodgers and, except for the rent, made all arrangements with her. At work, Harry and Morgan got on easily, but they were not often home at the same time, and in the first weeks saw comparatively little of each other. The Glynmawr box was worked in three shifts. Harry followed Morgan, and was followed by the third signalman, Jack Meredith, a bachelor in his forties who as well as the box had a smallholding – three fields and two others rented – on the edge of the mountain, above the entrance to Trawsfynydd valley, and bordering on the Kestrel. When Morgan was working from six till two, and Harry from two till ten, they shared the same house only to sleep. Then, in the next week, Harry worked nights, and would sleep at home in the mornings, getting up as Morgan was leaving for the afternoon turn. Only in the following week, when Harry worked mornings while Morgan was sleeping after nights, could they have any time together, on the patch. It was ordinarily a quiet house, with one of the men having to sleep two mornings out of three. But Mrs Lucas and Ellen worked together easily, and provided the real continuity.

Mrs Lucas had come into the house for Mary Rosser's confinement, and when Mary had died had stayed on, taking over the housekeeping and the care of the baby girl. She was sixty-one, and had been a widow for more than twenty years. She took over Ellen as if Ellen were her daughter, and the three unconnected generations – Mrs Lucas, Ellen, and the baby Eira – would have seemed, to a stranger, a single family. The two men came and went, in the routine of their work. Meals were always ready for them, at the inconvenient hours. To Morgan, especially, the arrangement was good, for his interests lay outside, and the house since his wife's death had been little more than a base. He was active in the railwaymen's union and in Labour politics, and went regularly to meetings in Gwenton and even in Newport. He was interested in his daughter, but with a certain reserve. 'The women understand this business, and I don't,' he said, in the box, to Harry. 'To lose a wife and get a baby strands you really; you have to remind yourself that it's yours.' Harry accepted this, but himself spent more time in the house, and with the baby. There was little to do in the garden in November, and in any case the garden was not his, and he didn't want to interfere. He went to an occasional meeting, at Morgan's invitation, but with no great interest. He seemed still deeply centred in himself, as if something in his mind drew in all his energy. But he was happy with Ellen, and to be settled in the valley.

In early December Ellen found that she was pregnant, and from this, suddenly, the feel of the settlement was altered. Harry knew, now, that the arrangement must be temporary, though Ellen seemed glad just because things were as they were, so that she could count on Mrs Lucas's help. In talking with the older woman, and in helping to look after Eira, she felt safe and prepared. On her own she knew she would be lonely and frightened: not only because Harry was so often withdrawn and silent, but because in any case he was so many hours away, and the nights, every third week, were especially lonely. Usually, now, she took Eira into her room on these nights, for the company, and the centre of her interest every day was again the child.

'It's lovely to see you with that little baby,' Mrs Lucas said one day, when they were together in the kitchen, and Ellen was nursing Eira who had been crying. 'It's just as if it was your own. I think sometimes like it is.'

Ellen smiled, and kissed Eira's head, among the dark down of hair.

'She'd have been glad,' Mrs Lucas said, coming over to the baby and quickly touching its curved, tiny hands.

'Mrs Rosser?' Ellen said, still drugged with the baby's nearness.

'Yes. She was lovely, Mary was. I've nursed her myself, like you're nursing her baby. Only at the end she held on to me so hard, like I could keep her alive. No, though. I didn't expect it.'

Ellen, only half listening, looked up at the tinted wedding portrait of Mary that hung beside the dresser: a dark, childish face, pretty and unformed, in a frame of thick, ringletted black hair.

'She loved so much, too much for a child,' Mrs Lucas said.

'Too much to have her child?' Ellen said, surprised.

'Too much for him,' Mrs Lucas said, and turned away. Ellen hugged the baby on her lap, and again kissed the sweet-smelling head.

'I expect he loved her,' she said, after a pause.

'Rosser? Yes, as his girl. He had plenty of girls. Mary was his best girl. That's how he is.'

'He's nice, and good-looking,' Ellen said.

Mrs Lucas moved to the big black range. Her lips were tight, and she seemed less to walk than to propel her squat body across the intervening space.

'Girls look for that,' she said, her back turned.

'Well?' Ellen said, looking down again at Eira.

33

'And what Mary said was he had so much to him. He was going to get on, she was sure of it.'

'I expect he will,' Ellen said, looking across.

'Get on where though?' Mrs Lucas burst out, and turned on the tap, which gurgled and then sent out a sudden rush of light brown water. 'Get on with her I wanted,' she said sharply.

Ellen hesitated, not knowing what to say.

'The water's bad again,' she said at last.

'Yes, every winter. It's a tank two fields up. Only the mud around there you should see.'

'It shouldn't get into the tank.'

'Look,' was Mrs Lucas's only answer, as she rippled her fingers in the muddy water. 'Now put that baby back and come and help me with these greens.'

Ellen obeyed, slowly. She tucked Eira in, and walked to the sink.

'That's Rosser, you see,' Mrs Lucas said. 'Tell him will he go and look at it, he'll tell you every house has got a right to clean water and you'll get it by voting.'

'Voting,' Ellen said, and laughed.

'I'd get up there myself, though it's Hybart's job,' Mrs Lucas said angrily.

'I'll ask Harry to look,' Ellen said.

'It's Hybart's job. He gets the rent.'

'Perhaps Harry can help anyway,' Ellen said, and went on with her work.

Going to look at the water was a regular job for the men on the patch. Bill Hybart, whose father had built all these houses, and who lived now in the first, tried to get it right, but it was only a brook at the edge of a wood, with a small tank. The cattle were often in the field, and the overflow from the tank made all the ground around it muddy, and the cattle could not be kept away. Ellen spoke to Harry, and he went to see Hybart. The two men walked up together and looked, but there seemed little enough that could be done.

'A proper scheme see, Harry,' Hybart said, 'and we'd solve it. But

I can't put that in on my own, and there you have it. Two, three hundred quid at lowest.'

'Aye,' Harry agreed, standing in the mud and looking down at the muddy overflow. Hybart was ready to go, but Harry kept standing there and looking. He turned at last, and they walked back together down the fields. A great cloud hung low over the black line of the mountains, and the distant spurs were hidden. They separated, without discussing the water again. Some days later, however, Harry went again to Hybart.

'I been up looking at the water.'

'We all go and look at it, Harry,' Hybart said, backing his horse into the shafts of his wagon.

'I know not much could be done,' Harry said, 'but there's a bit, if I got your permission.'

'You do what you like, boy. Long as you don't blow it up.'

Harry smiled and explained.

The following week, when he was on afternoons, he borrowed the wagon and fetched a load of old sleepers from the station, and dumped them beside the tank. Next morning he laid a sleeper track from the dry, higher ground through the mud to the tank. Then, under the overflow, he dug a deep channel, and lined it three sleepers high on each side. Finally he cut stakes and fenced off the immediate area, against the cattle. It was four mornings' work, and the water was still discoloured at the end of it. But there was some improvement, and Harry himself was pleased. Hybart also was pleased, though still doubtful. 'It looks tidier, but it's still dirty.'

'Keep the cattle out at least,' Harry said.

'Aye,' Hybart said, 'that.'

There were sleepers left, and when the turns were right Harry and Morgan cross-sawed them into two-foot lengths for firewood, and stacked them in the big shed where the hens roosted. More and more it seemed like the settling-in of a family. Working together on the sawing, the men became more friendly, though always within the limits of Harry's reserve. Morgan was quick and intelligent, well able to judge other men. Now that he knew Harry he liked him, with

35

something of the patronage of an elder and more capable brother. One day, as they changed turns in the box, he referred to the way things were going.

'It's working out all right, isn't it?' he said, confidently.

'We're all right,' Harry said, looking away.

'You ever thought, Harry, that money's not all that important, not really?'

'My money's important to me.'

'Aye, your money. But just take it now. I pay Hybart rent, you pay me lodging, I pay Mrs Lucas for the housekeeping. But the money between us is like passing the salt or something. We live more like a family.'

'Aye, it suits us,' Harry said, and turned away. 'Well, bed,' he said slowly, and went down to get his bike to ride home. As he rode through the dark, gripping the worn rubber at the ends of his handlebars, he knew his own life, and could feel it, but it was still, at any time, a kind of riding through the dark. All that was around him he had to wait to find, in his own time.

Later, he remembered this conversation, and again thought about it. This was at Christmas, and both men were at home, for on Christmas Day the box was closed, and there was through working from Gwenton to Pont Dulas, the next station north. It was a family dinner, with Morgan at the head of the table, Mrs Lucas on his left, and Harry and Ellen facing them, Ellen near the cradle where Eira was asleep. They had killed one of their own hens, and fetched in the vegetables from the shed. They drank wheat wine, eighteen months old, that had been bottled a month before from the big stone jar under the stairs. Morgan was gay and hospitable, flirting a little with Ellen, teasing Mrs Lucas, refilling Harry's glass.

'Well, the happy family,' he said, lifting his glass.

'We was lucky,' Ellen said.

'I was lucky,' Morgan corrected her, gallantly.

Harry said nothing.

Mrs Lucas got up and cleared the plates, and Ellen, after looking at Eira, went across to help. They were in the front room, and could see through the window the wide expanse of the valley: the dull winter grass, the grey woods, the wet red earth of plough. Beyond, the mountains were very clear and close. A train went through, north, whistling as it passed Glynmawr's open signals.

'Express a bit late,' Harry said, looking at his big pocket watch.

'Forget it, mun. It's Christmas. Keep the family party, forget the work. There'll be trains enough tomorrow, and if they're late, we're not on them.'

'It is like a family Christmas, after lodgings,' Ellen said.

'There you are, see,' Morgan laughed, and Ellen saw what she had said and laughed too. But when we are all here, Harry thought, staring out at the mountains, it isn't that really, not really.

4

In March, Will Probert and his wife, who lived in the nearer of the adjoining cottages across the lane, gave notice to move: they were going up Trawsfynydd to be nearer their son, a woodman. Harry heard of the notice from Probert, and at once, without consulting Ellen, went to see Hybart to ask for the cottage.

'Well, Harry, I'd be glad see. Only the missus does the letting and she's in town. If I said to you "yes" and she come back and had promised it somewhere, there'd be ructions now, wouldn't there?'

'I'll come round again when she's back,' Harry said.

'Well, all right. Only let me talk to her first. She don't like to be rushed. Then let your missus come round perhaps, that'd be the best.'

'I've not mentioned it to her,' Harry said. 'I come straight round when Probert let me know.'

Hybart looked at him, wiping his untidy moustache. 'They like to be asked, boy. If only for the fun of saying no.'

Harry nodded.

'They all do say no, see, at first,' Hybart added, winking. 'That's the fun, mun.'

'Not in houses,' Harry said.

Hybart laughed. 'It's a damp old place, Harry,' he said, more seriously. 'Not like Rosser's.'

'Maybe. Only I haven't got Rosser's.'

'You're all right there, aren't you?'

'Yes, for a lodging.'

Hybart looked away, and spat past his boot. 'What we all want to split up for, Harry, I don't know. All of us on this patch now, we could all get into my house, two or three a room. That's how it used to be, see.'

'You'd go out of job as a builder then.'

'Aye, of course, that's what I mean. We do it to make work. Like you now, on the line. Where do they want to be going, all them up and down in these trains? They only go, after, to come back.'

Harry moved impatiently. Hybart was a bigger man than himself, lean, long-nosed, sandy. He was well respected, but to Harry, watching him, it seemed that the life of the earth dribbled away in men like this.

'It's cunning though, Harry,' Hybart said, leaning close to him. 'We make all this work, see, and out we go. Then they're at home, cooking our dinner. Back we come see, patting our pocket. Money, girl, money – look! They don't say no.'

'Aye, well, I must be getting back,' Harry said. 'I'll look round this evening.'

'Better if your missus come.'

'I'll settle it, thank you.'

When Harry got back to Rosser's, Ellen and Mrs Lucas were in the kitchen ironing, and Eira was on a blanket on the floor, in a cage of chairs.

'Hullo,' Harry said, bending down to the baby, who lay kicking on her back. The baby smiled, unknowing, and Harry smiled and touched her nose with his slender finger.

'There's a father for you then,' Mrs Lucas said, to Ellen.

Ellen smiled, but without feeling. At five months she was already heavy with the child, and had gone much more quiet, at times almost sullen. Harry went to her, and put his arm across her back, squeezing her shoulder with his fingers. She went on ironing, unresponsive. Harry looked at Mrs Lucas, who showed no signs of moving. After a moment he turned back, and bent down again over the baby.

'You hear what happened to Lippy up the waterworks?' Mrs Lucas asked.

'No.'

Lippy was a Lancashire man in his thirties, very small and weak for the labourer's work that he was doing. He lived in an isolated cottage, away from the lane. His sick wife, a local girl, came from one of the two village families that were commonly regarded as poor: the Daveys, who lived in a hovel beside the river, just below the chapel, and the Loams, from a cottage far up on Darren, where Elsie Lippy had been born, the sixth child of ten. Tommy Lippy had met and married her in service, and they had drifted back to Glynmawr. He worked now on the dam that was being built far up in the mountains, west of Darren; he went up each day in a lorry, with other local men.

'Course it's Elsie's fault,' Mrs Lucas went on. 'She don't give him the food, only an apple and a bit of thin bread and butter she learned to cut thin in service, like a wafer. Course, Lippy brings this out and the others get on at him. Bring bacon, mun, they say. Not enough, the wife says. Then cheese, mun. Don't know about cheese. Well, eggs. Got no hens!'

Harry had stood up, and was watching intently. Ellen, he noticed, was smiling.

'Isn't only hens lay eggs, Lippy. All birds lay eggs. Well, I know that, Lippy says, know it as well as you, what you coming? Some too small, they say, some too sour, some got ballies in them. What's ballies? Ballies is like you, Lippy, born before their time. Lippy don't take no notice. But now moorhens, Lippy. Up here see, moors, moorhens. Lovely egg, rich.'

Harry laughed.

'Where d'you find 'em, Lippy says. We'll find 'em, give you some tomorrow. Next dinner, yesterday it was, I met Billy Davies he told

39

me. Here you are, Lippy, moorhen's eggs. Looks like hen's eggs, Lippy says. Aye, only better. Have to cook 'em, Lippy says, boil 'em. No, mun, not moorhen's eggs. Raw, mun, tip it back. They was all round him see now, and one of them got a knife out and clipped off the top. Gel, Lippy's nose. They was rotten hens' eggs, see. Nasty, Lippy says. Get away, mun, lovely. That Davey you know, George Davey, he done it. He'd got a good hen's egg ready see, and he clips it and tips it back. Be a man, Lippy, he says, tip back. Billy said he did it himself, I don't wonder if they pushed it down him. Anyhow Lippy takes it, and sick, well.'

'Poor little chap,' Ellen said.

'He isn't safe to be around,' Harry said, with a surprising edge of anger. 'He don't work, only brew tea and run errands. And getting thirty-eight bob, he's lucky.'

'Call you lucky if you eat a rotten egg.'

'Lippy can't get out of his own way,' Harry said, and went out.

He came back into the kitchen half an hour later, but Mrs Lucas was still there. He hesitated, and then said to Ellen, 'Seen them grey socks of mine?'

'What grey socks?'

'The knitted grey, you put in the drawer.'

'I haven't moved them.'

'I looked in the drawer, they're not there.'

'Well, you don't want them.'

'Yes.'

'Now?'

'Aye, might as well. These I got on are wet a bit.'

'Well, there's others. The black there in the basket.'

'The black are thin. I want the grey.'

Ellen looked at him, and he met her eyes.

'All right, I'll find them,' she said. She took her iron, and replaced it on the stove. Mrs Lucas, busy at the other end of the table, seemed to have noticed nothing. Ellen went slowly out, and up the stairs to the bedroom. Harry followed her, and closed the bedroom door.

'Here,' Ellen said, at once finding the socks in the drawer. 'It's not that,' Harry said. 'I wanted a word on our own.'

'What about for goodness sake? Dragging me up here for nothing when I'm tired.'

'The Proberts have give notice,' Harry said. 'That cottage is going.'

'Well?'

'I asked Hybart for it.'

'Asked him?'

'Aye, I went straight down, didn't want to miss it.'

'Not much to miss.'

'It's all right. Damp, Hybart says, but I don't think so. There's a guttering loose I noticed on the end wall, probably all it is.'

Ellen waited, looking at him, and then suddenly flung herself down on the bed and cried with her face in the pillow. Harry, holding his breath, looked away. The apple buds on the tree just below the window were moving. He looked down with a warm feeling at the short white tips.

'Is it you don't want to move?' he said, still looking at the buds.

Ellen did not answer, but her crying went silent, and she turned her face on the side.

'Is it?' Harry asked.

His voice was very strong, though low-pitched near the window. 'Well, say, is it?'

Still she did not speak, but he knew that she was looking at him. He struggled a moment, and then went across and sat beside her. Her fine hair lay disordered over the puffy eyes and mottled cheeks.

'Is it, girl?' he asked again, putting his hand low on her back.

'Did Hybart say yes?' she asked in return, her voice more controlled then he had expected.

'We're settling it this evening. When Mrs Hybart's back.'

'Do you want to go then, Harry?'

'I want my own place.'

'But with the baby coming, and here Mrs Lucas to help.'

'It's only across the lane, girl.'

'And the furnishing of the place, now, like I am.'

'I'll get that done.'

'Aye, somehow,' Ellen said, and even smiled.

'You tell me, I'll do it,' he said stubbornly.

She looked intently into his stubborn, heavy face, and at the deep blue eyes that were now very settled and clear.

'Well, Harry, I don't want to, and that's straight.'

'Why?' he said, getting up off the bed.

'I don't feel up to it, not with the baby coming. I'm safe here, I know I'm safe.'

Harry rubbed his hand over his face, and looked down at her.

'That rate we'll be here for ever.'

'Not ever. There's other houses.'

'Aye, and other babies, and this place damp and that place lonely, always a reason.'

'Why shouldn't I want my own house?' Ellen asked, facing him.

'Yes. That's what I said.'

'Only something a bit better than that, I hope, and when I'm all right.'

'Like this, say?' Harry asked, and Ellen saw for a moment a new expression, over the whole face, that made her catch her breath.

'When I'm better,' she said, putting out her hand and gripping his fingers, which stayed limp and cold.

'When it's time,' he said, and gently disengaging his fingers turned from the bed and went out. He closed the door quietly behind him, and walked softly down the carpeted stairs. He did not mean to go back into the kitchen, but Mrs Lucas called from near the door.

'She all right?'

'Bit tired, I think.'

'It's only natural, as she is. I heard her crying, they all do that. No use being hard when they get like that, just quiet.'

'You keep out of it,' Harry said, with a sudden open anger. It was the first angry word that had passed between them, and Mrs Lucas drew back quickly, but then wiped her hand on her apron and smiled.

42

'You won't do no wrong,' she said, and turned back into the kitchen.

5

That evening Harry went to Hybart's. Mrs Hybart, tall and dark, with bright red cheeks, answered the door and at once asked him in. He wiped his feet carefully, and took off his cap. He followed Mrs Hybart into the big, stone-flagged kitchen, where Hybart was sitting in a high wooden chair by the fire.

'Sit down then,' Mrs Hybart said, drawing out a kitchen chair from the long, white-scrubbed table. He sat on the edge, and put down his cap. Mrs Hybart sat opposite her husband, and folded her arms.

'I come about the Proberts' place,' Harry said at once. 'I'd be glad of it if it's going.'

'The Proberts are going, yes,' Mrs Hybart said, watching him.

'What rent would it be?' Harry asked, though he knew the rent from Will Probert.

'Five shillings the week the Proberts have paid,' Mrs Hybart answered. She was finding, to her surprise, that she could not stare this young man down. Hybart, although he was not being looked at, glanced away.

'That I can manage,' Harry said. 'My job's regular.'

'And your wife?' Mrs Hybart asked.

'She'll be glad of a place of her own.'

'Will be? She wants it then?'

'I come to ask you.'

'I told Harry it was damp,' Hybart said to his wife.

'The damp is nothing,' she said sternly.

Harry reached for his cap, and stood up.

'Well?' he said, looking at both in turn. 'Can I have it?'

'Sit down, boy,' Mrs Hybart said. 'What's the old hurry? Let's have a look at you.'

43

Harry stayed standing, but smiled. Mrs Hybart looked sternly up at him, her eyes bright.

'Bill,' she said suddenly, 'we'll have a glass of wine.'

Hybart looked surprised, but sat forward, pushing at his moustache.

'Go on, mun, get it,' she said, impatiently.

Hybart got up. His heavy boots were unlaced, and he stumbled a little as he moved.

'Sit down,' Mrs Hybart repeated.

'The elderflower?' Hybart asked, standing at the dresser.

'Aye.'

'I'd take on,' Harry said, 'from when the Proberts move. Only we wouldn't go from Rosser's for two or three weeks – I'd have to get the place right.'

'No furniture?' Mrs Hybart asked.

'No.'

'Sit down boy, sit down.'

She took the bottle that her husband handed her. She fetched glasses from the dresser, and set them on the end of the long table. Harry waited for Hybart to sit again, and then sat himself.

'There's a sale Friday week up Cefn, and another the Monday after, a good one, at Tretower,' Mrs Hybart said, handing the two men their glasses. Harry sipped at once, his slender fingers curved tightly round the glass.

'And you'll pay rent when you move in, not before.'

Harry nodded, and sipped the dry, scented wine.

'How long is it with your wife now?'

'July it's expected.'

'We'll get you settled by then, boy, don't worry.'

'Aye, should be plenty of time.'

'I'll take your wife to the sales. I know those houses. I know the things are worth.'

'I got twenty-three pound,' Harry said. 'That'll have to do it.'

'What you furnishing?' Mrs Hybart exclaimed, and for the first time laughed. 'This house?'

44

Harry smiled.

'Here's to the baby boy,' Mrs Hybart said, lifting her glass.

'Or girl,' Harry said.

'Or twins, mun, Harry,' Hybart broke in, laughing loudly. 'One of each, mun, as a sample.'

Though the others hardly responded to him, Hybart got up and stood with his back to the fire.

'We'll have a look round one of these days, Harry, see if there's any little jobs.'

'There's a guttering loose,' Harry said at once. 'On the end wall.'

'Aye, well guttering now,' Hybart began, but at once his wife got up.

'We don't want to keep the lad from his wife now. Go on boy, back and look after her.'

Harry put down his glass and got up, holding his cap. 'Thank you,' he said. 'Both.'

Mrs Hybart smoothed down her heavy black dress. 'Don't hang about, boy. Go on.'

Harry smiled and made his own way out. As he walked back up the lane, he whistled as he looked up through the bare branches at the spread of stars.

6

Ellen accepted the decision, once it was made. She had periods of crying, but Mrs Lucas took charge of her, and kept her settled. Morgan, when Harry told him, seemed genuinely sorry, but agreed that sometime it had to be done. Mrs Hybart, for her part, was as good as her word. She called on Ellen, and took her to the sales, buying and advising shrewdly, accepting all Ellen's preferences. Hybart lent Harry his wagon to bring the various articles of furniture home. He had done nothing about the guttering, but one day when he was out Mrs Hybart told Harry where to get the ladder, and came and held it for him while he did the comparatively simple repair.

Fires were lit, and windows opened, in the mild April sunshine. The end room, which had been damp, Harry repapered. By the third week in April the house was ready to live in, and Harry paid Mrs Hybart the first rent. On the same afternoon, the suitcase, the leather box, the wooden box, and the frail, with all their personal belongings, were carried across the lane, and the move was completed.

Llwyn Celyn, as both cottages were called, after the big holly tree that stood in front of them on the edge of the lane, had originally been Hybart's father's workshop. When Josh Hybart was a young journeyman builder, he had married Joan Thomas, the only daughter of Will Thomas whose son Jack still farmed at the top of the lane. At the wedding Josh had been given the two fields, then largely covered with bracken and bramble, on which all the houses of the patch now stood. He had hired men and, building first the large house in which his son still lived, had brought his wife there, and set up his business. The two next houses were those now occupied by the Powells and Rosser, in similar pattern but diminishing scale along the lane. Then, across the lane from his house, he built the long brick workshop, with two storeys, the top floor being used for the carpentry. In the following years, three cottages were built, one up the lane past the workshop, the other two in cleared ground behind the three larger houses. The building was all substantial, and well planned: all except the workshop were in stone. Now, half a century later, the patch was settled and pleasant. More houses might have been built on it, but the gardens were kept large, and there were big runs for poultry, and a long, open drying-green where the children of the patch played. Bill Hybart, after his father's death, had often talked of adding further houses, but did not. He built a row of four cottages under the Holy Mountain, near the church, and then moved gradually back to where his father had begun, employing no regular men, but working himself at repairs and minor alterations. He also dealt, quite profitably, in hay. With the diminished scale of work, the brick workshop was not needed, and in 1914 was converted into two cottages, with nine small rooms between them. A tall, wooden workshop, beside his own house, took its place.

An old couple, called Lewis, had lived from the beginning in the western end. The other end, into which Harry and Ellen moved, was slightly the larger of the two. On the ground floor, it had a built-on back-kitchen, which was entered from the long porch by a door beside the main door; this kitchen had no other communication with the rest of the cottage. From the main door a narrow passage ran to the stairs, and from the landing opened three bedrooms, one of which was over the Lewises' kitchen. Downstairs, the living-room, with two windows, opened off the passage, and at the far end of the living-room (always called simply 'the room') was a dark pantry – at the extreme end of the cottage from the kitchen. The pantry was matched by another, extremely small room, which had a door to it from the living room. Nothing could be done in so small a space, although it had a door to it and was a room in everything but size. Harry, walking round one day with Mrs Hybart, before the move, argued that this space should never have been walled-off at all, but left with the living-room. Mrs Hybart agreed, and added: 'I took less interest, see, then. I had the children in arms.'

'And the back-kitchen now,' Harry said. 'There could be a door through to it from the passage. Otherwise, want to eat anywhere but the back-kitchen, you got to carry the food about round the open.'

'You got the porch, boy.'

'The porch is open, the rain blows in it.'

'I know, yes. Only get settled in, look, before you start pulling the place to bits.'

Harry smiled. 'Aye,' he agreed. 'Only easier if it had been done with the original conversion.'

'It's always the case, isn't it?' Mrs Hybart said sadly, looking out through the open window at a cart passing in the lane. 'Not knowing what you ought to have done till it's gone too late.'

'I wouldn't say that,' Harry answered, and moved busily on through the rooms.

47

The disadvantages of the cottage were obvious, but when the furniture had been moved in it seemed very comfortable and attractive. There was good new linoleum on all the floors, except in the back-kitchen, which had a decent brick floor. There were several good chairs, and a kitchen-table and a round oak living-table, and bright yellow-patterned curtains. In the bedrooms were two good beds: one of them, in the main bedroom, a big mahogany tester, bought at Tretower, of which Harry was particularly proud. The small middle bedroom was still empty.

The Proberts had been tidy people, and the water-butts in the little front garden between the cottage and the lane were sound and newly tarred. The garden itself was crammed with flowers, and was bright, when they moved, with white and lilac sweet rocket, and sweet williams budding in a long bed under the holly. Looking back across the lane at Morgan's house, Harry felt no disadvantage. Ellen, for her part, took the place as it came, working with Mrs Lucas at the curtains and cushions, but centred increasingly on her own body bearing the child. It was a fine spring, and the crowded fruit trees on the patch were heavy with blossom, which the bees worked incessantly. Ellen waited, and let herself be carried, through the peaceful weeks.

7

More and more often, during the last weeks of waiting, Mrs Lucas moved across the lane and stayed with Ellen. The warm spring had matured into an unusually hot summer. The hay was cut, in the fields across the valley, and horses dragged the loaded gambos through the narrow lanes, to the barns where the dusty heat, even near the gables, was almost unbearable. Eira, when Mrs Lucas was at the cottage, lay in a cradle in the open porch, and usually stretched out beside her was Rex, the Lewises' collie, old and smelling in the heat. In the cottage, everything was made ready for the birth, and still the meals were prepared, and the men came at their odd times from work and ate them, going out quickly again, leaving the women on their own. At first, Morgan still ate in his own house, but as Mrs Lucas stayed more with Ellen he would often come to the cottage and take his meals there, while the house across the road stood temporarily unused. On the line, traffic was heavy, with the big summer shifting of coal. Several Sundays were worked, and the men were more often away.

It was on a Sunday, late in July, that the birth came. Ellen did not get up in the morning, and Harry fetched Mrs Lucas early. She at once got Ellen up and made her walk around the room, in which the big tester bed left only a narrow space. Morgan was at work, and Harry, due to relieve him at two that afternoon, stayed around the cottage, often standing near Eira, who was sleeping peacefully in the porch. Mrs Lucas had expected to cook Sunday dinner, but she could not leave Ellen for more than a few minutes, and Harry, under her directions, put the food on the stove. He wanted the birth to come before he had to go to work, but when he went up, soon after one, he found Ellen still being roughly walked about the room, then stopping and leaning on the end of the bed, looking across at him with the distant eyes of a child in pain. He said what he could, and went reluctantly back down. Soon after, he had to leave for the station.

Morgan promised, when he relieved him, to come back up when there was news, but Harry sat all afternoon and evening in the box, which on Sundays was always lonely, and no message came. At ten he closed up, for Meredith to re-open at five, and rode as fast as he could down the village, and up the steep dark lane. The yellow lamp shone out from the bedroom window; only a candle was burning downstairs. Eira was back in her own bed, and Morgan in his own kitchen. Harry stood in the garden, hearing a scream from the window open above him. He could not say he heard Ellen – the voice was strange and barely human – but he could hear Mrs Lucas's urgent voice, and knew that still he must wait. Above the garden and the trees, the summer sky was drawing into an intense deep mauve. Over the line of the Cefn, to the east, hung the pale full moon. Harry walked to the big water-butt, which was almost empty. He could smell, from the drying wood, a sourness which stayed separate from the night-sweet scent of the stocks and roses under the red wall. Above him the tall chimney stack seemed distorted and elongated. The screaming came again.

He went indoors and along the passage to the foot of the stairs. Then he knew he must turn back, and walked slowly out through the porch to the back-kitchen. He lit the hand-lamp, and stoked the fire of the copper, in which the water was still hot. There was a step at the door, and Morgan was looking across at him. They nodded, but hardly spoke. Harry saw suddenly how tense Morgan was. He looked away without speaking and put a kettle on the stove for tea. They sat opposite each other, in the poor light, sipping the scalding tea. Above them, the bedroom was silent. After some while, they heard footsteps down the stairs and along the passage. Harry stood, expecting to see Mrs Lucas, but it was Mrs Hybart. He had not known she was in the house. She came in, looked at them both, and smiled.

'You two making yourselves comfortable then?'

'How is she?' Morgan asked. Harry had asked only with his eyes.

'Not a she, a he,' Mrs Hybart said roughly. 'You got a boy, Harry.'

Harry smiled, looking past her shoulder.

'Don't you want to know how your wife is?' she went on, watching him with amused eyes.

'She's all right, is she?'

'Yes boy, all right and all over.'

'It's been such a time.'

'Aye, the first, and too big he is, see. What you want a boy like that for?'

'Big?'

'Aye. Now don't stand there gaping but let me have some of that water. You let the copper fire out?'

'No, I stoked it.'

'Thank goodness you're some use. Standing there, the two of you. Like dogs in the wet you are. Mind then, let me fill this bowl.'

The men stood obediently aside. They were used to this.

'Eira asleep?' Mrs Hybart said over her shoulder to Morgan.

'Aye,' Morgan said, gruffly.

'Mind then,' she said, as she came with the filled bowl from the copper and walked back out through the porch.

The birth had been difficult, but there were no compli-cations, although Ellen was very weak. Harry saw her briefly that night, and she smiled and looked for him to go to see the child. Harry went across, awkwardly, and stared down into the cradle. Mrs. Lucas lifted the lamp, and the yellow light fell across the tiny wrapped head.

'Right, get off to bed now,' Mrs Lucas whispered. Harry turned and smiled again at Ellen, who did not notice him. Then he went tiptoe out of the warm room. He did not go to bed until Mrs Hybart came down on her way back to her own house. He thanked her, and then took a candle and went up alone to the end room.

Ellen was slow in recovering her strength, though Mrs Lucas nursed her carefully. Harry sat with her for longer periods each day, and by the Thursday spoke of the one thing he knew he must do – registering the birth. They had talked generally about names, but without agreement. Ellen, for a boy, wanted Will, which had been her father's name. Harry wanted Matthew, though only he knew why, for it was not a name that meant anything in either family. When he finally raised the point, it was while Mrs Lucas was in the room, clearing up.

'I could go this afternoon to Mrs Evans, get it done.'

Mrs Evans kept the post office, and was also the registrar.

'Yes,' Ellen said, turning her head on the pillow.

'What you want me to put down?'

'He's Will.'

Harry hesitated, his deep blue eyes withdrawn.

'Only William, see, you got to put down,' Mrs Lucas explained. 'William you put down and then call him Will for short.'

'I thought Matthew though.'

Mrs Lucas looked at him, surprised.

51

'Aye, well Matthew's nice.'

'There hasn't been a Matthew,' Ellen said, stubbornly.

'Nice to have a family name,' Mrs Lucas said.

'Aye, Matthew Henry you'd put down,' Harry said. 'Henry being from me.'

'It's right to put the father's name,' Mrs Lucas said, looking back at Ellen.

'The second name don't matter,' Ellen said. 'Only his first name's Will.'

'She wants Will,' Mrs Lucas said, and smiled.

Harry stood up. Ellen's fine hair lay spread out under her on the pillow. Her cheeks were red and pretty, under the pale, still frightened eyes.

'Go on then, get it over,' Mrs Lucas said. 'I'll have your tea ready by the time you're back.'

Harry nodded, and looked down at Ellen. She seemed very small and alone, under the posts and canopy of the big bed.

'I stick to Matthew,' he said, but caught his breath as he saw tears start into her eyes.

'Go and do what you like.'

When he came back, about an hour later, his tea was ready in the kitchen, and he ate it and went out to work in the garden. It was not until late evening that he came back into the house. Mrs Lucas was in the porch, getting ready to go back across.

'Go up and see her. I'm off now.'

'Aye. When I've washed.'

'You done the registering?'

'Aye.' He washed and tidied himself, then went upstairs. Ellen was lying awake, in the big bed. The baby was beside her, its head turned under her arm. Harry leaned over and kissed Ellen on the cheek.

'All right, girl?'

'Yes.'

'He all right?'

'He hasn't been, but he is now.'

Harry drew back from the bed, and went and sat on the chair by the window, looking down into the lane. Mrs Hybart's two children, Alun and Muriel, were playing under the holly tree, drawing with a stick in the dust. Far up the lane, a dog barked frantically as if trapped.

'You see Mrs Evans?'

'Yes.'

'What did you put down then?'

The children below were quarrelling over the use of the stick.

Harry watched them, prepared to shout.

'Matthew Henry Price.'

There was a silence. The stale heat of the room hung heavily between them. Harry caught for a moment the bitter scent of the elderflower that was spread to dry in the unused middle bedroom. He looked round, confused.

'You never went against me.'

'I put that down.'

'How could you? After how hard it was.'

'Keep quiet down there, you young shavers,' Harry got up and shouted, leaning from the window as the quarrel broke out again. The children looked up at him and moved away.

'I'd said Matthew.'

Ellen did not answer.

'Anyway now it's down, girl, no use us quarrelling.'

Ellen smiled, and turned her face so that her cheek rested along the baby's head.

'What do it matter it's down?' she said as if to herself. 'He is Will whatever.'

8

There was a good flower garden in front of the cottage, but the rent also included a long vegetable garden at the side of the drying green. Harry worked at this, and in the following autumn persuaded Mrs Hybart to rent him for a pound a year a further strip adjoining it, which he put under fruit trees – apple and pear and plum. Also, that same autumn, he was able to rent two strips of garden behind the timber yard at the station, and these he put down one to gooseberries and currants, the other to potatoes. In the following spring he bought wood and made four hives, which by the end of the summer, buying swarms in the valley, he had stocked with bees. The hives stood among the young fruit trees at the edge of the home vegetable garden. Then, at the end of the strip, he built a poultry run, which would be Ellen's work.

Although he got on easily enough with his mates at work, he still had no close friends in the village. He never went to the pubs, and his gardens, added to the railway work, left him little free time. People got used to seeing him ride through the village, on his old high bicycle. He was always hurrying. The heavy body seemed under some violent pressure forward, and over it, in the frame of the black coat and the regular black cap, was the set, hard face with the distantly brooding deep blue eyes.

Ellen understood the life that Harry was making, for she had known his family at home, and they had always lived like this. The Prices were living in their cottage at Llangattock, while Ellen's father, Will Lewis, was a foreman at the Peterstone mill on the border river. As a farm labourer, Jack Price got twelve and sixpence a week, with milk and eggs. Although there were always children in the house, Mary Price also worked. She would take the children gleaning or hop-picking in the fields north of Peterstone, where Ellen as a girl also went. Or, on the rougher fields of Llangattock, she would pick stones by the day: a cartload would fetch a shilling or sometimes a shilling and threepence. Later, she got a weekly contract for washing from the big house, Llangattock Manor. The dirty clothes would be brought down each Monday in a donkey-cart, and by Thursdays, except in the winter when drying was difficult, were ready to be returned. Then, when Harry was five, his father had rented an acre of glebe land not far from the cottage. This was the family's mainstay, as the children grew. At the bottom of the little field, pigsties were built, and a hurdle enclosure. Two or three pigs would be kept for bacon, and the others as breeding sows, to give piglets that could be sold at market for seven and sixpence or sometimes ten shillings. In the rest of the acre grew the family's potatoes, and at the top barley or oats, as feed for the pigs. Ellen could remember being at the mill with her father, when Jack Price and two or three of his boys would bring down the corn harvest. She remembered Harry once, standing beside her father, watching the threshed grain coming through. One of the workmen shouted that that was the end of Price's, but her father had called, 'Leave it, it's still Jack's coming through.' She knew later that it was not, and that the Prices often carried home an extra sack. As well as the grain, the pigs were fed on acorns. It was Harry's regular job in the autumn to fetch a bucket of acorns before going to school. The seven Price children, three boys and four girls, grew up strong and healthy, although their mother died young, in 1917, while Harry was at home with his wounded wrist.

Now, as Harry made his settlement in Glynmawr, Ellen saw and accepted the pattern. She knew it was no use trying to stop him working, although it meant that he was not often in the house, and in the first years she was often alone with her child. Will, after one dangerous attack of bronchitis at nine months, was a healthy child, with his mother's bright hair and fine skin. As he grew older, he could be left at times with Harry, when he was working on one of the home gardens. Eira, almost a year older, was also often left in the garden or on the drying green. Or sometimes the two children would be put in Morgan's house, watched, though never closely, by Mrs Lucas. For Ellen liked to get away to the town, shopping, and took every chance she could.

'When we moved,' she said, 'I was having Will, and we just fixed things up anyhow. Now I've got to get it right.'

Most of her buying was for the house: curtains and cushion material, pretty china, a mirror, a set of ornaments. Her eye for these things was good, and the furnishing of the cottage came to be admired by the other women, though less by Mrs Lucas and Mrs Hybart, who were differently adjusted. Morgan, among the men, was always quick to notice and to praise. He often congratulated Harry on Ellen's good taste. Harry was pleased by this. He knew it was not his world.

So, slowly, the home and the gardens were made. It was four years, really, before Harry and Ellen felt themselves changing, and knew that the settling had come. One important factor in this was Ellen's decision not to have another child. She told Harry this, one morning when he found her crying.

'All right,' Harry said. 'That's your affair.'

'Only if you're disappointed, Harry...' she said, watching him. She had always this ability to recover very quickly from crying, and go on in a normal voice.

'Disappointed? Why should I be?'

His eyes fixed on the tiny window, fifteen inches square, in the back wall of the kitchen. Through this, beyond a young fir tree, was the dark line of the mountains. Ellen was papering the window, with semi-transparent, heavily-patterned window-paper, but at the top it was still clear, and a little of the distance could be seen.

'Only you grew up in a large family,' Ellen said.

'Too large for Mam.'

'Well then. What is it? Don't you like that paper?'

'No, no, it's all right.'

Will was sitting at their feet by the brass fender, cutting at cardboard with old, blunted scissors. Harry looked down at him and smiled.

'What you making, boy?'

'A train.'

Harry smiled, and bent down to him.

'I used to cut out cows like that. Shall I show you?'

'Mam showed me how to cut the train.'

Harry paused and stood up again. 'Aye, well. Later perhaps.'

He washed at the sink, and went out into the garden, where he had a row of seedling lettuce to transplant. He was due at work at two, and at twelve had dinner but went out again as the row was still not finished. He worked fast, his feet set wide apart in the soft

56

red earth, his body bent over the tightness of the broad leather belt. He seemed to forget time, and at five to two Ellen ran out, alarmed.

'Don't you know the time? I only just seen you there. I thought you'd gone.'

'What?'

'Five to two.'

'No?'

'It is. You're bound to be late.'

He rubbed his hand over his face, the slim, pale hand against the dark face. He looked quickly around the garden, and then across the valley at the line of the railway.

He stooped, and heeled in the loose lettuce.

'Leave them,' Ellen said. 'I'll fetch your bike.'

She ran back to the house, and as he came slowly into the lane, passed the old, high machine into his hands. Harry took the saddle, but still looked round reluctantly.

'Give them lettuce some water about six.'

'Aye, only hurry, boy. What's the matter with you?'

Harry nodded. He put his foot on the pedal, and then, leaning across, caught her shoulder and pulled her forward to kiss her on the lips and cheek.

'Go on with you, boy.'

'Aye, so long,' he said, laughing, and, pushing suddenly, jumped astride the thin, knobbed leather saddle, and rode fast away down the lane.

9

In the following autumn, Harry met Edwin Parry, who farmed far up on Brynllwyd, north of Brynllwyd House. Parry had come to the station with timber. There was a big trade just then in pit-props, and many of the farmers had turned to it. Edwin – tall, slow, fair-haired – came up into the box when he had finished his business. Slowly lighting his pipe, he stood near the door, waiting with the local reluctance to turn away from any man just met. Harry talked about the timber, and from that they moved on to Edwin's farm and its difficulties, talking so easily and at once taking to each other that Edwin stayed to the end of Harry's turn, and before they separated invited him to come up one day to the farm.

About a week later Harry decided to go up, and walked out across the valley, crossing the river by the bridge below the chapel, and making his way across the fields towards the rise to the mountain, where he could see the white front wall of Edwin's farmhouse. Few farms in the whole valley were big. The majority had six or seven fields, and the best farms were in the bed of the valley, near the river. Edwin's was far up. Not one of his fields was anywhere near flat. Those across which Harry walked to the house sloped so steeply that already, though it was meadow and ploughland, he seemed to be climbing the mountain itself. Everywhere there were signs of the seizure of this land from the mountain. From every hedge the bracken encroached, and brooks and watercourses, slow declivities of marsh, cut across the steep fields. At the edges of the water, bracken and bramble grew thickly. Farther up, in the last high field before the house, gorse grew thickly on the steep banks, which ran suddenly away from the general pitch of the field. The lane alongside, barely a cart wide, was so heavily grown that it was roofed with thorn and hazel to a green tunnel, and ferns and mosses grew thickly in its shadow, in the wet red earth.

As Harry approached the house, two black-and-white collies came tearing out at him, barking furiously and snarling as they came near. The older dog backed away at Harry's shout, but the younger jumped at him impetuously, baring its teeth. Harry laughed, and lifted his knee as the dog jumped. He felt the hard kneecap smack against the dog's lower jaw, and there was a yelp of pain which he cut across with an angry, wordless shout, that sent the young dog to its distance, where it followed, still barking furiously. The dogs came with him through the muck of the yard to the stone porch of the back door. Facing east across the valley was the front door, with heavily curtained windows and the small, neglected front garden.

The front door seemed to have been closed for years. It had last stood open when Edwin's father had died.

In the porch there were short, narrow benches, and a big stone scraper. Harry cleaned his boots and called in through the open door.

'Who is it?' a woman's voice called from the kitchen.

Harry stepped into the house, and across the stone passage to the kitchen. Edwin's wife, Olwen, was standing at the wide fireplace. She looked round at him, her red cheeks hot from the flame, her thin black hair loose.

'Edwin in?' Harry asked.

'No, he's up somewhere. The dingle I think he said.'

'We met down the station. Harry Price.'

'Aye, Edwin said about it.'

'Don't let me disturb you. I'll go on up and find him.'

'I'm sorry to be like this. Only the bread's just...'

'You carry on. Let me shift that fire for you.'

'No, no, I can manage.'

The bread dough was ready in tins in the hearth. Olwen had opened the iron door of the oven, which was at shoulder height in the wall at the far side of the fire. Now she lifted the red wood embers in the short-handled shovel, and scooped them into the oven, immediately closing the big iron door. She brushed off her hands, and pushed back her hair.

'You live by Hybart's, did Edwin say?'

'Aye.'

'You get the bread delivered down there, I suppose?'

'Aye, Saturdays. Bowen you know, he's got a little cart.'

'Edwin said for me to order some, leave at the caretaker at the chapel, only by the time I'd gone down and fetched it, and anyway it's a lot they charge.'

'Aye, though it's good enough bread.'

'I've eaten it, up my Mam's. You know them? James Cwmhonddu.'

'I've seen your Dad. Not to speak to.'

'Down there they're all right. When I come up here marrying

Edwin I made a proper mess. In the winter, see, up here, you got to lay in two months'. Well, Sundays, that winter, we had to go after chapel and eat with Mam, I'd got so short.'

'You look well stocked up now,' Harry said, looking round the kitchen. Sides of bacon and long strings of onions hung from the dark beams, above rows of open shelves stacked with bottled fruit and jam.

'Oh, I've done a bit! Only that lot'd go by Christmas, once Edwin started.'

'I doubt it. Mind, it's all right that the women think so.'

'Look out for us if we didn't.' She turned to the oven door, and opened it slightly to test the heat.

'Well, I won't keep you, look. On up, Edwin is?'

'Aye. Go out through the yard, and across you'll see the end of the sheep-wall, up by the Ship we call the pines. Go that way and give him a shout, he'll be somewhere.'

Harry made his way out. The dogs came to him, and the younger one, chastened, began to follow him as he moved across the yard.

'Come on then,' he called. 'Where is he?'

The dog lowered its shoulders, and came up to be patted.

'Where is he? Find him.'

The dog barked, and ran round in an excited circle. Harry walked on, avoiding the worst of the mud, and came out where he could see up the steep field to the dark line of the mountain. The low stone wall of the sheep fold stood out clearly, beyond the little group of pines that from the valley looked like a riding ship. He bent to the climb, with the dog at his heels. Up here the wind was stronger and fresher. With the exertion of the climb, and the deeper breathing, it seemed to flow into and chill his body. Thyme grew loose everywhere, under the burdock and nettles, and in the folds of bracken.

Harry rested, and looked back. The whole valley lay under him, gentler and more lovely. He looked far across to the rockface of the Holy Mountain, and could follow every rise of ground towards the isolated peak. He clapped his hands and shouted, and the dog barked excitedly. At his second shout there was a distant answer, and the dog, pricking its ears, ran off towards it. He followed, and soon Edwin came in sight from behind a straggle of wood, looking down towards Harry and waving. They walked towards each other, and smiled.

'Busy?'

'Aye, on my knees.'

'What is it then?'

'Praying,' Edwin said, and laughed into his big wind-reddened hand.

'Up here?'

Edwin spoke angrily to the dog, which was jumping at the torn end of his old, heavy coat.

'Look though, Harry. What you feel up here, mun, but pray or nothing? The water comes every bloody way, every field. And the bracken, well it's God's favourite, that's all I know. Me or the bracken it is, Harry, and he don't like me.'

'You got a lot of it cleared.'

'Aye, now. You wait spring, and all over, curled it is, like snakes or something ready to shove up.'

He turned, swinging his stick.

'These fields could go, Harry. Go and I'd hardly notice. A dog wouldn't get a living from them. It's only the sheep up there.'

They turned and looked at the mountain. From a hundred yards up, the bracken thickened into a dense mass, running away as far as they could see, along the line of the ridge. But beyond it there were the dark patches of heather and whin, and there the sheep were, eating the close sweet mountain grass.

'How many you got then?'

'Hundred perhaps. I've lost more than I'd tell you. Once they're up there, see, what have they got but ten or twelve mile the same? They don't say I'm Parry's, I must stick by him.'

Harry nodded. His eyes were clouded again, as he looked back down over the valley, and made out his own cottage, in the settled patch, that from this height seemed almost overgrown with trees.

Nearer, he saw the clean line of the railway, with a goods train, trailing its long dark smoke, running south.

'Come on down the house, mun, have a drop of cider.'

'Thanks,' Harry said, still watching the valley.

They walked down together, easy with each other but not speaking until they were into the yard. They moved towards the porch and were about to go in, when Edwin caught Harry's arm and whispered:

'What sort of chap's that mate of yours, Rosser?'

Harry looked into Edwin's face, which was suddenly cunning, the eyes narrowed.

'Morgan? He's all right.'

'Morgan Rosser. Aye. Course he talks, he's that sort. Only a decent chap you say?'

'Decent, yes.'

Edwin stared down at his boots, considering. Then he took Harry's elbow and moved him away from the house.

'Why I'm asking is, Harry, he's up a lot now seeing Edith. Edie Davies, you know?'

'Yes, I know Edith.'

'Well now, Edie's dad is Olwen's uncle. You know how it is here. You can't go into one house without finding somebody got a relation in all the others.'

'The farms, that is.'

'Aye, farming. Only old Jim asked me, see, what'd I make of this Rosser. Edie's, you know, taking it serious.'

Harry looked down at the patch. 'Morgan ought to marry again,' he said. 'There's the house, the little girl needs a mother, and he's in work.'

'Aye, only it isn't that, Harry. What Jim said was this talking, you know. Mind you, I reckon he goes up there and lays it on a bit. Thinks he's making an impression.'

'I don't know. I get on with him all right. He's a good mate.'

'Well, that's all right then. Only, you know...'

He stuck his thumb forward, under Harry's nose, and was about to go on when Olwen came out to the porch.

'What you two whispering about out there?'

'On about our best girls,' Edwin said, lowering his thumb.

'And who might they be?'

'We was trying to count them up,' Edwin said. 'We'd got as far as a hundred and one.'

'That all? You been quiet. Don't think I mind, so long as I'm not the one.'

'Wives not counted. Are they, Harry?'

Harry did not answer, but turned to Olwen. 'Bread all right?'

'Better'n stones anyhow,' Olwen said, laughing. She turned and led them into the kitchen. She had set the table for dinner – bacon and potatoes and a jug of cider. Edwin sat straight down, and Olwen asked Harry to sit. The two men ate, while Olwen waited. When the meal was over, Harry had to leave almost at once, to get back in time for work.

The friendship between the two men grew steadily. Soon after this visit, Harry borrowed Edwin's second horse, and they rode out together all day, over the mountain, finding and driving his sheep, which were marked with a red P of which the standard had been lengthened and turned into a Christian cross. They rode in file along the narrow, rutted sheep-tracks, far out until the valleys were left behind, until all around them was the silent expanse of heather and whin, with the occasional bird starting as they approached, and once in the distance a herd of wild ponies, which galloped furiously away. The sheep, when counted, were turned on to the mountain again, except the breeding ewes, which were kept in the home fields.

Two fields below the house Edwin ploughed that November, and in late February, when the snow was still deep on the mountain, ploughed another long field for potatoes, and arranged for Harry to have the three rows next the south hedge, in return for his help around the farm. With these rows, Harry could turn his own potato garden over to fruit; he planted more currants and gooseberries, and a new apple. The extension of his work to the farm, where he went now whenever he could, was fitted somehow into days that even before this had seemed overcrowded. He kept up his gardens and had now seven hives of bees, from which that summer he took nearly four hundred pounds of honey. Two of the hives he took in Edwin's cart to the mountain, for the flowering of the heather and its dark, rich honey. Within all this, the work in the box was only a part of his life. The cottage too, which was now so pleasant, seemed also only a part. But Will was four, and increasingly drawing his interest. Gradually in the winter evenings he moved back, through Will, into the home.

CHAPTER THREE

1

Matthew woke, suddenly, and at first could not realize where he was. He stared at the knot of blankets he was holding, and beyond it to the curved mahogany posts of the bed. The book he had read overnight lay open on the quilt, and he reached for it automatically, finding his way back. He was reading again as the whole memory returned.

That the church at Glynmawr is distinguished by its relics, including a gown and brooch of Jane Latimer, reputed mistress of Robin de Braose. That there is an interesting font, and in the Norman porch an illegible fragment of a Saxon tomb. The whole book in this style: the county history. That there is a Norman roodscreen and an ancient camp and the bloodiest of the border castles and the Stone of Treachery and the gown of the reputed mistress of Robin de Braose. Yesterday the pictures in the train, and now this: the pieces of past and present that are safe to handle. Here, in this living country.

He pushed away the book, and turned to the window. He had left the curtains open, but he was not expecting what he saw. The air was blue-grey with mist, and the wall of the mountains was sudden and sharp. The line of the sheep-wall curved along the scarp, and above it the group of pines, the Ship, stood out on the high skyline. An express train whistled, and drew out the sound to a cry. The silence of the valley, under the black wall of the mountains, seemed suddenly drawn and pointed.

He got up and looked down into the lane, which was empty. He stood for some moments, and then dressed quickly. He made his bed, and put the book away on the table. Then he went out, slowly, to the landing. For some moments he listened, and could make out Ellen's voice, downstairs, at the back door. He hesitated, and then tapped lightly on the door of his father's bedroom. There was no reply, and he looked quietly inside. The curtains were across, and the air of the room was dusk and heavy. Harry lay back on the heaped pillows sleeping, his mouth hanging slackly open. Matthew stood, looking down, and his hands moved into a known position that had succeeded the child's praying: the fingers of the right hand grasping the left wrist on the pulse. Then he turned and went downstairs. He walked into the kitchen, feeling the hush and tension of the morning. Ellen was talking to Mrs Hybart, at the half-open back door. As he came in they stopped talking.

'You're up then, Will. I'd have brought you some tea.'

'That's all right, Mam. Good morning, Mrs Hybart.'

Mrs Hybart smiled. She was tall and grey, still very erect, though she carried a stick. The cheeks that had been red were very pale now, with the translucence of age.

'There, every time I see you, Will...'

'I haven't thanked you yet. For ringing me yesterday.'

'Go on, boy, I don't need thanking.'

'Yes, you do, you know.'

'To pick up an old phone,' Mrs Hybart said impatiently, and turned away to Ellen. 'I remember when Harry come first for the cottage, he stood stubborn, like this grown-up son of yours. Only I was younger then, mind.'

She looked back at Matthew, her eyes amused, almost coquettish, under the thin grey hair.

'So was I, look,' he said, watching her.

'Aye, considering you wasn't born, I expect so.'

'It is a long time,' Ellen said sadly, but Mrs Hybart and Matthew ignored her, each concentrated on the other.

'And me on the old phone yesterday,' Mrs Hybart laughed. 'Calling you Mr Price like I was nervous of you. I should just have said Will, like I said Harry to your Dad.'

'Well, why not?'

'Because you've grown up, boy, and you've gone away from us. And I'm an old woman, I have to know the one and the other. You here and I can see you, you're Will again. You away, it's different, it's just an idea. So I watch out and say Mr Price.'

'You do it all right. Very formal.'

'Oh, for that,' Mrs Hybart said, turning and lifting her stick. 'But still I must be getting on, can't stand here lazy. I feed my fowls a bit more than they feed me. It's getting like pets, Will.'

'Aye, I expect. Tell me they're pets at Christmas.'

'Yes,' she said, looking sharply up at him. 'Yes, I'll tell you. If you're here to tell.'

'I'll make a special journey.'

'Aye, no doubt.'

There was a silence, and Ellen moved away to the stove.

'How is he, Will?' Mrs Hybart asked suddenly. 'What do you think of him yourself?'

'He's sleeping. I can't say. I know less than any of you.'

'And that's not much,' Mrs Hybart said bitterly. She pushed with her stick at a small tangle of cat's fur that had lodged in the doorstep. 'All the same, he'll be better for you being here.'

'You make it like magic.'

'And it is, too.'

She glanced at Ellen, and moved away to the lane. Matthew, staring after her, felt a sharp pressure of breath, as if he could not speak. At last, with an effort, he called to her.

'Only don't overfeed them, now, mind. You're getting too fond of them, I can see what it is.'

'It's allowed to an old woman.'

'I'm getting your breakfast, Will. Sit down, look,' Ellen said.

'Aye, in a minute.'

Ellen seemed suddenly young, as he remembered Mrs Hybart. For a moment, standing in the kitchen, he felt detached and distant.

'How old is she now?'

'Over eighty she is.'

'It's like an extra life, isn't it? After Dad's age.'

'Well, yes,' Ellen said sharply. 'Yes, it is.'

'We think first of two generations, then three. Then on top of the three there's this other, seeing us all spread out.'

Ellen did not answer. She stood in her familiar place by the stove, her yellow hair closely netted to her head. He watched her carefully, then looked out across the lane.

'Who's across home now?'

'Where?'

'Across home. The cottage.'

'Oh, I didn't think for a minute. Mrs Whistance it is now, you remember her.'

'No.'-

'Yes, Will. Used to live on the mountain. Up beyond the Ship.'

'No, I don't remember.'

'She remembers you.'

He looked across the lane at the cottage, at its warm red bricks, its absurdly high chimney, the rough lichened slates over the little back-kitchen, and the slanting porch in front on its black wooden posts. From the water-butt the trailers of a climbing rose reached to the window of the middle bedroom, where he had slept and worked. As he watched, across the lane, he saw a white head cross the back-kitchen window. Was there nobody left young here? Was the whole patch of old people, that we have all gone away and left? The lane, once, would have been busy with shouting children. Now it was empty and quiet.

'It's ready, Will. Sit down.'

'Thank you.'

'I'll go up and see your Dad. I'm hoping he's asleep.'

'He was when I came down.'

'You didn't disturb him?'

'No.'

He sat at the table, while his mother went upstairs. As he picked up his cup, he looked round for a newspaper, but the daily paper, he remembered, did not arrive till eleven. There was a pile of old papers on the dresser, and he picked out the last local *Times*. On its closely-printed front page there was a small two-column headline: *Rent Strike by Council Tenants – Threatened March on Town Hall*. With the paper propped against the bread, he settled to read and to eat. He was still reading, half an hour later, when Ellen came down.

'You'll get the ten bus will be best.'

'Oh, yes. I'm sorry, I'd forgotten.'

'I've made the list. And he wants you to get him a bell.'

He put down the paper. He was aware, suddenly, of the distance he had travelled, and of how urgency, unnoticed, had been slipping away. The crisis of yesterday, the tension of the journey and the arrival, seemed suddenly far back. He had seen his father for a few minutes only, exchanged hardly a score of words, when in his mind on the journey the words had been endless, in the long crisis of coming back. Now, in so short a time, on this ordinary morning, even the purpose of his coming had slipped away. It had been easy and normal to talk to a neighbour, to look out at the day from the door of the kitchen, to eat breakfast, to read. The paper had been the decisive stage, removing him, as so often, from all the immediate situation. He knew, of course, just why he was here. But it was not what he had expected: to sit at his father's bedside. He was here to be in the house, and this meant to take up the life of the house, to settle to it as if he had really come home. But it was reluctantly now that he got up from the table: a reluctance that Ellen noticed, and quickly interpreted in her own terms; she had dragged him from print so often. Now that he was on his feet again, the situation changed. If he could not talk to his father, at least he could do what was necessary; not only the extras, but the other things Harry himself had intended to get done. He was here not only to be in the house, but as a kind of replacement, to carry life on. Standing now, holding the list, he thought again about the reluctance of which he had just been ashamed.

'Well, I can do this. And get a bell, you say?'

'Haven't I written it on there? I will, look.'

'I can remember.'

'Well yes, he wants it, Will. He's seen one he's often liked. A door bell, works from a battery. He says while he's in bed he can have it to save calling. In Davey's by the Monument. You're to say it's for him.'

'All right.'

'Ask for Mr Davey. Say it's for Harry Price, Glynmawr.'

'You mean not pay?'

'Oh yes, pay.'

'Then why say who it's for? It's just ordinary buying.'

'Well, yes it is, I suppose. Only we ask like that.'

He folded the list, and put it away in his pocket.

'I've got money,' he said. 'Fortunately I'd just drawn.'

'Yes, but you mustn't spend your money, Will.'

'It's money. We'll talk all that over later.'

'All right.' She seemed suddenly nervous of him, as, for a moment, Mrs Hybart had been. At this, more than at anything else, he felt disconcerted and helpless.

'Only now you'd better get on.'

'Yes. When's the bus?'

'Well, the ten, that's just before the quarter-past from the corner.'

'I see. And back?'

'On the half-hour. You'll get the twelve.'

'I'll shave and get tidy. Can I go in and see him?'

'Not now, Will, better. He seems very weak. Go in when you're back, you can show him the bell.'

He nodded, and walked to the door of the passage.

'Have you got your shaving things? You can borrow his.'

'I've got my own. I'll get off.'

'Not up, Will. The pipes disturb him.'

'But I must get my things from the case.'

'All right. Only shave down here. I've got a kettle on.'

'Right.'

He went upstairs and took his washing bag from the suitcase. On the landing he hesitated, swinging the bag. He wanted suddenly to push the other door open and go in to his father. But he stood

70

waiting, and at last went quietly downstairs and along the passage. Ellen had cleared the breakfast things, and propped a mirror on the table, with a folded newspaper in front of it. Water was steaming in the big shaving mug that Harry always used.

'All right,' he said, and sat at the table.

2

When Matthew got back from town, he walked slowly up the lane. In the bus he had known so few people that he felt like a stranger. Even the faces he recognized were altered, or belonged to a different generation. In Gwenton he had met nobody he knew, and the simple shopping had been difficult, after London: the conventions were different. He had felt empty and tired, but the familiar shape of the valley and the mountains held and replaced him. It was one thing to carry its image in his mind, as he did, everywhere, never a day passing but he closed his eyes and saw it again, his only landscape. But it was different to stand and look at the reality. It was not less beautiful; every detail of the land came up with its old excitement. But it was not still, as the image had been. It was no longer a landscape or a view, but a valley that people were using. He realized, as he watched, what had happened in going away. The valley as landscape had been taken, but its work forgotten. The visitor sees beauty; the inhabitant a place where he works and has his friends. Far away, closing his eyes, he had been seeing this valley, but as a visitor sees it, as the guide-book sees it: this valley, in which he had lived more than half his life.

He stopped at a gate and looked down. Lorries were moving along the narrow road to the north. A goods train was stopped at a signal on the down line, just beyond the Tump (a round barrow, tufted with larches, that he had not known was a barrow when he went away). The line-gang were working about a hundred yards from the train, and there was grey smoke from their hut. Around them stretched the fields, bright green under pasture or red with the autumn ploughing. He saw the woods, the treeline of the river, the intricate contours of slope and fall, and these slowly distinguished themselves as farms – Parry's Tregarron, James's Cwmhonddu, Probert's Tynewydd, Richards' Alltyrynys, Lewis's The Bridge. Then the other houses, away from the farms: grouped, in their patches, along the lines of the roads and lanes. There, in Hendre, people were busy around their houses, and the marks of their work were everywhere: in the untidy sheds, the stark posts of the washing-lines, the piles of red earth beside the unfinished ditch, the sprawl of netting wire and old troughs in the fowl-runs, the dirty lorry parked in a field corner, with black tarpaulins beside it on the grass. In the general loveliness that was so clear across the valley, he found himself narrowing his eyes to blur out this disfiguring debris around the houses. Yet, as he did so, some quality vanished: it was now neither the image nor the actual valley. He turned and looked up at the mountains. On a low skyline a tractor was moving, in an area that he remembered as wooded but that now had been cleared and fenced. Farther north, below the high barn, several dogs were running, in a steeply sloping field. Since the rabbits had gone, hares were coming down from the mountains, and the dogs were chasing them now in great circles, the whole hunt in this one field. Lower down, a field was being ploughed by tractor, and a strip at the edge of it was spread with lime, the quick white standing out sharply against the turned earth. He looked down again, into the weathered wood of the gate. This was not anybody's valley to make into a landscape. Work had changed and was still changing it, though the main shape held.

He turned and walked on up the lane. Now, higher, he looked out to the spurs of the far mountains, that fell in wave after wave into the wide haze of the valley. Now, at that distance, everything was suddenly still. Even the column of blue smoke, from a far bonfire, seemed part of the stillness, its colour the colour of the mountains under the pale sun. He stood, held and divided, and then walked on to the house.

As he opened the gate he heard voices, and hesitated. But he had been seen, obviously, and must go in. In the kitchen, sitting opposite Ellen, was Mrs Davies, Jane Davies Campstone, stout, sandy-haired, her big hands crossed in her lap. 'Well then the morning,' Ellen was saying, 'he got up as usual, half past five, and went off.'

It was the ritual voice, and the repeated story, that must be offered, in full, to everyone who called. He stood by the door waiting, but Jane Davies had stopped listening and was looking round at him.

'Here's Will back then,' Ellen said.

'How are you, Will?' Jane Davies asked.

'Very well, thank you. And you, Mrs Davies?'

She nodded and smiled.

'And the family?'

'Yes, thank you.'

'You've got two nice boys, Will. I bet you're proud of them.'

'Oh, yes,' he said, putting the shopping on the table. 'Yes, of course.'

He was wondering how Jane Davies, who was not a close friend of the family, hardly more than an acquaintance, knew so much of the detail of his own life.

'Your Mam lent me the photos, that you had in Cornwall. I took them up home to show Phyllis.'

Phyllis? Phyllis Davies? No, of course, Phyllis Rees, Jane's younger sister, who had been with him at school, in the same class.

'How is Phyllis then?'

'Oh, doing very well, Will. They've got three children of their own, all girls.'

'They're lovely little girls, Will,' Ellen said, with a note in her voice that seemed to plead for his attention.

'Yes, I can imagine. Phyllis was pretty.'

'And still is mind. Don't you let me go telling her you said she used to be.'

Would she mind? he wanted to ask. If we met in a London street should we even know each other? It was only here, in this network, that the memory held.

'Well yes, I suppose so. Only to me, you see, she's still what, about fifteen. Something like that.'

'That's how it is, of course. With you being away.'

'Yes,' he said firmly. He saw Ellen watching him, and found the sudden pressure intolerable.

'And now with your Dad.'

'Yes. My mother was telling you, I believe. If you'll excuse me, I must just go up and see him.'

Ellen moved, nervously. Jane Davies glanced at her, and then back at Matthew.

'Yes, it's a comfort for him to have you. And for your Mam.'

'Thank you. And thank you for calling. If you'll excuse me, I'll just go up.'

'You go on, Will. I'm not in your way.'

'That's right. Perhaps I'll see you again.'

As the door closed behind him, he stood in the passage, fighting down his anger. He had learned very thoroughly to be ashamed of anger, and certainly it could be blamed, here in this anxious house. Yet he could not much longer go on accepting the unacceptable terms in which he was received. But the thread of this anger was confused. If he worked it loose, he could not know where it would lead.

He looked down at the bell in his hand. With some difficulty he had persuaded the man who had sold it to him to fit the battery and make all the connections, so that it could be used at once. He estimated the distance, and then hung the bell on a coat-peg by the pantry door, and took the long lead and the switch upstairs in his hand. At the bedroom door he paused, and passed the lead under the stair carpet. Then he knocked quietly, and opened the door. This would be only the second time he had talked to his father, in all the rushing strangeness of the return.

Harry was propped up in bed. His face was stronger, and his skin a more usual colour. As Matthew came in he was staring at the ceiling, with a fixed intentness.

'Mam?'

'No, it's me this time.'

'Aye,' Harry said, smiling and looking at him. 'Sit down, Will.'

'Yes.'

He sat on the edge of the bed. The pressure had gone, suddenly, and was even difficult to remember.

'I'll just put this bell by you. Then you can ring when you want.'

Leaning across, he wound the lead round the bedpost, and laid the switch on the pillow.

'What bell's that?'

'I got it in town. At Davey's. The bell's downstairs. This is just the press.'

'Aye, I can see that,' Harry said, fumbling for the small white bakelite switch.

'Here,' his son said, picking up the switch and putting it into the groping hand. The fine long fingers grabbed at it, as they touched his hand. The fingers were cold and seemed stiff and unco-ordinated.

'How are you now?'

'I see,' Harry said, staring down at the switch. 'This is a button, a push.'

'Yes, you put the little plate on the outside of the door. Only now, while you're ill, you can use it up here.'

'Aye, it's all right, Will. Thank you very much.'

Matthew held his breath, looking down at the bed. Harry had withdrawn again, and had closed his eyes. There was a grey stubble down the cheeks and on the loose skin under the mouth. The bristles under the nose were darker and closer.

'Don't go away, Will, I like you being there.'

'I'm glad to be here. You get your rest, don't worry about me.'

'I can't say all I want, Will. But I want you to know it's made a world of difference, you coming.'

'I hope so, anyway.'

There was a silence, and then the eyes opened suddenly.

'You can tell,' Harry said, in a quite ordinary voice. 'You can tell if it's only coming to put yourself right. It isn't what's said. You can feel.'

'Yes, I think so.'

'I can feel,' Harry insisted. 'It isn't what's said.' Matthew sat, hardly daring to breathe, as if the voice was beyond him.

'You know what I feel,' he said at last. He was still short of breath, and the words were hard in his throat. There was another pause. The breathing in the bed was deep and heavy.

'Yes, this way and that,' Harry said. 'It isn't as if any of it was easy.'

'No, of course.'

'We don't altogether understand,' Harry said. 'It goes this way and that, in your mind.'

Matthew stared down at the bed, waiting. He was breathing normally again, but the tightness was still there, across his chest. Outside, across the valley, a train passed on the up line, an express. Harry jerked to attention, and looked across at the clock. Then almost before he had completed the movement, he relaxed and sank back.

'That's right. Let them run,' Matthew said.

'What's that?' Harry asked, screwing round to look up at him.

'The trains. Let them run. They're not your worry.'

There was a long silence, and the eyes clouded again, before closing.

'That's right, Will, they're not. Yesterday, now, I heard every train, and worked out...' His voice trailed away, and he moved uneasily on the pile of pillows.

'Today I hear them,' he went on, his voice slurring. 'I hear them but I don't think I've...' Again the voice trailed away. The bell-switch was still grasped, between the long, pale fingers.

'Can you eat anything? For your dinner?'

'Aye, perhaps, Will. Later.'

As he spoke, Harry opened his eyes, and looked down at his hands. He seemed surprised, suddenly, to see the bell-switch there. He turned it over carefully, and examined it on both sides. Then he laid his thumb on the button, and pressed. The bell rang downstairs, and there was the sound of a door opening.

'Do you want anything, Dad? Can I get it?'

Harry looked up at him, making an obvious effort to collect his thoughts.

'No,' he said slowly. 'No, I don't want anything.' Matthew went out to the landing. Ellen was coming along the passage to the stairs.

'It's all right, Mam. He was just trying the bell.'

'I'd better see.'

'It's all right, it's really all right.'

Ellen went past him, into the bedroom. He heard her quiet voice over the bed, and again the deep, wordless voice, the hard effort of breath. Slowly he went downstairs, and said good-bye to Jane Davies who was leaving. He stood at the back door, looking out across the lane and at the mountains. Some minutes later, Ellen came into the kitchen. When he turned and looked at her he could see how frightened she was, more deeply frightened than he had seen her at all. He saw in her face how she, with everyone, had taken her husband to be utterly strong.

'It was nothing, was it?'

'No, he was just trying the bell.'

There was a short silence, and Matthew felt the change in himself. He was beginning to realize the depths of his own fear.

'Well, at least it got rid of our visitor,' he said, harshly. 'I really don't know how you stand it, Mam.'

'Stand what? It was very nice of Mrs Davies to call.'

'It's nice of them all to call. But what is this, an illness or a tea-party? You can't be kept running upstairs and at the same time have a whole stream of them in the kitchen. Not just asking how he is, mind, but settling down in the chair for every detail, and then going on to whatever interests them, just a good general gossip.'

Ellen smiled nervously. 'Yes, Will, it is a strain.'

'Then why put up with it?'

'Only it's nice that the neighbours call.'

'The neighbours! It'll be half the parish at this rate.'

'He's very well liked, Will.'

'If they liked him, they'd keep away. They come to put themselves right. His illness is just an excuse.'

'They all say can they help.'

'But in fact they're hindering. They must know you've enough to do.'

'Well, yes, I have.'

'Our whole attention should be on him. Not on receiving whoever cares to come.'

'I know, Will. But it's natural for them to ask.'

'If they want to know how he is, I'll write it out, on a card, and pin it on the door.'

'No, Will.'

'All right. Only for heaven's sake, if they're all to come in and settle down. Half the time they're not asking about him but about me, as if...'

He stopped, and looked away.

'Well, of course, Will, they like to ask.'

He went across to the stove.

'What are you making him?'

'That's our dinner on, Will. I'll make him an egg custard in a minute.'

'See to him first. I'm not hungry.'

'I can see to it both, boy. I'm used.'

He looked round the kitchen, which seemed very settled and complete. The shopping he had brought from town had already been tidied away, and the little table was laid for dinner.

'I've been away too long,' he said, sitting down at the table. 'I've forgotten it all, and I can't bring myself back.'

Ellen stood at the stove, breaking an egg into a basin.

'He was saying now when I was with him. He told me he'd thanked you for coming.'

'Thanked me! For God's sake! What do you both think am?'

'It's the worry, Will. But it is, it makes the difference to him. He was crying yesterday, when I told him you'd said that you'd come.'

'Did he think I wouldn't come?'

'He said not to worry you, Will.'

Matthew drew in his breath. As he looked away he heard the

separate language in his mind, the words of his ordinary thinking. He was trained to detachment: the language itself, consistently abstracting and generalizing, supported him in this. And the detachment was real in another way. He felt, in this house, both a child and a stranger. He could not speak as either; could not speak really as himself at all, but only in the terms that this pattern offered. At the same time, and quite physically, the actual crisis took its course.

'Shall I take that up?' he asked, as Ellen was laying the tray.

'No, Will, I'll take it. I may have to stay with him.'

'Then I can do it. You need to rest. You'll wear yourself out.'

'Well, but he may need to be fed.'

'But I can do that.'

He carried the tray upstairs, and backed through the door of the bedroom.

'Aye, come in,' Harry said, quite strongly. Matthew smiled and put the tray on the side of the bed, within reach.

'How much was the bell then?'

'I don't remember. Not a pound.'

'I'll get that out for you,' Harry said, moving on his pile of pillows.

'No. Eat your dinner. What does the money matter?'

'You've got your family to keep.'

'And you're my family.'

'Well, I know that,' Harry said. He was silent for some time, and his eyes had closed. Matthew waited and then reached and lifted the hand that lay nearest to him.

'Come on, try and eat.'

'Aye, all right.'

'Shall I help you? Pick it up?'

'Aye. Try.'

Matthew took the bowl, and lifted a spoonful of the custard. Harry bent towards him, not looking at him, and gulped the food from the spoon. Matthew also looked away so that they were close to each other, passing and taking the food, but as if by agreement ignoring the process, simply getting it over.

'Aye, that'll do,' Harry said, sinking back.

'Sure?'

'Put the bowl down. Put the tray away.'

'All right.'

'You looked round the gardens then?'

'No, Dad.'

'Don't bother. I don't want you working there.'

'I'll do whatever you want.'

'I've made it my job,' Harry said, sharply. 'I'll be up and finish it.'

'You must rest,' Matthew said, looking into his eyes. Harry held the look, steadily and gently.

'Aye, I suppose I must,' he said, turning his heavy body away. 'Only rest, Will, and it all to come clear. Too much comes back to lie patient. I only wish I could tell you.'

CHAPTER FOUR

1

In the spring of 1926, in Glynmawr, the green of the meadows was fresh and cool, and the blossom was white in the orchards, and on the thorns and crabs in the hedges. Along the banks of the roads the violets were hidden in overgrowing leaves, but the primroses were out, though not so thickly as on the banks of the railway, where they flowered most richly, as if the cuttings and embankments had been made for them. All over the valley, and far up on the mountains, innumerable birds sang and flew. The Honddu was high, as it had been since midwinter. The low-lying cottages near the river had already been flooded.

Here was the ordinary history of the valley, sheltered and almost isolated under its dark mountains. But now, with this May Day, a different history exerted its pressures, and reached, with the railway line, even this far. The troubled years of strike and lock-out, which had affected the village only slightly, moved now to their crisis, and touched this valley under its lonely mountains. As April ended, the Government's subsidy to the coal industry ended with it. The miners refused the owners' new terms, and lock-out notices were already posted at the pits. Up beyond the mountains, little more than ten miles from this farming valley, lay the different valleys, where the pits and the colliers' houses were crowded. At dusk, above Darren, the glow of the steel furnace spread up each evening into the sky, and many turned now to watch it more seriously, and to think of the black valleys that lay hidden beyond. There was the trouble, that the eye could almost see, and in the papers the trouble was recorded, to be read in the sun of mid-morning among flowers and blossoming trees.

The coal negotiations in London had broken down. That afternoon, at two o'clock, the executives of all unions affiliated to the Trades Union Congress were meeting again in the Memorial Hall. That night, when Harry went to work, two telegrams had reached the Glynmawr branch of the National Union of Railwaymen, and had been pinned up on the noticeboard in the box. Morgan showed them to Harry, who went across and read them.

Negotiations with Government on miners' dispute having broken down, Executive Committee now considering our attitude along with other unions. Circular letter in post outlining position, meantime our members must continue their ordinary work. Spasmodic action can only defeat our object. Prepare your members for action, but only on instructions from this office.

The second, and later, telegram read:

Executive instructs all our members not to take duty after Monday next. Arrangements to be made locally so that all men will finish their turn of duty at their home station on Tuesday morning. Circular in post.

Harry stood re-reading the telegrams, above the low fire.

'General Strike then, is it?'

'Aye,' Morgan said. 'And about time.'

Harry turned and took off his coat. 'All right,' he said. 'It's straightforward enough for us.'

'So long as we know what we're doing,' Morgan said, coming nearer. 'Only I tell you, Harry, this is no ordinary bit of a strike. This is us against the Government, no penny-an-hour job.'

Harry rubbed his hand over his face. 'We're with the miners, isn't it?'

'Aye, but with them why? Because we're the working class, Harry, united for common action. The miners are fighting their own battle against their employers. We're not, mind. We're not fighting the companies, we're fighting the Government.'

'The country they said,' Harry answered, half to himself.

He wanted, in one way, to hear Morgan talk, yet the real argument was in his own mind, and in different terms.

'The country, Harry! We're the country. And mind you, if we come out, let's realize it's that we're saying. We're saying that we're the country, we're the power, we the working class are defying the bosses' government, going on to build our own social system.'

'I don't know about that,' Harry said.

'How many know it, I wonder? Do the union leaders know it? Have they got the courage? We're not miners see, Harry. We got no right to strike, only for the working class.'

'I'll stand by the miners, if it comes to it.'

Morgan looked at him, doubtfully, and then threw up his hands.

'If that's all it is, mun, we shall lose. We're out for the power, the power in our own hands.'

Harry walked to the far end of the box.

'Shall we be all out here?' he asked, staring out into the darkness down the line.

'If I know anything about it, we shall.'

'Meredith?'

'You leave Meredith to me.'

'Aye, only Jack's a funny chap, mind. Don't go talking to him about the working class and power and that.'

'Why not?' Morgan asked. 'He's a worker, isn't he?'

Harry hesitated, and looked slowly round the box.

'Aye, only it's not the way we talk, so watch him.'

'Look, Harry,' Morgan began, and then stopped. 'All right, boy. It's too late for it now. Branch meeting tomorrow, three o'clock.'

'Sunday?'

'Aye, Sunday. Here's a major crisis, affecting the whole country. Do you think they mind what Glynmawr does on Sunday?'

'It's not what the country thinks. What the chaps will.'

'Get on, mun. Leave Sunday School to the kids.' As he spoke

Morgan picked up his bag, and went to the door. 'It's what we need in Glynmawr, Harry. A taste of common action for a change. Leave just working for ourselves.'

'I don't know about that.'

'It's what you need certainly, Harry. You know what I think of you: that you're a good chap, a good worker and so on. But yourself, Harry. You work here, you draw your money, you ride home and you dig your garden. All right, for a time it makes sense. But you're what, twenty-nine. Look ahead a bit. What'll you be doing, what'll you be doing it for, in twenty or thirty years?'

'Aye, you can look at it like that.'

'People need an idea, mun. Something outside them-selves. You settle here, and you dig yourself in. And then what? Just work out your time, and then throw aside?'

'I suppose it all comes together. I hope so.'

'Not on its own it doesn't. But a thing like this now, it might really work out. Good night, boy.'

Harry heard the door slam, and Morgan's boots down the steps. He stood alone in the box looking out where the light threw its framed shape into the general darkness. An express was asked from Gwenton, and he accepted it and pulled off the up signals. Then he made up the fire from the bucket, and sat down on the small wooden chair. He found himself staring at the worn patch of dirty brown linoleum, which had torn where the legs of the chair were catching it. He leaned forward, and put the big kettle on to boil. The express came through, and he stood at the open barred window to watch it pass, and then put back the signals. As he was doing this, the lamp that hung in the centre of the box sputtered and faded. He crossed and reached up to it, shaking the bowl. As he had expected, it was empty. His look moved for a moment to the door that Morgan had slammed, and he smiled. It was the afternoon man's job to trim and fill the lamp, but again and again, in taking over from Morgan, he had found it empty. He pulled the chair across, and reached up to unhook the lamp. Then he went down in the dark under the box, and felt for the drum of paraffin. He filled the lamp, testing the level by dipping his finger in the hole. When he had carried it up again, he gave it a quick clean with a handful of cotton waste from his locker, then lit it and hung it up. He pulled the chair back in front of the fire where the kettle was beginning to sing. Before he sat down, he looked again at the telegrams, and read them carefully through for the third time.

The branch meeting on the Sunday afternoon was quite well attended. Everyone wanted instructions, and Morgan's effort, as secretary, to explain and interpret the general issues of the strike was sat through impatiently. All that was wanted, by the other men, was a direct order about stopping work. The discipline which operated in their work was now to operate in their leaving it. A time to withdraw their labour, as Morgan described it, was like a time for booking on. Still, until the promised circular arrived, even this could not be settled. The only other thing discussed was whether they would all be out. Bill Thomas, the ganger, promised all the platelayers: 'You just leave my chaps to me.' The new porter, Will Addis, was not at the meeting, but they expected no difficulty with him. The two doubtfuls, as Morgan called them, were Jack Meredith, and the stationmaster, Tom Rees.

'But Rees,' Morgan said, 'can't run the station on his own.'

'Rees may surprise you,' Harry said.

'We'll see.'

On the Monday morning the circular arrived. During his morning turn Morgan drew up the detailed instructions. All but the signalmen would stop that evening; the last turn worked in the box would be Jack Meredith's, ending at six Tuesday morning. This was set out in a notice, that was pinned to the door under the steps of the box. Beside it, when Harry came to work at two, was a new telegram:

Stoppage appears inevitable. Unless we advise otherwise every man must act on instructions already given. No trains of any kind must be worked by our members. Acting in full agreement with Associated and Railway Clerks' Unions. You must do likewise in districts. Allow no disorderly or subversive elements to interfere in any way, maintain perfect order, and have confidence in your own representatives. Perfect loyalty will ensure success.

As Harry went to put in his bike, Tom Rees was standing reading the notices, and Morgan stood above him at the top of the box steps.

'All clear then,' Harry heard Morgan call down, while he was wheeling his bike along the dusty ramp, beside the lower rods of the signal levers.

'Clear enough,' Rees said, lighting his pipe.

'Only you notice what it says about agreement with your union,' Morgan called. 'That means you'll be with us, I suppose.'

Rees drew carefully on his pipe. 'We'll have to see about that,' he said.

Harry came out, and took off his clips.

'Nice day, Harry,' Rees greeted him.

'Aye. Only a bit too warm for what I been doing.'

'What's that?'

'Digging.'

Morgan came down the steps, and Harry passed him and went up into the box.

'We don't want no trouble, mind,' Morgan said, to Rees.

'Trouble,' Rees said, looking out along the quiet platforms. Two of the platelayers were working near the crossing. On the down platform Will Addis was working on the flower-beds. He had pulled up most of the wallflowers that had been in bloom there, and these lay now in little heaps around the waiting-room. Some of the plants still carried a few last red and yellow flowers, and bees hovered around them, in the warm, still air. On the cleared beds, sparrows and chaffinches hopped busily for the disturbed worms. Across the valley the Holy Mountain was clear in the sun, but to the south-west, beyond the line of the shining rails, the hills above Gwenton, that covered the mining valleys, were indistinct in the rising haze. Harry stood at the window of the box, looking down.

'What's these subversive elements you got to watch out for?' Tom Rees asked Morgan.

'You can read what it says, can't you?'

'Disorderly,' Bill Phillips shouted. 'That's old John here Saturday night, turning out of the Skirrid.'

Harry smiled. The bar on which he was leaning was warm with the sun, and he could smell the wallflowers from across the line.

'Just come about right for me,' John Jones said. 'Missus been on at me three week or more to fetch down that ash by our gate. Said we'll have it on us.'

'He don't keep up with much, do he, Harry?' Bill Phillips shouted.

'I keep up with myself,' Jones said. 'When you're my age see if you'll say as good.'

Tom Rees walked away to his office, but he came out again almost immediately. He walked to the door of the parcels office, and unfolded a large poster and pinned it up. It was of a familiar official kind. Harry, from the box, could read only the headlines in black:

Great Western Railway. Whom do you serve?

'What's that thing, then?' Morgan called, and walked across.

'You can read for yourself, can't you?' Rees said.

'Whose is it? Why you put it up?'

Morgan looked up at Harry, then walked over to the poster. The two platelayers rested their shovels and watched him. Morgan was silent for a minute, reading it through, while Harry shifted his arms on the warm bar.

'What's it say, Morgan?'

'It's just bloody insolence.'

'What?'

'Listen,' Morgan said, and began to read.

Great Western Railway. Whom do you serve? The Agreement of Service provides that each man will abstain from any act that may injuriously affect the interests of the Company, and that seven...

'Louder, mun,' Bill Phillips shouted.

And that seven days previous notice in writing of termination of service shall be given. Notice to the Staff. The National Union of Railwaymen have intimated that railwaymen have been asked to strike without notice tomorrow night. Each Great Western man has to decide his course of action, but I appeal to all of you...

'Hold it,' Harry shouted. 'Look out there, John. Fishguard coming through.'

Morgan turned, by the poster. The platelayers moved quickly on to the platform, and stood near him. Soon the train could be heard, coming fast. Harry moved back in the box for a minute, and then returned to the window to see the express through. As it passed, he stared into the half-full compartments, where most of the passengers were sitting indifferently, only a few glancing out. With a rush of noise and of following wind, the Fishguard was through, and went quickly away out of sight.

'Shall I read you the rest of the stuff?' Morgan called.

'Aye. In a minute. I'll just see her clear.'

When Harry returned to the window of the box, Morgan was talking to the two platelayers, and there was a wait before the rest of the notice could be read.

I appeal to all of you to hesitate before breaking your contracts of service with the old Company, before you inflict grave injury upon the Railway Industry, and before you arouse ill feeling in the Railway service which will take years to remove. Railway companies and railwaymen have demonstrated that they can settle their disputes by direct negotiations. The Mining Industry should be advised to do the same. Remember that your means of living and your personal interests are involved and that Great Western men are trusted to be loyal to their conditions of service, in the same manner as they expect the Company to carry out their obligations and agreements.

'Can you beat it, Harry?' Morgan shouted up.

'Aye. It's like the war.'

'You got it, boy, and they'll be getting it. Half a minute, I'm coming up.'

Harry looked across at the poster.

'What's that the other side?'

'That? That's the Union stuff.'

'What? On their poster?'

'Aye. Letter from the union. *I am conveying this intimation to you in order that you may be cognizant of the fact that in ceasing work the men are acting upon the instructions of the National Union of Railwaymen.* From Cramp.'

'What do that mean?' Bill Phillips asked.

Harry was staring out into the distance.

'And there's a bit more,' Morgan added. *'Miners' Crisis. Members of our Union must handle no traffic of any kind, foodstuffs or otherwise.* Signed Cramp again.'

'Well,' Harry said, 'that's fair enough.'

Morgan looked up at him. 'I'm coming up,' he said. 'Whom do you serve, indeed. I'll show them who we serve.'

In the box Morgan took a foolscap sheet from his locker, and with the official pen scratched busily at a capital-lettered notice. He handed it to Harry without comment.

Reference the above. Men are reminded that we are not anybody's servants. We stand together now for our own cause, and <u>no Company masters, national or local,</u> can stop us. We are not the Company's servants; this is a free country. Stand together and be loyal to your Union, which is yourselves.

(Signed) Morgan Rosser,
Secretary, Glynmawr Branch,
National Union of Railwaymen.

'All right, Harry?'

'Aye, I suppose so.'

'You see where I underlined?'

'Aye.'

'Rees'll get it, don't worry.'

He went across the line again to pin up the notice, below the large poster. Some minutes later Tom Rees came out, and read the notice. As he finished reading, he looked at Morgan without speaking, and then glanced up at the box.

'All right, Harry?'

'Aye, Mr Rees, everything all right.'

'Where's the pickup then?'

'Signalled now.'

'Right. There's them three empties, remember. You're stopping her?'

'Aye.'

'I'll be down the yard,' Rees said, and crossed the line and walked down under the box to the siding. Morgan went home to the dinner that Mrs Lucas had been keeping for the last hour, and work at the station continued.

In the last half-hour before his relief at ten, Harry was busy with various jobs about the box. He cleared and made up the fire, swept the floor, refilled the kettle, emptied and refilled the fire bucket that was used for washing, and cleaned and filled the lamp. At two minutes to ten he saw the light of Jack Meredith's bicycle crossing the bridge and coming down the zigzag path to the platform, then along under the box. A few moments later came his heavy step on the stairs, and the opening doors.

'Evening, Harry,' Meredith said, pulling off the frail that was slung around his shoulders.

'Evening, Jack.'

'Everything in order?' Meredith asked, going straight to the register.

'Aye, fairly normal.'

Meredith looked down the register. He was a small, dark man, with a large, broad nose and very deep, bloodshot eyes. Harry looked at him carefully: at the seamed, dark, ugly face; the old, loose, grey jacket; the white flannel shirt without a collar but with a big loose stud; the dark brown breeches; the tight black leggings and boots. As Harry buttoned his own uniform coat, Meredith stood astride by the fire, lighting his short black pipe.

'What's this talk about a strike then, Harry?'

'General Strike, Jack. To stand by the miners. We take no duty from tomorrow morning.'

Meredith said nothing for some minutes. He was busily tamping the black shag in his pipe.

'You a miner then, Harry?'

'It isn't that, Jack. It's the principle.'

'Principle?' Meredith repeated, drawing noisily. 'Fine bloody principle, taking my wages and throwing them down some bloody mine.'

Harry smiled, but his eyes were clouded and distant, and his whole body was attentive.

'It's been worked out, mun. If we let them go, they let us go. Then it's our own wages next.'

Meredith rubbed his tight black legging against the edge of the high steel fender, watching Harry closely yet without meeting his eyes.

'It was that bloody war did it,' he said. 'You all come back the same, squaring up to anybody. Where are you, boss, I'll knock you down?'

'Aye, that may be.'

'You can't earn a bloody living, mun, with your fists. What's come over you all? And another thing, mind, they'll beat you. First round, knock out. Country's not going to be run by a lot of young gawps.'

Harry stood very still, as if waiting for something in himself.

'It'll work out,' he said at last. 'Anyhow, we're stopping tomorrow.'

'You are,' Meredith said. 'I'm not.'

'That's your own affair, to decide.'

'You mind bloody well it is, Harry. Go on home, boy, look after your family.'

Harry opened the door, and then looked back.

'We'll get it agreed,' he said.

'Go on, boy,' Meredith said roughly. 'She's waiting for you.'

Harry went down the steps.

2

It had been arranged that on the following morning Morgan would arrive at six, and see that the box was closed. Then he would stay at the station, with the ganger, and see that nobody took work. There was no more for Harry to do, but as he lay that night, staring out past the edge of the canopy and the curved mahogany bedposts to the dark outline of the window, thinking over again his talk with Meredith, he decided that he must after all go to the station in the morning, and on that slept. When he woke at half past five, and got quietly out of bed, Ellen also woke and asked him where he was going.

'Station, for a bit. Got to see it all right.'

'It's nothing to do with you, though, Harry.'

'I'll be back for breakfast. Nine at the latest.'

In the dim light of the bedroom, Ellen was pale. Her hair lay loosely around her face, and her eyes were puffy and red-rimmed. Harry hesitated, and then reached across the bed to kiss her cheek. She turned away from him, but he held her and quickly kissed her shoulder and neck.

'Go on,' she said, pulling away and closing her eyes.

He took his boots and went quietly out of the room. As he reached the landing, Will called to him through the open door of the middle bedroom.

'Good-bye, Dada.'

'You awake?'

'Only now.'

Harry went in to his son, and stooped and kissed his forehead.

'Go on back to sleep now. You'll get all your sums wrong else.'

'No, I won't,' Will said, pushing back his fringe of coppery hair. 'Lie quiet anyhow.'

The house was chilly, in the early morning light, but when he had put on his coat and boots, and got outside, there was already a pale, filtered sunlight, and the air was fresh and clear. He took the big high bicycle, and wheeled it out through the front garden, looking down at the red tulips which were growing along each side of the path. A missel sat pertly on the near gatepost, flying up and away into the dark green mass of the holly, at the last moment when Harry came. Along the line of the privet hedge, the Hybarts' big white cat, Snowman, crouched and sidled in the shadows, baulked of the bird.

'Cooch away, you won't get him,' Harry said under his breath to the cat, which turned and looked straight up into his eyes. He launched his bicycle forward, running beside it as he loved to do, and then jumping into the saddle. He freewheeled downhill and swung round into the road. Along the line of the river a thin mist was breaking up into wisps. As he rode, the sun came up out of the cloudbank by the Holy Mountain, and the day was suddenly there.

It was five to six when he reached the station. Bill Thomas was already there, standing by the edge of the platform. In the box, the window was closed, and there was no sign of Meredith.

'Come to see the fun, Harry?' Bill Thomas asked.

'Not much fun.'

Tom Rees, in full uniform, walked stiffly down the zigzag path to the platform, from his official house.

'Everybody up early,' Bill Thomas said.

'Aye.'

'Well, boys,' Rees called as he came nearer. 'Anxious to work?'

'Aye, we're the blacklegs,' Bill Thomas said. Rees nodded, and stood near the edge of the platform, swinging his shoe at a loose stone on its corrugated edge, and at last sending it flying down into the ballast of the track.

'No Mr Rosser arrived?'

'He'll be here,' the ganger said, looking at his watch.

It was six o'clock, and the three men walked down the platform, and stood under the box. A window of the box was opened, suddenly, and Meredith stood there looking down.

'Wanting a train?' he said, flatly. A browned cigarette was stuck to his lower lip.

'That's right, my man,' Bill Thomas shouted up. 'See that it hurries along, will you?'

'See that my mate hurries along,' Meredith said.

'He'll be here.'

'Much about, Jack?' Rees asked.

'Nothing since half past three. Might as well have been in bed.'

'You go to bed, do you, Jack?' Bill Thomas asked.

'Them as work do.'

'What the other boxes doing, Jack?' Harry asked.

'Closed, both ways. They just rung through.'

'Well, come on then,' the ganger said. 'Close up yourself.'

'I'm waiting for my relief.'

At seven minutes past six, Morgan arrived. He rode down on to the platform, his head bent forward. As he stepped off, he looked round and smiled.

'You here, Harry? You should have come and woke me.'

'I took it you'd be up.'

Morgan smiled, pleasantly. All the intelligence of his face was concentrated now, and controlled.

'Well, come on. Let's get this over.'

He looked up at the window, but Meredith had disappeared. 'He's up there, I suppose?'

'Yes,' Rees said. 'Doing a bit of overtime, I fancy.'

'Right,' Morgan said, briskly. 'I'm closing the box, you know why.'

'I'll come up with you,' Rees said.

'No need, I can manage.'

'I'll come all the same.'

They walked to the steps, and Bill Thomas nudged Harry. 'Come on, Harry, we might as well go too.'

They followed the others up to the box. Morgan had left the two doors open. All the men stood close inside. Meredith had his coat

94

on, and his frail slung on his shoulders. He stood at the far end of
the box, waiting.

'All right,' Morgan said. 'You can go now.'

Meredith did not answer, but looked across at the little clock
above the desk, which now showed eleven minutes past.

'Look, you've seen the notices,' Morgan insisted. 'No duty to be
taken from now, till further orders. You needn't come tonight.'

'You're relieving me now, are you?' Meredith asked, after a pause.
'Relieving me at, what, twelve minutes past?'

'I'm closing the box,' Morgan said distinctly. 'All you have to do
is go home.'

'If you'll relieve me,' Meredith said, 'I'll sign off. Till then, I'm
staying.'

Morgan hesitated, and Bill Thomas stepped forward and spoke.
'Look, Jack, the notices, you saw them.'

'Only notices I'm interested in is these,' Meredith said. He rapped
his fingers against the dusty, yellowing notices on the official board.
'Notices for the working of trains.'

'I'll handle this,' Morgan said. 'Now I'm not telling you again,
Jack. Stop fooling about. I'm closing the box, and you got no option.'

'Relieving me, are you?' Meredith repeated.

'Not relieving. Closing the box,' Morgan said again, as if to a slow
child.

Meredith looked away, wiping his mouth with the back of his hand.

'Then I'm still on duty,' he said, looking round. 'And while I am,
I'll have no unauthorized persons in this box.'

'Unauthorized. What the hell you playing at? Come on, get going.'

Meredith smiled, and faced Morgan silently. For some moments
nobody moved, and then Tom Rees spoke.

'There's no trains, you say, Jack?'

'Last was a parcels, half past three.'

'Well, Morgan's here, look. You sign off, he sign on. Then you're
in the clear.'

'If he'll sign on, I've offered,' Meredith replied, his dark eyes
glancing quickly over the other men.

'Right, Morgan, sign,' Rees said.

'Sign on? I'm not signing on. My orders are to take no duty after midnight. I'm standing by that.'

'You can sign just to put Jack right,' Harry said. 'Then do what you like.'

'I am doing what I like, and what the Union says. I'm the branch secretary, and am I to be the first to scab?'

'No scabbing, mun, just sense,' Harry said.

'So you won't sign on?' Rees asked, after a pause.

'No. Certainly I won't.'

'Then I will,' Rees said. 'Jack, will you hand over to me?'

Meredith looked surprised. He shifted his feet.

'Aye, if you say so, I suppose. But I don't understand.'

'Right then,' Rees said, and went to the register.

'And you'll take over?' Morgan shouted, stepping forward. 'You'll take over the box when the Union's called us out?'

'Shut up,' Rees said harshly.

Meredith shrugged his shoulders and walked to the register, where he signed off. Morgan looked round angrily at Harry and Bill Thomas.

'Are we going to let him get away with this?'

'Hang on,' Harry said.

Tom Rees stood at the desk, and tilted back his bright, official cap. Then he wrote quickly in the register, and with the round black ruler drew a line across the page. He walked across to the instrument panel above the signal grid, and closed the instruments. Morgan hurried to the register, and read what Rees had written

Box closed, 6.18 a.m., 4th May, 1926, owing to General Strike.
T. J. Rees, Stationmaster.

'You mean you're closing up?' Meredith shouted. 'You're helping them with this daftness?'

'I'm responsible for that,' Rees said. 'Now come along all, we'll lock up.'

Harry went at once, and Bill Thomas followed him down the steps. Morgan walked behind them, frowning. Finally, Meredith appeared, with Tom Rees behind him.

'You're responsible for keeping this station open, not closing it,' Meredith was saying. 'Call yourself a bloody stationmaster!'

'Go on home, Jack,' Rees said, as he turned and locked the red outer door. 'You got work to do there, haven't you?'

'I'd better have, with this bloody lot,' Meredith said angrily, and pushed past the others to his bike. He rode away without speaking again.

'Only the thing is,' Rees said, coming down the steps with his bunch of keys, 'all this has got to be done right. No sense otherwise.'

Harry looked at him, and smiled. They all stood together under the closed box, looking along the empty lines and the deserted platforms, and at the home signals set at danger. For some while, none of them spoke.

Later, Rees locked the waiting-room, the parcels room, and his own office, and went back to his house for breakfast. The others waited on the platform. Two or three of the platelayers arrived at normal time, to make sure that they were not to work. The men were standing together talking, when the porter, Will Addis, came down carrying a big parcel wrapped in newspaper. He went to the door of the parcels office, and tried to open it. When it would not open he kicked it and rattled the handle, then at last walked over to the others. He was squat and sandy, with an awkward, rolling walk. The others grinned as he came.

'It's locked,' Addis said. 'What's on?'

The men roared with laughter, and Addis looked even more puzzled, staring nervously into each face in turn.

'What it is, Will,' the ganger said solemnly, 'they've decided, sudden, to do away with trains.'

'Do away with trains?'

'Aye, from now on, Will, all goods and passengers will fly.'

'Fly, go on,' Addis said, looking round suspiciously.

'Cut it, mun,' Morgan said, impatiently. 'Will, can you read?'

'Aye, Morgan, I can read.'

'Well, don't you know you're on strike then?'

Addis looked at the others and then smiled. 'Oh, aye, I know about the strike.'

97

'It's started, Will,' said the ganger. 'You can go home.' Addis looked round and shifted his big parcel.

'But I can't go home. I got these snaps to put in.' At this, everyone laughed loudly again. Harry glanced back up the platform at the cleared flowerbeds.

'You mean you've come just to plant up the flowerbeds?' Morgan asked.

'Aye, of course. I lifted the snaps this morning, I can't leave them out.'

Morgan smiled, and smacked his pocket. 'Well, now I've seen everything. What d'you say, Harry? A life-and-death struggle for the workers of this country, and Will wants to plant his snaps.'

'Well, what's wrong wanting that?'

'Wrong, Harry? Only that no man's to take duty, that's all. The plants'll have to wait.'

'But they can't wait. What harm does it do?'

'Look, Harry, keep out of this. I know how it is, I've got the experience. Once you start making exceptions in a strike, you're done for. Next it'll be oh, just one train, with perishables, and before we know where we are we'll all be at it.'

'It's only the three beds,' Addis said.

'Three or three hundred, they're still the Company's beds. And planting the Company's beds is work, and there's to be no work.'

'I made the beds myself. They're not Company.'

'You made them in Company time on Company property, and that's that. So shut up, will you, and leave it.'

'No, I won't leave it. The plants'll spoil.'

There was a silence, and then Harry spoke. 'What you want to get in the parcels for, Will?'

'My line, Harry. I got my spade.'

'Well, shove them in without a line, why don't you? Go on, I'll give you a hand.'

'Aye, come on,' the ganger said, 'we'll all plant them. No use them spoiling.'

'We'll do without the line,' Harry said. 'Draw with your foot.'

'Aye. Come on, John,' the ganger said to the old platelayer. 'We'll get them in and then get home.'

Morgan started to speak but stopped, knowing that he was defeated. Yet he did not go away. Will Addis untied the big parcel, and separated the raffia-tied bundles of moist, slender antirrhinum plants, rooted in packed red earth. The others got sticks, and dibbed in the plants.

'Fetch us some water, Morgan,' the ganger called back joking.

Morgan hesitated, and then took a firebucket and filled it. He brought it up to where the men were working, and joined in.

'I don't know, though,' he said. 'You oughtn't to be planting these in the morning, with this sun coming up.'

'They'll do,' Will Addis said. 'I'll raise them.'

With so many hands, the work was soon finished. The men walked back together, easily. For a while they stood again, looking round the silent, deserted station. Then they separated to go home. The strike had begun.

3

As Harry rode back through the village, he passed Will on his way to school. He was in a group of children, walking together up the narrow road. There were the Jenkins children, Gwyn, Glynis and Beth, from the cottage next to the Lippys; Howard Watkins, Will's age, from the chapel cottage; and little Cemlyn Powell, son of the widowed schoolmistress who lived next door to the Hybarts. Cemlyn was better dressed than the other children, but smaller for his age, and pale. Will walked in the middle of the group, carrying a stick. He was proud to be walking beside the leader of the group, a big boy of thirteen, who was already the size of a man. This was Elwyn Davey, from the poor family, the Daveys, whose earth-floored cottage by the Honddu had been flooded several times this past winter. Elwyn was exceptionally strong and resourceful, the acknowledged master of the school in the playground, and a match, if it came to it, for William Evans the schoolmaster himself, who simply waited resignedly for this impossible boy to leave. On Will's first day at school, Elwyn had taken him under his protection, warning the other boys off him and teaching him how to start to wrestle. Often, on the way home, he carried Will on his back, taking him down sometimes to the river, where he would wade in among the stones, with Will on his back, or sometimes, leaving Will on the sand near the acrid 'wild rhubarb' leaves, wade out himself into a deeper pool, and bend to tickle for trout. Whenever he could, Elwyn took off his boots and went barefoot, though in the winters at least there was always an old pair of boots that more or less fitted him. Often he would carry Will home and put him down in the porch, breathless and laughing. Ellen did not like him, and asked Harry to tell him not to take Will off to the river. But Harry did nothing; he thought Elwyn was a fine boy.

'Hurry up, you young shavers, you'll be late,' he called as he rode past.

'Ain't shaving quite yet, Mr Price,' Elwyn shouted back, laughing.

Harry's regular term for the children was gradually being attached to Will: in school now, most of the boys called him 'Shaver'. But Elwyn always called him Will, and offered to stop the nickname if the little boy wanted it.

'No, I got lots of names,' Will said to him. 'My real name's Matthew Henry. It's on my birthday paper. Honest, I saw it. Dada showed me.'

'Making out you can read,' Elwyn laughed.

'I can too. Dada showed me how before I came to school.'

'Reading,' Elwyn said, and laughed as if it were the greatest joke in the world.

'It's all right. What's wrong with it?'

Elwyn looked down at him, and put his hand across his shoulders. 'You like what you want to, Will. Don't let them stop you.'

Will smiled, showing his missing front teeth. 'And we've got a book,' he said, 'called *English Authors*. We read each other out of it.'

'Aye, English,' Elwyn said. 'Only here we're Welsh.'

'We talk English, Elwyn.'

'That's different.'

'How's it different?'

Elwyn hesitated, and then laughed. 'Come on now,' he said, 'race you to the gate, give you half-way start.'

'Aye.'

Farther down the road, some way behind the children, Harry passed Mrs Powell, small and thin-faced, her head down as she hurried.

'Morning then.'

'Oh, yes, good morning, Mr Price. Not working?'

'No. All out today.'

'You'd say something if we sent your kids home, not teaching them.'

'That's different,' Harry called back, and rode on. The answer came easily, but for much of the morning he went on thinking of what she had said.

As for money, the strike could not have come at a worse time. He had been saving regularly, but only a few weeks before had spent all his reserve, and a bit from his wages, on a new honey extractor and a season's supply of jars. By autumn, these would show a profit, but there, now, was the money locked up. There would, of course, be the strike pay – twenty-four shillings a week. But while for a week or so this might be enough, it would mean postponing payments and even getting into debt, which he could not face. Ellen had not complained about the strike, but she doubted whether she could manage on the twenty-four shillings, and he knew that he must get what other money he could. In the gardens there were ten dozen sweet-william plants, and about eight dozen hearted lettuce, that he could take to market to sell. Later, though it was the wrong time, he might sell some of the hens. Meanwhile, and likely to be easiest, he might get in advance his May wages as groundsman at the bowling green – a part-time job he had started in the autumn, when the old groundsman had died.

The rent was due on the following Monday, and since he now paid monthly, he planned to take a pound from the strike-pay and replace it with the pound he hoped to get from the bowls club. But he did not want to ask for this at once. He had drawn his April money only a few days before, at the end of the month, and William Evans had made so much of a formality of it that Harry did not want to go back again so soon. He decided to go on the Saturday, when he had prepared the green for the usual Saturday afternoon game. But in case he did not get it, he put the pound from the strike pay aside at once – in the usual place behind the caddy in the back-kitchen.

On the Friday the old couple next door, the Lewises, asked Will to go to the shop. They had got into the habit of asking this errand, and Will was always keen, for he got a penny for sweets out of the change. That Friday, as he came home from school, Mrs Lewis called him and Will went in to tell his mother.

'Go on then,' she said, 'get it done before your tea.'

Harry was up with Edwin on the farm, and tea might be as late as six or half past.

'Anything you want, Mam?'

'No, boy, no. Got to go easy now with the strike.'

Will ran off, and into the Lewises. Ellen saw him come out soon after, carrying a frail and a long leather purse. Then she could only see his hair above the hedge as he walked away down the lane. She was making a dress, sitting in the back-kitchen with the door open on the warm, quiet evening. As she went on working she did not notice the time, and though once or twice she thought that Will should be back, she was not worried till Harry arrived. Looking up at the alarm clock, she saw that it was past six.

'You didn't see Will down the lane?'

'No. What's he, playing?'

'The Lewises sent him down the shop. He ought to be back long ago. I just didn't think the time.'

Harry put down the bag of greens he was carrying. His forehead was covered with sweat, and his clothes were dirty and heavy on his body.

'He'll be all right.'

'He's gone to play, I expect, with that Elwyn,' Ellen said.

'Elwyn'll look after him.'

'Well, it's late. I want him back.'

He stood for a few moments, and then went out to his bike. 'I'll run down and get him then. Got tea ready?'

'Aye, soon as you're back.'

Harry free-wheeled down the lane, letting the stiffness go from his legs. At the road he turned right, and rode slowly, looking around. He reached the shop without seeing any sign of Will.

The shop was a room in an ordinary house. It was run by a widow, Mrs Preece, who had served in the old shop next the chapel, before old Mrs Jenkins died. Preece had been a platelayer, and had been killed on the line.

Harry put his bike against the wall, and went up the steps and through the door, on which the big spring bell jangled. The usual smell of the shop greeted him: leather, bacon, cheese, sweets, oil, fresh bread. Mrs Preece came from the back room, through the tasselled green curtain. At thirty she was still the exceptionally beautiful girl Harry remembered from the few months of her marriage.

'Oh, Mr Price, come after Will?'

'Yes. He been here?'

'He came, now just after four. For some things for the Lewises. Only he'd lost the money.'

'How much?'

'Well, a pound. Of course I'd have let him have the things, I said take them. Only he was upset you know. I told him go back and tell his Mam.'

'He hasn't come. A pound, did you say?'

'It was too much to give him, wasn't it? I thought that. Only he come in, see, with the purse, like he always does, put it on the counter. I got the things, and then picked the purse up and opened it. There wasn't nothing in it but a hair-pin, only he said there must be, Mrs Lewis had said there was a pound note.'

Harry listened, staring past her, feeling the sweat across his forehead and the tightness of his chest.

'I must find him,' he said. 'Thank you.'

He ran back to the road, and crossed over to a glat in the hedge. The Daveys' cottage was at the bottom of the field. He hurried down, calling for Will.

'Here.'

He looked round, but could see nobody. Then Elwyn appeared, crawling from the foot of a holly bush.

'He's here, he's all right.'

'Bring him out.'

Elwyn helped Will out through the narrow passage from their hide under the holly bush. His bright hair was dishevelled as he looked up and avoided his father's eyes.

'You lost that money. Why didn't you come home and say?'

Will did not answer. Harry could see that he was nearly crying.

'Money,' said Elwyn. 'What money you lost now, Will? Come on.'

Again Will said nothing. As Elwyn put his hand on his shoulder, he turned his face and rubbed it against Elwyn's sleeve.

'The Lewises give him a pound to go to the shop. When he got there, he'd lost it.'

'A pound?' Elwyn said, his eyes widening. 'No, Will, why didn't you tell me? If he'd told me, Mr Price, I'd have brought him straight back. I'd have looked for it, Will. We'd have found it.'

'That's what we better do now.'

'Aye. Come on, Will. No use being a baby.'

'I didn't lose it,' Will said. 'I couldn't have. I didn't open the purse.'

'How d'you know it was there then?' Elwyn asked, sharply.

'Mrs Lewis said. I saw her get it down from the mantel.'

'Then you must have opened it,' Elwyn said impatiently. 'Or it'd be there in the shop.'

'There was only an old pin, hairpin Mrs Preece said,' Will insisted, and at last looked up at his father.

'We'll look,' Harry said. 'Come on.'

'Where's the purse now?' Elwyn asked, as they walked to the road.

'I hid it, Elwyn. Inside the frail.'

'Where?'

'Them nettles by the hedge.'

'Will boy, you're daft. Come on, show me.'

The boys ran ahead, and at once recovered the frail. Elwyn felt inside for the purse, and opened it.

'That's right. Only a hairpin.'

Harry climbed the hedge in front of the boys, and jumped down into the road. Elwyn, turning, helped Will over, and they ran to catch up. Harry went back to the door of the shop and looked carefully along the path and back down the steps.

'Which side the road did you walk, boy?'

'This side, Dada.'

'All the way?'

'Yes.'

Elwyn looked suspiciously down at Will. 'You didn't go off anywhere else now, Will? No fibs now mind.'

'I walked straight down here, Elwyn. Honest.'

'You sure?'

'I'm sure. And I didn't open the purse either.'

'You must have.'

Harry had gone ahead, walking along the side of the road, looking down in the camber, and along the scythed grass bank.

'Come on, you two.'

The boys followed. Elwyn looked carefully along the bank as he walked. Will did not look, but walked head down. They reached the lane, but found nothing. Elwyn had collected three old Woodbine packets, and several other dirty scraps of paper. Harry barely looked at them. In the lane, he again asked where Will had walked, and brought him up beside him to show. They made their way slowly up the lane, with Elwyn busily searching some yards behind. But nothing had been found when they reached the houses. Ellen was out standing with old Mrs Lewis at the Lewises' gate.

'You found him then?'

'Aye, found him, only he's lost the money.'

'Lost the pound note,' Mrs Lewis cried. 'Oh, Will, you never.'

'I didn't lose it,' Will said, looking straight up at his mother. 'When I took out the purse in the shop there was nothing in it. Only an old pin.'

'But there must have been, Will. I put it in myself. I remember folding it.'

'You must have opened the purse and dropped it,' Ellen said.

'We've looked all the way,' Harry said impatiently. Then he turned back and looked at Ellen. She met his eyes, and he saw her suddenly as very young still, almost a child herself, with a child's expression of helplessness and fright.

'You shouldn't have given a child so much,' Harry said roughly, to Mrs Lewis.

'Wait, Harry,' Ellen pleaded.

'I know, Mr Price, only there wasn't the change,' Mrs Lewis said anxiously. 'It's all the money we got in the house see.'

Harry looked round, letting his eyes fall on Elwyn. It was only with Elwyn, now, that he could feel any contact.

'Still, since you give it him and he took it, I'm responsible. I'll pay you the pound.'

'Harry, wait,' Ellen said.

'And I got to go back down for my bike. What was it you wanted?'

Mrs Lewis looked up at him with tears on the edge of her eyes. She pushed her fingers back over her thin hair, unable to speak. Will, meanwhile, had moved a little away and was stroking the head of the old collie.

'I'll fetch your bike, Mr Price,' Elwyn offered.

'No. Now, what was it, Mrs Lewis? Don't make it worse now.'

'Half-pound of tea it was, two boxes of matches, and a half a pint of vinegar, the bottle's in the frail.'

'Right,' Harry said, and walked on to his own gate. Ellen turned and followed him.

'Will,' Harry called back, 'come on in with your Mam.'

Will left the dog and followed. Harry went into the back-kitchen and took the pound from behind the caddy. He came out and met Ellen and Will on the path.

'Will, go on in,' Ellen said, and the child obeyed. 'But, Harry,' she said urgently, 'you're not giving her the pound back. Not now?'

'The change from it.'

'I don't know what you think we're going to manage on.'

'That can wait. I'll see to it.'

'I tell you,' Ellen said, and lowered her voice. 'You don't think Elwyn got it off him? You know what that family's like?'

'I know they're poor.'

'Well, then?'

'So are we poor, and Elwyn's a decent boy.'

He went past her and out into the lane. Mrs Lewis had gone back into the house, but Elwyn was waiting, holding the frail. Harry took it, and Elwyn walked beside him down the lane. For a long way down they did not speak, but then Elwyn said suddenly: 'You believe me, Mr Price, don't you? If I'd have known, I'd have brought him straight up. I thought his Mam knew, see, he was out to play.'

'It's not your fault. Don't think about it,' Harry said.

He was walking fast, still watching the ground. They did not speak again until they reached the shop. Harry went straight in, and the bell jangled again. He realized that he had pushed too hard at the door.

'Found it then, Mr Price?'

'No. It's gone.'

'It's a shame now. A pound!'

Harry looked at her, and was at once strangely relaxed. She must have felt his look, for she flushed slightly, and put her hand nervously to her hair.

'I've come for the stuff anyhow.'

'It's all here ready, Mr Price.'

'Give us the change from that,' he said, and put down the note he had been holding.

'You paying it yourself then?'

'This the lot?' Harry said, packing the things into the frail. 'What about the vinegar?'

'Oh, yes, I didn't take the bottle, did I?'

He passed the bottle across, and Mrs Preece filled it from a stone jar, behind a hanging rack of dresses, aprons and coats. 'Right,' she said, wiping the bottle on her apron, and putting it on the counter. She took the note, and counted the change. Harry put the change in his pocket, without counting it.

'Good night, thank you,' he said, and went out.

Elwyn was waiting for him at the foot of the steps, holding the bike.

He took it and stepped over the saddle. He rode back quickly, and at the pitch in the lane, where he usually dismounted and walked, he stood on his pedals and rode, glad to feel his strength. He was breathing hard when he reached the houses, and the sweat had run down into his eyes. The first thing he saw was Ellen running out to him, laughing.

'It's found,' he heard her shout, and as he heard the words his strength seemed to ebb. He drew back and got off the bike.

'Found?'

'She never put it in. She took it down ready, and left it on the table.'

Harry seemed not to be listening. He stared down through the frame of the bike, then: 'Catch!' he said suddenly, and threw the frail across. Ellen, surprised, nearly dropped it.

'And here's the change,' he said, grabbing the money from his pocket. 'Bring back the pound.'

She watched him, surprised. She had expected pleasure, or at least relief. This hard edge of withdrawal and anger was frightening. He walked on without speaking, and put his bike away under the porch. He went into the back-kitchen, which was now almost dark. Will was sitting on a chair between the table and the copper; far back against the wall, his feet not reaching the ground. Harry went to him and bent down.

'You know it's found, Will?'

'Mam said she didn't put it in.'

'I'm sorry. Honestly, I'm sorry,' Harry said, and bent forward so that his head touched the boy's shoulder.

'Not for you to be sorry, Dada,' Will said but pushed the head away.

Ellen came in behind them, quietly.

'I got the pound, Harry. And the twopence she made me bring, for Will's sweets.'

'I don't want her old twopence,' Will shouted.

'Leave it all,' Harry said, sharply, and got up. 'I'll hear no more about it. Now get the lamp lit, and we'll have some food.'

Ellen, suddenly quiet, obeyed.

4

On the next day, the Saturday, they had an early dinner, and Harry went up to the bowling green, to mow and roll it and set out the rink-strings and the mats. While he mowed, Will sat by the roller watching him. Since the previous evening he had been very still and quiet, and in this mood his face was remarkably like his father's, though with the contrasting brightness of the hair. Harry mowed one of the three rinks, and then rolled and set it ready, in case anyone came early. Before he mowed the other rinks, he took off his waistcoat and set it down beside Will.

'Mind my watch in the pocket.'

Will nodded. As his father bent over him he could smell the sweat from his body. He kept his head down till Harry went back on to the green. He knew, having watched this work before, that today his father was racing through the job, at times almost running with the mower, but he did not know why. Then, when the mowing was finished and Harry was dragging the heavy roller, Will heard him curse under his breath as the schoolmaster, William Evans, arrived. Will got up at once and hurried away to the shed, to bring out the remaining markers and mats and the three shiny white jacks. He got these ready by the door, but did not go further, preferring to stay for the while in the hot, dusty shed.

'All right, groundsman?' William Evans asked, putting down the leather bag that held his woods, and sitting beside it on the grass bank.

'It's all ready,' Harry said, swinging back the roller handle, and setting off again down the green. It was the last journey; up once more would finish it. He bent far forward, dragging the roller, walking with quick, short steps. He was glad, when he turned, to see that nobody else had arrived. As soon as the markers and mats were down, he would ask for his May money.

'Will,' he called, as he came back up the green.

Will ran out from the shed.

'Just bring them markers and the mats, then go back for the jacks.'

Will turned, and picked up more than he could carry. As he came across, a mat slipped from his grasp and William Evans smiled.

'Got a mate, I see, Harry.'

'Aye.'

He ran the roller off the green, and hurried towards Will. The sweat was pouring down his face and neck, and his breath was quick and harsh.

'How much an hour do you pay him then?' William Evans asked, pulling his nose in the habit that everyone in the village knew.

'What he's worth,' Harry said, taking the mats and hurrying down with the markers. Will ran back for the jacks.

Tom Rees appeared, carrying his woods.

'It's a pleasure,' William Evans said, 'to see the railwaymen here. A real pleasure.'

'And why not?' Rees asked.

'Why not indeed?' William Evans said, pulling again at his nose. 'Come to that we could make this the new station, more convenient, see, for the passengers.'

'Take on a job as porter?' Rees asked, putting down is bag.

'Well, at least,' William Evans said, 'the strike's good for the bowls.'

Rees smiled and sat down beside him.

'You'll find the schoolmaster here any day, I'm told. Isn't that right, Harry?'

'I'd rather mow a billiard table, that's all I know,' Harry said, wiping his forehead.

'The green looks lovely, boy,' William Evans said. 'A credit to you.'

'Have a game?' Rees said. 'I'll fetch the slips.'

Harry waited for Rees to be out of hearing, then said quickly, 'You'll excuse me asking, Mr Evans. You can be sure I don't like to. But could I have my May money in advance? I don't need to tell you why.'

William Evans looked at him, raising his eyebrows. 'May? Why, yes, it is just May, of course. By a few days.'

'If I could have the pound, Mr Evans, it would be a great help.'

William Evans was about to answer when the policeman, John Watkins, walked up to the fence. A few moments later, Tom Rees came back with the slips.

'If you could manage it, Mr Evans.'

'Of course, boy, of course.'

'Have you come then, John, to arrest these dangerous men on strike?' William Evans asked, smiling broadly and showing his long yellow teeth.

The policeman rested his bicycle against the long fence of the green.

'Green looks well, Harry.'

'Not bad.'

'And I'd promised myself a game too, this afternoon.'

'Why not then?'

'On duty.'

'I'd have thought,' William Evans said, 'they'd have fetched you by now, for the Rhondda. Don't they parade you all through the streets, showing the miners who's boss?'

Watkins took off his helmet, and wiped his forehead and neck.

'I had enough of that, Mr Evans. Sirhowy, in twenty-one.'

'Well, you know,' Evans said quietly, 'law and order have to be kept, after.'

'And who's not keeping it?' Rees asked.

Harry looked for Will. The boy had gone back to the shed and was sitting by the open door.

'There's troops coming through this afternoon,' Watkins said. 'That's why I'm out.'

'Soldiers?'

'Aye, I suppose. Military convoy, they said.'

'Which way?'

Watkins pursed his lips and gestured with his thumb over his shoulder, up in the direction of the long ridge of Darren and the mining valleys beyond.

'Going to play the miners at rugger, I expect,' William Evans said, breaking the silence.

'Soldiers?' Watkins said.

'The Government knows what it's doing. All it wants is to prevent trouble. Only agreed, it is a dangerous situation. You men don't know what you've started.'

'Well, what I'm starting,' Tom Rees said, 'is an end of bowls. None of us is playing soldiers here.'

'I'm with you,' William Evans said, following him on to the green. As he passed Harry, he winked, and lightly patted his pocket.

'Constable Watkins,' came a shout from the road.

They all turned, to see Major Blakely, from Brynllwyd House, walking up towards the green. Watkins put on his helmet.

'The lorries are due in twenty minutes, constable.'

'Yes, sir.'

'We'd better get down to the road then. They might be early.'

'Right.'

Major Blakely hesitated, looking round at the others. He would probably have turned away if William Evans had not spoken.

'Military convoy I hear.'

'Yes.'

'A precaution, of course?'

'Quite.'

Tom Rees moved impatiently. Harry took his coat, and stepped off the green.

112

'Or it could be intimidation,' he said as he reached the bank.

Blakely hesitated, glancing at the two older men.

'Any intimidation, Price, is on your side.'

Harry stood pulling on his coat. Will had come up beside him and was standing in his shadow.

'Aye, you always turn it to that,' Harry said angrily. 'If I was selling you honey now, you wouldn't call it intimidation to stick for my fair price. On the line we sell our labour, and that's to be fair too.'

'But that isn't the dispute,' Blakely said patiently. 'You fellows always manage to get the wrong end of the stick. There's no dispute about the railwaymen's wages.'

'He's right, Harry,' William Evans said. 'Want to watch, these things are very difficult.'

Harry stood very still. His lips were set, and his eyes had lost focus.

'I don't claim more understanding than I've got, but I know this. Part of the fair price for any man is a fair price for his brother. I wouldn't want it if the miners went without.'

'Then are the miners your brothers and the rest of us not?' Blakely asked.

'The miners are locked out. That or take a cut in wages. It's your owners, isn't it, your government, holding the rest of us up?'

'I agree with Harry,' Rees said sharply. Both Blakely and William Evans looked at him, surprised. Rees only touched the stiff, waxed ends of his moustache.

'I know you men think you're being loyal,' Blakely said evenly. 'I admire you in a way, but you're quite fatally wrong. The coal owners can't afford more. The whole industry is depressed. And the Government can't let our national life break down. You may think your motives are good, but the facts, unfortunately, are against you.'

'You're so sure, aren't you?' Harry said.

Blakely looked at him, flushing a little and moving involuntarily.

'Well, are you sure?'

'I am. I'm sure because I was brought up to it.'

113

'To what? To striking?'

'To what has to be done.'

There was a pause, and then Watkins shouted from the road. Major Blakely at once hurried down. Harry turned slowly and took Will's hand to follow. When he and the others reached the road, an Army despatch rider was passing. Watkins stood stiffly at the edge of the road: a commanding figure in the uniform stretched tightly over his huge body. A light armoured car, with an officer standing in it, staring down at his map, came round the bend past the school. Behind him came eight open lorries, with about twenty steel-helmeted infantrymen in each. As the lorries passed, the soldiers looked tired and resigned. Then from the fourth lorry, two or three men waved.

'They open up the road?'

Harry had no time to answer, but he lifted his arm and waved back.

'Where the soldiers going?' Will asked.

'Just to a new camp,' Major Blakely said, smiling down at the boy and wanting to touch him.

'Let's hope it's that,' Harry said. Blakely nodded, closing his eyes for a second.

Before William Evans could go back to the green, Harry went up to him again.

'I'm sorry. We got interrupted.'

'The discussion about the strike?'

'The money.'

'Oh, that, yes. I been thinking, Harry – mind I know how things are – only it seems to me I ought to put it to the committee. It's their money after.'

'I need the May wage. You needn't think the work won't be done because I get it in advance.'

The schoolmaster looked down at Will, who was drawing with his boot in the dust.

'Would ten shillings in advance be any help?'

'I could do with the pound.'

'Yes, of course, but...' Evans hesitated, and again looked round. 'Well, perhaps,' he said quickly. 'Seeing it's in a good cause.'

He took out a big leather purse, and unfolded a pound note.

'Come in one day and sign the receipt.'

'Aye. Thank you,' Harry said. 'Only what did you mean a good cause?'

William Evans smiled, and carefully pulled at his nose. 'Ask no questions, get no lies. That right, boy?'

He patted Will on the shoulder.

5

So the money, if not enough, was as much as Harry had counted on. On the Monday the rent would be paid, and that was that. For food, they would not go short. They would manage.

That Sunday was the Baptist anniversary, and Will, with the other children, was to recite. He had been christened in church, but went to Sunday school at the chapel because it was nearer. Before they set out, Harry tested Will in his piece – a little Welsh poem of two verses – and then they all walked down to the chapel, with Mrs Lucas and the Hybarts, who were leading members. Many people were standing outside when they arrived, and everyone shook hands before going in. The choir, the solos, and the recitations went as arranged. Will, like many of the others, stood nervously under the arch by the pulpit, and said his poem clearly. At the end of the service, all the children were given a book: Will's was in green, with the title, *The Holy Child*. Harry was very pleased about the book, but Ellen, who had been watching Will more closely, was uneasy. She took care on the way out to get close to him and to admire it. Everyone waited outside, to shake hands again. Mrs Hybart, while the conversation continued, looked down at Will. He was turned away looking down through the railings at the river.

'You got a nice book then, I see, Will?'

'No.'

'Yes, it is, Will,' Ellen said quickly. 'You'll be able to read it at home.'

Will looked up stubbornly. 'I'm church, Mam, not chapel.'

'Well, yes, we all know that,' Mrs Hybart said.

'I'm never going in the chapel again,' Will shouted. 'And I don't want their old book.'

Holding one cover, and letting the rest of the book hang loose, he reached to the fence and threw the book down into the river. For several seconds there was a shock of silence so absolute that the flow of the water seemed the only sound there had ever been. Will looked up at the faces which stared down at him, but the only eyes that he met were his father's. He saw, for a moment, an expression he could not give a name to. It frightened him, not because it was angry but because he could not understand it.

'Shall I go after it, Harry?' Edwin asked.

'I will.' He moved reluctantly to the fence, and scrambled over. The bank was steep, and he slipped at the last step and felt the water come in over one boot. The book was floating a few feet out. He grabbed it and shook off some of the water. Then he turned slowly to climb back up. Edwin reached to give him a hand. Will now was looking white and frightened. 'You got a tartar there,' Edwin said, as he pulled Harry up.

'I'll tartar him all right,' Ellen said.

Harry shook his wet boot, and looked at the soaked trouser-leg of his suit.

'I'll say good evening,' Edwin said. He shook hands, formally.

Harry took Will's hand. They had to pass several of the standing groups to get to the entrance to the lane. Ellen walked self-consciously, feeling that everyone must be staring at them. When they were out of being heard, she spoke angrily to Will, but Harry said nothing.

'He's got his punishment,' he said at last, as they reached the cottage.

The book was dried on top of the copper, but it was hopelessly stained and curled. Will was put to bed, still tense and white. Ellen, when she came down, started talking to Harry. She wanted relief from the strain and its reaction, but he hardly answered.

'One thing anyway, Harry, you'll have to take in the rent. I honestly couldn't face Mrs Hybart after that.'

'You'll have to sometime.'

'I want you to take it, Harry. Please.'

Next morning, straight after breakfast, he went down to the Hybarts.

'Who is it?' Mrs Hybart called from the kitchen.

'Harry Price.'

'Come in, boy.'

Mrs Hybart was ironing at the long table. She went on working as he came in.

'I brought the rent.'

'Rent, is it?' She was turning the sleeve of a shirt.

'And to say we're sorry about last night.'

'Last night?'

'The book.'

'The book was given to him. He can do what he wants with it.'

'And what he said.'

Mrs Hybart put down the iron, and went across to the fire. 'Well, they always say, boy. Like father like son.'

'I don't know what you mean.'

'The father goes on strike, the boy throws away the book.'

'That's altogether different. I'm not apologizing for the strike.'

'Well you ought to. Such daftness.'

'I apologized to you about the book,' Harry said. He was staring down, unconsciously, at the half-ironed shirt.

'And where's the rent money come from, if you're out on strike?'

Harry shifted his feet.

'That's my business, isn't it? Anyway here it is.' He held out the pound.

'Put that note back in your pocket.'

'Why?'

'Do what I tell you, boy, or I'll have to shout.'

117

'Shout what? About the boy?'

Mrs Hybart took her second iron from the fire, and wiped it with her sleeve before putting it by her cheek to test the heat. She turned it, with her strong wrist, and spat down on the hot face. The spit sizzled and wrinkled dry.

'You got a wife and child to keep, haven't you?'

'Well?'

'Well, put that back in your pocket then. If you're so daft as to strike and go without your money, then I'm not taking it off you.'

'We pay the rent because we live in the house.'

Mrs Hybart laughed. 'Go, you look like Will, mun. Sulking at me.'

Harry looked away. 'If I don't pay the rent I can't keep the house.'

Mrs Hybart laid down the iron. She put out her hand which was as big as his own, although he was a head taller. She took his fingers, and folded them over the note.

'When it's all over, boy, you can pay me then.'

'I'd rather not get debts.'

'Debts? Here?'

Harry hesitated.

'Now get on and do some work,' she said, going back to the iron. 'And get back to the box as soon as you can. Forget this old strike.'

'I shan't forget anything.'

6

Comrades, the struggle has begun. Today the whole body of British workers stands united as one man in their unconquerable determination to resist demands which were a calculated and de- liberate attack, not only upon the miners but on every worker in the country and upon the very existence of the Trade Union movement itself. There is no need for us to call for your assistance, for you have already given it. With you we shall stand firm to the end in defending the rights of the organized workers. With you, we know that justice is on our side. With you, we are confident

that the resolute action of a united movement will bring victory to
the cause of the workers.

This declaration – part of the manifesto of the Miners' Federation, extracted from the *British Worker* of May 5th – stood pinned to the parcels office door in the now deserted Glynmawr station. Morgan had put it up and had added a notice of his own:

> *Railwaymen's response magnificent. Take no notice of lying wireless propaganda. All grades have acted well. But, apart from white-collar men, signalmen have worst record. Though out of 4,843 on the G.W.R., only 384 still at work. Keep this up and we shall win.*
> *Morgan Rosser,*
> *Branch Sec., Glynmawr.*

Hardly anyone came to read the notices. The Glynmawr men were out until they were told to go back, and meanwhile there was plenty to do, in the gardens and the fields. Morgan had called one meeting, and it had been well attended. But there was so little to do, except listen to extracts from speeches in London, that they decided to have no further meetings until there was some new development. Morgan found this inactivity difficult to bear, and he rode twice to meetings at Tredegar, and once went on to make contact with delegates of the miners. He discussed plans for the transport of food from Glynmawr.

Every railway worker in Glynmawr was now officially on strike, including the stationmaster, who had written a letter to Newport notifying his decision. Even Jack Meredith was officially on strike, though he indignantly denied this. After leaving the station on the first morning, he had worked in his fields. He went back that night at the usual time, only to find the box locked and the station deserted. Next morning he wrote to Newport, stating his readiness to work. In reply he got instructions, telephoned to Major Blakely and personally delivered by him, to report next morning at Ponty-pool, sixteen miles away.

'Are they daft or what? I'm not going down there.'

'But you offered yourself for work, Meredith. Here it is.'

Meredith got angry. Blakely had offended him by calling him 'Merridith', in the English manner, and in any case he did not like him. He seemed to hold Blakely personally responsible for the absurd instructions.

'I got my stock. What do you know about it? I can't trip all over the country like some people. Open Glynmawr box, and I'll work it, but that's my job and I'm going nowhere else.'

'You refuse the instructions then?'

'Those instructions, yes. I want my own job and my own wage. What do they think I am?'

Blakely gave up, and went. Meredith, still indignant, learned two days later that he was officially regarded as having withdrawn his labour.

'Withdrawn,' he exclaimed. 'I'll withdraw my fork in some of them, with their daft bloody ideas.'

Blakely tried once more, with a suggestion that Meredith should take over duties as a carrier between Glynmawr and Gwenton. But this was dismissed so angrily that Blakely, anxious to avoid trouble, hurried away. Even the strikers were not as offensive as this; indeed they were generally polite.

The life of Glynmawr was so largely centred on itself that adjustment to the strike was quite quickly made. In the lovely weather, it seemed that it might go on for weeks or months. So that when, on the Wednesday of the second week, news came on the wireless that the strike had been called off, Harry and the others were greatly surprised. Ellen, who had been in at Mrs Hybart's, where there was a crystal set, ran excitedly out to find him.

'It's over, Harry. The strike's over.'

He put down the hacker with which he had been splitting an old ash stump.

'Official, boy. On the wireless.'

He wiped his forehead, and walked back with her.

'What's happened then, I wonder.'

'I don't know, but do it matter? The miners must have won. There, don't look like that, boy. It'll be all right, you be sure.'

She was very excited, and hugged his arm. They walked down to the Hybarts' to listen.

'Stop fiddling with that whisker, will you,' Mrs Hybart said angrily to her husband. 'You'll lose it and here's people waiting to listen.'

Hybart stood up, looking sour and long-suffering. He took off his headphones, and passed them to Harry. For some minutes there was distant music, and then the official announcement of the end of the strike was repeated. A message from the King followed:

Forget whatever elements of bitterness the events of the past few days have created... Forthwith address ourselves to the task of bringing into being a peace which will be lasting because, forgetting the past, it looks only to the future with the hopefulness of a united people.

Harry waited for more news, but the only item was an announcement from the Cardinal Archbishop of Westminister that a *Te Deum* would be sung in Westminster Cathedral on the following morning, which would be Ascension Day. He took off the tight headphones, and stood up. He stayed for some minutes in the cool, dark room, and then went to find Morgan. He was not at home, and Harry rode to the station. Only Rees was there, and he knew no more than the bare announcement. During the afternoon the other men began to arrive. By four they were all there except Jack Meredith. Two of the young platelayers went to kick a football in the timber yard. Will Addis was laying heaps of poisoned tea-leaves to keep the slugs from his snaps, which had gone back a good deal since planting. Morgan arrived from Tredegar, and sat waiting by the phone.

'Only one thing more I know,' Bill Thomas said. 'The miners' choir are singing the Archbishop's *Te Deum*.'

'Don't be so bloody insulting,' Morgan said, quickly.

Bill Thomas smiled, and winked at the other men. All but Harry smiled back at him. In this situation, he found his respect for Morgan steadily increasing. It was he and not the others who in fact understood.

At last news came through. First a telegram, from union headquarters in London:

T.U.C. notify strike called off. Members must present themselves for duty at once. Keep me advised if necessary. Cramp.

While this was still being discussed, the phone rang. Tom Rees took it, and sat listening for some time, writing notes on the back of an old leaflet of an excursion to Barry. When he had finished, he read out his notes:

Company instructions on resumption of work. One, men return to work absolutely unconditionally. Two, in some departments individuals will be selected for dismissal. Three, men only taken on, on condition they lose all previous privileges of service. Four, men may be shifted from grade to grade, or place to place, as the Company require.

Morgan went over and stood beside him. The others watched him carefully; Morgan would know what to say.

'All right. Only on those terms they can keep their bloody railway. None of us is going back on that.'

'Your union has ordered you back.'

'Whose bloody side are you on, then? Or them for that matter. I'm telling you now, you as stationmaster, we're not working on that lot.'

'Before you go on about your stationmaster, make sure, I should, who he is. One note I didn't read. Men in salaried grades who joined the strike will have their positions considered individually.'

Morgan hesitated, and then clapped his hand on Rees's shoulder. 'You stick with us, Mr Rees, we'll see you right.'

'Perhaps,' Rees said, turning away. 'Meanwhile, I'm locking the office and going home. We'll see in the morning.'

At half past seven next morning they met at the station, still without Meredith. At nine a formal meeting was held, and a resolution passed refusing work on the conditions stated. But they were really waiting for news from outside. At eleven it came, and they met again, sitting round the walls of the parcels office. The conditions announced last night were withdrawn. Instead, any man reporting for duty was required to sign a form of re-engagement:

You are re-engaged on the understanding that you are not released from the consequences of having broken your contract with the G.W.R. Company. Under this condition please come on duty at the times stated.

'Polite to put in "please",' Morgan said, angrily.

'There's more,' Rees said. 'For the time being, only permanent way men and two signalmen required.'

There was a short silence. Rees looked across at Harry.

'Two?' Morgan asked. 'Which two?'

'My instructions are to re-engage on seniority.'

'That means Jack and Morgan,' Harry said.

'But Harry's been with us and Jack against us,' Bill Thomas protested.

'It don't arise,' Morgan said. 'None of us is signing that form.'

'You're right we're not,' Bill Thomas seconded. 'None of us is to sign nothing, understood?'

'I shall be in the office,' Rees said. 'Any man wishing to sign on can come in and do it.'

He went into his office, leaving the door open. Nobody followed him. A new mood of anger, that had not previously been evident, was slowly emerging. When they went out into the sun, and talked, there was a new and corroding bitterness. They all stayed at the station. They seemed to know instinctively that it was important to be with each other. In the afternoon a union telegram arrived, and Morgan read it out, standing on the weighbridge:

Do not sign any form of re-engagement. All to resume work under the old conditions only.

123

At this, for the first time since the beginning of the strike, there was a quick cheer. During the rest of the day, the new feeling hardened. In the evening another telegram arrived.

In view difficulties concerning reinstatement, Joint Executives call upon all railwaymen to continue strike until we receive satisfactory assurances.

'So we needn't turn up here tomorrow,' Morgan said. 'The strike is still on.'

Still, on the Friday, everyone went to the station again. Even Meredith turned up. They were all bitter and determined now. It was a more definite issue. A further statement came from the company, but added little. 'Rights in re broken contracts' were still reserved, as also were all decisions on salaried men. 'So are our rights reserved,' Morgan said. In the afternoon, strike money was paid out, and most of the men went home. Harry went back to the station in the evening and found Morgan jubilant. Another, apparently final, telegram had come in:

Complete reinstatement secured without penalties. All members should report for duty immediately. Full details to follow.

'That's all right then,' Harry said.

'Seems so. Without penalties: well, that's all right. And complete reinstatement: that means everybody.'

'It's all right,' Harry said. 'So far as we're concerned.'

'What d'you mean?' Bill Thomas asked him.

'He means the miners,' Morgan said.

'Yes. I thought that was the object.'

The three men were silent. Harry stared up at the black ridge of the mountains. Above them, high into the sky, was a great bank of loose white cloud, shot jade and rose with the fragmented colours of the sun.

'That's national politics,' Bill Thomas said.

Morgan said nothing. He was looking intently into Harry's face, in which the eyes were withdrawn and misted, as if he were looking far back into himself.

'Anyhow, Harry, for the time being, I'm taking duty at six, Meredith at two. You come on at ten.'

'Right.'

On the Saturday morning, as arranged, work was begun. But Harry did not go back that night. The full details that had now arrived read differently from the telegram. Morgan brought the papers over when he came off work.

First: those employees of the Railway Companies who have gone out on strike to be taken back to work as soon as traffic offers and work can be found for them. The principle to be followed in reinstating to be seniority in each grade at each station, depot or office.

Second: the Trade Unions admit that, in calling a strike, they committed a wrongful act against the Companies, and agree that the Companies do not by reinstatement surrender their legal rights to claim damages arising out of the strike from strikers and others responsible.

Third: the Unions undertake (a) not again to instruct their members to strike without previous negotiations with the Company; (b) to give no support of any kind to their members to take any unauthorized action; (c) not to encourage supervisory employees in the special class to take any part in the strike.

Fourth: the Companies intimate that, arising out of the strike, it may be necessary to remove certain persons to other positions, but no such persons' salaries or wages will be reduced. Each company will notify the Union within one week the names of men whom they propose to transfer, and will afford each man an opportunity of having an advocate to present his case to the general manager.

Fifth: the settlement shall not extend to persons who have been guilty of violence or intimidation.

Harry folded the papers, and passed them back to Morgan. Morgan looked down at him, his lips drawn into despair.

'I'd never have thought it, Harry. It's shameful.'

'It's bad, certainly. As bad as what we said "no" to.'

'And now they've said "yes" for us. The strike's over. What chance have we got?'

Ellen was standing near the door. She dried her hands on the towel, and looked across at Morgan.

'How will it be at the station then?'

'That's just it. It's not all back. They've said they only want two signalmen.'

'That means Harry won't work?' She looked across to where Harry sat looking down at the brick floor.

'No use blaming anyone,' he said, looking up.

'We can blame the Union,' Morgan said. 'Blame them, blame the T.U.C. What they call it off for, sell us and the miners out, when we were strong?'

'They're all in London,' Harry said. 'They see things different.'

'Will it be long though?' Ellen asked.

'I hope not long,' Morgan said.

'It could be months,' Harry said. 'While the miners are out, they're right. There won't be the traffic to justify.'

Morgan turned to Ellen. Since they had first met, they had liked each other, but now, under pressure, the pattern of feeling was shifting. They were both very conscious of Harry, as they might be of a parent.

'Rees is in for it, mind,' Morgan said. 'He got a tip on the phone he was one for special consideration.'

'What would that be?' Ellen asked.

'They'll move him, I expect. Just to show.'

Harry got up, and stood buttoning his black waistcoat. He had not shaved, and the beard was dark over the collarless shirt. He went across to the tap and washed his hands. There was a noise at the door and Will ran in.

'Mam, Dada, can I have a hoop?' he asked breathlessly. His cheeks were flushed from running.

126

'A what, boy?' Morgan asked. He put out his hand and ruffled the boy's hair, but Will drew away.

'Don't bother your Dad now,' Ellen said.

'Brychan's got one, Mam, you should see it go. I tanked it for him down the pitch, you ought to see it. And Eira's going to ask for one.'

'Is she with you?' Morgan asked.

'She's waiting over your place, Mr Rosser.'

'Hoops,' Morgan said indulgently, and smiled at Ellen.

'Leave it for now, Will,' she said. 'Don't bother your Dad.'

Harry walked past them, and dried his hands at the door. 'What sort is Brychan's?'

'Iron, Dada.'

'All right, I'll try. My dad used to get me hoops from the old barrels. I'll try up the pub.'

'Only run along now, Will,' Ellen said. 'We're busy.'

Will went out, looking up at them, and then they heard him calling Eira as he broke into a run along the lane.

'I'd better go too,' Morgan said. 'I'm sorry, Harry.'

'That's all right.'

Morgan put out his hand, and Harry took it, smiling.

'It was all to come out so well, wasn't it?' Morgan said.

'Do it ever?' Harry answered, and laughed. 'Anyhow we're all right,' he said. He turned back to Ellen and put his arm around her. She moved away a little, but then stayed.

Morgan walked out to the porch. 'One thing, Harry, I've sworn. The miners need food, and here it can be collected. I'll set that going if it's the last thing I do. If I can get an old van, see, and collect around.'

'If you can get a van.'

'I got a bit put by. We'll manage it. If we could get a depot in Gwenton. Get the stuff brought in as far as there, then run it up as we could.'

'It's worth trying,' Harry said, but his eyes were distant again.

7

For the next five weeks, Harry was out of work. Traffic on the line was light, and there was no immediate prospect of him getting back. In the third week the decision about Rees came through. He was to be transferred to Llangattock, as stationmaster, from the beginning of June. His house must be given up by the same date. The move was only twenty miles, and there would be no loss of pay, but the effect of the decision was heavy, and Rees showed it in his face and walk. The face became thinner and older, so that the waxed points of the moustache seemed more prominent and more artificial. The tall body was stooped, and the hunched shoulders seemed thinner. He discussed the affair with nobody, but everyone could see how much it was costing him, to leave the village and his garden. In fact the deepest hurt was the loss of confidence. A man with Rees's kind of pride in his job was being found at fault, was being moved as an example and a warning. It was this mark that he carried away when he left quietly, one Saturday, on the twelve train.

Harry did not see him in the last week. He could not bring himself to go to the station until he was wanted for work, and Rees avoided the bowling green and the rest of the village. In any case Harry was busy: working long hours with Edwin at the farm; cycling to market with lettuce and spring onions, bunches of sweet rocket and lupin, an early crop of broad beans, and finally the twenty jars of honey he had kept back for use in the house during the summer. Mrs Hybart found him a job, felling and chopping an old oak by the Lippys' cottage. This, she said, took care of the May rent. But every day, though he did not talk about it, he waited for the message from the station, that seemed increasingly unlikely to come.

The way it happened in the end was entirely unexpected. Jack Meredith, who since the strike had not spoken to Morgan, leaving only written messages for him in the box, was working afternoons in the sixth week after the return to work. On the Friday, he was due to close the box at ten as usual, but at half past nine a message came on the phone. A banker engine was to run a heavy goods train up the gradient from Gwenton, then drop off and turn in Glynmawr siding and go back to the sheds. This was routine, and Meredith hardly listened until the clerk said:

'He's a bit delayed, but he'll get to you about ten or quarter past.'

'Past what?'

'Past ten, what do you think?'

'I can't shunt him then, can I?'

'Why not?'

'Because I book off at ten.'

'We know that,' the clerk said. 'That's why we're ringing you up. Keep the box open till the banker's turned, then that's it.'

'I keep open till ten.'

'Yes, we know that. Only tonight you see there's this banker.'

'Aye, well, that's your problem,' Meredith said, and hung up the phone.

He sat down by the empty grate. To look at him, nobody would suppose that he was thinking or feeling anything. The hands hung down between the breeches and the tight black leggings. The dark, ugly face was wholly unmoved and unexcited. When the phone rang again, some ten minutes later, he got up to answer it as if he did not know what it would be about. It was a different, more authoritative voice.

'Meredith.'

'Meredith here.'

'This banker now. You know how it is. If he can't turn at Glynmawr he's got to go on to Hereford. There's the crew out all night, and the banker's wanted here first thing in the morning.'

'Aye.'

'Well now, you stay open till he's turned and back. Twenty minutes at the most. And not for nothing, mind you. You'll get your overtime.'

Meredith hesitated. 'That's how you look at it, is it?'

'Well, yes, that's how it is.'

'How what is?'

'How we got to work the banker.'

'How you want to, aye.'

'Now, look, Meredith. You're a reasonable chap. It's common-sense, isn't it, we got to get that engine back. You wouldn't want the crew stuck at Hereford all night.'

'It isn't what I want. It's how you arrange it.'

'Well, I'm arranging it now. Your orders are to stay open till that banker's turned. Right?'

'Right nothing. I'm closing at ten.'

There was a pause, and Meredith was about to hang up. Then the voice came again.

'Let's just get this straight. You're refusing an order, are you?'

'I'm refusing nothing. I booked on at two to work till ten.'

'But look, Meredith, use your sense. This goods is delayed, or she'd have been through you by now. For quarter of an hour you wouldn't cause all that trouble.'

'There's a signalman at home,' Meredith said. 'If you want I'll get him called out.'

'For a quarter of an hour? As late as this?'

'That's up to you. You said it was important.'

'We don't need a new man on. You can do it perfectly well.'

'Aye, I can. If she gets here before ten.'

'You can do it just the same at quarter past.'

'What, from up the mountain?'

'You can stay open, as I've told you to. And don't try and get funny. By playing obstinate you'll lose that crew their night in bed, and hold up the work here in the morning.'

'That's your business,' Meredith said, looking across at the clock. There was a short pause.

'You bet it's my bloody business, Meredith. Now, look, I'm giving you one more chance. Are you keeping that box open?'

'Till ten o'clock, aye, as I signed on.'

'You think you're bloody clever, don't you? You think, perhaps, this'll help this mate of yours. Well, it won't, let me tell you. And it isn't the last you'll hear about this. If you close that box, you'll regret the bloody day you were born, and you can take that from me.'

'I'm not listening to be sworn at,' Meredith said, and hung up the phone.

It was now six minutes to ten. The goods, with the banker attached, was asked from Gwenton, and Meredith accepted it. He pulled the up signals for it to go through his section. Then he packed his frail, bolted the window, and stood waiting. As the minute hand reached the hour, he signed off and went out, locking the box. He got his bike from underneath, and wheeled it along the platform. From behind him, down the valley, he could hear the approaching train. He stopped, put his bike against the parcels door, and waited. Some minutes later, the train reached the station. The front engine stopped just beyond him. Meredith walked along, through the cloud of discharging steam, and climbed up on the step to the footplate.

'The box is closed,' he shouted to the driver.

'What?'

'The box is closed. You can't drop the banker here.'

'How's that then? We was told.'

'I don't care what you was told. The box is closed.'

The driver hesitated, pushing back the peak of his cap. 'All right, mate, you know best. I'll go back and tell them on the banker.'

'Aye,' Meredith said, 'then you're right away for Hereford.'

The driver looked at him, then wiped his hands on a lump of waste.

'Good night then,' Meredith said, and went for his bike. He wheeled it up to the road, and stood waiting by the bridge. There was a long delay, and then the driver came back. The front engine whistled, and from down the line the banker replied. With a heavy blow of steam, the engine drew forward. Meredith watched it pass under the bridge, and the steam rose around his face. Behind the long engine came the line of trucks, jerking noisily at their couplings. At the end, behind the guard's van, came the banker, still attached. Meredith turned to his bike and rode home.

No one at Glynmawr ever knew exactly what happened the next day. But in the late afternoon a message came through that Signalman Price was to report for duty on the Monday, and that the box would return from the same day to normal working, with three shifts. Harry got the message the same evening, and later, from Morgan, heard a version of what had happened in the box. Much of the story had come out, and was common knowledge along the line, where the other signalmen had been listening on the phone. Harry was surprised, both to be getting back, and about Jack Meredith. On the Monday, at two o'clock, he reported for duty, relieving Meredith. Meredith was much as usual, awkward and untalkative.

'I heard about Friday night, Jack. I want to thank you. I owe you a lot.'

'Owe me?' Meredith said, slinging his frail on his shoulder.

'It got me back to work. I won't forget that.'

Meredith looked at him. 'Only your own bloody silliness got you out of it, didn't it?' As he spoke he rubbed his fingers across his broad nostrils, and his small, bloodshot eyes stared.

'Aye, well that,' Harry said. 'Perhaps it's always silly to go helping your mates.'

'Of course,' Meredith said, and walked to the door. 'People ought to learn to look after themselves for a change.'

Harry smiled and signed on in the register, for the first time in nearly seven weeks.

'Get on home now, Jack. You'll find your sheep on the road, I wouldn't wonder.'

'Don't you worry about my sheep,' Meredith said, and he pulled on his cap and opened the door. He turned suddenly, his face under the low peak still set and sour.

'Haven't forgot how to work the box I suppose?'

There was the trace of a smile at his mouth as he slammed the door.

CHAPTER FIVE

1

Matthew stood on the bridge above Glynmawr station, looking down at the box and the lines. A wind was blowing from the mountains, which were dark and close under the leaden sky. He turned down his collar, to make sure that he would be recognized, and walked down the zigzag path to the platform. Across the lines, by his hut, Bill Phillips the ganger saw him and waved. Matthew returned the greeting and hesitated. Was it right now, he wondered, to wait and talk?

He reached the platform and waited. Bill Phillips hesitated, then after looking each way on the line came across. Matthew watched him as he jumped up on to the platform: a lithe, weathered man, with heavy, blunt hands. As he came up, Matthew put out his hand and it was gripped, firmly.

'I'm glad and I'm sorry,' Phillips said.

'Yes, I know. I've come to fetch one or two of his things.'

'Aye. In the box. All right.'

Matthew looked away. Perhaps he had been wrong to wait.

'How are you keeping yourself?'

'Not bad, Will. Mustn't grumble.'

'Why not? We all do.'

'Aye, only not at each other. Not now.'

'Perhaps you're right.'

'Aye, of course,' Phillips said, and went back across the line.

Matthew walked down the platform, past the waiting-room and the parcels office to the steps of the box. With his hand on the steep wooden rail, he stopped. In the old days he had gone up these steps so often: bringing his father's dinner; waiting in the box while his mother went shopping in Gwenton; later just to sit and talk, through the long hours. It was almost a part of home, this box in which for thirty-six years Harry had spent almost a third of his life. Yet it seemed, looking up, quite separate and commonplace. Once in early childhood, it had been a place of magic.

He walked quickly up the steps. At the top was the red door, with its square metal notice forbidding entry to unauthorized persons. He opened the door, and closed it quickly against the wind. He was in the little square between the two doors, and the place came back to him. On the wide shelf stood the three red fire buckets: the nearest filled with sand, with shreds of tobacco decaying on the moist yellow surface; the next with water, with a faint iridescence of oil. The third was the washing bucket, blue and milky, with a curd of lather around the rim. Beside the washing bucket was the yellow tablet of hard gritted soap, and the two pieces of cotton waste, tangles of multi-coloured threads. The atmosphere of the box began here: a faint, sweet smell of dust, soot, lamp-oil, food. He opened the inner door.

Jim Price, the signalman on duty, was about Matthew's own age. He had come first as a relief signalman, and then had married in the village and got the regular job. He came across now, with a quick smile. He was about Matthew's height, and they looked carefully at each other as they shook hands.

'It's good to meet you, Will. I've heard a lot about you from your Dad.'

'I just came for some of his things.'

'Aye. In the locker. You carry on, Will.'

'It's the middle one, isn't it?'

'Yes, he's always had that.'

Matthew took Harry's keys from his pocket, and bent and opened the locker. The bottom was filled with cotton waste and a big roll of brown corrugated paper. On the shelf were the usual possessions: the stump of yellow comb, the glass jars of tea and sugar, the blue cup, the rule-book, the old bone-handled razor, the pencil and signal pad, the spare spectacle case, the heap of saved string. He stared over them, not knowing what to do.

'I don't really know what to take, Jim. He just asked me to bring back his things.'

Jim was slow in answering. He had carefully avoided looking into the open locker. The privacy of the lockers was absolute.

'It's all bits of things, Will. You get attached to things like that.'

Matthew took the comb, the razor, the spectacle case and the pencil, and put them in his overcoat pocket.

'That's the personal things anyway.'

'Better take it all, Will. If he asked.'

'What, the cup, and this tea and sugar?'

'Well, the cup, certainly.'

'All right. But the tea and sugar? I can leave them, can't I, for you?'

'No, better take them. And the rule-book, he'd want that.'

'No, surely,' Matthew said. 'He wouldn't have asked, you know, if he thought he was coming back.'

'No, I daresay.'

'Then the rule-book?'

'Yes, we hold on to that.'

'All right. If you say so. I'll manage.'

He took out the other things, and put them together on the shelf above the lockers.

'He could come back,' Jim said. 'He's still strong, he could get over this.'

'But he asked for these things.'

'Yes, well, it's how he feels.'

Matthew looked round the box. He recognized the flap-table, under the little window, where he had hidden when his father had teased him, saying the Inspector was coming, or when his mother had got off the train and been told he was lost. He saw the dusty, threadbare red and green flags, and the heavy black megaphone, with its brass lip. He saw the four telephones, and the notice board above the fireplace, with its grimed and yellowing schedules. He saw the high clerk's stool; the open register with its thick, large writing; the round ruler and the white pen. He looked last at the grid, with its twenty-six levers: the shining handles and clips, the distinguishing plates in red, blue, yellow and black, the two check dusters to grip the polished handles; then the line of instruments above: the model indicator signals, the bells mounted in wooden clocks, with swinging notices in the face; the central master-key, with its looped brass chain.

'How are you managing now? Are you working twelve hours?'

'Aye, we've worked twelve hours since July. When your Dad was here, Bill Owen was off. There isn't a regular relief.'

'Bill Owen's back?'

'Aye. Just four days before your Dad went down.'

'Twelve hours is a strain.'

'Aye, but you know what we say, Will. We're here, but we're in the dry.'

'Yes.'

The down bell rang, above the grid: a train being asked from Pont Dulas.

'Can I take it?' Matthew asked quickly.

Jim hesitated. 'Well, aye, Will, go on. You remember, do you?'

'I remember the bell. Is it all right?'

'Aye, carry on.'

Matthew hurried to the grid, and returned the signal. He waited, tense, until the next signal came.

'Goods? All right?'

Jim was smiling now as he watched him.

'Aye, take it, go on.'

Matthew returned the second signal, and glanced at the clock. Then he went to the end of the grid, and pulled off the five levers in turn. The pull of the distant was harder than he remembered, and he watched anxiously for the little indicator signal to drop.

'I used to get that distant stuck sometimes.'

'Aye, if you don't get the smooth pull you do.'

'All O.K. then?'

'Aye, you'll train up, Will.'

Matthew moved away, embarrassed. He had no right, after all, to come playing at a man's work. Yet the impulse and the memory had been overwhelming, when the bell rang.

'I'd better not stay here and interfere,' he said.

'Might as well stay now, Will. See your train through.'

'All right,' he agreed, and suddenly the tension was gone, the air was light. He went to the open window, and leaned out, his elbows on the bar. The little station was quiet. In the yard, where there had always been a great pile of timber, there was only an empty area of dust and ragged grass, with the gaunt crane rusting above it unused. Along the platforms the flowerbeds were closely planted with young green wallflowers. In the station building the office windows were dirty, and the rooms were quiet. He looked at the Ladies' Room where he had always left his bike before catching the train to school. You could use the room but not the lavatory. Always go in the men's next door, there's a piece of flattened wire you can open the lock. And stay if you like to see them pigeons let go. They'll scatter up high, then wheel and back over the mountain. Grey pigeons, but see the colours now in their necks.

Jim moved behind him. 'I haven't really said I was sorry about your Dad. Only you don't need telling, Will.'

'Yes, you'd got to know him.'

'We always talked when we changed. He's told me a lot, Will. He always had something to tell me.'

'I know. I remember.'

'Of course, me being younger, it wasn't the same. See, a signalman's real mates aren't in his own box. They get on all right, I'm not saying that, but it's only the bit each day. Your real mates are in the box each side. It is with your Dad, it's years been with them.'

'I've heard him say that.'

'Aye, Ted Evans the Junction and old Sam Prosser Pont Dulas. They talked, like we all do, half the night together on the phone. Harry and Ted used to tease old Sam, make out he'd got a woman in the box, they could hear her. They got a fireman once, took up a bunch of flowers for her. Sam cusses now when the two of them is at him.'

'Aye, I've heard about Sam.'

'Only not only that. I mean, signalmen, we talk about everything. Long you know, sometimes, Will, when we get on a thing that is serious.'

Matthew looked out, far down the line, to the wood below Campstone, where the smoke of the train would first show. As he watched the smoke came, and soon the train could be seen in the distance. He watched for the moment when the first signal was passed and the arm of the track indicator swung, then pushed back the first lever. He stood by the levers, pushing two more back as the train, a fast goods, came noisily up to the station. Then he hurried back to the window, and the driver lifted his arm as he passed the box. The habitual gesture seemed to release a whole world of feeling. The long black engine, the line of trucks loaded with scrap, seemed now to fill and dominate every part of his body and mind. He watched the fireman's cap as he turned to the bunker, then the wheels, the greased springs, the thick couplings. There was a sudden noisy clap of buffers, singly back down the trucks, as the gradient changed where the line swung away towards Gwenton. Then at last came the open guard's van, with the guard turning away inside. The lamp was in place; always check that. Recovering slowly from the power of the train, he turned and waited to push back the other two levers. Jim, at the desk, was entering the time in the book.

'Well. There she is.'

'Aye. She's all right.'

Matthew completed the signals, and stepped down from the grid. 'I'd better get on, now. I'll take these things.'

'Aye, that's right.'

'I'll see you again, Jim.'

'Any time, Will.'

He hesitated, and Jim opened the doors.

'Sure you can manage?' Jim asked. The first nervousness had come back, to them both.

'Yes, fine. Thanks.'

He made his way back up to the road.

2

A car was standing in the lane outside the house. Matthew went in at the back door, and put the things from his pocket on the dresser. He could hear voices from the bedroom. It would be the doctor, Evans, whom he had not met.

He took off his coat, and brushed his hair at the mirror above the sink, suddenly conscious of his appearance in a different way. Here was another adjustment; yet another way of speaking.

He went to wait in the front room. It was cold, it hardly ever had a fire. In the bay window, half-covered by long red curtains, stood several pots of chrysanthemums, brought in to flower. The tight, flat buds already had colour in them: pale bronze and yellow. On the table stood two framed photographs: a studio portrait of Susan and himself, taken just after their wedding, and an enlarged snapshot of the two boys. He went over to look at the photographs. That of the boys was delightful: Jack with his hair in his eyes and his impudent mouth, defying the camera to get him, though it had; Harry relaxed and graceful, the finely shaped head easily poised, the trained hair emphasizing the confidence of the face.

But if the snapshot had life, the studio photograph was dead. It was not even like them: some trick of lighting had narrowed and glazed their faces. They looked quite separate: indeed looked like two people being photographed, each concentrated on the act in itself. Perhaps this was the last of the rituals, this arrangement to the camera: confirm me, frame me, receive my image.

The door opened upstairs, and he heard a stranger's voice: Evans taking leave of his patient. A Welsh voice, but very different from the Glynmawr accent: smoother with narrower vowels, and with the intonation of the mining valleys – persuasive in every rhythm, ingratiating even, whereas here the rhythm is an unfinished truculence – you're not going to believe what I say. Dr Evans, all right I can meet you.

Ellen hurried downstairs.

'The doctor's coming down, Will, you'll talk to him.'

'Yes, if you want me to.'

'Well, yes.' She hurried out of the way to the kitchen. Evans hesitated on the landing, and then came down.

'I'm sorry, could you spare a minute?'

Evans stopped and looked at him. They were of equal height, and of about the same age. Evans's hair was jet-black, and his face was pale and narrow above the dark suit and the stiff white collar. Matthew's voice, obviously, had interested him. He looked quickly up and down this other man's clothes.

'Why, certainly. You'd be Mr Price's son?'

'Matthew Price, yes.'

'Matthew Price? But now...'

'I'm called Will here. You probably heard...'

'No, no, it's just... Matthew Price. Yes, of course.' Evans looked away. Matthew wondered what could have been said to put him at so obvious a disadvantage.

'I just wanted to ask about my father. I've only heard the facts second-hand.'

'Yes,' Evans said, still preoccupied. 'Yes, of course.'

'How is he?'

'I don't need to tell you it's serious. Very serious indeed.'

'Yes. What exactly are the chances?'

'The chances? Let me put it like this. A man can have an attack of this kind, and it can be, you see, the end. Or on the other hand he can have such an attack, get over it, and perhaps die ten years later of something quite different.'

'Depending then on what?'

'On a great many things. It's not really possible to say. It's a matter, really, of general strength, though in fact... It's no use me telling you a few comforting words, now is it?'

'I should be glad to hear them. If they were true.'

'I shouldn't tell you anything untrue. But you're probably in a position to distinguish me from some figure of magic. All I could say, about the future, would be essentially a guess.'

'But he's holding his own?'

'Well, yes. He is. But there are so many factors. If it came again...'

'I understand.'

'On the other hand, you see, I've no grounds at all to stop hope. In three months, quite ordinarily, he could be about and quite fit again. One can never tell. Medicine is examination and treatment, it can't really be prediction.'

Matthew was watching Evans closely. The face was controlled and intelligent, and his whole impression was favourable. Yet he had felt suddenly that Evans was not really talking: that the words were a screen behind which some more complicated process was engaging him. Evans looked at him again, and seemed about to say something quite different.

'But there's nothing more we can do? Everything is being done?'

'We'll do everything we can,' Evans said. 'We have a good chance.'

Still he was not wholly there. The matter had become something different, almost directly personal.

'Look, I mustn't keep you. Though I hope, while I'm here, you'll tell me everything you can. As a matter of habit I prefer the facts as they are.'

It was a kind of ascendancy, and sounded like that: a way of speaking irrelevant to the case they were discussing. Yet it seemed that nothing more could be said.

'The facts are,' Evans said, with a sudden neutral formality, 'first, that he's had a very serious attack, which has all the symptoms of a coronary thrombosis; second, that I've injected with morphia against the pain; third, that he needs prolonged rest and quiet, which I'm helping with tablets; and fourth, that I shall be seeing him regularly.'

'I can see he's in good hands,' Matthew said. Evans looked at him, and suddenly smiled.

'People look to a doctor. That's why I said about magic. It's a bit of a weight.'

Matthew smiled. 'Of course. Thank you.'

They went out together to the lane. As he was putting his bag in the car, Evans turned, almost casually.

'I've been wondering. I think you know my wife.'

'Do I?'

'Eira. Eira Rosser.'

So at last the difficulty was clear. Matthew looked away. 'Of course I know Eira. In fact she was born in this house.'

'In *this* house?'

'When her father lived here, before he moved to Gwenton. After Eira's mother died.'

'I knew, of course, that they'd come from Glynmawr. But I hadn't realized it was this house.'

'We lived across the way then. In the cottage.'

'I see. But I hadn't realized, when I came to attend your father, that it was this Price. I'd heard about you, of course.'

'And I hadn't realized. I understood you'd only just come here.'

'Yes, it's my second practice. I began near home, in Llanelly.'

'I knew Eira had married a doctor, but again I didn't connect. And Rosser could have told me, he brought me out here last night.'

'He saw no need perhaps.'

'No, maybe. Though your name was mentioned.'

'Well, anyway, Matthew, we know now.'

He turned away to the car. 'You must come in and see us one day.'

'Yes. Thank you. Though I shall only be here a few days.'

'Let's fix something then. I know Eira would be glad to see you.'

Matthew wished now, that the recognition had not come. This, more than anything else, would drive back over old ground. And it seemed wrong that the initiative should be coming from Evans. Any other way would have better fitted his feeling. Could they really meet, the three of them, on ordinary terms?

'Look, come in the day after tomorrow. That's the one day I may not be able to get out here.'

'Yes, thank you,' Matthew said. 'I will if I possibly can.'

Evans got in the car, with a quick gesture, confirming and reassuring. He started the engine and turned in the narrow lane.

3

Matthew walked back to the kitchen, where Ellen was waiting.

'You had a long talk then?'

'Yes.'

'Did he say anything?'

'The usual things. Rest, quiet.'

'He seemed a bit more pleased with him, I thought, today.'

'Yes, but of course it will be a long struggle.'

In Ellen's tired face, the eyes moved and blurred, in a sudden trembling. Matthew stood, holding back, and then crossed and put his arm round her shoulders.

'Will,' she said brokenly, and then her shoulders moved and she eased away, touching her eyes with her fingers.

'Mam, you knew he was married to Eira?'

'Evans? Oh, yes.'

'You didn't say.'

'I didn't think, Will. There's been so much to think about.'

'Yes.'

'Eira's very good. I've seen her, several times, since they moved back here.'

'I see.'

'They've got a boy, Mark, just between your two. She brought him out here once.'

Matthew cleaned and refilled his pipe.

'There's a photograph somewhere she sent me before they moved back here.'

'You kept in touch with her?'

'Oh, yes, Will, always. She used to write every Christmas, when she was away. When she was in Cardiff, nursing, where she met Evans, she used to write more to me than to her home. She and her stepmother have never got on.'

'Then why move back?'

'Well, it's a better practice. And they wanted the country, for the boy to grow up in. Morgan heard about it, he told them.'

'There's other country.'

'Well, it was near all her friends.'

'What I don't understand is all this going on, and neither Evans nor I knowing. He didn't know, when he came here, who Dad was. I didn't know he was Eira's husband. We had to find out, like fools, for ourselves.'

Ellen did not answer.

'This is supposed to be a place where we know all about each other,' Matthew went on angrily. 'But a thing like this, it's almost as if it were concealed.'

'Well, there wasn't anything to conceal,' Ellen said.

'All right. We know now. He asked me to go in there one day. To see them.'

'He's a nice chap, Will. There's no side.'

'No.'

'Your Dad likes him. He's different from old Powell. Old Powell was very, you know. Well, Evans was telling your Dad now, his own Dad was only a bus-driver. He had this same thing, and got well of it.'

'Only?'

Ellen looked at him, not understanding.

'It's all right, Mam. Go on.'

She took the electric kettle from the shelf, and filled the teapot.

'You'll have some tea here? Or shall I lay inside?'

'No, here.'

'I'll just take a cup to your Dad. He thought he might try it.'

'Can I take it?'

'All right. You take it up, Will. He'll be glad to see you.'

144

He waited for the cup to be poured, and then carried it carefully along the passage and up the stairs. He went into the bedroom without knocking.

'Here, I've brought you some tea,' he said as he went in.

'Thanks, son.'

'You're looking better now.'

'Am I?'

'I had a talk with Evans. You like him?'

'Aye, I heard you starting to talk.'

'He seems a decent chap.'

'Aye, very good.'

He leaned forward, bringing his lips down to the cup. With some difficulty he gulped a mouthful of tea. Matthew saw that his hands were trembling.

'Shall I hold the cup?'

'Aye, perhaps if you will.'

He took the cup, and held it higher, pushing it gently forward towards the dry lips. Harry drank again, with an obvious effort, and at once lay back and closed his eyes.

'I shan't ask what he told you, Will.'

'Well, only what you'd expect.'

'Never mind, I shan't ask. I know what I've got to do, to lie here and rest. I don't want to know anything else. That's not to do with me.'

'Well, you know that it's serious, and you know that rest can get you better.'

'Aye, well, never mind,' Harry said firmly, his eyes still closed. 'I'm quite content just to lie here and rest. If I don't work again, never mind. I've done forty-six years, that's a fair share.'

'Yes.'

'And whatever happens, I know... well, I don't know. It'll be all right, either way.'

'You're going to get better. You're strong.'

'I have been.'

'You still are.'

'You seem to know best,' Harry said, looking up.

'Yes,' Matthew said. 'Yes, I know that.'

'Only there's one thing,' Harry said, again closing his eyes. 'Just lying here and thinking. It's more like in your job. You get a different way.'

'Yes.'

'It was always there, Will. Like from the box I could see the sheep-wall, and beyond it, where you can't see, I remember riding with Edwin, those miles all empty, riding all day and only the heather and the whin. And the buzzards, Will. They went but they're back nesting.'

'Yes. Yes, they're back.'

'I was only saying just now. Old Sam Prosser. We told him the buzzards was nesting. He? Well. Old Sam I don't know. Tell us, Harry, how do you spell colts? Two cawlts on the line, he put. And when he read Peek Frean he made it Pike and Fireman.'

'Like the firs, furs and furze,' Matthew said, smiling.

'Aye,' Harry said, his eyes lighting up. 'You remember that, Will? In which Canada abounds. He give it us, dictation, the day we left school.'

'It's a silly trick.'

'Aye. Though I got two of them. That was as many as you got, mind, when you were that age.'

'Yes, you told me the third. Furze is so many things.'

'Aye, I expect so.' He closed his eyes again, and Matthew watched him carefully.

'Will you finish this tea now?'

'No. No thanks.'

'I'm going in to see Evans. Day after tomorrow. He asked me to call on them.'

'Aye, of course. And with Eira there.'

'It's funny to think of him as Morgan's son-in-law. We've had so much to do with that family.'

'Aye, here, from the beginning.'

'Do you find Morgan all right?'

'Aye, we still get on.'

'You're so different really. I've thought a lot about it, since I've been away.'

'We went our own ways. We always knew we were different.'

'You knew you were.'

'Aye, well, with Morgan it was make or break. You get men like that.'

'I know. It's happened to me.'

'Has it? I don't blame him. I watched it happening, back in the Strike.'

'I mean breaking away. Going out and living differently.'

'So long as we don't regret what we chose,' Harry said.

'You don't anyway.'

'No. Maybe,' Harry said, and drew further down in the bed.

'I'll leave you to rest now, Dad.'

'Aye, I could sleep I think.'

'All right. So long.'

He moved away, but suddenly Harry reached out and caught his wrist.

'Don't worry, Will. I'll try to make it out. But being here, helpless, just the words racing.'

'Yes.'

'It's as if, all the time, I have to watch myself working. Then like watching the sky, Will, and the edge of the cloud moving up to the tree.'

The grip of his fingers relaxed suddenly, and he closed his eyes.

147

CHAPTER SIX

1

The end of the strike had changed Morgan. Harry had lost most, by being off work, but recovered quickly. The way he had got back, through Meredith's defiance, had pleased him, and he often thought about it. It was the kind of action he himself was most used to. But for Morgan, really, there was no satisfaction. A struggle had been lost; a common effort had failed. And it was not only the failure that broke him, but the insight this gave, or seemed to give, into the real nature of society. His life had been centred on an idea of common improvement. The strike had raised this to an extraordinary practical vividness. Then, suddenly, a different reality had closed in. The brave show was displaced, in an hour, by a grey, solid world of power and compromise. It was not only that the compromise angered him: not only that he was sickened by the collapse into mutual blame. It was that suddenly the world of power and compromise seemed real, the world of hope and ideas no more than a gloss, a mark in the margin. He had lived on his ideas of the future, while these had seemed in any way probable, and they had seemed probable until now. And a man could bear to lose, but the sudden conviction that there was nothing to win – that the talk of winning was no more than talk, and collapsed when the real world asserted itself – this, deeply, was a loss of his bearings, a change in the whole structure of his life. The change was slow to clarify, in all its implications, but the restlessness was there from the disillusion of the last days of the strike. Left virtually alone, in this close pre-occupied valley, he could feel the hardening. You could talk about creating the future, but in practice, look, people ran for shelter, manoeuvred for personal convenience, accepted the facts of existing power. To see this happening was a deep loss of faith, a slow and shocking cancellation of the future. You could live only by what you could find, now.

There was still, for a time, one simple course. Beyond the mountains, the miners were still out. They were short of food, and here in Glynmawr it was plentiful. He kept to his promise to get food up into the starved valleys. Drawing out all his savings, he bought a small second-hand van. At first, he collected food himself, and when he had a load, drove up to the valleys with it, often going straight from the box. Then, slowly, he organized a more ambitious scheme of collecting. He got representatives, in all the villages around, to collect what they could. In Gwenton itself, through the Trades Council, he organized house-to-house collections, and set up a special stall, each market-day, looked after by voluntary helpers, where gifts of food and clothing could be left. Many were anxious to help, and his organization was good. By mid-June there was a regular depot, in the hall of the Labour Club, where food and clothes and other gifts were sorted and stored. Almost every day he loaded his van and drove up over Black Rock to the valleys. He worked, throughout, to the limit of his strength, but he was glad of this. Like Harry with his gardens, Morgan found, as the summer months passed, that the journeys with the van were his real work, his actual centre, while the work at the box was just done in the margin, for a wage.

Autumn came, and with it the sharpening of need in the valleys. He went on, as before, but often, as he drove alone in his van, he thought that the first frosts were the beginning of the end. Under cold and sharpening hunger, the miners would go back. Yet the pain of these last weeks strengthened him. He would go on, he decided, as long as he was needed, but he saw the pressures too closely to have any illusion about lasting the winter. When at last, bitterly, the miners went back to the pits, he could hardly bear to turn his van and drive back, to go over the scarp and down into the gentler country. But all he could carry was still needed, and he went back, forcing himself, for each new load. Until Christmas the scheme he had organized went on as before, but then the extra giving at Christmas became, unintentionally, a climax, and was followed by a gradual decline, with the miners back at work, food everywhere scarcer, and the roads more difficult. He still took what he could, but his trips became less frequent, until they were down to one a week. By the end of February there was almost nothing to take, and the time he had been dreading had come. Now at last, under forced inactivity, and with the added scar of the miners' defeat, his restlessness deepened until he hardly knew himself, or what to do. Deliberately, he turned to Harry again. When they were both off work, he would go across in the evenings and sit talking, until much later than Harry and Ellen usually went to bed. Yet they sensed his crisis, and were glad that he came. To Ellen it seemed that he ought to marry again. If he married Edith, as had once seemed likely, he would have more to keep him to the house. But Morgan now hardly ever went up there. His regular visits had stopped when he started with the van, and now, though obviously lonely, he did not resume them. It was a part of his gradual turning away from Glynmawr. He did not want to marry here, and settle as Edith would expect. Even Harry and Ellen were already at a certain distance from him. He had turned too far.

'The thing is, Harry, I can tell you this. I enjoyed those trips in the van, quite apart from thinking it was right to do.'

'Meeting the people you mean?' Harry asked. He was watching an ash log burn that he had sawn in May, while he was out.

'The people, yes. Only not only that. The loading up, say. And the feeling, you know, once I was on the road, that I was going somewhere, taking something: the business feeling of it.'

'Well, you still got the van.'

'Aye. The thing is, Harry, I could do a job like that.'

'Why not?'

'I mean, I know my way about up there. I know the sort of stuff that's needed. And I know this end where I can get it and what I'd have to pay.'

150

'Dealing, you mean?'

'Aye, that's the word.'

'Why not?'

'It's like this, Harry. I could do it, I'm sure, and make a nice little bit in the bargain. Only I hesitate, you see, because...'

He stopped and looked around. Harry looked across at Ellen, who was knitting, farthest from the fire.

'Go on, Morgan,' she said.

'Aye. Now Ellen would understand, see. Women always do, it's a funny thing.'

'You haven't told what we got to understand yet,' Ellen said.

'No.' He was holding up his cigarette, and looking intently at its coils of smoke. 'As I say, I've got the van, I've got the contacts, I could do what Harry calls dealing. Only then...'

'You need the bit of capital. Is that it?'

'No, no, Harry. I got all that worked out. It isn't that at all really. It's just, well, whether it's right.'

'Right?'

'Dealing I mean. See, I started this as a sort of outcome of the strike. Now, if I take it up on my own, well, it's different, that's all.'

Harry was staring into the fire, watching the bark peel and rise, as if it was really alive.

'Do you mean take it up full-time?' Ellen asked. 'Give up the box?'

'No, no. I shouldn't make enough for that. Mind, the way I look at it is this, Harry. In the strike the miners needed the stuff as a gift, agreed. But I saw enough, when I was up there, to realize the need is there all the time. To get good stuff, see, Harry. Fresh, good quality, and cheap, cutting out all the handling.'

'What would you reckon to take?' Ellen asked.

'Oh, I know the stuff. Vegetables, see. Eggs, rabbits, bit of poultry, butter, chutney. You know.'

'Fruit,' Ellen said. 'And honey of course.'

'Aye, honey,' Morgan said, and smiled.

Harry sat back, so that his face was in shadow. He looked carefully at them both, but said nothing.

151

'From the practical point, see, I got it all worked out. Only it's still just nagging me a bit. Dealing, you know? The idea of it.'

'What's wrong with dealing?' Harry asked.

'I've thought a lot about this sort of thing, Harry. My idea of myself, see, has always been a worker.'

'Dealing's work.'

'Aye, it's work. Only that's not my point. It's a different class, see, Harry. Different altogether.'

'No, I don't see.'

'Well, a dealer's a kind of *capitalist*, Harry. Small, yes, but that's his economic basis.'

'I don't see that. Stuff has to be got from one place to another.'

'You don't see my problem, do you, Harry?'

'Mind you, fair. That's for granted.'

Morgan threw his cigarette in the fire and lit another. 'I wish it was all so simple, Harry.'

Harry moved and looked at Ellen. He wanted to go to bed; there was nothing left to sit up for. It seemed obvious that Morgan wanted to deal, knew how to deal and would deal. The only question was why he pretended otherwise.

'Well, bed,' he said, and got up.

Morgan looked at the clock. He still had nearly half an hour before work. 'Aye,' he said, not moving. 'I'd better pick up my stuff and get on to the box.'

Harry stood above the fire and wound the clock. Reluctantly Morgan stood up beside him. He kicked out his legs, in the heavy uniform trousers, getting back his circulation. He started the conversation again, but Harry went out to lock up. Morgan said good night to Ellen, and went slowly across the lane to his own house.

For some weeks Morgan delayed, but by early April there was produce on the market again, and at last, in his week on nights, he bought a vanload and set off. He made a point of including, in this first vanload, some stuff of Harry's, mainly early lettuce. He got back late that night to the box, with much of his produce unsold. It was harder than he had expected, to establish this new kind of contact. But he was still optimistic. Within a month, he reckoned, he would have all the selling-points he needed. Some losses must be expected while he was getting things going. He went once a week, then twice, and gave the work all his interest and energy. By midsummer he could buy precisely, for a known market, although still his profit was small. The big step forward came in the autumn, with the apple glut. In September and October he went three times a week, easily extending his business. By the winter he was well established, though supplies were now scarcer. He carried on with rabbits, preserved eggs, bottled fruit and cooking apples. By spring he had added flowers, which found a much readier sale than he had expected. He got Eira and the other children picking violets, primroses, cowslips and field daffodils, paying them threehalfpence a bunch. On his van, now, he had painted *Morgan Rosser. Fresh Produce. Direct from the Countryside*. In Glynmawr his enterprise was generally welcomed. It was so much easier to sell to him than to take small produce to market. Within a year he had become an institution in the village.

Harry saw, as the months went by, how much this new life was meaning to Morgan. His work in the box was becoming more and more of a tie. Still, as Morgan said, if Harry in his spare time could manage his bees, four gardens, and part of a field, he, easily enough, could manage his dealing. The point came, though, when some rearrangement had to be made. In the autumn, with the apple crop especially, he needed a collecting point, as there had been during the strike. In the ordinary way he could use his own sheds, but he found it paid to buy over a wide area, and much of his stuff was now being delivered in Gwenton, on market-day, from other villages. To drive it home to Glynmawr, and then back through Gwenton to sell, was obviously wasteful, yet he had to do this because he could never give a full day, whatever shift he was on at the box. He began to look round for storage in Gwenton and at last heard of a vacant shed, near the market. He called on its owner, the ironmonger, Frank Priddy, and found himself forced up, steadily, to a rent of six shillings a week. He complained, but took the shed. He was used, now, to the way business had to be done.

Priddy, a tall white-haired lay preacher, was the leading shopkeeper in Gwenton. He had a large shop in the main street, and a depot for agricultural machinery near the market. Also, he had recently opened branches in Tredegar and Ebbw Vale. He had relatives, through his wife, in Glynmawr, and this made Morgan's approach to him easier, though leaving the bargaining unaffected. Priddy had married a widow, Audrey Davies, whose first husband had been a farmer on Campstone. She had brought with her to Gwenton her niece Janie, whose parents had left her a small hill-farm which she could not manage and had sold. Soon after his marriage, Priddy had moved from the house over the shop, where he had been born, into a new middle-sized bungalow on the outskirts of the town, facing the mountains. Slowly, Morgan got to know him better, and helped him occasionally in his business, when something had to be carried to one of the branches, or when small orders were urgently needed in Glynmawr. Eventually, he was invited to the bungalow, and introduced to Mrs Priddy and Janie.

'Nice this,' he said, looking round the bungalow.

Priddy nodded, without enthusiasm.

'You used to live over the shop, didn't you say?'

'Aye.'

'I couldn't take to that, Mr Rosser,' Mrs Priddy broke in. 'Mind you, Frank was attached to it, I knew that. Only with the business doing so well, you know...'

Morgan nodded. He glanced across at Janie, who was tall and ungainly, but carefully and attractively dressed.

'You'll find it different from the village,' Morgan said.

'Oh, we miss it,' Janie said, glancing at her aunt.

'Well, we do and we don't, Janie,' Mrs Priddy said contentedly. 'It's the women feel the change. Take here now. No old stone floors, no muck in the yard, no miles to go to the shops. We got the electric, see, and the gas for cooking, and the car and the good water, and the you know, the proper w.c. I often say to Janie I was born in

Glynmawr but I wouldn't go back there to live for anybody. Not if they paid me. Don't I, Janie?'

'Yes, Auntie, you do.'

'Janie knows as well as I do, I'm sure. Where her poor Mam and Dad used to live, right up the mountain. I said to her when it was hers, didn't I? Now you sell, girl, get the money in the bank. I wasn't wrong, now was I? Nine hundred pounds she cleared, mind. She was lucky.'

Janie looked quickly at her aunt, and then avoided Morgan's interested eyes. She twisted her body helplessly, as if she wanted to make herself smaller and less noticeable.

'There was the walks, Auntie. Up the hill,' she said quickly. But before all the words were out she seemed ashamed that she could have said anything so silly.

'We can walk anywhere. Can't we now, Mr Rosser?' Mrs Priddy said comfortably.

Her husband was standing on the far side of the lounge, holding his pipe so that the smoke curled away through the open window. Morgan sat forward in the hide chair, smiling at each woman in turn.

'There's a lot in what you both say, you know.'

'Well, yes,' Mrs Priddy agreed. 'The advantages is only natural.'

'It's what I've often said myself, mind. Out there in Glynmawr you know, talking. Why, I ask them, do we put up with dirty old water, and oil-lamps, and the buckets, you know the buckets?'

Janie twisted again. Mrs Priddy put her short red fingers to her whitened hair, which had been cut short and carefully waved.

'You can't tell me, Mr Rosser. I was a farmer's wife. Ten I've cooked for, that was.'

'I've seen a bit of it,' Morgan said, nodding. He wanted to smoke, but from Priddy's position judged that he had better not.

'What is it then, Mr Priddy didn't say, what you do?' Mrs Priddy asked, her eyes lively behind her glasses.

Morgan hesitated. He saw that Janie had looked up.

'You don't mind me asking?' Mrs Priddy said.

'Mind? Just look at me. Do you think I'd mind? I've always been on the railway, since the Army. Signalman. Only now, see, I've started this bit of dealing your husband has helped me with.'

'The little van.'

'Aye, well, that's a start. I'm building it up, see, gradual. As it is, mind, I wouldn't say I'm doing so bad.'

'No, I'm sure,' Janie said politely. Priddy turned, glanced at her, and turned back to his window.

'If there's one thing I like, Mr Rosser,' Mrs Priddy said warmly, 'it's a young man starting out on a business. Course, an established business, we know, brings in more. Like Mr Priddy, well that's only natural. But a young man, starting out, making his way. You'll laugh, but it's like a son to me.'

'Auntie, now!' Janie protested.

'I'm always shocking them, Mr Rosser,' Mrs Priddy said, and laughed again.

'Shock? Why?'

'I never had a son, you know. Mind, Janie, she's a good girl, she's like a daughter.'

'I couldn't have got on without you, Auntie.'

'Well, it's what my Mam said,' Mrs Priddy conceded. 'The Lord give me my eyes in the front.'

'We must get on,' Priddy said suddenly. He knocked out his pipe into the garden, and turned to Morgan.

'Aye, business won't wait,' Morgan said.

'That's what I like to see. Mind you come again, Mr Rosser, we're always here.'

'We go to the pictures, Auntie,' Janie said, breaking into the conversation like a child. Morgan looked at her tall, awkward figure. She was in her early thirties, but still had a child's intonation and manners. Janie saw him looking at her, and twisted away.

'You go to the pictures, Mr Rosser?' Mrs Priddy asked.

'No, no. No time.'

'It's for the women really,' Mrs Priddy explained. 'Mr Priddy, now, he doesn't like it, but Janie and me go. Only the Coliseum, mind. The Gaiety we don't think's quite clean.'

'Used to be a corn store,' Priddy said.

'It isn't that,' Mrs Priddy said. 'It's what you bring home on you.'

'No,' Janie said quickly, her dark eyes pleading and hurt.

'Well, you did, Janie, so I don't mind saying. But the Coliseum's very nice.'

Priddy went to the door. Morgan shook hands with the women, and followed. As he walked he felt the thickness of the bright red and blue carpet. White paint gleamed on the half-open door.

'So long then, both.'

Janie's mouth was open as he turned. She closed it suddenly. Mrs Priddy smiled and sat down. Morgan walked on behind Priddy, noticing the good dark cloth of his suit.

'I'll see the stuff in the van,' Priddy said. 'Then Wednesday, is it, you're through again?'

'Wednesday, yes, about three.'

They got into Priddy's car, and drove back to the town, which lay below them in a blue haze under the hills. The green copper dome of the town hall stood out like a beacon. Morgan kept his eyes on it as they drove down.

2

The entrance to the school, Glynmawr Non-Provided, was through an elaborate grey arch, which rose from the dirt playground to announce the porch. A cross was carved in the weathered grey stone, and below it the date of foundation, 1853. Above and below the cross were two scrolls, with the legends, *Laborare est orare* and *Benedicite, omnia opera*, but the carving was now barely legible, for it was filled with dirt and moss. The porch was narrow and dark. Part of its limited space was taken up by an old harmonium, over which William Evans gave his boys their more severe beatings. At the western end stood the small room for the infants. The rest of the school was one large room, divided by a green curtain. On the far side sat the Second Class, children up to nine or ten, taught by the sharp Mrs Powell. On the near side was the First Class, up to fourteen except the few who left at eleven with scholarships, under William Evans. The main door from the porch opened into the First Class, and William Evans had his desk facing it. Second Class children entered by the same door, though there was another at their end of the room leading to the boys' playground and the drinking tap. The stove was also in the Second Class end. This, though William Evans often regretted it, was unavoidable. Beside the stove, Mrs Powell had her desk.

From the patch now went Will, Eira, Cemlyn Powell, and the three Jenkins children, Gwyn, Glynis and Beth. Will, Eira and Cemlyn had just been moved up, early, into the First Class; Will sat with his friend Brychan, who lived farther up the lane. Their desk was right back against the curtain, nearer Mrs Powell's desk than the Boss's. It was difficult sometimes, if their attention wandered, to know which lesson to listen to. This morning, with the May sun slanting across their desk, throwing a long shadow from the window-frame and the flower bowl made from a melted-down gramophone record, they were listening to neither. A note had been passed to them, from Phyllis Rees:

Sweetheart now, who you may be,
Sign and pass it back to me.

This was usual, but they had to think of a good answer. They looked at each other, widening their eyes. At last Will took the note and scribbled:

I cannot sign,
I cannot write,
I lost my pen
Last Sunday night.

Brychan wrinkled his nose disapprovingly, then folded the paper and carefully passed it back. They watched as the girls in front bent quickly together to read. Eira, who sat by Phyllis, turned and whispered to Will, and William Evans paused and looked round.

'A halfpenny and a farthing, not a halfpenny and a farthing,' Mrs Powell was saying, with emphasis, just behind the curtain.

'Silence,' William Evans ordered, and looked down again at his book, in which he had lost the place.

'Not a halfpenny and a farthing,' the loud voice continued, 'a farthing and two farthings. Three farthings.'

Brychan nudged Will and looked over towards the door. The big ring handle had moved slightly. This, every morning, was what the boys waited for. Tegwyn Evans, their friend, whose father, a hedger, lived far up on the northern slope of Brynllwyd, came to school late almost every morning. It was a three-mile walk, but this was not the reason, for Tegwyn was sent off at seven. He was late because there was so much to do on the way: bird-nesting, throwing for conkers, fishing for bullyheads under the Honddu bridge, watching a fox. Each day, when at last he reached the school, he was frightened by his lateness. When he could, he would open the door quietly and peep in, watching for a favourable moment. Now, as William Evans began reading again and Mrs Powell went on with her arithmetic, the boys watched the door. 'A halfpenny see is two farthings. So not a halfpenny and a farthing, two farthings and a farthing. Three farthings.' The big iron ring trembled and turned. The boys held their breath while, slowly, the door opened inwards. Suddenly, Tegwyn's face appeared in the narrow opening, looking straight at them. The face was pale and sharp-nosed. The ears, which were the colour of lard, were big and spreading. The straw-coloured hair was cropped to a stubble of brittle ends. The thin lips of the narrow mouth gaped a question.

'For the valour and the honour of the Cymry,' William Evans was saying, looking over his glasses at the book.

Tegwyn's head, which was still all of him that could be seen, turned in the direction of the voice, and then looked back at Will and Brychan.

'Here's my head, my arse is coming,' Brychan whispered to Will.

Will sat without moving a muscle. He wanted to laugh, but dared not, in case Tegwyn should be seen.

'"The Saxon hordes, what are they?" Gruffydd asked, his face proud as an eagle is proud,' read William Evans.

'Watch now, I'll write it up,' said Mrs Powell, behind the curtain. 'A penny can be divided into four farthings. Watch.'

Will heard the chalk squeak on the board. A plan had come to him, to try to help Tegwyn. If, quietly, Tegwyn opened the door and came in, then down behind Will's desk to his own, the usual punishment might be avoided. He did not stop to think whether this was really possible, in the long run; he was too excited by the immediate chance.

'Teg,' he whispered.

The face turned towards him, the eyes wide, the mouth still open.

'Quick, Teg, down by here,' Will whispered, sweeping his hand downwards to show the way.

Tegwyn's head shook, briefly. His cheeks reddened a little with the refusal.

'Aye, Teg,' Will insisted. 'Come on. Quick.'

He gestured again, this time with both hands. Tegwyn's face suddenly went a deep red, and the staring eyes closed. Will, still turned, felt the classroom go suddenly silent. He looked back slowly, straight into William Evans's eyes. He tightened his lips, and looked down, waiting for the voice.

'Willy Price.'

Will said nothing. There was nothing he could say. The master's voice was gentle, a kind word to a frightened child.

'Willy Price,' the master repeated, his voice a shade firmer, but still not harsh.

Will looked up. From the corner of his eye he could see that Tegwyn was still there, looking round the door.

'Willy Price, tell us what you were doing.'

'Looking at Tegwyn, sir.'

'Looking at Tegwyn Evans? Yes, yes. Looking at Tegwyn Evans. But why, boy, why did you wave your hand like a windmill?'

The last words were sharp. Looking up, Will saw the master pulling his nose between finger and thumb. The class was very silent, watching. Even Mrs Powell seemed to have stopped.

'I was telling Tegwyn, sir, to come into the school.'

'Into the school? Yes, yes. To come into the school. But how was he to come in? How? Tell me that.'

'Through the door, sir.'

There was the beginning of a laugh from the class, but it was cut short, with a quick general intake of breath. William Evans got down from his chair, and walked forward.

'Through the door and down by me, sir,' Will said as he came. 'Only he wouldn't, sir.'

William Evans stopped, and again pulled at his nose. 'Down by you?' he said. 'Yes, yes. Down by you. Only without me seeing him, I suppose?'

'I didn't think you'd see him.'

'You didn't what, boy?'

'Didn't think you'd see him,' Will repeated, raising his voice.

Now, suddenly, William Evans came forward. He took hold of Will's ear, and led him out to the open space near the desk.

'Stand there, boy. Now. Tegwyn Evans.'

There was no reply.

'Evans. Tegwyn Evans. You,' William Evans shouted, pointing furiously at the door.

Tegwyn seemed stuck. He did not move, although he went on staring, his face pale.

'Evans,' William Evans shouted.

'Yes, sir,' Tegwyn said smartly, as if he had only just heard.

'Evans, have you only brought your face to school this morning, or can we have the rest of you?'

The class laughed. Even Will smiled. But for all the effect the remark had on Tegwyn, he might have been deaf.

'Evans, come inside,' William Evans shouted. 'Come in, come in, come in, come in.'

Tegwyn, certain at last, pushed open the door and entered. He walked up to the master, his feet shuffling, his shoulders hunched forward, his neck pushed out.

Here's my head, my arse is coming, Will remembered.

Tegwyn wore a darned grey jersey, dark brown breeches, thick grey stockings, and heavy black boots, caked with fresh mud. He stopped about a yard from William Evans, and looked up.

'Stand by Price,' William Evans ordered, and Tegwyn obeyed. He and Will looked at each other, and moved very close together.

'Brychan Thomas,' the master said gently.

'Yes, sir,' Brychan answered, standing.

'Brychan, are you a good boy?'

'Yes, sir.'

'Brychan, have you got a knife?'

'Yes, sir.'

'And can you cut sticks with it, Brychan?'

'Yes, sir.'

'Then go outside, Brychan, to the hedge by the bowling green. You know where I mean?'

'Yes, sir,' Brychan said, and moved at once to the door.

'Wait, boy, wait, wait, wait, wait. You don't know what I want, do you?'

'Yes, sir. No, sir.'

'Then what's the good of rushing off?'

'I don't know, sir.'

'All right, Brychan,' William Evans said gently. 'Now watch me, Brychan. I hold up my arm.'

'Yes, sir.'

'You see how long it is?'

'Yes, sir.'

'Good. Now, Brychan, I hold up my thumb.'

'Yes, sir.'

'You see how thick it is?'

'Yes, sir.'

'Then go, Brychan, to the hedge, and cut a stick for me. As long, now, as my arm. As thick, see, as my thumb.'

162

'Yes, sir,' Brychan said quickly, and darted out through the door.

Will and Tegwyn stood very still. William Evans, ignoring them, went back to his desk, and took up his book. He continued to read aloud.

'"They have not," continued Gruffydd, "the sinew for our sinew, the hearts for our hearts, the blood for our blood. On the mountains they are lost. In the valleys they are fearful. We, by the shadow of this rock, by the light of this sun..."'

Will was not listening. He was thinking of Brychan, following his movements. It was normal, in the school, to send a boy out to cut a stick for caning. Sometimes, even, you cut your own, the one you would be hit with. The precise instructions William Evans had found necessary from experience; without them, the merest switch would be brought. 'Couldn't reach up to no others, sir, my knife's too blunt.' But the ruling majority of the boys had a method which had been passed from brother to brother. A thick enough stick would be cut, if ordered, but then they would take a bud, about a foot from the thin end, and cut a T, carefully, in the soft skin around it. Lifting the edges of the skin, they would bore in with the point of the knife, cutting across the fibres, and then the skin would be smoothed back, and a lick of mud smeared over the T. As the stick hit the hand, it should break. The victim, forewarned (a tampered stick was always handed thick end first) would then yell as if he had been hit too hard. Always, when a stick broke, William Evans failed to send for another. He knew his own temper, and was quickly cautious. An obvious trick, such as ducking the hand so that the stick hit the desk, was certain to be punished, but 'boring 'em', so far as the boys knew, had never been discovered. Will waited, thinking of Brychan, knowing he could rely on him. He seemed almost to see the fine incision in the freckled skin. The door opened, and Brychan was back.

William Evans stopped reading, and put out his hand for the stick. Brychan gave it to him, thick end first. Will felt Tegwyn close against his body. There was a smell of fresh cow-muck, from his boots.

'Discipline,' William Evans said, standing above the boys.

'Discipline, now, in every walk of life is essential. Hold out your hands.'

The boys obeyed. Will noticed that Tegwyn's hand was much thicker than his own. On the ends of the fingers there was a smear of bright yellow pollen.

'You, boy, for lateness,' William Evans said, and swung the stick.

Tegwyn took the cut on his fingers, without cry or movement. The stick did not break. Will saw Brychan anxiously watching.

'And you, boy, for inattention and disturbance.'

The stick swung again, and Will, looking at Brychan, yelled before it even reached his hand. At the same time he pushed his hand forward, so that the cut came on the bottom of the palm. The stick broke, and Will turned and jumped about, lifting his hand to his mouth and licking. The palm in fact hardly hurt at all.

'Now, now, boy,' William Evans said anxiously, looking down at the broken stick.

'It's all right, sir.'

Eira was watching him with concern, but Phyllis Rees, beside her, was smiling and looking round at Brychan, whose face shone in the sun.

'Back to your desk, now. Quick march.'

Tegwyn, as if nothing had happened, and Will, keeping his hand in his armpit, obeyed. From behind the curtain came the steady chant of the Second Class, in its four times table. William Evans, back at his desk, went on with his reading. For some time Will did not listen; but at last the cadences entered, and he sat forward, attentive.

'And thus,' William Evans was concluding, 'in the year of Our Lord one thousand and sixty-three...'

Years later, Will was to remember it, word for word:

'"...The good Gruffydd ap Llewellyn, the head and shield of the Cymry, fell through the treachery of his own men. The man who before was invincible stood now in the glens of desolation, after taking vast spoils, and victories without number, and countless treasures of gold and silver, and jewels and purple robes. The body

164

of the brave Gruffydd ap Llewellyn died, but his memory will live for ever in the hearts of the sons and daughters of Wales.'"

'Right. Break,' William Evans said, shutting the book. Will and Brychan, pushing, were first through the door and out.

3

When Harry and Morgan met now, in the box, Morgan was full of the excitement of his new life. He stayed on, often talking of the ways the business could develop. Often he asked Harry to change turns, to fit in with his travelling, and Harry was usually willing to change, for Morgan would offer to do nights. But the strain of the double job was beginning to show, and soon, obviously, some decision would have to be made.

In that spring they were all at a wedding party, one of the regular weddings between the farming families, and Morgan had brought Mrs Priddy and Janie, who were relatives of the bride. Towards the end of the party, Morgan announced his own engagement, to Janie. When the party was over, they all walked down together to the patch.

'You've not seen the house then?' Ellen said to Mrs Priddy.

'No, not to go in. Mind, they're not going to live *there*.'

'No?'

'No, no. Janie wouldn't want it. We've got used now, to the *modern* houses. I told Janie she couldn't think of coming back out here.'

Ellen did not answer. She was looking at Harry's back as he walked beside Morgan and Priddy. She wished that his suit had been better; the wear showed now in the sun.

'There'll be Morgan's work though,' she said. 'He'll have to be in reach of the box.'

'No, no, he's giving up all that. There's no future, I told him, in that.'

'I see.'

Ellen was still looking at Harry's suit. The jacket was stretched across the heavy shoulders. In the last year, suddenly, he had broadened a good deal; his weight had gone up over fourteen stone, and none of his jackets fitted, though the trousers were still good. He had been very much slimmer when he had first worn this suit, ten years ago at their wedding in Peterstone. Ellen, seeing the breadth of the shoulders, felt suddenly that she might easily cry. But she could find no reason, except perhaps that a wedding always brought things back. Morgan's suit, she noticed, was new. He wore it well, as he wore all his clothes, and his hair was tidily cut. He had started going to a barber in Gwenton, which very few men in the village did. Normally they cut hair for each other, with one or two specialists; Bill Thomas the ganger was very well spoken of. Of course, Ellen saw, Priddy's suit was old too, but he wore it as if it had been made for him. Harry really, when they could see their way, must go in for another.

'With the dealing now,' Mrs Priddy was saying, 'he's doing really quite well. And of course now, marrying Janie, he can give his whole time to it. He's got all sorts of plans.'

'Morgan always was very go-ahead,' Ellen said.

Will and Eira, in front, were walking self-consciously on either side of Janie.

'Do you like school?' Janie at last managed to say. She had found the earlier conversation, especially with Eira, very difficult.

'I don't mind it,' Eira said. 'Will can do it better.'

'Can you, Will? You getting on all right?'

'Not bad, Miss Thomas,' Will said, kicking a stone.

'You'll try for your scholarship, I suppose?'

'We're both trying,' Eira said. 'We're two out of five from the school.'

'Yes, I know,' Janie said awkwardly. 'But by then of course, Eira, you'll be in Gwenton. You'll be taking the scholarship from there.'

'What do you mean?' Eira asked, stopping and looking up.

'The wedding, stupid. Didn't you hear?' Will said.

'But we won't be moving, will we, with the wedding? We've got a house already.'

166

'It's to be better for your Dada's work, Eira,' Janie said carefully. She wished that she had not spoken at all.

'I don't want to go from here,' Eira said. 'I don't want to live in the old town.'

Janie stared helplessly. She wanted so much to get on well with Eira, but she was still very nervous of her. A child a few years younger or a few years older would, she thought, have been easier. Awkwardly, she looked round at Morgan, who had heard but merely smiled. For a moment she was angry. His expression said so clearly that he was leaving it to her. But she had learned the dangers of anger. She turned to Eira, and nervously touched her arm.

'You'll see now, Eira, it'll be nice. When my Mam and Dad died, I had to go to the town. I used to live out here, just like you. Only we all got to do what's best. In a few years' time, you see. You'll like it.'

'It's not as if it's far,' Will said. 'If I was you, I'd go.'

'Well, you're not me,' Eira said sharply. She did not speak again until they were back at the patch.

After this first visit, Janie and Mrs Priddy were often at the house. Some of the furniture would be taken – there was no sense in wasting – and besides, there was Eira, who no longer protested, but who had still to learn to accept. Ellen had thought there would be trouble with Mrs Lucas, who would be losing her home. But she and Mrs Priddy got on well, and some arrangement was made between them – Ellen did not know what. Bit by bit, all the details of the change were coming out. After the wedding, Morgan and Janie were to take over the Priddys' bungalow. It was very nice, Mrs Priddy said, but not quite what she and Mr Priddy wanted. She had seen rather nearer the town just the place which would suit her: a very similar, rather larger bungalow – she was sure she would be happier there. Priddy, who had thought she was happy where she was, bought the new bungalow. The old one was to be left on mortgage with Morgan and Janie.

There were also to be changes in Morgan's business. The van, which was still serviceable, was to be kept, but a lorry was to be bought, more adequate to the scale of business he could now do. For the time being the shed would be kept on, but another store was to be rented in Tredegar, and the buying was to be put on a different basis. The difficulty with this kind of trade was that it was too seasonal: at one time there would be too much to carry, a few months later nothing like enough. Morgan, after talking things over with Mrs Priddy, had a new plan. The fresh produce would be carried as before, but he would also carry much larger supplies of bottled and preserved fruit and vegetables, and jams and chutneys. He intended to place small local contracts with the farmers' wives and the other women in the villages. If the women knew that twelve dozen bottles of plums or pears, six dozen pots of jam, a few dozen chutneys and pickles, would be taken at a fixed price, they could easily increase their normal making by that amount. The fixed price was low, but jars and preserve bottles were provided – Morgan got these wholesale through Priddy – and the sale was definite, collected from the house, and paid for on the spot.

Morgan explained his system, in the course of making an agreement with Harry to take three hundred jars of honey. 'What it is, see, Harry, I'm staking on faith. Up there, when money's short, they're offered poor old stuff – jam that's hardly seen a bit of fruit, bottles of stuff that have been coloured and spiced up with chemicals – and yet it's not all that cheap. I can beat that, see, even for price, if my quantity's enough – I've got to have quantity. That's for the working people mind. There is just a bit of a better class of trade: people that can't touch the factory stuff and want a bit of country quality. Take your honey and some of this imported stuff: they're not the same thing. And if we label the heather honey now, separate, under its own name, and a bit of the stuff in the combs – I'll get you those little frames, with a deckle, you know, for the table – well, there's a good sale for that at good prices. Only still, see, Harry, faith. Faith that people need stuff of real quality – the old country stuff. And, of course, as well as needing it, that they'll take it, when it's offered to them.'

Harry agreed, though he couldn't see what faith had to do with

168

it. The good food was there, and to organize its distribution was sensible. So far as he was concerned, the arrangement with Morgan saved him his annual outlay on jars, and he got his whole yield taken at once instead of having to take a few dozen jars at a time to the market. The jars, like all the containers Morgan was providing, came labelled with the distinctive sign: *Morgan Rosser – Country Foods*. The lettering was in red on white, with a gold border. Behind the lettering was a line-drawing of the valley and the Holy Mountain.

In the following June, at West Street Congregational Church in Gwenton, Morgan married Janie. There was no honeymoon; the business was at too important a stage. The bungalow, 'Mountain View', was ready for them to move into. Morgan had finished at the box at the end of May. Eira, after the wedding, stayed on a few weeks with Mrs Lucas, and then went to Gwenton to join her father. The house across the lane was left empty, and Harry and Ellen wondered who would come there. Mrs Hybart said nobody had asked, and at eight-and-six a week there would obviously be no rush. The garden, since Morgan had taken up dealing, had been badly let go. Mrs Lucas, after taking Eira to town, cleaned up and went to live with her sister, eight miles up the Trawsfynydd valley, near the ruins of the abbey. A new signalman, Bill Owen, in his middle twenties, came to replace Morgan, lodging with Bill Thomas the ganger.

At thirty-six, Morgan's close-curling black hair was beginning to be streaked with grey. He spoke and moved, now, with an added authority. There were rumours, particularly among the farmers, that in terms of money he was not really doing well. All Janie's nine hundred pounds had gone, and there was really very little coming into the house; everything that could be spared was going into the development of the business. Yet the rumours made little headway against Morgan's appearance of confidence. He was now a figure in the district, and few doubted his success.

At last the house on the patch was let. The Baptist minister, Joshua Watkins, who since coming to the village had lodged at Penydre, called on Mrs Hybart and asked for it. The inquiry was immediately overshadowed by the reason he gave, in the strictest confidence (but there were many people in Mrs Hybart's confidence). He intended shortly to marry Edith Davies. The date would be fixed once the question of the house was settled. Well, at ten shillings a week, Mrs Hybart thought, the house could quite easily be arranged. Ten shillings? A rent of ten shillings? Joshua Watkins had not been thinking of quite so much. But there, to start your married life in, Mrs Hybart pointed out. Well, yes, perhaps so. Perhaps it might be managed.

So in the spring after Morgan had married, Edie Davies, now Mrs Watkins, moved into Morgan's house. Ellen was pleased, not only because she liked Edie but because she could not bear to see the house standing empty any longer. The winter had made it very damp, and she and Mrs Hybart lit fires in it for a week before the new tenants moved in. Harry was less pleased. He'd have preferred, he said, with unusual bitterness, a man to come there. The garden, just watch, would get worse than ever. He had no use for Watkins, even as a minister, and a few weeks' experience of him as a neighbour was more than enough to confirm this. There was the incident in the lane, when Harry and Lippy and Bill Hybart were spreading ashes; in the bad winter, with the carts up and down, it had been almost impassable. With half the job done, Watkins had come up the lane and stopped to congratulate them. 'You've made a real good job there,' he said, and Lippy was pleased and answered him, but Harry and Hybart turned away. A few days later, there was almost an open row. Edie, obviously embarrassed, came across to ask Ellen if Harry would mind emptying their lavatory bucket. 'He isn't sure, you see, where it's got to go.'

'I'll show him,' Harry said, thinking of the dingle beyond the drying green where all the buckets from the patch were emptied. But this was not what had been asked.

'You know better than me,' Watkins said, self-deprecatingly. 'I'm no good at that sort of job. You know how it has to be done.'

'You carry it to the dingle, tip it and bring the bucket back,' Harry said.

Joshua Watkins waited. He knew how these men had to be humoured.

'Shall I show you where?' Harry asked.

'Well, no, you see, Mr Price. It isn't exactly that...'

'All right, I'm busy,' Harry said, and walked away.

That evening, as it was getting dark, Harry stood in his garden watching, while the little minister, in the black he always wore, carried the bucket across the drying green, looking round to see that he was alone, but missing Harry where he stood in the shadow. Harry laughed, but was angry again next day when, standing in the garden, he heard from the house Watkins's high voice rehearsing his prayers and sermon. It went on for more than an hour, in Welsh, although the eventual delivery would be in English. This practice, it seemed, was to get the first flow right. Harry cursed when he went back in, and both Will and Ellen were frightened. Still, usually, he was dark and silent, with the characteristic clouding of the deep eyes. But occasionally – and every occasion was remembered – he would break out and curse, with extreme violence, never touching anyone or anything while the rage lasted, yet always, it seemed, only a few inches from touching, the heavy body held tense and strained. Joshua Watkins was always enough to bring this out in him, beyond, as he recognized, any limits of fairness.

Then, in that same spring, there was a different kind of outburst. Will, with three others, had sat for his scholarship to the Gwenton grammar school. William Evans did not know what chance there was. Will and his friend Brychan were probably the best boys; 'but there, Brychan see, his parents won't let sit.' Harry sat with Will in the evenings practising sums. He had been, since his own days at school, an unusually quick calculator. He also talked about grammar and words.

'Take I said to you now, "the son of Pharaoh's daughter is the daughter of Pharaoh's son". Is that right?'

Will repeated the sentence, and shook his head. 'It's nonsense, Dada. Isn't it?'

'Well,' Harry said. 'Take this one, it's the same. "The river of Glynmawr's valley is the valley of Glynmawr's river."'

'Yes,' Will said doubtfully. The freckles stood out in heavy blotches on the originally fine skin of his face and neck. The reddish hair, now less bright, hung in a fringe on his forehead. Harry leaned over, inscribed the sentence in his quick, clear writing, and bracketed the clauses. Will watched the strain and movement of the words.

They came to enjoy working together. They competed in mental arithmetic, up to sums like seventeen times a hundred and seventeen, glancing and laughing at each other to see who would be first. Then, on the last evening before the examination, Ellen made Harry stop and prepared her son in her own way. For a special occasion like this, she washed his hair with beaten egg, as she often washed her own. Next morning she took him to Gwenton and as far as the gates of the school.

The result was better than Ellen had expected, though Harry had always been confident. Will passed easily, with very high marks. Harry rode to Gwenton, to buy the local paper, and when he arrived back he was extraordinarily excited, throwing his bike at a run along the hedge under the holly, and shouting the news to Ellen and Will and the neighbours. Will was made a great fuss of by everyone, and several neighbours gave him presents. He himself valued most his father's excitement; he had never before seen him quite like this.

Next day Ellen went to Gwenton and brought back a present of two books. They were strange to Will, and he did not understand, either then or later, quite how they had been chosen. They were translations, in green paper covers, of the *Trojan Women* of Euripides, and the *Prometheus Chained* of Aeschylus. These made, excluding Will's story books, the fifth and sixth books in the house. The others were the Bible, *English Authors*, *Everybody's Home Doctor* and the *Manual of Beekeeping*. Will read the plays, still numb under the tension of his father's excitement. Harry said they must now really start to get some books together; before there hadn't been the need.

From the window of the box Harry saw Morgan's van cross the bridge and draw up. As Morgan came down to the platform, he moved away from the window, whistling nervously under his breath. He heard Morgan calling across to Will Addis, and then his heavy steps up to the box. He picked up a paper, keeping his back to the door.

'Well, all right, Signalman?'

'You, is it?'

'Aye. Thought I'd come to relieve you.'

Harry smiled and moved away to the far end of the box.

'What's the matter with you, Harry? Every time I see you now, you're closed tight like you used to be.'

'No, I don't think so.'

'Your new neighbour getting on your nerves?'

'Watkins? No.'

'Look, be straight, Harry. Loosen up, mun. It's got that you don't ever say what you really think.'

'How do you know what I think?'

'Aye, go on. Stare me out. I'm used to it.'

Harry looked away.

'You've been here too long, Harry. You're getting, I can see you, like all these people.'

'Am I?'

'Look, if I thought you'd hit back I'd punch your nose for you. Anything to get some reaction.'

'There's nothing to fight about.'

'No? Well, all right then. You've heard, I suppose, these rumours going about?'

'What rumours?'

'About me.'

'All sorts of things get said.'

'Aye. And you're one of the few men I'd trust to judge for himself. Still, I wanted to tell you.'

'About what?'

'It's no use denying there have been difficulties,' Morgan said and settled himself on the hard chair by the grate. 'Only I want you to know, you, Harry, particularly, that I'm doing all right and can see what I'm at. Business is a new thing to us. It's not a set job, but making your own job. You've got to keep pushing on or get pushed back.'

'Nothing new about that.'

'I had to spend capital, Harry, and it wasn't mine to spend, not in the ordinary way. It come through my wife, and it's that the rumours are playing at. These people don't like what just had to happen. Here was land turned into money, but then turned back not into land but into something else. Land they value, but not anything else.'

'I suppose so,' Harry said. He was looking up to where a cloud-shadow was moving over the rockfall of the Holy Mountain.

'Which is why, among other things, they're so backward. It's always been so in Wales. There's never been the capital, Harry. Our coal and iron had to be got out with English money. The English, see, always understood money better.'

Harry was listening now, but still warily. He was waiting for terms he could feel.

'They're strong enough, Harry, in their own little patch, their own fields. But what they don't realize is there's far stronger things, not like people at all, breaking in from outside. If a man digs hard enough he'll eat: that's all they see of it. But a miner digs, just as hard, and it isn't the same. The coal has to go out and come back as meat, and a lot can go wrong with that. Even here it's the same. It isn't just what they grow, but what happens out there, places they've never seen and know nothing about.'

Harry smiled suddenly, but to himself, and following some line of thought of his own.

'What is it, Harry?'

'I was thinking about old Lucas. You know, up Cefn. He was here the other day. Going on about what he'd got for his wheat. Made out it would ruin him. "What we want, see, Harry, is another war. Not a war would hurt anybody mind, but to bring the prices up a bit."'

'What did you tell him?'

'I didn't tell him anything.'

'Why?'

'Well, if old Jack come to me and said, "Harry, what we want's a river running up the mountain", would I tell him?'

'But that's just where you're wrong, Harry. I've often told you, and I know you take no notice. But take the strike. We saw what happened there, you as quick as anyone. Stuck here, turning over the same bloody clods year in year out, they're just like babies really. You know, reaching and reaching for the same tossel, and when they got it they don't know what to do with it. But you, Harry, you've seen how it goes. You're here, in the box, an industrial worker, and that's a fact. Your gardening's neither here nor there. Your future's a matter of the whole national economy, not how hard you dig.'

'What I grow I sell to you. I get the shillings.'

'Aye, shillings, that's the point, but you don't live on shillings. What I'm saying is, take a long look at it all. Ask yourself, honest now, where the future is. That's what I did, after the strike, and I tell you it's working out.'

'Aye, you're getting what you want.'

'And this is only the start, mind. There's no limit, none, so long as we see the real situation. Here, I'm saying, you can't. Your eyes are down all the time, on the muck or the dust. If you look up, what is it you see? Mountains. Miles and miles of barren, bloody mountains. You got to break out of it, Harry, before it's too late.'

'That was right for you,' Harry said.

Morgan got up, and walked across to the narrow bench under the window.

'Why is it, Harry, you won't talk this out straight? What is it really you're afraid of?'

There was a shout from the platform. Harry went to the window, and saw Will Addis.

'Three for the pickup, Harry.'

'Right.'

'How's your old snaps?' Morgan shouted, leaning past Harry at the window.

'Can't you see?'

'What you want for half a dozen bunches?'

'What I'd get is a week in the clink.'

'Snaps don't make good bunches,' Harry said.

Morgan smiled, watching him. 'I might have known it was no use talking.'

'Who to? Addis?'

'You or Addis. You're all the same.'

'He's better than he was. Them beds this year is pretty good.'

Harry looked out at the beds along the platform, bright with the pink and yellow antirrhinums.

'Let's talk business, then, if you won't do the other.'

'Business?'

'Aye. That's what I come for. Sit down a minute.'

'I got the pickup to see in.'

'You can do that with your eyes shut. Now just you listen.'

Harry went on making his preparations for the train.

'I've come to a turning-point, Harry, and I've come to you. What I've got to do is reorganize and I've got to do it quick. Up to now I been running all over, buying and selling. But now, see, with the stuff I've got to handle, I've got to concentrate and reorganize before I can go on and expand.'

'Yes, I saw that would come.'

'The selling depends on me, naturally. I've got the contacts and I know the market. But to use all that I need my whole time. It's there, see, asking to be expanded, and here am I running up Trawsfynydd for three dozen eggs or Campstone for a dozen rabbits.'

'Aye, I've thought about that.'

'Well, now look, Harry. What I need, see, is a buyer. A chap I know, a chap I can trust, a chap with the background. Somebody that knows where to go, what the stuff's worth, all that.'

'Yes.'

'I'm putting it to you, Harry.'

'Me?'

'I'm putting the offer of the job to you.'

'I got a job.'

Morgan closed his eyes. 'If you was to use this for buying, mun, you'd make both our fortunes.'

'Use what?'

'This bloody stubbornness. This pretending you don't understand.'

'Aye, that.'

'Look, Harry. Be serious. I'll go through my books with you, you can see exactly what's what. And I'll offer, guaranteed, four pounds a week and the expenses of the van. What d'you say?'

Harry hesitated, looking down at his hand, where a bramble scratch was healing. He rubbed his thumb along the still reddened skin, and then pushed his hand back over his thinning hair.

'That's thirty bob a week on what you're getting, mind.'

'Aye. Seventy-eight quid a year. I'm thinking of that.'

'I know it would work, Harry. I'm sure of it. We've known each other now, what, twelve years. We'd get on, mun.'

Harry moved to see the pickup into the siding.

'Thanks for making the offer,' he said, as he locked the black lever of the points.

'It's for my good as much as yours. I know your value, Harry.'

Nothing more was said, for some minutes, while the pickup operations continued. Morgan stood in the centre of the box, waiting.

'I appreciate it,' Harry said at last, walking across to the register. 'Only I don't see my way to it.'

'Why not? What's wrong with it?'

'Just I don't see my way. There's nothing wrong.'

Morgan looked at the stiff, heavy figure, and at the strong, coarse face. Harry's eyes were very dark and withdrawn.

'Take your time, Harry, think about it. The end of August is time enough.'

'No, I won't hang you about. It's fair you should know now.'

'But think, Harry. Think of Ellen, think of Will. This could be the making of all of you. You know you could do the job.'

'Aye, it's not that.'

'Well, what is it, then? I've a right to know, surely.'

'Nothing. Nothing against it.'

'You don't like the idea of business, is that it? Or you think it wouldn't be secure enough?'

'What's secure?'

'You think dealing's wrong. Is that it?'

'No, I told you all that when you were starting.'

'You did, yes. You told me. But for yourself, I suppose, it's different?'

'No, Morgan. Dealing's all the same.'

'Then why not?'

Harry hesitated. Morgan, watching him, saw what he had so often seen before in this man: an extraordinary tension between what was felt and what could be said. Whenever the eyes were dark, like this, the old, losing struggle was being waged.

'You put it to me as why not,' Harry said slowly. 'I put it to myself as why.'

'Well, that, I'd think, is soon answered. There's the money to start with, that's the first consideration.'

'Is it?'

'Then the work, Harry. Getting about, seeing new places, being your own boss.'

Still Harry was watching him, his lips very full and pressed slightly forward.

'There's every reason, Harry. Don't tell me, for instance, the money don't weigh with you.'

'Aye. The money weighs all right.'

'Well, then?'

Harry walked across to his jacket, which was hanging behind the door. He stood, silent, for some moments. A swift was flying above the bridge. He saw it against the lines of the telephone wires, with their short, irregular black joins.

178

'It's only fair I should say no now, Morgan. And to say again that I appreciate you offering it to me.'

'Blast you, Harry,' Morgan said, and walked across the box. There were small beads of sweat along the lines from his nose to the corners of his mouth. Harry glanced up again at the swift.

'You say that's your attitude, Harry. Only don't think I'm taking it as final. I've had this thought out long enough, I can tell you. I've gone over it every way, and I know it's the right thing. And I'll say it to Ellen, mind. You watch, she'll be on my side.'

Harry stiffened momentarily, and then relaxed. 'We won't quarrel about it, Morgan, whichever way it goes.'

'You see, you're admitting it's not final.'

'Nothing's final. Only I've given you my answer.'

'We'll see,' Morgan said, and went past him and opened the door. 'You see, you'll be in that van up there by Christmas, I bet you.'

'Always glad of a ride,' Harry said.

'Working in it, that's what I mean.'

'No.'

'Yes, Harry. Yes. Yes. I tell you, it's meant to work out like I said.' Morgan's voice was broken, and the rims of his eyes were startlingly red. Harry looked at him, and then moved away.

'Anyway, thanks for looking in, Morgan.'

'I'll be back.'

'I hope you will. I'll have some stuff for you.'

'It isn't the stuff I want, Harry. It's you.'

Harry smiled and walked away to the far side of the box. 'And keep your feet well stuck in that mud, mind,' Morgan shouted.

'Aye, perhaps.'

Morgan slammed the door and went away down the steps and along the platform. Harry saw the van turn and move back over the bridge. Above it, the swift still darted against the wires and the sky.

CHAPTER SEVEN

1

Standing at the window of Harry's bedroom, Matthew saw the milk-van draw up in the lane. Until the end of the war the milk had still come by cart; you took out a jug to be filled from the churn. Now, in the back of the van, were milk-crates and shiny-topped bottles; he was glad to see them. He started as he saw the driver walk round. The walk came through even before the name, and for a moment he was back in the schoolroom, with Mrs Powell's voice loud behind the high green curtain, and the ring-handle turning on the door from the porch. Tegwyn pulled one of the crates, lifted two bottles from it, and walked as always, his legs stiff, his head thrust forward, to Ellen at the back door.

'Tegwyn's the milkman, then?'

'Aye, doing very well.'

Matthew had come up after breakfast to shave Harry and it had been tiring for them both: for Matthew because he had never shaved anyone else, and the angle seemed always wrong, yet he could not grip, for fear of hurting the aching shoulders; for Harry, because the effort of sitting up tired him, and he had got impatient, once grasping the razor and using it with several quick, violent, scraping strokes, before it slipped again from his hand. Now Matthew was wiping the blade, while Harry lay back to rest.

'Not late still, is he?'

'Tegwyn? No, he's a reliable chap.'

Tegwyn was talking to Ellen at the back door, but when he turned Matthew tapped the window, and he looked up, startled. The face of this man in his thirties reproduced, for a moment, the frightened stare of the boy who had looked round the door. Then he smiled, as Matthew waved, and through the glass they gestured to each other. Tegwyn lifted his thumb towards the bedroom and, with his expressive face, successfully mimed the question about Harry. Matthew nodded and turned to go down. But when he reached the back door, Tegwyn had got back in his van and driven on up the lane.

There was plenty to do, in the new day. Harry had said not to bother about the gardens, but still the jobs must be done. He went out to the strip beyond the drying green, and began the day's work. The first job was to finish planting the savoys Harry had been working at with the first attack. He dibbed the stalks in the soft red earth, following Harry's pattern. It seemed particularly important that these should grow well.

On the next strip there were late apples to pick and carry back in boxes, then wipe and store on the slatted shelves in the shed. On his way back down the lane, Tegwyn had left a sack of potatoes from Jack Thomas. The heavy sack stood blocking the shed door, and he strained to get it back into the depth of the musty shed. As he came with his last load of apples, Ellen called him for dinner.

After dinner he went back to the garden. There were the lettuce for spring to transplant, and the dead canes to cut from the raspberry strip, that was badly overgrown. When the light showed the first signs of fading, he moved to the hives by the lavender hedge. There were mouseboards to fit at the entrance to each hive, and, though each job was simple, it was dusk when he came to the end of the row. The mountains were black across the valley and mist was rising in the low fields by the river.

He went back across the lane and into the house. Tea was ready, and he sat with his mother in the half-dark kitchen, lit only by the crackling flames of sleeper wood in the grate. As the fire burned lower, neither of them moved to put on the light. Matthew sat in his father's chair, his hands loosely resting on the wooden ends of its arms. It was very quiet, and they sat for some time without speaking.

Then, after six, they moved into the living-room, where there were various insurance and club forms, stored in Harry's desk, to be examined and seen to, and letters to write. Matthew sat writing, and Ellen stood opposite him, telling him what to say. Soon after eight, they went back to the kitchen and Ellen prepared to go up to bed. She was filling a hot-water bottle at the sink when the bell from the bedroom rang loudly.

'I'll go.'

'All right, Will. Only take up the bottle. It might be that.'

When Matthew reached the bedroom Harry was sitting up, his arms stretched forward over the covers. After the shave and the long sleep, his face looked younger and easier.

'Was it the bottle you wanted?'

'Aye, I woke sudden.'

'You've had a good sleep. You look better.'

'I was dreaming, I think.'

'What about?'

'It's just things come back.'

'Good things?'

'It don't seem to be here, Will. In Llangattock, always.'

'Yes. Always where we grow up.'

'But not feeling like a boy, Will. Feeling like now, and the same things happening, but as if they were happening there.'

'Yes, I know.'

Harry was quiet, looking away at the dark square of the window. 'When I go, Will, I want it to be that way.'

'What do you mean?'

'You know what I mean. I shan't say it again.'

'I understand.'

The room was very silent now, and the valley beyond the window was an empty darkness.

'You been working in the garden?'

'Yes. Done a good day.'

'Good job there are no pigs.'

'I agree.'

'At home it was all pigs. I've never liked them.'

'You've kept them though.'

'Aye, for the bacon. I've never liked them.'

'Could anybody?'

'He did,' Harry said sharply. 'Fetch a bucket of acorns, Harry. Fetch a bucket of beech-mast, Harry. Cut them cabbages for them, Harry. We used to laugh at him at it.'

Matthew sat very still. He wanted to look at the photograph of Jack Price, but could not risk it.

'Well, Gran was a good man.'

'Aye. You could say that.'

'You sound a bit doubtful.'

'It was harder then,' Harry said, and his eyes clouded. His fingers moved impatiently at the edge of the covers.

'There's a bit of that in it always,' Matthew said.

'Yes. Naturally.'

'We just have to put up with it, I suppose.'

'There's worse than that,' Harry said.

The silence settled again, and they sat waiting. Matthew looked past the bed at the photographs on the walls, then down again to Harry's fine hands, that lay crossed over his thighs.

'It's hard to be right with the ill,' Harry said, suddenly.

'Is it?'

'You've done right. You've been straight with me.'

'I hope I have.'

'Being straight is difficult when it comes.'

'You mean telling the truth? If the truth's unpleasant?'

'Aye, that. Though that can be solved. A man knows his own pain. If there's comfort given, he takes it as comfort, not as anything else.'

'Yes.'

'It's different being straight, Will. It's like turning a focus, and it's all there to look at. Only the focus is pain, and you daren't really touch it. You daren't move anything, if you don't like what you see.'

'No, it's late then.'

183

Harry turned and looked into his face. It was the look, suddenly, of a father bending over his child, watching for sleep or for pain.

'I went through the decision,' Harry said. 'When Mam was going.'

'Yes, you told me.'

'Not it all, Will. I go back now, confused, as if it was all still happening.'

'It was cancer, wasn't it?'

Harry's hands moved quickly along the edge of the covers.

'Will, I've only that once been angry. Not temper, temper is easy. Her with cancer, and picking stones in the fields. Picking stones a shilling a cartload, I still can't get past it. I can see her now, bending over, picking the stones. I can feel them, feel their edges, feel the stones in my hands.'

'Yes.'

'Dad and us three boys went in to the hospital. But only I went inside, to her bed. He would never go in. I begged him to go in. He hated hospitals. Hated them like a child.'

The pale hands moved again, slowly.

'It was a hot day, I remember. You could smell the horses in the streets. The four of us stood there, outside the hospital. There was a high blank wall, and we stood under it, in our black suits and the high collars chafing us. Go you on in, Harry, you do the talking.'

'Yes.'

'I went in and saw her. There was nothing to say. I just took her hand and held it, till it was time to go. In the corridor outside, the doctor spoke to me. He talked like talking to a fool. He said it over, three times, like talking from the top of a tree. I understood it the first time. If I didn't answer it was I didn't know what to say.'

'There, take it easy,' Matthew said, for the fists were tight, and the blood had come up into the face.

'I went out and said it to Dad and my brothers. Without an operation, no hope. With an operation, fifty-fifty, no promises. We stood down there in the street. I had to go back up and say.'

'They agreed?'

'He wouldn't say. He didn't want her cut up. That's all he kept saying. My brothers said they'd agree what we decided. And I had no right. She was past asking.'

'You decided?'

'I said we had to decide, standing there in the street. Dad looked at me suddenly and said make up my own mind. I went back and said operate. "You're very wise, Mr Price." Not that it was kindly said. Then we went and walked in the market, not talking a lot. She lived three more years.'

'And even if she hadn't, you'd still have been right.'

'It's easy to say that. Like that doctor talking. "You're very wise, Mr Price."'

'I didn't mean that.'

'No. But you say, take the knife. I'd been holding her hand and I had to get up and decide. What I mean now, the focus of pain and we say we daren't touch it. And the wall quite blank, no windows over the street. I said go on, and we walked in the crowds in the market.'

'You were right. You know you were right.'

Harry looked up at him, surprised, as if this was not the face he was expecting to see. Matthew looked back at him, and then Ellen came quietly in behind them.

'All right, then?'

'Aye, with my company,' Harry said, looking away, and caught both their hands.

CHAPTER EIGHT

1

Jack Price, after his wife's death, lived with his eldest son Owen, who had stayed in Llangattock as a roadman. Harry occasionally visited him there, once or twice taking Will. It was a small, quiet, very formal cottage, filled with what Will remembered as a curious brown light. Even Jack Price was subdued and untalkative in it, and he took the first opportunity to leave. Owen's wife died, and within a season Jack Price was sixty-five and could leave the farm where he had worked since before his wedding. He sent for Harry, and said that he wanted to live in Glynmawr. Two days later he came down alone on the bus. The bus had to stop for several minutes, at the bottom of the lane, for all his things to be unloaded.

For Will, the arrival of his grandfather was strange and exciting. Jack Price turned to him and talked, as the others had not heard him talk since their childhood. The end of work seemed to have released his spirit. He read Will's school-books, talked of the politics he remembered, teased both Will and Harry with dialect words that he had known as a boy but that had gone out of use. Then, as the spring came, he began working in Harry's gardens, on the bees and pigs and poultry, and sometimes in the house itself. Often Harry came home from the box to find some alteration made which he had not been asked about. In his easy way the old man dominated the house, and Harry saw coming back to life the father he remembered – the quick, excitable, incalculable man who had been submerged for so many years in the morose silence of the cottage in Llangattock. Watching his father, Harry felt a straining of spirit in himself; a movement where for years there had been deadlock. Since he had first left home he had never laughed so much as he now did, when his father took over an evening, talking extravagantly, bringing the past back until it seemed that living had always been exciting and easy. Will, who had known only the silent, bowed figure, listened as if in a new world, and asked for particular stories again and again.

One day as he rode up the lane from school, he heard a strange high shouting, beyond the patch. He ran his bike along the hedge by the holly, and followed the shouting. Across the drying green, by the apple trees, Harry and Jack Price were shouting and dancing, clapping their hands above their heads. Above them, twenty feet in the air and still rising, a swarm of bees moved in a gathering brown cloud. Will had seen many swarms, but the first thing he noticed, now, was the way his father and grandfather were dancing; the bees seemed only an excuse. And then Ellen arrived, carrying a zinc bath full of pans, and they all took the pans and began a furious drumming and clattering on them. The brown cloud rose steadily higher, above the apple trees. Still, the tanging continued, and the excited shouting. Then suddenly, 'they're going,' Ellen shouted, and at once the tanging was stopped and Harry was running away down the green, through the hedge by his garden, and into the field beyond. The cloud was against the sun, flying west to the mountains. 'And you, boy,' Jack Price shouted. Will ran back through the patch, and fetched his bike. The excitement was still racing in him, as he rode down the pitch to the road. At the shop Harry was waiting, and took the bike. Will went on, across country. The swarm was far ahead of them now, but they had got its direction.

Will ran down the field, past Elwyn's cottage, to the plank bridge over the river. He made for the opening through the railway embankment. A goods train was passing on the down line, the engine labouring and sending out a great grey cloud of smoke. The fireman was shying knobs of coal at the scurrying rabbits along the embankment. Elwyn always said how much coal they got there, 'coal and rabbits from the same bank'. Stubby stalactites hung from the grey arch under the line. Beyond was a wide view of the rising ground to the mountain. He climbed on a stile and looked up into the sky. There was nothing, not even a bird. He looked back towards the patch and then at the trees to see the direction of the wind. But it was very slight, hardly more than a breath. After two more fields he reached the deep cutting of the old road. It was deserted and silent.

He called, but there was no answer. He walked north, listening. Then, round a bend, he saw his bike lying on its side in a bed of nettles, the back wheel still slowly spinning. There was a glat beyond the nettles, and a path to the mountain. He called again, and then ran up the path. A long narrow wood lay ahead, and as he passed through it, to the steep bracken rise, he heard Harry call. At the end of a narrow field, on the edge of a dingle, Harry stood looking up at the bees. They were settling on a branch about seven feet from the ground, the brown crawling beard slowly growing in size. As Will came up, Harry was laughing exultantly. The sweat had made little runnels of dirt down his cheeks, and his hair was wet and matted to his head. The leg of his trousers had been torn, and Will could see the dotted red line of the scratch underneath. But the luck of finding the bees was everything.

The bees settled slowly, and the branch looped grace-fully with their weight.

'Watch them, but keep away!' Harry said. 'I'll go back for my kit.'

'If they go again shall I keep after them?'

'Just stay.'

It was forty minutes before Harry got back to the swarm. He came up the field, carrying the two-handled zinc bath at his chest. In the bath was a box, with his gauntlets and veil and blower.

'All quiet?'

'Aye, it's humming now, not buzzing.'

'Aye, they're settling.'

Harry took the bath and carried it down into the dingle. He set it upside down, immediately below the swarm. Then, setting the lid very carefully against the bath, he put the box beside it. He stuffed the cloth into the waistband of his trousers, then tucked his trouser ends inside his socks, and put on the veil, which was sewn to the brim of an old felt hat. He drew the bottom of the veil tightly around his neck, then crouched and took up the blower. He unscrewed the back, and pulled out an edge of the rolled corrugated paper, and lit it with a match. He screwed it up again, and stood testing the bellows. A thin trail of acrid blue smoke came from the long spout. Putting the blower under his arm, he pulled on his gauntlets, and looked round the dingle.

'Shall I come, Dad?'

'No, you keep right back.' The voice was muffled by the veil.

Harry walked carefully around under the swarm, seeing how the branch lay in relation to the main bush. Then he touched the lid again and bent and picked up the open wooden box. He got up on to the bath, and slowly lifted the box past his chest, until it rested at one end of his shoulder. The bees were already disturbed; several were flying around his hands, and the noise had thinned and sharpened. He shifted his feet on the bath, and reached up past the swarm to grip the branch. He tested it with a very light pull, and checked again the position of the box. Scores of bees were now flying around, but he could not use the blower, which was in the hand holding the other end of the box. He hesitated and then suddenly pulled downwards on the branch, with his whole weight. At the same moment, with a heave of his shoulder, he thrust the box up around the swarm. There was an immediate violent buzzing, and a cloud of bees around his head. With his right hand he was now violently shaking the branch, getting the swarm free. He stepped down, one foot slipping from the bath as he staggered under the weight of the box. He let the box go down and grabbed for the lid, clapping it over the box. He pulled the cloth from his waistband and spread it quickly over the lid. He was surrounded now by a cloud of angry bees: so many, indeed, that there might almost be none in the box. He stood up and used his smoke blower, moving away. Slowly the bees circled away from him, and then went down to crawl over the box and the cloth. Puffing the thin smoke, Harry walked up the dingle, a strange figure in the veiled hat and the long gloves.

'Mind, keep away, till they've settled down.'

He stood picking bees from his clothes, throwing them lightly down towards the box, in which the angry buzzing continued. Then he picked a stone and set it on the lid. Walking away, he smoked carefully all over his body, and then started taking off the gauntlets. Finally he took off the veiled hat, turned it upside-down and picked a bee from inside it.

'They'll take some carrying home, won't they?'

'You keep away. I'll manage them on the bike.'

'Shall I carry the other stuff?'

'No, you can't manage that. We'll leave the bath, get it tomorrow.'

'I can take the blower and the hat and so on.'

'Aye. In a few minutes.'

Harry squatted, and eased his shoulders. Down on the box, a hundred or more bees were crawling over the cloth. After a few minutes he put on the gloves and hat again, and, sliding back the lid a few inches, got most of the stragglers in. Then he crouched by the box, feeling under its edges with his fingers. Will saw him take the strain, and then lift suddenly.

'Go on, get away,' Harry shouted, coming straight up the dingle.

Will walked beside him, carrying the blower and sending out smoke at the bees that were still loose and following them. While he was enjoying this, he caught a glimpse of Harry's face, and stopped. He was walking awkwardly, with the box across his chest, but all the strain seemed to be in the face: the lips drawn back, baring the big teeth; the eyes narrowed; the forehead knotted and red.

'You'll have to rest them, Dad. You won't get all the way down.'

Harry did not answer: he was watching the ground ahead of him, choosing his path. Will walked beside him, seeing the road come nearer. At last they reached the fence and Harry bent to put the heavy box on the grass.

'Get the bike. We shall be all right now.'

Will scrambled over the fence and wheeled the bike over the grass. Harry lifted the box to the fence, and climbed over, balancing it.

'Hold the bars.'

When the bike was firm, he lowered the box across the carrier. He pulled out a length of the hairy white string he always carried, and took two loops around the box and over the saddle.

'There's a couple of hundred pounds of honey, if I can keep them.'

He steadied the box while Will pushed, and they turned on the circle for home.

2

For many reasons, and to many places, people left the village. The most recent to go from the patch was the Hybarts' boy, Alun. As they walked to the Eisteddfod that autumn, Harry, Ellen and Eira were talking about him.

'Only it shows something for the village,' Ellen said. 'And now to see him back.'

'Aye,' Eira said. 'They're proud of him in Gwenton.' Alun was a footballer and had played at centre-forward for Gwenton. Big and reckless, he was the best forward in the local league. It was often said that scouts for bigger clubs had been watching him. Nobody wanted to lose him, but it was taken as only right.

Soon after the start of the 1934 season, a stranger arrived at Glynmawr station: a man in his fifties, dark, urban, his heavy face purplish with burst and swollen veins. He asked for the Hybarts' house, and walked down through the village. William Evans was taking his evening walk when he came on the stranger leaning against the wall of the Baptist chapel, staring over it at the headstones of the graves.

'Good evening,' William Evans said.

'Ah, good evening, Mr Davies,' the stranger said.

'Davies? My name is Evans.'

'Look,' said the stranger, and pointed over the wall. The schoolmaster followed the pointed hand and saw the near row of headstones: Martha Davies, beloved wife of James Davies; also James Davies, husband of the above; William Davies, Pantycelyn;

Mary Davies, wife of the above; Thomas Davies; David Davies; Mary Ann Davies; William Davies, Pentre; Elizabeth Davies; Sarah Davies; John Davies; Reuben Davies.

'Well?'

'You'll agree,' the stranger said, 'it was a sporting chance.'

'My name is Evans,' William Evans repeated coldly, and prepared to walk on. The stranger took a pipe from the big pocket of his overcoat, and began to fill it.

'Know a family called Hybart?'

'Yes. Just up the lane.'

'I ought to introduce myself. Trefusis. Cardiff City.'

'Cardiff?'

'Cardiff City.'

William Evans looked suspiciously into Trefusis's face, and then moved away. Trefusis, watching him go, lit his pipe, threw the match over the wall into the graveyard, and crossed the road to walk up the lane.

Next day the news was all over the village. Our Alun had been offered a trial with Cardiff City, and might sign as a professional. Alun, of course, jumped at the offer, and the trial was successful. By mid-October he had signed professional forms.

'Only you just see mind,' was the general opinion in Glynmawr, 'by Christmas he'll be in the first team.' That this did not happen was not Alun's fault. He had a great deal to learn, in a different class of football, and was satisfied, for the time being, to win and hold his place in the third team. There, in small print at the bottom of the columns in the South Wales papers, was the evidence: Jones (P); Willis, Lucas; Dove, Harvest, Lewis (T); Wells, Griffiths (M), Hybart, Peel, Pugh. It would not be long though, obviously, before Hybart went into bigger type.

When they reached the hall, Will hung back, talking to Brychan. Alun was standing in the porch, and everyone who went in was shaking his hand. Tall and ruddy, with short black hair, Alun smiled and acknowledged his welcome. Will watched as Eira went up to him, and suddenly left Brychan.

'Eira, you're due on, I see,' he heard Alun saying.

'Aye, trying somehow, Alun.'

'You going to win for us then?'

'No, I don't think so.'

'Come on, don't be shy about it.'

'No, Alun, honest.'

'It isn't the winning, it's the taking part,' Will said.

'What you know about it, Shaver?'

'Playing is for music, not for prizes. The Eisteddfod's more than a tinpot competition.'

'That's what they say who can't win.'

The afternoon session of the Eisteddfod was less emotionally charged than the evening. A succession of children sang, recited and played, but, though skilful, they lacked the finish and pressure of the adult performers, and the whole atmosphere was relaxed. The proceedings, in fact, could almost be looked on as entertainment. There were the stiff little gestures of the reciters – usually the hand a second or so behind the words. Then the contained, decorous singing of the girls, their faces subdued to routines practised again and again in their kitchens, as their bodies were subdued to the surface flare of satin. There were awkward moments when a violin string broke, or a small foot slipped from a pedal. Only towards the end, towards adolescence, came the first signs of that conscious emotional attack which would later be so fully and so devastatingly mounted. There were signs of this even in Eira, whose natural simplicity was obvious. Will was embarrassed as he watched her sit forward on the edge of the piano chair, looking down at the keyboard. She paused deliberately, and carefully stroked her long white fingers, as if making a mime. Will saw the adjudicator look up and pencil a note. He supposed, sadly, that it would be favourable.

At last the children's choirs caught up the ragged informality of the afternoon. From their first hushed pause at the note, the beginnings of general emotion were evident. Against his determination, Will felt himself caught up in that movement and pressure of the audience by which, in response, they became virtually part of the choir: the united voices quickening them to a common awareness which had little to do with their physical presence in the drab, watching rows. Sound was master.

The conductor of the Eisteddfod was saving himself for the evening. I. Morgan, Watch Repairer, as visitors to Gwenton might find him, became, for these occasions, Illtyd Morgan y Darren. In the afternoon session he was masterful, but as yet contained. His gleaming wing collar stood sharply up under his prominent chin. Above his long fine nose, his dark eyes were caverned under jutting white eyebrows. The sleeves of his black coat were pulled back to reveal several inches of gleaming white cuffs, and from these, sudden as a snake, emerged thin wrists and long, chalk-white hands, which seemed arranged always in a position to clap. When he clapped, as he did with great frequency, his palms were hollowed to a resounding, slapping violence, and he would seem borne up from his chair on this explosion of sound, itself only a preliminary to the sudden coming of the voice, of which even a whisper seemed to vibrate in the farthest corners of the room. Over the whole range every human feeling seemed at instantaneous command. There was the tumble of laughing words into any of the known jokes; the slow spaced hiss of the incitement to applause; the strong, harsh break into sadness and condolence: and each was punctuated by the darting wrists and the quicksilver, chalk-white fingers, and by the explosion of the laugh, which set a period to everything – statement, ribaldry, lament. As yet, in this ragged afternoon, there was a familiar restraint. Illtyd Morgan conducted with perhaps twice the intensity of an ordinary man, instead of the unimaginable degrees in which he would later spend himself. And with the children there was a particular ceremony which took most of his attention. As each child came up, Illtyd Morgan identified her family, and recalled older members of the same family, who had come as children to this platform.

'Elinor Watkins. Come up, Elinor. Elinor Watkins. Elinor Watkins, Tremaen. Tremaen, yes. Where the white barn, the *white* barn, stands by the bend of the river. Elinor, yes. Elinor daughter of Mary who was Mary Rees when she went to marry John Watkins, the son of my very old friend John Watkins the Bridge. Mary herself, I remember, Mary with red hair, red to her shoulders, singing here where I am standing, eleven years old. Mary Watkins, Elinor's mother. She's down there, Mary Watkins. I can see her now, looking about five years older. And this is Elinor, her daughter. Mary Rees, Mary Watkins, Elinor Watkins, Tremaen. Come up here now, Elinor. Come up by this old man who remembers your mother singing for him.'

Will looked round uneasily. He could see Mrs Watkins, in a low brown hat, with a brown, square-shouldered coat, not betraying by so much as a movement her intent reception of this memory of herself. He knew how much this ceremony of identification and memory meant to the silent and apparently unresponsive listeners. This, centrally, was the meaning of life. And Illtyd Morgan was never out in the smallest detail. Half-ashamed, Will found himself wishing that there could be some extraordinary blunder: the child given to the wrong mother; the parents mixed up; bastardy and confusion flung across the valley by that compelling voice. But always – there it was – he was right, and a stranger coming into the room would learn, in the course of the day, the greater part of the complicated family relationships by which Glynmawr lived.

At nearly six the afternoon session ended. The evening session, announced for seven-thirty sharp, would begin as usual soon after eight. Eira and her stepmother were coming to tea with Ellen. Will walked with Eira up the lane, behind Harry and Alun. She had come equal first in the piano solo; it was better than she had expected.

'What you do with your fingers before you started?' Will asked sharply.

'What with my fingers?'

'Holding your hands out and pulling at them. Just for the adjudicator to see.'

'You got to do that, Will, before you play.'

'Why?'

195

'It helps the fingers, honest. You got to keep them flexible.'

'Fingers are flexible.'

'Don't go on at her, mun,' Alun said, turning.

'It's all right, Alun,' Eira said. 'I depend on Will to tell me what's wrong.'

'It wasn't wrong, though. If he could play the piano he'd know you've got to do that.'

'It is just a habit though, I suppose, really,' Eira said uncomfortably.

Will walked on beside her, looking down at his father's boots. Harry said nothing. He went to the Eisteddfod as a matter of course, but it was not his world.

'I nearly cried, though,' Eira said suddenly, her voice very simple and unguarded. 'When old Illtyd Morgan said that about my Mam. Every year it's the same and I say I won't cry but I do.' Will did not answer. He was waiting for Alun to turn off to his own house, so that he and Eira could go on alone. Ellen and Janie Rosser were in the cottage already. There was a light in both rooms as they walked through the garden. Tea had been laid in the living-room. Will and Eira went in there, and stood by the fire. Soon the two women came in from the porch with the teapot and kettle, and they all sat to the table, rather formally. Jack Price came in last, and at once presided. He had been stimulated by Illtyd Morgan y Darren, who was a man after his own heart. Will caught echoes of the conductor's gestures and intonations, and began awkwardly to doubt his grandfather. Eira was very conscious of her manners at table, and he could see, looking round, how in this the women divided from the men. His father and grandfather might have been eating, self-absorbed, in the fields. But the women, somehow, seemed to be eating for each other, showing each other what they were doing.

'You do keep it nice here, Ellen,' Janie said.

'Do you think so?'

'Oh yes. Isn't it, Eira?'

'It's lovely,' Eira said, colouring. 'I've always loved this house. Always, for me, it used to be like home.'

196

'Well, the house is nothing much,' Ellen said. 'It's inconvenient.'

'More tea,' Harry said, holding across his cup. Ellen took the cup and filled it. Will watched the pursing of her lips.

'When we came here Harry was talking about a door through the passage to the back-kitchen, save going out through the porch with everything. Only we haven't got it.'

'Do you good, girl, to get the night air,' Jack Price said.

'That's Hybart's job,' Harry said. 'I can't knock holes in his walls.'

'Well, it's like that with everything,' Janie said. 'I mean out here you expect things to be inconvenient.'

'Naturally,' Jack Price said. 'In London, see, they're growing wheels instead of legs. It'll be wings next. That's the real answer.'

Will looked at Eira, and smiled. She smiled back quickly and then turned away. Will saw the colour in her neck, above the border of the olive-green woollen dress.

'It's not that at all,' Harry said. 'Improvements are necessary, but you can't pick one thing out. You have to take account of it as a whole.'

'What, houses you mean?' Janie said.

'Houses and the rest.'

'Well, I know one thing, Ellen. Life feels different, like my auntie says, when you got a nice modern house.'

'The bathroom we got at our house,' Eira said suddenly, seeming hardly to realize that she was speaking aloud, and looking round awkwardly as the others turned to her. 'Well,' she went on in an embarrassed rush, tumbling over her words, 'when I first saw it, I was just scared to use it for getting it dirty.'

'It is nice,' Janie said.

'Mrs Lucas used to bath me in the brown one, you know, like you got,' Eira said breathlessly. It was as if she could not help going on, yet could not bear what she was saying.

There was a general silence. The last of the bottled raspberries were shared between Eira and Will. Jack Price lit his pipe.

'Morgan still says, you know,' Janie said, 'how he wishes Harry would come in with him.'

197

'Yes,' Ellen said.

'The business is going so well now, but he needs somebody reliable, for the buying. Jack Thomas, that he tried you know, he's no good. Harry, he keeps saying, is the man to do it.' Ellen looked across at Harry, waiting for him to speak. And Will looked at his father, who was leaning back on his chair, staring down at the lace edge of the tablecloth.

'I heard about that,' Jack Price said. 'Dealing, Harry told me.'

'Morgan's built up the business very well,' Ellen said.

'Only I've always reckoned Harry could do anything, if he wanted. When he was at school, I remember, the master come to me and told me about him. "He can do whatever I set him. With the right chance, he'll really get on."'

'Old Wilkes,' Harry said.

'Well, he was right, wasn't he?'

'How should I know? He never told me that.'

'Wanted to keep you at it, see,' Janie said.

'Aye, that or something.'

'Only dealing now,' Jack Price said, 'might be the one thing Harry couldn't do. He never took to it, not when he was at home. Like when your Dad, Ellen, was at the mill, he and I used to get on all right – counting the bags, you know, coming to an agreement. Harry, when I'd send him down, might have been anywhere. Watching dragonflies he said one day, when I caught him. There wasn't the interest.'

'If we're to get back,' Harry said, 'I must get round and shut up.'

'There's plenty of time, Harry.'

'Aye, well I'll get it done.'

The tea things were carried out through the porch, and Will walked out down the garden, where he could see his father crouching on the narrow brick path, cleaning his acetylene lamp. As Will came up, he caught the foul smell of the old tipped-out carbide. Looking up, he saw the dark ridge of the mountains, and the way the shadows were lying there, following the fold of the land into the climbing fields.

'Anything I can do, Dad?'

'No, son, that's all right.'

Will looked away. There was a lump in his throat, and he could feel a tingling pressure behind his eyes. But he did not know what this feeling was, that threatened to overwhelm him. He heard the bowl of the lamp being tapped on the edge of the brick path, and looked down at the spent grey dough of the carbide.

'Look, tell me. Why was I called Matthew?'

Harry looked away, his fingers busy with the lamp.

'Just a name, Matthew.'

'Aye. Only then you all called me Will.'

'Matthew's still your name though,' Harry said, getting up and edging the carbide off the path.

'I know. That's why I'm asking.'

'Now mind the way,' Harry said. 'I got to get on and lock up.'

He pushed past his son, on the narrow brick path. Will turned and called after him.

'Can I do some, though? Let me.'

'No, no. You go on back to the house.'

Will did not want to go in, but the dark evening was settling, hiding the valley, and it was suddenly colder. He went in, and got a book to read until it was time to go back to the Eisteddfod. When they all set out, he was very low and dispirited. The mounting excitement, as they mixed with the others making for the hall, seemed wholly apart from him. He sat between Eira and Harry, wishing the evening would never start.

At last Illtyd Morgan was on the platform again. Now, in the close atmosphere of the crowded oil-lit room, the tension was immediate. Everyone stood to sing the English national anthem, put at the beginning so that at the end, when they were really involved, they could sing the Welsh. Then the solo singing began. But now it was not a matter of shy boys and girls. Now there were such personages as Madame Maisie Jones, from the other side of Hereford, who always won the contralto solo, and was virtually a professional. Tenors, baritones, sopranos, came and went: all developed in face and in stance as well as in voice, used to travelling from distant villages and from the mining valleys. Illtyd Morgan was now at the peak of his commitment: laughing, congratulating, condoling, expounding. The recitations came next, and here there were more people from Glynmawr itself. Many of the farmers, ordinarily slow inarticulate men, recited regularly. On the little platform, under the single oil lamp, they became intent and strange in the practised, formal eloquence, which was warmer, more pressing on the heart, than even the singing. Will kept his eyes down. As the moving of a voice, he could accept it, but what was difficult, always, was to look up and see the man himself: Ieuan Davies, Josh Evans, Evan Preece.

The set piece was the twenty-eighth chapter of Job. It was recited nine times in all:

He putteth forth his hand upon the rock; he overturneth the mountains by the roots.

He cutteth out rivers among the rocks; and his eye seeth every precious thing.

He bindeth the floods from overflowing; and the thing that is hid bringeth he forth to light.

But where shall wisdom be found? and where is the place of understanding?

Man knoweth not the price thereof; neither is it found in the land of the living.

The depth saith, it is not in me; and the sea saith, it is not with me...

Will repeated the words to himself, continuing to stare down. He setteth an end to darkness and searcheth out all perfection. Surely there is a vein for the silver, and a place for gold where they fine it. The moving voices continued, and the applause, when it came, was concentrated.

It was time now for the choirs, and Will knew, looking up, that it was no use at all even trying to stay separate. Each choir moved into position, into dark settled rows, and the set faces turned to the conductor, eyes widened and lips poised; men and women surrendered, asking for movement and control. The drop of the raised hand, and then not the explosion of sound that you half expected, but a low, distant sound, a sound like the sea yet insistently human; a long, deep, caressing whisper, pointed suddenly and sharply broken off, then repeated at a different level, still both harsh and liquid; broken off again, cleanly; then irresistibly the entry and rising of an extraordinary power, and everyone singing; the faces straining and the voices rising around them, holding, moving, in the hushed silence that held all the potency of these sounds, until you listening were the singing and the border had been crossed. When all the choirs had sung, everyone stood and sang the anthem. It was now no longer simply hearing, but a direct effect on the body: on the skin, on the hair, on the hands.

Will stood by Eira in the crowd pressing to the door. For a minute, as they were pushed together, he held her hand, without looking at her. Once they were through, and the night opened above them, their hands separated and dropped. The car would be just up the lane, Eira said. Morgan was standing by it, smoking a cigarette.

'Eira? Get in. Will, is that?'

'Yes.'

'Been making a bit of noise in there, from what I could hear.'

'Not me, no. It was the singing.'

'Aye, singing's the opium of the Welsh.'

'Don't take no notice of him, Will. He says things like that.'

The others came up the lane.

'It's not the training,' Mrs Priddy was saying. 'They don't do the training.'

'Too much wireless I think it is,' said Edith Watkins.

'There now,' Mrs Priddy said. 'It's nice, isn't it, to have the car. Eira, you get out and go in the front. You and me, Janie, go in the back with the rug. You got the rug?'

'It's in there, Auntie.'

The good nights were said, but in a minor key against the instructions and counter-instructions of getting into the car.

Will had not noticed his father, but now in the headlights he saw him directing Morgan down the lane, and waving. When the car had moved off, they walked home together up the lane.

3

Morgan had taken over a new building in Gwenton, partly as a depot and partly for bottling and jam-making. Janie worked there, in the busy time, with four or five other women. Morgan was sure, in this way, of standard quality. The amount of fruit, the quantities of sugar or other sweetenings – for some things substitutes were better, making a better colour for instance – could now be properly controlled.

He had still, however, to rationalize the buying. He was working towards large-scale contracts for the fruit he needed, in particular soft fruits. But it was proving difficult to persuade farmers to lay down a field of black currants, even with a guarantee of purchase of the whole crop. Fields of black currants were unknown, and that, normally, was the end of the discussion. Still, with his extraordinary energy, and with adequate resources from the profits of the earlier years, Morgan was making some headway. Three contracts had already been placed, in different villages, and he was now negotiating with Major Blakely in Glynmawr.

'What I had in mind, Major,' Morgan said, sitting back comfortably and brushing cigarette ash from the points of his waistcoat, 'was this park that you call—'

'Yes,' Blakely said, 'the park.'

'What you got? Three or four cows there? Grazing for your horses?'

'Yes, I sold most of the timber. That used to be a very fine avenue, but needs must, you know.'

'It's out of place, Major. That kind of thing nowadays. What's important is that the soil's good and there's a southeast slope. Dug up there could be what, three or four hundred currant bushes. That's a big crop.'

'Too big?'

'I can handle whatever I get, Major. You leave that to me.'

'Well yes, as you say, you know your own business. Only it's a quite considerable initial cost. One needs to be sure.'

'We could make a five-year agreement,' Morgan said. 'I take your whole crop, at a price to be agreed annually a fortnight before picking.'

'Not a fixed price?'

'At a fixed price you might lose, I might lose. This way we're both all right, letting the market decide.'

Blakely was silent for some time.

'Well now, Mr Rosser,' he said at last, 'I don't deny the prospect's attractive. One gets stale, you know, in a place like this. I should enjoy something a bit more active.'

'You won't regret it, I promise you. Nobody has, who's ever dealt with me.'

'I can believe that. All right then, let's get out and do a bit of a recce. There's a lot to be decided.'

Morgan got up at once and took Blakely's hand. Blakely seemed embarrassed, but was trained to this kind of social concession.

'What about the picking, Rosser? Will that be a problem?'

'No, no. You've only to say in the village, they'll all be up here. The women and children especially.'

'That'll add to my costs, of course.'

'I'll suggest a price, Major, when we make our arrangement each year.'

'That will help, of course. Your knowing these people.'

'I know what they'll do for money,' Morgan said, smiling. 'And that's almost anything, you'd be surprised.'

'Good. Let's get out and look over the ground then.'

'I'm with you, Major.'

That autumn the park of Brynllwyd House was ploughed and harrowed. By Christmas the long rows of currant bushes curved away down the slopes, making a new pattern in the fields. Since the quality of the fruit was an essential consideration, Morgan himself acted as agent in buying the bushes, from a North Wales nursery. The price was a little higher than Blakely had expected, but as an investment the scheme was still very attractive. On his first year's crop, when the pickers from the village had been paid (they came, as forecast, in great numbers) and when Morgan's price had been agreed (a low price, but then the whole crop was taken at once) Blakely recovered almost a quarter of his capital outlay, and was delighted. In September he went to Morgan with a proposal to expand the original agreement. In addition to the park, there were two fields, part of the Brynllwyd House property, now let. Blakely proposed to end the letting of these fields – this was simple, since the let was annual – and to plant them with currants and gooseberries.

'Who's got the fields now, you say?' Morgan asked.

'Meredith, you remember him.'

'Aye, I remember Jack Meredith. He won't like it, will he?'

'No. He's an awkward customer.'

'But you really want to do it, is that it?'

'Certainly. The fact is, I'll admit, I've rather taken to this kind of thing. It's so obvious a place for this sort of growing, though it needed a man like you to see its possibilities. Besides, I've really enjoyed the work, as an interest. It's been like a new lease of life, everyone tells me so.'

'Well, Major. What you do with your own fields is your own affair.'

'Yes. Yes it is. On the other hand the whole scheme depends on your taking the crop.'

'I'm not the only one in the market, Major. There's the big jam firms, they're crying out for contracts like this.'

'You needn't fear I'd go to them. You gave me the idea. I feel at least a moral obligation to you.'

'Aye. A moral obligation. But what about Meredith then?'

'Meredith? Well...'

'What else has he got? Two fields, is it?'

'Three, I think. I believe they used to be his brother's.'

'It'll cut down his scope a bit. Still, that's your business. If the fields were his, he'd take them back off you.'

'Not that I want unpleasantness, at all costs. Only everyone seems to think that because I'm English and an Army officer I'm made of money. Good Lord, Rosser, I'm treated sometimes as if I were a great landowner or something of that kind. I'm just a pensioned officer, with a small family capital. And I have children still to educate. If the fields are there, and I can use them, isn't that all perfectly above board?'

'It's your business, Major.'

'But not altogether. It's only a proposition, for me, if you'll contract for the crop.'

'Yes. And I'll think it over. I'll come out and see you one day next week.'

Morgan came again, and walked out with Blakely to look at the fields. They looked across at Meredith's own holding: the two long fields, running down from the white cottage, and a third field, above the cottage, little more than an enclave in the mountain bracken. Blakely's two fields were poor rough pasture, but they had the same south-eastern slope as the park.

'Well, what do you advise?' Blakely asked, as they walked back.

'I'm in the market for fruit, not advice.'

'It couldn't be done at once, of course. I've seen my lawyer; it needs six months' notice from the end of the year. That would make it July, and I could get the land ready for planting next autumn.'

'Yes,' Morgan said. He was chewing a stem of grass that he had picked as they walked. 'Currants, of course, are the thing. With gooseberries you've got the harder picking.'

'There's a sale for them though, surely?'

'Well, yes, bottling. Only in two years' time, say, I shall be over mainly to jam. I've got a few schemes of my own I've not exactly been broadcasting.'

Still chewing the pale shining grass stem, he stopped and looked at Blakely.

'Yes, if all goes well I'm going to build. I've got an option on a site, and now it's just the finance. What I want, you see, is a small modern jam factory. Nothing on a big scale, not yet. Only it's in jam, I've found, the money really is. It's the way they eat.'

'You'd advise both fields under currants then?'

'If you're to sell to me, yes.'

'All right. I'll get on with my own part of it. I'll get in touch with you again.'

'As you like, Major.' He shook hands and walked away, refusing an invitation to go back to the house for a drink. Blakely watched him go, and waited to hear his car start up before walking back. Next morning he called on his lawyer, and made the necessary arrangements about the fields.

Harry first heard of this plan about a week later, when Meredith was relieving him in the box.

'You've heard what our friend Rosser's been up to, I suppose?'

Meredith's ugly features had narrowed and sharpened in these last years. His habitual moroseness was more cutting and more offensive.

'No,' Harry said, as he picked up his coat. He did not like discussing Morgan with others. He knew that Morgan was not really liked in Glynmawr, though so many people dealt with him. But much of the dislike seemed to him to be envy.

'Him and Blakely,' Meredith said. Always now he called Blakely 'Blackly': well he calls me 'Merridith', don't he?

'What, the park?'

'Never mind the bloody park. They're starting now on my bloody fields.'

'What?'

'Six months' notice, Harry, and I've heard what it's for.'

'What then?'

'Currants,' Meredith spat, as if the very word was dirty. 'Currants. I could pick up some bloody sheep currants for him. That's more his mark.'

'Blakely's give you notice from the fields?'

'Aye and I've got to take it, too,' Meredith said, slinging down his frail. 'And don't think I don't know who put him up to it. What did that bugger Rosser ever do here but bring trouble? First, it was strikes, now it's currants. Christ!'

'Look, Jack, it's not his fields, it's Blakely's fields.'

'Blakely. Him! What do he know about farming? That sort don't know what's under a mare's tail.'

'Maybe. Anyway I'm sorry it's happened. Sorry for you.'

'Ah, get out of it. You're one of the same bloody sort, aren't you? Him and you always was.'

'Me and Morgan have been friends, yes.'

'That's what I said. Well, when you want my bloody shirt off my back, let me know.'

Harry buttoned his coat, looking away.

'See you tomorrow,' he said and went out.

On the next Sunday evening, he was standing in the lane with Lippy, when Morgan drove up and stopped beside them.

'Just the man I want to see,' Morgan said, winding down his window.

'Aye?'

'Hullo, Mr Rosser,' Lippy said, but was ignored.

'I was just off to see the trout jumping,' Morgan said.

'Trout?' Lippy said, frowning.

The Sunday convention of going to see the trout jumping was well known in the village. In Wales, on Sundays, none of the pubs were open, but only three miles away, where the border river curved in towards the village, lay England, and just across the bridge was the Silver Fox. To go to see the trout jump under the bridge had become something of a habit.

'Care to come along, Harry?'

'No, I don't think I will.'

'Where's Ellen?'

'At chapel. With my Dad.'

'Come on, mun. There's something particular I want to ask you.'

'Well, all right,' Harry said, and walked round the car.

'You coming?' Morgan called, offhand, to Lippy.

'Coming where, Mr Rosser?'

'To drown your sorrows.'

'Drown?'

'For a drink, mun. Come on, wake up.'

'Oh, aye,' Lippy said quickly. 'I'll come for a drink.'

'Then get in the back and hold on. Don't fall out now mind.'

'Righto, Mr Rosser.' He ran round the back of the car, following Harry. After some difficulty with the handle he got in and sat up very straight, holding on as he had been told. Morgan winked at Harry, and turned the car. They went off down the lane, and along the road to the border.

'Seen Jack these last few days, Harry?'

'Aye, I have. He's got it in for you.'

'It's Blakely's business, not mine. After all, I went to Jack and asked him to grow for me. He wouldn't.'

'So I suppose.'

'Black currants, is it?' Lippy asked eagerly.

'Come on, Harry. Spit it out. Say what you think.'

'I don't think nothing. It's hard on a chap to lose his land.'

'Aye, but Christ, Harry. Land's there to be used, isn't it? In the industrial areas people need this stuff, so why not grow it? And if Jack won't Blakely will.'

'It's the way it's arranged.'

'Harry, mun, you've lived here too long, you've got too set. The world's changing, Harry. Why not keep up with it?'

'You're quite right, Mr Rosser, there's a lot of changes,' Lippy said.

If there were any trout in the pool, it was too dark to see them. Morgan drove straight over the bridge, into England, and pulled up at the Silver Fox.

'And go steady mind, Lippy, or you know what your old woman'll do to you.'

'I can manage her.'

'Go steady for your own sake then.'

There was no bar in the Silver Fox. In the front room, furnished with benches and a table, the landlord, Eddie Lewis, sat drinking with the others. When you wanted a drink from the kitchen, he would fetch it. Several men from Glynmawr were already sitting along the benches. The three sat down and exchanged a few words with them. After a proper interval, Morgan asked Eddie Lewis whether there was anything left to drink. Lewis said there might be a drop of something; he'd go and see.

'Cider, if you could,' Morgan called.

'Aye. There's a cask now from Richards Alltyrynys.'

'Christ! Poison.'

'Aye, only it acts quick, cuts down your agony.'

He came back with three pints of the farmhouse cider. Morgan did not pay; that would be done when he left. The men took the tankards and set them on the table. Lippy drank thirstily.

'Quiet tonight,' Harry said.

'Aye. See a few more after chapel.'

'Go, what a country,' Morgan said, and drank.

The talk continued, slowly and generally. It was mostly about a new forestry scheme, in the valley beyond Trawsfynydd.

'The wages is good,' Lewis said.

'Aye, have a bash at it myself,' Lippy said.

'There was a letter in the *Gwenton Times*,' Morgan said. 'From Blakely. You see it?'

'He's a friend of yours now, isn't he?' Lewis said.

'I do business with him. I do business where I have to.'

'I can't see he's right,' Harry said. 'Pines it is they have to grow. Why not?'

'Aye, only Blakely said "the uncivilized intrusion of an alien landscape into one of our unspoiled native valleys".'

'Native!' Lewis said. 'Him!'

'I've seen pine forests, what's wrong with them,' said one of the other men.

'There's a vested interest, I tell you,' Morgan said, tapping his cigarette. 'A vested interest in keeping this countryside barren. They've mucked up half Wales and half England, and now the Black

Mountains they say is good, it's empty. So keep out of it, it's for us to look at.'

'I'll be up there, you watch me,' Lippy said. 'Three pound a week they reckon.'

'Aye,' Morgan said. 'Only that's for working.'

'That's what I said.'

'Aye, that's what you said.'

The door opened, and four men came in. One of them was Jack Meredith. Harry leaned forward and finished his cider.

'Evening, Jack,' Morgan called.

Meredith swung round, looking first at Harry and then at Morgan.

'I don't want no bloody words from you mate. You can keep them to sell your currants.'

'Have a drink, Jack,' Harry offered.

'I'll have my own drink,' Meredith said, and turned away.

Morgan smiled and looked round the room.

'Come on, Lippy,' he said suddenly. 'Do us a bit of boxing.'

'I can't,' Lippy said, getting up.

'Come on, mun, come on. Liven things up. Here's old Jack Meredith now. He likes a bit of fighting.'

'Shall I?' Lippy asked, looking to the landlord.

'Don't hurt me, mun.'

'Righto then,' Lippy said, and took off his jacket. He walked to the open stone floor by the window. He raised his hands and began squaring and hunching his shoulders. He was so small, his chest and forearms so thin, that this in itself was always enough to set the others laughing.

'Promising flyweight, they called me,' Lippy said. 'In the paper up home.'

'Fly on then,' Morgan shouted.

'Right,' Lippy said, and lifted his fists into a guard. With a sudden intense concentration, he scuffed his boots along the stone floor, and began to dance backward and forward, his thin body weaving, his fists leading and guarding, his face grim.

'Warm her up,' Morgan shouted.

Lippy wiped his nose with the back of his hand, and went into an intense flurry of shadowed blows, his body weaving continually, his boots scuffing on the stone floor.

'You've got him. Finish him off,' Morgan shouted, laughing. Lippy seemed to respond to the call, although by now he was so closely shut in by the imaginary circle of his boxing, his eyes half-closed with the effort, that he seemed beyond reach. Faster and faster came the flurry of blows on the air; faster and faster the weaving of the frail body; fiercer the expression on the weak, blurred, sweating face. The other men watched stolidly, while the furious exhibition continued.

'That's enough now,' Harry said at last, but Lippy was past stopping. Stumbling on the uneven flagstones, he continued to launch his flailing attack on the air, sniffing repeatedly, and once letting out an angry gasp, as if he had been hit. Harry got up. Lippy was now quite beside himself, as always at the climax of these exhibitions. As the frantic movement continued, Harry walked across, and held Lippy's shoulders. Lippy continued to lash out, staring strangely up into his face.

'Righto, that was fine.'

Lippy stopped suddenly, and looked around.

'Was it, Harry? Was it really all right?'

'Most promising flyweight I've seen in years, mun,' Morgan said, from the bench.

'Aye, only Rosser's a liar,' Meredith said loudly, 'so what's that count?'

There was a sudden silence, and Morgan stood up. Meredith looked across at him, holding his glass.

'Say that again, Jack.'

'I said you was a liar. A liar, an underhand dealer, and no bloody good to anybody.'

Morgan had gone very white, but did not move.

'Jack, you're an old mate of mine. But if you wasn't older than me I'd thrash you for that.'

'Try it, Rosser. I've dealt with yappy dogs afore.'

'We're going,' Harry said. 'Come on, Lippy.'

Morgan was still white, and his fists were clenched.

'No, wait, Harry. You're a fair-minded chap. Act as a judge now, straight, between Jack Meredith and me.'

'I'm not a judge. Come on.'

'No, but fair, Harry. You got to be fair. He reckons I've done him down, but before God I've not. He could have had what Blakely's having, and he turned it down.'

'You put him up to getting my fields,' Meredith shouted. 'For years they've been mine. We don't need you telling us what to grow. Get home where you come from.'

'You see, Harry. It's no use. No reason in it.'

'Men get across each other,' Lewis said. 'No use making it worse.'

Harry was looking down at the floor where Lippy had been fighting.

'I've told Jack,' he said. 'He knows how I feel.'

'Then tell your mate.'

'I've told him, too. But he's gone his own way, and now he's got his work, like we all have.'

'Leave it, Harry,' Morgan said.

Harry looked at Meredith.

'Jack done me a good turn. Years back. He knows I've not forgotten it.'

Meredith smiled.

'I done you no good turn, nor nobody else. One thing I've learned, I'll tell you. That's every man for himself. Nobody else will help you.'

'That's what you made out then. That's what's happening now.'

'Come on,' Morgan said, 'let's get in the car.'

'Yes. Good night, Jack,' Harry said.

Meredith did not answer, and he turned away awkwardly.

'Good night all, then,' Morgan called.

There was a general murmur of good night. The three went out, and got into the car. A minute later, with the headlamps shining along the steep banks of the hedges, they were back across the border.

4

In Will's fifth year in the grammar school in Gwenton, Harry was called in by the headmaster to discuss future plans. There was a possibility of a university scholarship, but obviously this would be a serious commitment, and a great deal would depend on the attitude at home.

'It's what I want.' Harry said.

'Well, that's something. It's also what we want, here at school. Only you see how it is, Mr Price. This is the local school, the boys come in here and it helps them to get decent jobs. But that's just here, the world they know. Going away altogether, into a quite different world, that would be very much more difficult.'

'He'd go for a degree, is that right?'

'Well yes, yes. Of course if he got the scholarship.'

'It's what I want,' Harry repeated, sitting up very stiff on his chair. 'As for going away, we all have to do that when our work makes it necessary.'

'Is it only that, though, Mr Price? Like me say, moving to a school in Gloucester, or you to a signal-box in Swindon or Merthyr?'

'It's moving,' Harry said. 'None of us is doing what our fathers were doing. None of us is living quite as they lived.' The headmaster looked carefully at him, across the desk.

'You may be right. I don't know.'

'That's how it seems to me.'

'Well, if you're happy about it, that's the main thing. Who's the vicar now, in your parish?'

'Pugh.'

'Yes, I have met him. Matthew goes to church, of course?'

'Yes. Not regularly though.'

'It might be an advantage – you know, getting all the help we can – to get Pugh, if he would, to talk to Matthew. It might help.'

'Yes.'

'And we here will do all we can. It's been very pleasant meeting you, Mr Price.'

'Thank you,' Harry said. 'And I'll talk to Mr Pugh, and to Matthew.'

It was the first time he had used the name, in talking about Will. He found, as he went out, that it had pleased him.

Later that week, he called on the vicar and found him very willing to help.

'Though I don't know what I can say, Mr Price. Don't want to bring him up here just to talk at him.'

'I appreciate that.'

'Would he be interested, do you think, in my telescope? I've got a little telescope, it's a hobby you know.'

'I'm sure he would.'

'Do you ever look at the stars, Mr Price?'

'Yes. On nights when it's clear.'

'It's a bad habit, in one way. It throws you out a bit, don't you think?'

'From what?'

'From the way we think in the day, when we're working.'

'No, I've not felt that. Unless you mean religion.'

'I wasn't meaning religion.'

'Feeling alone perhaps?'

'That, yes. And then just wondering about it all.'

'We get to live with that.'

'Yes, I think you do,' Pugh said.

'Only I don't find it helps. The religion.'

'I know. I accept that,' Pugh said, and got up. 'But at times it helps me.'

'Yes.'

'Anyway, send Matthew up any evening except Wednesday. I'll be glad to have him.'

Will went up for the first time on the following Friday, when there was less homework. At first the telescope was the main interest. Pugh set it up on the tower of the church, to which they climbed on the dusty ladders past the bells. It was wonderful to come out on to the roof of the tower and look out over the valley to the mountains.

Everywhere above them the sky was clear, though at their backs, to the east, the mass of the Holy Mountain shortened the horizon. Standing on the leaded roof, Pugh showed Will the major constellations. The first effect was a heightening of the quality of the valley. To see, in the winter sky, the great shape of Orion, walking above the ridge of Darren, was to move into a different dimension. To look up on the great starlit nights, and see shapes and patterns which he had not known, was a new and unlooked-for growth.

He knew very well the village opinion of Pugh. He seemed a man isolated from them, sad and indifferent, with few of their interests. But where at one extreme this was contempt, Will had taken from Harry a different opinion: Pugh was withdrawn, but for reasons that ought to be respected. Pattern was the word that Will grasped at, through the crowded impressions of these first weeks. There was never any talk of religion, and very little of books. But there were the stars, endlessly exciting, and when the sky was overcast there was the microscope, in the untidy study, with slides left haphazard on shelves and chairs and sills, and again there were shapes and patterns that had been closed to the eye. Arthur Pugh was a collector, rather than even an amateur scientist. But the different ways of seeing, whether from the tower or through the microscope in the study, had their deep effect. And at no time was there any kind of personal demand in the growing relationship. Pugh's very withdrawal, which made him so strange and unliked in the village, served now as a virtually impersonal medium, through which Will passed to new bearings and new interests. Pugh himself might have forgotten the original point of his invitation. Certainly, for some months, nothing of the kind was mentioned.

Pugh brought the matter up at last: obviously deliberately, but in his own indirect way.

'Formerly, you know, Matthew, I should have been educating you, and then sending you on, later, to the cathedral.'

'What for, sir?'

Pugh misunderstood the question.

'What for? Yes, now we ask what for. I've had to learn, since I came here, that they always ask what for, when they think of me or of the Church.'

Will said nothing. He was too shy to rephrase the question, to give the meaning he had intended. Also, he knew the truth of what Pugh was saying. It was an attitude he had absorbed.

'The real life here, Matthew, is the growing and the selling. At least it often seems so, seems no more. But that isn't fair. The real life, for these people, is each other. Even their religion is for each other.'

'Isn't that right, sir?'

'I'm not saying it's wrong, I'm just looking at it. The members of the chapels now are all good people, very good people, and there are far, far more of them, I'm afraid, than ever come to my own services. But then, when I look at what the chapels do, I understand this. The chapels are for people to meet, and to talk to each other or sing together. Around them, as you know, moves almost the whole life of the village. That, really, is their religion.'

'Is it, sir?'

'The chapels are social organizations, Matthew. The church here is not. I don't mean that their religious professions are insincere, but they could equally, it seems to me, be professions in almost anything – any other system of belief, for instance. What matters, what holds them together, is what their members do, through them, for each other. God, you might say, is their formula for being neighbourly.'

'Being neighbours is right, though.'

'Yes, it's right. That's why they're so successful. But here, for instance, what can I offer of the same kind? Almost everything I've tried to do in the village – less than I should have done – has broken down on that. They're the real local organization, you see. I'm just a sort of outpost.'

'Outpost of what, sir?'

'There are ways of thinking,' Pugh said, 'ways that have no roots here, but are nevertheless alive. Religion, I would say, is one of them.'

Will hesitated, looking across at this sad, awkward man with something of the excitement of when he had first, from the tower, been shown the figure of Orion.

'You wouldn't want to say that to them, sir. That they haven't got any religion.'

'But they have, you see. In their own terms. And they are good people. The thing is, can you expect people to have religion. It always surprises me.'

'Why, sir?'

'Because it really is a very rare thing to know God. Can we expect it to be otherwise? But it's an easy thing to go with your parents to chapel, and to grow up in that. Knowing the things you say when you are there; learning, there and elsewhere, your duties as a person. With that as religion, they are of course religious. But to know God, to know what we mean when we say we know God: that on the whole is almost incredible.'

'There are people who don't believe in God.'

'Yes. There are good people who don't. I, you know, may even be one of them.'

'That's impossible, sir.'

'No, no. In an English parish, with a full congregation, I'd have enough to do for it to work out in the usual ways. I'd know I was doing good work and could say I was serving God. Here, with so little to do, I'm not granted that. I have to put these questions to myself, and there are so few answers.'

'My father says that.'

'That there are so few answers? Yes. Your father is a very unusual man.'

'Do you think so?'

'He takes the usual ways, Matthew, as far as he can. He lives, I have seen him, in a very full way, with his work and his neighbours. But I have seen him, also, at the very edge of his understanding, and he is not the man to pretend.'

'I suppose that's right, sir?'

'Right and wrong have so little to do with it. There isn't that much choice; at least I've learned that. And there is more than one kind of outpost. Your father is not a religious man, in any way. I know enough of religion to insist on that, and not to mind about it.'

'You keep saying outpost, sir. I still don't quite understand.'

Arthur Pugh went to the window, where the curtains were undrawn. The silhouette of the tower stood faintly up against the night sky, and above it, very dark, was the mass of the Holy Mountain.

'They call that mountain holy,' Pugh said, 'because once in a time of persecution men met there, secretly, to worship and build an altar of the stones. We make too much of persecution, Matthew. Every cause, good and bad, has had its martyrs, yet there are some foolish enough to think martyrdom sanctifying. Just as I said outpost. There are outposts of everything: many of them are bad.'

'Which is this you mean, sir?'

'I meant the Church, Matthew. But I don't know, it seems an extravagant way of talking. If there were a cathedral out there, but still the mountain would dwarf it. Yet the cathedrals, the universities. Perhaps I am too much away from them. Perhaps they are only the Glynmawr chapels, better built. Only as institutions, sometimes, they seem more. That, at least, you must go and see for yourself.'

'I should like to go, sir.'

'It'll be all right. If not for one reason, then for another. We can tell them, can't we, you're doing it to get on?'

'My dad would say yes to that, sir.'

'Yes, he would. I said he was honest.'

'They told me once, you know, sir, talking. If I did well at school I could get a good job: five pounds a week even.'

'That's enough reason, isn't it?'

'Yes, sir, it is.'

'Let's leave it at that then. Because it's never a choice between the letter and the spirit. Besides, your choice was made, years ago. I don't need to advise you.'

'My father asked you to, sir.'

'You don't need another father, Matthew. He asked me not for the way, but for the start.'

'But it's outside his experience, sir, isn't it? This sort of going away?'

'You could say that. But experience isn't only what's happened to us. It's also what we wanted to happen.'

Will did not answer. They were standing together near the door.

'I think it's for him as much as for you,' Pugh said. 'And I want you to see that, as I saw it in him. That a life lasts longer than the actual body through which it moves.'

5

Eira was eighteen, and Will seventeen. Every weekend, now, they went out somewhere together. Will had drawn up a list of places they should visit, that were written about in the county history but in ordinary life only rarely visited. They went to each of the border castles, to the old churches, to the ruined abbey in Trawsfynydd, to the Kestrel and the Stone of Treachery. They had known each other so long that they got on easily, but the relationship was changing, in each of them, and they were both aware of this and yet inarticulate. Always, at each weekend, there was the new place to go.

One day in early summer they had been walking on Darren. They stopped in a favourite hollow out of the wind, where they could look down over Glynmawr to the Holy Mountain and Gwenton. Eira sat spreading her legs, her hands cupped in the billlow of her wide yellow skirt. Will looked down at her and then walked a little away. A stream was trickling from a small outcrop of rock just above them. At a black ledge, it fell in a white jet of water, and then spread again into a dark, shallow pool. Will went to the ledge and lay beside it. He cupped his hands into the jet and brought a little of the sharp cold water up to his mouth. Then he eased forward, twisting his body over his arm. He lowered his head and turned his lips until he could drink. The water came in ice-cold spurts against his teeth, and splashed over his face and neck. As he drew up, he saw Eira coming across to him.

'You going to try?'

'Yes. Mind.'

He went back on his knees, and she lay beside him. She cupped her hands as he had done, then reached forward and turned her head. He put his hands on her shoulders, and held her as she strained down. As the water touched her face she cried out, shocked by the cold, and jerked back her head.

'Go on,' Will said, gripping her shoulders.

'Yes. Only it's so cold. Hold me.'

Her hair fell loose as she strained to the sharp white water. Will felt under his hands her quick breath, and saw the water splashing on her face and hair. Widening her mouth, she drank quickly, feeling the cold of the water back through her body. Will felt the movement of her shoulders under his hands, and his fingers tightened as he drew her up. She turned to him, laughing, and for a moment rested her head against his arm. Then she stood up and brushed down her dress. He stood by her, watching her.

'We'd better get on down, Will.'

As she spoke she was pushing back her thick hair, which had fallen around her face.

'Yes. If we must.'

'You coming in with me on the bus?'

'Why not?'

'You don't have to.'

'I'll come.'

Eira smiled, and turned on to the path. Will bent down, and pulled at a stem of bracken. He felt the sharp cut of it in his hand.

'Watch, Will. That can be bad.'

'Can it? I always do it.'

'Come on. Is it all right?'

'Yes,' he said, looking down at his hand. The skin was crossed by a sharp red line, but was not broken. Eira took his hand, and looked at it for a moment. Then they walked on down.

As they were getting near the road, Eira said:

'There, Mam said Alun was coming to tea.'

'Is he?'

'You know they're not keeping him at Cardiff?'

'So I heard.'

Eira stopped and looked into his face.

'What's the matter, Will?'

'Nothing.'

'Well there is, I can see.'

Will looked away, and they walked on for a while without speaking.

'Why do you call her your Mam?' Will asked. 'She's not, so why call her it?'

'But she's been my Mam, since they got married.'

'It's still wrong. What they do doesn't make it different.'

'What should I call her? Stepmother sounds nasty.'

'If it's nasty, say it.'

'But it isn't nasty, it only sounds it.'

'If it sounds it, it is.'

'No, Will,' Eira said, stopping. She smiled and looked carefully up at him. 'What is it? What's really the matter?'

Will moved away. He had picked up a stick and was bending it, to near breaking-point, between his hands.

'Nothing's the matter. What could be the matter? You're like my own Mam, getting at me.'

'She doesn't, Will. Really she doesn't.'

'I know. If anyone feels anything, tell them they don't. Or in any case that they oughtn't to. Then rub it all out. Be a good boy. Be somebody else.'

'Tell me, Will. What is it?'

'It's nothing I can tell you.'

'Is it Alun?'

'Alun? Him!'

'Well, when I said he was coming you started like this.'

'No, I don't think so. It was sooner.'

'When?'

'When we came off the mountain.'

'We had to come down.'

'Did we?'

Eira remembered suddenly the cold of the water against her mouth. She looked away, confused, and they again walked on.

'Not retained,' Will said. 'Hybart A. not retained.'

'Well, that's not Alun's fault, is it?'

'Not his fault, no. If you're not good enough, they send you back. It's not your fault, you've just got to go back.'

'Well?'

'What did they take him for, if they don't want to keep him? What they start it for, if they can't go on?'

'It was a trial. They said that.'

'No. He had the trial and they said he was good enough. Then a few games in the third team, and everybody waiting for him to go on up. Then no they say. Go home. We don't want you.'

'You talk as if you liked Alun.'

'Do I?'

'You don't like him, Will, and you never have.'

'What makes you so sure? What do you know about who I like?'

'You make me mad, Will. Look, it's me, Eira. You don't have to pretend.'

'We do damn little else, seems to me.'

'Pretend? Us?'

'What else, Eira? What else do we do?'

She turned away, putting her hand up to her face.

'Come on, we'll get the bus.'

Will stopped and brought the ends of the stick round till they touched. The bark and the first fibres split and cracked. He whirled round, holding the stick, and then threw it high and far away across the field.

'Dear, come on,' Eira called, holding her hand out towards him. He hesitated, and then walked up to her. He took her hand, and they walked to the road.

222

As they waited for the bus, they did not talk. It was much warmer in the valley, and they sat in the long grass of the hedge bank, content and rested. When the bus came they found a seat together, but again they did not talk, for the bus was crowded. They got out at the Town Hall, and walked slowly through the quiet streets to the bungalow.

Morgan was standing with Alun by the neat white gate, on which the name, 'Mountain View', stood out in black letters on a deckled walnut board. Morgan's new car, gleaming in the sun, stood where the grass met the steep unmade road. They were walking hand-in-hand as they approached the bungalow, but Eira pulled her hand away when she saw her father and Alun. The men stopped talking, and watched them as they came up.

'You're back then?' Morgan said.

He was deeply interested in Eira, and nervous of his interest. He liked Will, but saw him mainly as an aspect of Harry. He was often aware, now, of how much of himself had been left behind in those early days when Harry and Ellen had lodged with him. That was something to look back to, like a childhood. To see Will bringing Eira home took him back to that best part of his days in Glynmawr.

'Been far, Will?' he asked.

Will hesitated, and Eira answered.

'Up on Darren.'

'You're growing up, Shaver,' Alun said, smiling. He had got much heavier and his face was redder since he had been away. Will looked at him awkwardly. It was a long time since anyone but Alun had called him Shaver. He remembered how Elwyn had offered to fight anyone who did.

'Still at school then?'

'Yes.'

'Getting a bit fed up with it, I expect?'

'No.'

Morgan smiled and looked from Alun to Will. Eira had gone on to the gate, and he turned and spoke to her.

'Your Mam could do with some help, I expect.'

'Yes,' Eira said, and went in.

'Won't you stay, Will?' Morgan asked. 'Have some tea with us. Or at least not with me, I've got to be off. But go on in with Alun.'

'No, I ought to get back, thank you.'

'How's your Dad keeping?'

'All right, I think.'

'And your Mam?'

'Yes.'

Morgan hesitated. Will could see that he was nervous, but he could not imagine why.

'Tell your Dad I met someone the other day he'll remember.'

'Yes?'

'Old Rees, the stationmaster. You wouldn't remember him, I expect.'

'Yes, just about.'

'He's coming up to retire this autumn. And you'd hardly believe. He looks a real old man.'

'They kicked him out, didn't they?' Alun said.

'No, no. Transferred him. After he joined in the strike.'

'I remember Dad talking about it,' Will said.

'They were bad times then, mind,' Morgan said. 'And don't either of you forget it. They don't have no mercy on you if they can pick you out.'

'You're glad to be rid of it I expect,' Alun said.

'No. No, I wouldn't say that. If I believed the workers of this country could win – and I do believe it, mind, in the long run – I'd chuck all this up tomorrow, and go back.'

Will looked at him, carefully.

'What for, mun?' Alun asked. 'You're doing a lot better at this.'

'Aye, perhaps. What you think, Will? You going to take up politics?'

'No, Mr Rosser. Not as far as I can see.'

Morgan threw down his cigarette, and carefully ground it out with his heel.

'There's only one real politics, and that's politics on a weekly wage. All the rest, well. We can all talk.'

'I keep out of it,' Alun said. 'They're all the same. Just out for themselves.'

'So you see it,' Will said. 'Just people trying to get on.'

'You know nothing about it, Shaver. Your old man's carried you. You've never come across it.'

'How do you know what politics is then?' Will said. 'You said you keep out of it.'

He felt an anger behind his eyes, that was also the risk of crying.

'When you get out from behind your books,' Alun said, 'you'll find it all a bit different, I promise you. You don't know you've started yet. At school they drag you on as a kid.'

'I've heard about it. I can read it.'

'Reading is nothing. You don't feel it till it happens to yourself.'

'All right, then. Let it happen.'

'That's bloody hero stuff, boy. Wait till they really size you up, see what they'll give you. Then you'll howl.'

'All right, Alun. We'll howl together.'

'Don't you give me no lip now. I'm telling you for your own good.'

Will looked past him, at the bungalow. He could see Eira moving in the room on the right of the door.

'Different people tell different things. I'll make up my own mind,' he said.

'All right, only I'm telling you. Don't think you're something special. It'll come to you like the rest of us.'

'I heard you.'

'And when it does, mind, you'll wish you were back in school. Still behind your books, with ideas of yourself. It comes hard when you're really out on your own. I've had a taste of it.'

'Well, no use us quarrelling,' Morgan said, walking across. 'You're both right, you know. And I'm not just saying that to make it up. It comes hard, as Alun says, and yet still you have to have a go at it. I've had more experience of both than either of you.'

'He's had none,' Alun said.

'We're all unfair to each other, that's what,' Morgan said. 'When you're Will's age you think a man like me's not quite real. Morgan

Rosser you know. Got his little business. What else's he want? And me the same, looking at you two. Two lads, just starting out, what they worried about? Wherever it is, Will, it hurts.'

Eira came to the front door and called that tea was ready.

'Aye, you go on, Alun,' Morgan said. 'Sure you won't stay, Will?'

'Sure.'

'Come on, boy, I'll give you a lift down.'

'Won't it take you out of your way?'

'How could it now? Look,' Morgan said.

It was hot in the car, with the sharp smell of the bright leather seats.

'Try and see it from Alun's side,' Morgan said, as the car drew away. 'A man disappointed in the life he thought was opening up for him. No use turning it back into something general. When a man's known that, nothing else seems important. We look at it from outside, but it's inside that it hurts and goes on hurting. What is a man for but that? He wants to be himself, not somebody else's idea of him.'

'It looks like just getting on,' Will said. 'Being praised and noticed.'

'Do that matter, Will, if it feels wrong inside him? Notice or money, do they matter against that?'

'I don't know, Mr Rosser.'

'Think of your Dad, Will. Think of it his way.'

Will did not answer. He was not used, from a man, to this touching of open feeling. He had often watched his father, wanting feeling to come. But now, when Morgan moved closer, he wanted the feeling to stop. The usual distances seemed preferable.

'I liked seeing you bring Eira home, Will.'

'Yes?'

'When your Mam and Dad lived with me, she was just a baby, and you born a few months after.'

Will could not answer. He was watching the green dome of the Town Hall below them. It seemed a safe, fixed point.

'Your Dad and me have always got on well, through it all. He'd be glad.'

Glad. Will said over to himself. Glad of what? He stared out through the windscreen, and Morgan did not speak again. In the town, the car drew up at the market bus-stop. Morgan leaned across Will to open the door.

'Tell your Dad I'll be out to see him, soon as I get a chance. What's he on this week?'

'Nights, I think.'

'You think. Aye, well, it may be some time. Only there's two or three things I want to tell him about.'

6

Morgan came out a fortnight later, with Eira. She carried a case of jars in to Ellen, while Will stood with Morgan in the lane.

'Your Dad's just coming,' Morgan said. 'I passed him on the pitch.'

'Aye, been doing the green.'

'How he rides that old bike of his! Slam on those pedals like he's breaking a horse.'

'Aye, he don't waste much time,' Will said, looking back to the house for Eira. Harry came into sight, riding carefully now, with a half-sack of grass clippings slung over his shoulder.

'Catch,' he shouted to Will, and threw the sack. He was laughing as he ran his bike along the hedge under the holly.

'You still on with the green?' Morgan asked. 'I shouldn't have thought it was worth it.'

'It's nothing much,' Harry said, getting his breath.

'What they pay you? They've raised it a bit, I suppose?'

'No, still the same.'

'Go, mun, they're making a fool of you. Ask them for double.'

Harry took the sack from Will, smiling at him.

'It's easier than it was. It's come lovely and level, and the rolling's nothing like so bad.'

Morgan lit a new cigarette from the end of the one he had been smoking.

'What shall we do with this father of yours, Will?'

'It's no use arguing with him anyhow.'

'Never give up hope, boy.'

'I don't ask him to do it,' Harry said. 'Or you.'

Morgan laughed, moving along past the side of the car.

'Nice little job for Will, that'd be.'

Harry smiled again. Looking at him Will thought how pleasant his smile was, so easy, so open, and still very young. It was the surprise, perhaps, of the sudden break from the ordinary seriousness. The lines of the face were set very deeply now, and the black hair had thinned and receded, leaving a high, prominent forehead. He had thickened considerably in the body, especially in the chest and shoulders. The grey shirt, with no collar, was open all down the chest. The braces were drawn tight on the heavy black serge trousers, of which the top button, at the waistband, was always undone. The belt was wide and stained black. The black boots were clean but not polished, light working boots. As Harry stood by the hedge, the contrast with Morgan was sharp. Morgan had gone grey, but the hair was still thick and closely curled. He also was much heavier in the body, but the fit of his tidy, dark suit controlled the weight into a neat solidity. The face was plump and the skin fairly smooth and clear, shining a little above the gleaming white waxed collar. It was still a very pleasant face, open and regular. The teeth were good, even and white. Only in the hands was there less difference than might have been expected. Morgan's were actually larger than Harry's and quite dark-skinned. Harry's were pale and slender, as if they had never worked.

'Aye, well, dump your things, Harry. I want to take you all for a bit of a ride in the car.'

'Now?'

'When d'you think, mun?'

'A bit later would be better. I got one or two things.'

'All right, all right. I've got all the time in the world. Go on, I'll stand and watch you.'

'Billy's waiting in the back-kitchen, Dad.'

'Who?' Morgan asked.

'The Hybarts' new lodger,' Harry said. 'Billy Devereux. You should see him.'

'What's he here for then?'

'I have to shave him. They don't let him have a razor.'

'What, dangerous?'

'Aye, to himself.'

They walked through the garden to the porch. Billy Devereux was sitting very upright on a hard chair by the copper. He was about fifty, very small, with grey hair. He had a drooping moustache, pale watery eyes, and an ugly pocked nose. It was said that he came from a very good family, and there was certainly plenty of money to maintain him. He could be trusted to do very little for himself, but he came in every other day to be shaved by Harry, and proudly handed over his own threepence. When he talked, as he sometimes did, Will listened intently to an accent he had only heard in the voice of one other actual person, Major Blakely. But Devereux's accent was gentler than Blakely's; softer, more liquid, more evidently refined. Devereux seemed to resent Will staring at him when he talked, and would move peevishly, wrinkling his big nose.

'By the window, then, if you would,' Harry said. Devereux looked round suspiciously, and then sat with great care and precision on the hard chair facing the sink. Harry took an apron of Ellen's and tied it round Devereux's neck. A kettle was ready boiling on the stove, and he filled his big shaving mug from it.

'Look up, will you?' he said, lathering the brush on the side of the mug. Morgan moved around to watch, and winked at Will. Devereux noticed this, and moved uneasily.

'Still now,' Harry said, and began lathering the slack jowls and chin, and the scrawny neck. Will watched the lather coming up, as the brush was dipped again and again in the scalding water.

'You like Glynmawr, Mr Devereux?' Morgan asked cheerfully.

'Yes,' Devereux said, in a quick, frightened voice.

'It's a nice place, isn't it? But you ought to get about a bit.'

'I get about,' Devereux said, with a startled gentleness.

Harry put down the brush, and unfolded his big razor, which he stropped on his stained belt, drawn out from a hook by the sink. Will watched the long shining blade of the razor, turning over and over on the black leather. Devereux, he noticed, was also watching it, his light blue eyes intent and fixed.

'Right then, your head right back,' Harry said, moving behind the chair. He had torn a piece of newspaper and laid it over the edge of the sink.

The shaving began, the bristles grating at each stroke. When the blade was charged with the lather, in which grey and brown bristles stood out in a mottling grain, he wiped it on the newspaper, and then went back to the face. His hand rested lightly on top of Devereux's head. When the razor was at the face, neither of the others dared to speak.

'There, you look very nice,' Morgan said at last, when the shaving had finished. Devereux sniffed, looked up at him and did not answer.

'Wipe your face with this towel,' Harry said, untying the apron.

'I expect you find it a bit dull here,' Morgan tried again.

'Dull?' Devereux said wonderingly. As he looked up, Will could see that his nostrils were still clogged with lather.

'Not much to do, I mean.'

Devereux looked at him again and got up, wiping nervously around his face with the towel.

'Your nose. In your nose,' Harry said.

'Oh yes,' Devereux said, embarrassed. 'Yes, of course.'

He wiped his nose with the towel, while Morgan smiled. Then he put the towel down, and felt in his pocket for his purse. He looked down into the purse for a long time before at last drawing out three pennies.

'Thank you, Mr Price,' he said, holding out the pennies, but almost taking them back as they touched Harry's hand.

'Thank you,' Harry said.

Devereux looked around nervously. His grey suit was of a fine cloth, though the white shirt and black tie were ordinary.

'My hat,' he said, still looking around.

'Here,' Morgan said, taking the small bowler hat from the lid of the copper.

'Thank you.'

Devereux snatched the hat, looked inside it, then placed it carefully on his head.

'Good day,' he said, nodding to Harry and Will. Then, still looking nervously round him, he walked out through the garden to the lane.

Morgan watched him through the window and then turned.

'You'll have a funny idea of the world, Will, if you go by this place.'

'Billy's harmless,' Harry said, putting his razor away.

'Only the rate of madness,' Morgan said, 'in this sort of healthy country, would be worth counting. And that's just straight bloody lunatics, not the things they get up to in public and expect you to admire.'

Will smiled but said nothing.

'Why don't you count it then?' Harry said and put the chair back under the table.

Morgan laughed, and walked out to the porch. He rested his hand against one of the old wooden posts and then pulled it away quickly.

'Be bringing this down if I lean on it,' he said to Will.

'It'll stand a good many years yet,' Harry said from inside.

'All right, all right, Harry. But now are you ready to come?'

'No, I promised to wait here till half past three. Young Elwyn might come.'

'He'll be all right, mun.'

'No, I'll wait till the time.'

Morgan looked at his watch.

'All right, I've got one more call. I'll be back half past three.'

He started down the path, calling Eira as he went. She was upstairs with Ellen, and seemed not to hear.

'Eira,' Morgan shouted again.

'Yes,' she answered, startled, from the window of Will's bedroom.

'Hurry up, girl. We're going to see Blakely.'

'I thought we were all going in the car.'

'Aye, after.'

'Well, do you want me now?'

'Would I call you, girl, if I didn't? Come on.'

'Right,' Eira said and hurried downstairs. Will moved away, so that he would not see her as she went out. He stayed round the corner, by the big damson tree, until he heard the car start and move away. Then he walked slowly back into the living-room, where Harry and Ellen were talking. They looked round, disturbed, as he came in.

'I think I'll go out, Mam.'

'No, they'll be back soon.'

'Do they want me? Why?'

'Morgan's taking us in the car.'

'Blast his car. Do we have to wait for free rides? It makes me sick, the way you both let him order you about. You'd think he was God Almighty, the way he talks to you all.'

'It isn't ordering, Will. He's a friend.'

'If he's such a friend,' Will said, looking straight at his father, 'why didn't you go in with him, like he kept asking?'

Harry hesitated, looking at Ellen.

'That's different,' he said at last. 'You don't have to do what your friend does. You make up your own mind.'

'You'd have made more money by it, wouldn't you?'

'Aye, perhaps. Only there's other considerations.'

'Such as what?'

Harry pushed his fingers back over his thin hair.

'Don't keep on at your Dad now,' Ellen said.

'I'm only asking a simple question.'

'You do what you see your way to,' Harry said. 'I'm not telling you what to do with your life, and I never told Morgan.'

'That's no answer, is it?' Will said quickly. 'Anyway, you did tell me. You wanted me to go on at school. You sent me up to Pugh's for him to persuade me. Why deny it when you did?'

'It was for your own good, Will,' Ellen said. 'It was what you'd really want.'

232

'That's what I'm saying. Only it's one law for me and a different one for you. You'd got this course mapped out for me, and that was that.'

'Don't shout at your Mam,' Harry said.

'I'm shouting at you, Dad. Everything in this house is kept under so much, it needs shouting.'

'When you go from here,' Harry said, 'it's your own life. Till then, it's ours. What we've done for you we've done as we thought best. If you don't think so, you can go your own way. Only don't, since this is our house, try and tell us what to do in it.'

'It's mine too, isn't it? I can have my own say.'

'You're having it.'

'Yes and I've a damn good mind to clear out. I'm sick of blasted school and swotting and the whole outfit. I could clear out now and get myself a job.'

'Better not do anything in haste, Will,' Ellen said quietly.

'If a thing's worth doing, it's worth doing straight out.'

He was answering his mother, and looking at her, but it was his father's response he was waiting for.

'Well?' he asked, as Harry still looked down. 'Shall I do that? Shall I leave school and get a job?'

Harry moved across to the hearth. He reached up to the clock and wound it slowly. Will watched him, staring at the heavy neck and shoulders.

'I asked you a question, Dad.'

Harry turned with the key in his hands. He hesitated and then put the key back on the mantelpiece: gently, so that it made no sound.

'You might at least answer him, Dad,' Ellen said.

'He'll answer himself.'

'What does that mean? Nothing,' Will said.

Harry rubbed his hand over his eyes, which were sore and reddened. In the last few months, this soreness had been noticeable, particularly after nights, with the shortened sleep.

'All right,' he said. 'You set yourself a job, you finish it. Agreed, the job may be wrong, you might have done better. But get the habit when it's difficult of stopping and going off somewhere else, then it's not the job's useless – that may not matter – but you, you yourself. Nobody sets himself what he doesn't want. What you set yourself you wanted, or you seemed to want it. And now it isn't the chance you'd be missing, I don't care so much about that. Only once turn aside from what you've set yourself, once keep back just a bit of your strength, and then whatever happens, succeeding or whatever it is, whatever the others say, still it don't matter what you get, you're finished with yourself. You can get everything, only never get over stopping that one bit of yourself, saying no to that and letting the no grow through you, whatever the rest say yes to. So go on. I can't say it. Choose for yourself.'

Will looked away, and Harry watched him carefully.

'I'll try, Dad,' Will said at last.

Soon Morgan and Eira were back, in the car.

'You're back quick,' Ellen said, as they came down the path.

'I don't waste time, it's valuable,' Morgan said. 'You ready, Harry?'

'Aye, more or less. Get a collar on.'

'I'll leave the washing-up,' Ellen said. 'It's my fault, I was late with the dinner, and then we were talking.'

'I'll turn the car. Go on, Eira, you and Will get in.'

Harry took his collar and tie from a peg above the long dresser. Ellen hurried upstairs and came down in her new blue coat and hat. As Harry came out, she was standing with Morgan.

'Come on, mun, I been talking secrets with your wife.'

'That's as good as with me then,' Harry said, shutting the door.

'You know where I'm taking you?'

'Aye, more or less.'

'The glass isn't all in, mind, and there's the clearing around to do, but apart from that it's ready.'

'Aye, so I heard. Rosser's new place. They won't say factory.'

'Aye, well, factory seems a bit big. But it's the idea we've all been frightened of.'

234

'Don't tell me you've been frightened, Morgan,' Ellen said.

'Not frightened, Ellen. Just plain terrified. Go on, get in.'

As they went down the lane, Morgan hooted at Lippy, who was clearing the ditch below the Hybarts'. The little man swung round, startled, and did not seem to recognize them.

'This is it,' Morgan said, as they turned into the road. 'This is what I've always wanted.'

The car moved up through the village, and Harry looked out, surprised at the speed with which the familiar ground was being covered, and at the different look this gave to the village. On the corner by the school, three big red lorries were coming in the opposite direction. Morgan slowed to the bank and the lorries brushed noisily past. Harry turned and looked at them.

'Now there, Harry, there, if you ask me, is the future of this place.'

'The lorries?' Ellen asked.

'Aye,' Morgan said, changing down as the car reached the long pitch. 'In ten years, if there's no war...'

'There will be,' Will said.

'Don't say that, Will,' Eira cut in.

'Of course, it's all set up,' Will said, leaning forward.

'Whether or not,' Morgan said, 'this place is finished, as it was. What matters from now on is not the fields, not the mountains, but the road. There'll be no village, as a place on its own. There'll just be a name you pass through, houses along the road. And that's where you'll be living, mind. On a roadside.'

'There's a difference already,' Ellen said. 'With the deliveries from town.'

'Aye. My van was only the start. But even that was local. This won't be. This'll just be a trunk road, you watch, between the mining valleys and the factories in the Midlands. So look carefully at it, you're seeing the last of it.'

'That heavy stuff ought to go by rail,' Harry said.

'Always on the look-out for business, isn't he?' Morgan laughed. 'But a trunk road, you say. Just look at it.'

235

'You're right there,' Morgan said, negotiating the difficult corner near the station. 'It's a nightmare, this road, but they can build a new one. Straight through the middle of you all, you watch. And that'll be it.'

'We'll have to see,' Harry said.

'Harry, if I'd a bit of spare capital, I'd buy one of these pubs by the road, and a bit of land near it. Then I'd set up a pull-in and a bit of a café and just wait. In ten years, I tell you, I'd have scooped the business.'

'You got too many ideas for all at once, Dad,' Eira said. Morgan laughed, letting the wheel run reasily through his fingers.

'It isn't I get the ideas. They're just there, waiting to pick up.'

'It's a way of seeing things,' Harry said. 'You always had it.'

'Perhaps,' Morgan said, and hooted as he went over the bridge above the station. 'Who's on there, Harry? Honest Jack?'

'Jack's on, yes.'

'Merridith as old Blakely calls him. Merridith. He's so damn merry he turns his own milk bad.'

'He'll last.'

'Aye. And if the war comes, him and old Lucas Cefn and the others'll be sitting pretty. Nice little war to put the prices up. Remember, Harry?'

'Lucas said it, yes. He didn't mean harm. He just don't understand.'

'Not understanding is making harm. That's what I've always said, about this whole place. They're back in the past. It's the same wherever you look.'

'Some things change. Some don't.'

'What, for instance?'

Harry did not answer. He was staring out at the high banks of the road. They were on the old road now, under the black ridge of Darren. To the east the valley was wide, curving slowly up to the sharp peak of the Holy Mountain.

'What don't change, Harry?'

Harry shifted in his seat, but did not answer.

'Well, the mountains won't, anyhow,' Will said, behind them.

'Mountains! What do mountains matter? And have some faith in the future, Will. If they're in the way, we'll move them.'

'They won't be in the way.'

'I couldn't bear the mountains to be spoiled,' Eira said.

'Morgan's right,' Harry said suddenly. 'The mountains don't much matter, except to look at. I wasn't thinking of that.'

'You've lived under these mountains all your life and you can say they don't matter,' Will protested.

'It's a feeling about things, that's all. The mountains are just there, that's all about them.'

'You wouldn't talk like that if you went up there more often. All you ever go up for is your bees. If you went up there and looked, really looked, you'd see it.'

'See what, Will?' Morgan asked.

'Well, a different view of things, that's all. Something more than keeping your nose to the ground.'

'Grindstone's the word,' Morgan said. 'And of course, certainly, it's a good view, and the air's nice. Only you can't live on that. At your age, Will – I don't want to go on about your age, it used to annoy me, but still – at your age you get set on things like that. Mountains, stars, seas, distances. A sort of longsightedness. The things close-up are all too difficult.'

'They stay difficult,' Harry said.

'Aye. Only you don't solve them by going and looking from a mountain.'

'No,' Harry said. 'I've had too much to do down here.'

'And that's the size of it. It's what we've all got to come down to.'

Will smiled, nervously. Eira looked at him and pressed her elbow against his arm.

'Well,' Morgan said, 'round the next corner you'll see it.'

They sat forward, feeling their closeness. They went round a long bend, that was fenced with new concrete posts and taut shining wire. The ground fell away towards Gwenton, and at the top was the level field on which Morgan had built. The factory was small, but stood out with its sharp red-brick walls and white asbestos roof. All around it, the site was churned up into ruts of red earth, where the lorries had turned and tipped. Morgan drew the car up by the fence, which had the same concrete posts but now diamond-netted wire.

'Well, here we are.'

'It looks nice, Eira, doesn't it?' Ellen said.

'Oh yes, Auntie. And you should see the boilers in there, all lovely and big and shiny. I told Dad when they once see this there'll be no more old jam-making over the stove.'

'Yes, it's a terrible lot of work the old way.'

Will had walked forward to his father, who was standing inside the fence, testing the ground with his foot. Morgan came up behind him.

'There's a drain over the far side, see, Harry. That line of hedge there.'

'Aye.'

'This'll be all right cleared up. What I'll do is have all this front down to lawn, with a few flowering trees and a bed along the drive. Then round the side and down the back I'll have a sample, as you might say. You know, for show, though we'll use them of course. Currants, raspberries. Strawberries'll be too much upkeep.'

'Aye. Do all right.'

'I wondered, in the front here, about a floral clock. You know, and a sundial or something.'

Harry was walking on, hardly listening. Morgan walked after him, pulling a bunch of keys from his pocket.

'This now,' he said, going in front and unlocking a small door under a small concrete porch. 'This is the staff entrance. Come on, you two girls.'

'Girls indeed,' Ellen laughed, walking up with Eira.

'Well, we look it, anyhow, Auntie.'

Morgan pushed the door open and they went inside.

'Cloakrooms, washplace,' Morgan said, pointing round in the unfinished, hollow-sounding entrance. 'Where you off to, Harry?'

Harry turned and stopped.

'Impatient, isn't he, Ellen? Won't even stop and wash his hands.'

They came out into a square space, with big double doors at the near end. Along the walls, under the high windows, were wide benches and open wooden bins.

'The lorries drive in and back up to the doors, see,' Morgan said, going across to the double doors, and unbolting them. He began pushing them open, though one stuck and he had to heave at it.

'Get that right. Anyhow, unload and then sort.'

Will stood beside Eira on the dusty, concrete floor. Little heaps of wood shavings lay about, and there was a stack of glass against the wall – only half the windows were set.

'Then through here,' Morgan said, moving across. 'Through the arch here, and into the boiling-room.'

Harry led, and they followed through the arch. Eight boilers were set in two rows down the centre of the long room, with a passage between them. At the sides under each wall were wide tables, with cupboards built under them, and shelves above to the level of the higher window-sills. Ellen went across to one of the boilers, and looked inside.

'What you think, Ellen?'

'Lovely. I could come here myself.'

'We jar up see, here, at the side. Then on through, this way, to labelling and packing.'

He pushed back a wide sliding door, into a smaller room lined with narrower work-benches.

'Then the drive continues round the back, see, and we load up again here, at this door, and take away.'

He pointed to the outside door, and then walked to a line of three smaller doors, with a long window above them down from the roof.

'This corner's the offices,' he said, and opened the nearest door. 'Two doors for the main office. One, private, for me.' The others followed, and looked into each of the small rooms in turn.

'And there you are,' Morgan said, standing by the window of the empty office that would be his own. 'Good view from here, look.'

'You can see across home,' Eira said. They all looked out, past the site, to the fields running down to Gwenton. Beyond them was the road running up to 'Mountain View' and the other bungalows, set in their gardens and trees.

'I wanted to see it from the house,' Morgan said to Harry.

'Aye, get up and see it.'

Gwenton station lay where they were looking. A train had stopped in the station and was sending up a line of spreading white smoke. Beyond the box another engine was stopped by the high water-tank.

'Come September and it'll be a bit livelier in here, Harry. I can't stand it now, empty. It don't seem real yet. As it is, it's still in my mind.'

'It's good as it is,' Harry said, staring down at the station. Morgan walked round the bare room, his hands clasped behind his back. Will went out into the packing room, and looked down the length of the building. It seemed to him unimaginably bare and desolate.

'I'm glad you all like it, anyway. I particularly wanted Harry to see it.'

'I should think you're proud of it, Morgan.'

'Yes, Ellen, I am, I don't mind saying. Though I never thought I'd be.'

'It's what this area needs,' Harry said, as they walked back into the packing-room.

They made their way back through the building, and Morgan relocked the doors. When they were in the car again, Morgan sat for some time before starting the engine, but did not speak. When at last he started, he was still silent, and the others, used to him leading the conversation, hardly spoke. The journey back seemed quicker than the one out. The village, as they passed through it again, seemed less unfamiliar. Morgan drove up to the patch and they went into the cottage. Ellen and Eira went to the back-kitchen to get tea. Morgan and Harry and Will sat in the cool, shaded living-room.

'You really like it then, Harry?' Morgan asked, after lighting a cigarette.

'Certainly I do.'

Morgan hesitated, and looked across at Will.

'It's been a bit of a business, I tell you. Four or five of them in Gwenton have come in with me, through Priddy. And the bank's been reasonable. It all really depended on them.'

'Aye, there's a lot to see to in that sort of thing,' Harry said. He had noticed that Morgan's words seemed directed at Will. He saw also how nervous he seemed.

'I don't know, Harry. I've thought and thought about all this. I'd reckoned, as you know, that you'd come in with me.'

'We went into all that. And now, with the factory, you can carry straight on.'

Morgan nodded, and got up. Harry was sitting on the sofa in the middle of the room. After taking a few paces with no obvious purpose, Morgan sat beside him. Will, in a chair by the window, looked across at them as they sat together.

'Aye, Harry, it is different, with the factory. Though the job's there, mind, if you want it. I've never gone back on that.'

'I'm a bit too set in my own ways,' Harry said, sitting forward.

'Go, you talk as if you're an old man,' Morgan said, touching his arm. 'Don't you think so, Will?'

Will could not say anything. It was as if he had no breath. He did not know why he should feel this extra-ordinary tension. It seemed that something was trying to get through to him, some strange pressure that was not even a voice yet that carried an unmistakable attention and warning. He saw Morgan and his father sitting side by side, looking across at him. How would it have been, he thought suddenly, if Morgan had been my father? He immediately looked away, as if the thought had been spoken.

Harry got up and loosened his collar. He was uncomfortable with a collar on in the house for more than a few minutes. Morgan stared out at the lane, which was empty and quiet.

'You haven't said, Will,' he asked. 'Did you like it?'

'Like what?'

'There you are, see.'

241

'When you're young,' Harry said, 'you just see things. There's nothing much to say about them. You don't realize then all the life that's gone into it.'

'The factory?' Will said, coming back.

'I meant the factory,' Morgan said.

'I liked it, of course.'

Morgan shrugged his shoulders and sat back.

'It don't mean much to you though, do it? Like Harry said, what's all the fuss about?'

'I said I liked it.'

'Why?'

'Because it's a nice place. Because, well – it's what you wanted, isn't it?'

'Why did I want it, Will?'

'How should I know? To make jam, I suppose. To make money. That's your work.'

Morgan clapped his hands together.

'Christ, they can be cruel at that age, Harry.'

'Well, what is it for then?' Will asked. He could not focus on the two men in the room. Arguing with Morgan was like arguing with his father. He seemed never to know what the real argument was.

'What do you reckon a man works for, Will? To you, I daresay, the world seems open, there's plenty of time. But there never is, not really. You're into it, you're a man suddenly, and with a wife and a family. Then it's not next year to worry about, or the next stage. It's just the end of the week; that's far enough. People get driven, see, but not just for the money. That's what we don't understand now in politics. We see it as a system, but what it is, at the start, is a man working for his family. Caught, see, and anxious, and knowing he's got to go on.'

'Go on to what, though?' Will said. 'There's more than one kind of work.'

'Is there? There's you, and there's where you are, and that's your answer.'

'A different answer then in every case. You chucked one job, didn't you, and took up another? Dad had this offer from you, and decided to stay where he was.'

'You can argue, Will, but you haven't lived it yet. You don't work for yourself, see, that's what I'm trying to say. For a year or two now, you feel on your own. You think that's all it is, you out on your own.'

'Will's right that there's a purpose to it,' Harry said.

'All right, Harry. Then let's start again from that. You've had a good chance now, Will, at school. What are you going to do with it?'

'I don't know. If I could get to university.'

'That costs money, Will. Lots of money. And what is it, after? Just more school, moving away, getting in with a different lot of people.'

'What's wrong with that?'

Morgan leaned back, smiling. 'You don't know yet, do you? Now I had a point, see, Will, taking you out there this afternoon. You say about university and so on. But look, Will, I've known you since – before you was born, I was almost saying. I've known your Dad and I've worked with him, and it's been always to me like my own family. You as much as Eira.' He looked directly across into Will's face. Will met his eyes, and then looked away. He, too, had been thinking of Eira, but all he knew was that he did not want her, while this lasted, to come into the room. It was risking too much even to face her now.

'Never mind that so much perhaps. Only what I'm trying to get round to, Will, is that there, in the factory, is your opening, if you'll take it. And I don't mean the job I offered your Dad. I mean something different.' Will, completely surprised, stared across at him.

'You've got the education, Will, and you know the country, you know the people here. You could come in this summer with me, and start really learning the business. We're going somewhere mind. Don't forget that. Even this, though it's more than I expected, is only the beginning. And there you are, Will. Not as anybody's employee, but getting ready, when the time comes, to take things over. That's what I'm offering you, Will. That's what I've been trying to say.'

Will looked up at his father, but Harry had turned and was looking out at the lane, his eyes clouded.

'What makes you think I'd be any use?' Will asked.

'I told you. You've got the education and you know the people here. And you're your Dad's son.'

Harry moved suddenly, and walked across to sit by the window.

'What do you think, Dad?' Will asked.

'Morgan's made a good offer,' Harry said.

'I mean for me, Dad.'

'Aye well, for you.'

'You think I ought to do it?'

Harry hesitated. 'Well, that's for you to decide, boy. I shan't interfere.'

'You'd rather that than me go to university?'

'You don't know that you can go yet,' Morgan said.

'Well, if I can,' Will said, still looking at his father. 'If I get the scholarship, what then?'

'I'll tell you what then,' Morgan said. 'There'll be three more years for your Dad to keep you, and after that...'

'That's not in it,' Harry said quickly.

'It will be, Harry. And after, shall I tell you? You think when you've done that, the world'll be at your feet. It won't be, Will. You might as well know that now. What you'll get, in fact, is a start at the bottom of something, just as you might now. Don't think you'll get one of the good jobs. They keep them for themselves, like we might do.'

'It isn't only for a job, is it?' Will said.

'Aye, I thought you'd say that. Like what you said about the mountain. You get such an idea of yourself you think everybody owes you a living.'

Will flushed and looked away. He could hear his mother moving in the porch and calling back to Eira. Let them keep away, now this had happened. Let them not see him at a disadvantage like this.

'It isn't altogether true,' Harry said suddenly. 'I mean that going would make no difference to him for a job. There's all sorts of jobs depend on the degree, and he could get that.'

244

'You know nothing about it, Harry. How could you know about it?'

'I know that much, anyway. For the rest, we're both guessing.'

'So you're against it, too, Harry?'

'Will hasn't said he's against it.'

'Let him say then. Come on, Will. Answer up.'

Will looked back, slowly.

'It is a good offer, Mr Rosser, and I'm grateful. Only, to be honest, it isn't just what I'd thought of doing, and that's a bit difficult to explain. It would be all right, I know, but it's what you have in your mind to do, that's all.'

'Making jam, I suppose, isn't high enough for you. Is that it?'

'No, I hadn't thought of it like that.'

Morgan got up, and stood between father and son.

'It's the same with you both, come down to it. It's Harry I blame, and I don't mind saying it to him. There's always been this idea that business isn't good enough. And if there's one thing makes me mad, it's this looking down our noses at business. What's our politics mean if it's not good business, raising our standard of life? You know where it comes from, this attitude you've both got? Not from people like you, working people, but from them that have always lived on the work of others: too proud to make jam but not too proud to eat it. You've worked hard, Harry, admitted, but only a kind of punishing yourself. You haven't worked *for* anything, not really. And Will is going to grow up turned away from all the real things of the world, with his mind set on God knows what, being carried.'

'Will has worked hard in what was set him.'

'School is different. What I'm talking about is work.'

'Have I kept you waiting too long?' Ellen asked from the door. She was carrying a tray of tea things; Eira was behind her in the passage, with a plate of bread and butter and another of Welsh cakes. Ellen stopped, feeling the tension in the room.

'I'll give you a hand with that,' Harry said, getting up.

'Come on, Will, you help too,' Eira said.

'There's no need,' Morgan said suddenly. 'We're not staying.'

'Not?'

'Put that stuff down, Eira, and come on.'

'When we've just got it ready, Dad?'

'You heard what I said. We're not wanted here.'

'Not wanted?' Ellen said. 'Morgan, Harry, what on earth's been happening?'

'Ask this husband and son of yours. I'm sorry, Ellen. I know it's not your fault.'

Ellen put down the tray. There were bright points of colour at her cheekbones and her hands were trembling.

'What is it, Harry?' she asked.

Harry looked at her, and then at Morgan, but did not speak.

'Say, Harry, please.'

'I'll say it, Ellen,' Morgan broke in. 'You won't get anything out of him, you ought to know that by now. I come here, see, with an honest offer, to do with Will. I meant only the best by it, that he should come in with me, learn the business and perhaps one day take it over. I had him and Eira in mind, I will say, but never mind that. I was only thinking of the good of everybody.'

Ellen looked across at Harry, who had not moved. Eira could not help looking at Will, and he met her eyes. He remembered how she had looked by the stream on the mountain. It seemed a long way back, in childhood.

'Do you want me to do it, Eira?' he asked, suddenly.

'You must please yourself, of course, Will.'

'But you, Eira. What do you want me to do?'

'It would be nice, Will, for you to be working with Dad.'

'He won't,' Morgan said. 'It isn't good enough for him.'

'Nobody said that,' Harry interrupted angrily.

'What other reason is there then?' Morgan shouted, turning on him.

'Will's own reasons. He must say for himself. In fact, if you listened, he has said more or less. But you say one thing makes you angry, there's one thing makes me. A man makes up his own mind in his living. He can't make up another man's, or try to force him.'

246

'There's others would jump at the offer.'

'Yes, it's a good offer.'

'Then why insult me by refusing it?'

'Nobody's insulting you.'

'To hell with it, anyway, Harry. Get on with your own way. Get on with this narrow, self-satisfied way you've settled for. I don't care what happens to you.'

'Is there any point quarrelling then?' Harry asked, smiling.

'No,' Ellen said. 'Whatever happens we needn't quarrel among ourselves.'

Morgan turned to her, shaking his head.

'Why is it, Ellen? Why I keep coming back here, keep coming and asking, I don't know. I should have learned more sense.'

'We've known each other a long time now,' Ellen said.

'Yes. And it was good, wasn't it, in the start? We've come a long way from that.'

Harry moved suddenly, and pulled out a chair from the table.

'Sit down, mun. Have your tea with us.'

Morgan hesitated.

'All right,' he said. 'What you got?'

'Enough,' Ellen said. 'Or if it isn't there's more.'

Morgan looked across at Will.

'Come on, Will. Come and sit between me and Eira here.'

After the open row, it was easier to settle down than any of them expected. They were all used to Morgan's mobility, and he could usually create any atmosphere he wanted. Still, when they got up after tea, Will knew that some stage had been finally passed. The quarrel had been only superficially about the job. The real substance, and its roots, seemed to lie far back. This was a border defined, a border crossed. It felt like a parting, whatever might actually follow. As he walked with Eira to the car, everything was easy again, but in a different world. Morgan knew this, and Eira seemed also to realize it, against her will. Only Harry did not seem conscious of the change, perhaps because he had reached it before the others, and had been living with it, already, for many years.

247

7

After a warm, rich summer, that seemed at the very height of the valley's life, autumn came early and was unusually hard. Before the end of September there were several sharp frosts, and all through October, when the apples were being picked, the cold persisted and the leaves went quickly from the trees. In the gardens the high summer foliage was dark- brown and withered; the down of the michaelmas daisies lay thickly along the edges of the paths. From the first week of November Harry had to work twelve-hour turns in the box, and the autumn work in the gardens fell largely to his father who himself seemed older and more tired. Will helped whenever he could, and was given the rough jobs – striking the bean and pea foliage, bundling the sticks, sweeping the leaves. The digging Jack Price would not let him help with: 'You can't dig yet, boy.' Will watched and thought about it. Harry at least worked quickly, trenching and double-digging, bending for weeds and stones. But Jack Price worked so slowly that nothing seemed to get done. Only if you went away and came back could you see the advance of the beautifully clean ground.

One cold afternoon a strip was being made ready for the first planting of broad beans. When he thought it was done, Will fetched the beans and the line, but his grandfather had started on the strip again, moving incredibly slowly, raking and raking at the earth until it seemed he was trying to change its nature. Already there was nothing larger than a marble, but still, endlessly, the slow raking and fining went on. Though he said nothing, Will doubted whether in the growing this would make much difference. It was less this, he thought, than some ritual of service. And he saw how separate, in these ways, he had already become. For whatever purpose, he would never dig like this. The jobs which satisfied him were those involving an immediate sharp effort – hauling at a grubbed root, heaving a load of leaves to the heap, forcing along a heavy bundle of sticks. Harry worked like this sometimes, but Jack Price never. To him there seemed all the time in the world, though already the blue damp air was thickening, and evening was drawing along the valley.

Slowly, the gardens were made ready for the winter, and still the cold intensified. The grass now, each morning, stood up in stiff rimed spikes. The apple trees were black and bare, though here and there a few small apples, at the very tops, still hung in a heightened colour. The only green in these trees was the mistletoe, which stood out now very clearly in its dull clumps, with a few pearly berries. The holly in front of the house was thicker with its bright red berries than any of them remembered. Through the dressing of ash, the lane deepened in its winter ruts.

On the first Saturday in December, when Will came down at dinner from his books, Ellen sent him to look for his grandfather, who had gone for a walk by the river. Will walked down the lane and into the fields over the road. He went past the pool that they called the Stubs, where the sheep were dipped; then on into the next field, looking down at the unmown border next the hedge, thick with bramble and bracken and the brown spikes of sorrel. Ahead lay a small dingle, with an oak tree and a few low thorns. Glancing ahead, Will suddenly saw his grandfather. He was lying face downward, at the edge of the dingle.

'Gran,' he called, hurrying forward. There was no movement or answer. Holding his breath, he reached him and bent down.

'Gran,' he said again, urgently, reaching out and touching the shoulder that lay nearest to him. He hesitated as his fingers felt the rough cloth, and then suddenly pushed hard at the shoulder, trying to turn it, so that he could see the face. But he drew back midway in the effort. He knew now what he would find.

Slowly he stood up and looked around. There was nobody in sight; the field lay empty and desolate. Looking down again, he saw the hand tightly holding two sweetbriars, that were being brought for the garden. Beside the hand lay the big single-bladed pocket knife, with the yellow bone handle carved with initials. The knife had been bought, he remembered his grandfather saying, after his first year's work, when he was twelve. Once he had lost it while hedging, and found it again months later. Narrowing his eyes, Will bent down and again pushed at the shoulder. Then, reluctantly, he touched the clenched hand, which was cold.

On the line, a hundred yards away, the down distant signal dropped to off. He heard distinctly the sharp sound of its movement, and thought of his father's hands on the lever, far up in the box. He looked down, and then broke into a run back across the field. He ran fiercely, driving himself, making the shortest way to the road. He was still running when he reached the lane, though he had to slow on the steepest part of the pitch. At the house he burst in breathless, pushing open the door of the back-kitchen. Ellen looked at him, and without speaking put down the plate she was holding.

'Quick, Mam, we must get him back.'

'Where is he?'

'In the long field by the dingle.'

'You shouldn't have left him, Will.'

'But it was no use, Mam. He's dead.'

'Come on,' Ellen said slowly. 'We'll get Hybart.' They went down the lane, walking quickly and without speaking. Hybart was at dinner, but came out at once with Ellen.

'Where do you say, boy?'

'I'll show you.'

'Wait, boy. We must get a hurdle.'

Hybart went to the back of his workshop and came back carrying a hurdle, taking his time. Will put out his hand to take one end, and they walked with Ellen down the lane.

'When we've got him home you must fetch your Dad from the box,' she said, as they crossed the road.

Will nodded. He did not know how to answer. He was as tall as Hybart as they walked together, but he felt only his inadequacy and inexperience. They reached the field, and Ellen hurried ahead. When they came up with the hurdle, she was bent over the body, which she had turned on its back. Will watched as she loosened the sweetbriars from the clenched fingers. Still he could not look at the face. Hybart set the hurdle down.

250

'You'll have a bit of a carry, boy.'

'Yes.'

He looked, now, into his grandfather's face. The intense blue eyes stared up unmoving. The moustache and beard seemed to have no substance, to be only an effect of light round the hard, weathered face. He could see, as he looked, the likeness to Harry.

'Bring the hurdle here, at the side,' Ellen said, getting up. Hybart pushed the hurdle across, until it was touching underneath the body. Moving to the other side, she lifted the arms and crossed them. Then bending with Hybart she turned the body on to the hurdle, rolling it completely over until it lay in the centre.

'Can you manage, Will?' she asked anxiously.

'I can manage, Mam.'

'I'll go in front,' Hybart said. 'We'll set down where we can.' Ellen wiped her eyes, and picked up the knife and the sweetbriars. Will bent behind Hybart and waited for the word to lift. The weight when it came was much heavier than he expected, but he followed as Hybart stepped away. He was looking down as he walked, at the snub toes of the heavy black boots, the thick khaki cord trousers, the thongs which yorked the trouser legs just below the knees. The weight was heavy on his arms, but he held it, thinking of the way Harry carried.

It was a slow journey home, with many halts. The pitch in the lane almost defeated them, and when they reached the house they were exhausted. They set the hurdle down in the porch, while Ellen propped open the main door. Then, with difficulty, they carried in through the passage and into the living-room.

'You go now for your Dad,' Ellen said, and Will, without answering, went out. He got his bike, and turned out into the lane. The effect of the death came slowly over his body as he rode up through the village.

Harry saw him arrive, and was at the window of the box as he walked along the platform.

'Brought some dinner, Will?'

'No. Gran's dead.'

He had not known how to say it, but now he looked steadily up. There was hardly any reaction in the face. Only the eyes darkened and clouded.

'How's that then?'

'He was in the field. I found him. We've carried him home.'

Harry turned from the window, and Will went up the steps into the box.

'I'll see if I can get Mr Jones. You stay here.'

'Right.'

Harry hurried out of the box and along the platform. He came back almost at once with the stationmaster.

'Don't bother about here, Harry. Off you go.'

'Thank you.'

'You found your Gran, Will, Harry tells me.'

'Yes, Mr Jones.'

'It's a bad business. I wouldn't have expected it. He was a strong old fellow.'

'Yes.'

'Come on,' Harry said. 'Thank you, Mr Jones.'

Will followed his father down the steps, and waited for him to get his bike from under the box. On the road, Harry was away first, and Will pedalled hard to catch him. They rode together, very fast and not speaking, down through the village. Harry was just in front when they reached the house, and threw his bike along the hedge under the holly. Will stayed back and watched him walk inside. He put his own bike away and stood waiting in the porch.

But when, he was asking, when will the voice come? When, to take away this weight, will the feeling rise where it can be seen? We can stand and sing on the formal occasions, but now, when the pressure is desperate, we cannot even speak. The house is quiet, the patch quiet. And the valley quite still, the mountains dark. When will the cry come? Let it come now, let the voice come. In silence now, taking the strain, we risk being broken. Let the cry come, let the son cry.

Harry came, out, awkward, talking to Ellen.

'I'll get the dinner,' Ellen said, 'though I expect it's spoiled.'

'Never mind that.'

'You'll write the letters when you've eaten, will you?'

'I'll write them.'

Will moved as his father stood close beside him. Harry noticed the movement and turned, looking into his son's face. 'There,' he said, touching Will's arm. 'Come on.' They went together into the back-kitchen, which seemed suddenly overcrowded as they stood there. Ellen began putting the dinner on the table. The alarm clock, resting with its tilted dial against an old yellow hairbrush, ticked loudly from the mantelpiece. Will looked at the brick floor, following the lines between the bricks. He remembered suddenly the cry at the bees, and the tanging, the clap of the hands, the excited shouts as they ran. The clock ticked loudly on, in the silence of the room.

The funeral was fixed for Tuesday. Hybart was to make the coffin. There was so much everywhere to arrange. They moved around the house, separate, practical. Will, with least to do, went out and planted the sweetbriars by the hedge under the damson tree. They sat that evening in the back-kitchen, by a big wood fire.

On the Monday afternoon, Harry's sisters, Gwen and May, arrived together. Harry went to work at six, for the twelve hours. Will sat with his mother and his aunts, who seemed to know everything about him, everything he had ever done, though he would hardly have known them if he had met them in the street. That evening, about nine, it began to snow. When he went to bed at ten, the roofs and trees were already white, above the white lane. The snow was still falling, driven against the window by the rising wind. He took the warming-pan from the bed, and put it out on the landing. He was not asleep, but pretended to be, when his aunts came through on their way to the end bedroom. He could hear them talking, on the other side of the wall, late into the night.

When Harry came home at six it had stopped snowing, but the overnight fall lay several inches deep. On the road he had been able to ride, but in the lane there were drifts. Will was awake and saw him arrive at the house, the black cap and black coat standing out sharply against the general whiteness. The face was set and reddened as he walked in along the path. A few minutes later Will heard his step on the stairs, and Ellen's voice as Harry went into their bedroom. At eight, everyone but Harry got up, and had breakfast. Harry got up at eleven, soon after his brothers Owen and Lewis had arrived, walking from the station. Will looked at the three brothers as they stood talking. The family likeness was so clear that it was strange to think of them as three separate men, one of them his father. He remembered his grandfather's face as he had lain by the dingle.

Already the neighbours were arriving, carrying meagre winter wreaths. The snow was stepped in everywhere, along the passage and into the living-room. Edwin Parry arrived with the horse and cart that would take the coffin down to the chapel. Edwin was cheerful in the tingling snow-lighted air. Will stood at the gate, watching him turn the horse. The snow that had been undisturbed in the lane when Harry came home was kicked about now and dirty.

Ellen called Will back into the porch where the mourners were standing. Harry, his two brothers, and Edwin went into the living-room. They came out carrying the coffin. They had to stoop to get it under the low porch. The coffin was slid into the body of the cart, and then the wreaths were carried out and laid on top of it and around it. Edwin went to lead the horse, and the brothers stood looking back at the people in the porch. Harry's sisters, with Ellen and Will, walked out along the path, and the others followed. Edwin led the horse down the lane, looking anxiously down as it slid a little in the snow. Everyone watched for footing, as they reached the pitch.

Will looked past the cart with the coffin and the flowers, and past the black coats of the men and women walking in front of him. He could see the whole bed of the valley white with snow, and above, seeming closer, the strangely different white ridges of the mountains. He could feel the tingling of the cold air against his cheeks and eyes; all the faces around him were cold and pinched. Slowly following the cart, the black procession moved on. Looking down, Will saw the black parallel lines of the cart's wheel track, that had cut through the snow to the ash surface of the lane. The lines seemed to hold his feeling, and he kept his eyes fixed on them, as they drew out ahead, down to the road and the chapel.

CHAPTER NINE

1

Next morning he found his father better. When he dressed and went out to the landing, Harry was sitting propped up in bed, shaving. Matthew stopped, surprised.

'You're looking much better.'

'Aye, better with this stubble off.'

The voice, too, was stronger, almost the ordinary voice.

'I mean, you must be feeling better.'

'Much better, Will. I had a really good night.'

'So did I. Though I heard the cockerels once or twice.'

'Aye, I got eight down there, young ones. They're lovely birds, Italian.'

'Do they often crow while it's dark?'

Harry did not answer at once. He was shaving the awkward hollows under his mouth. At last he put down the razor and rested. 'Aye; cocks will crow almost any time. I hear them often, nights, in the box.'

'I thought it was the light made them crow.'

'They do, yes. But often at other times, or if anything disturbs them. You must go down and see these, mind.'

'All right. Is there anything you want now?'

'No, I'm fine. Go you on down and get your breakfast.'

Will went downstairs. The kitchen was empty, though the kettle was boiling and bacon was grilling in the stove. He looked outside, and saw Ellen bending in the shed.

'You're up then, Will?'

'Aye. He seems better.'

'He had a really good night. I'm so pleased.'

'What are you doing there?'

'Getting the stuff for his cockerels. He's silly about them.'

'He was telling me. Italian did he say?'

'Yes, they're really lovely.'

'Can I take the stuff down? He said I should see them.'

Ellen came out of the shed, with the half-filled bucket.

'Well you can try, Will. But they've got to know him, that's the trouble. Yesterday when I went, they flew up like mad things. I thought they was gone over the wire.'

'I'll try, shall I?'

'Yes, if you like. I'd rather, really, be in the house in case he rings.'

He took the bucket, and went to the drying green. The cockerels were in the far corner, in a small triangular run. He walked across to them, keeping very quiet. He got to within ten yards, but then the alarm went up. He halted and stared at the sudden unbelievable fury. Certainly they were wonderful birds; beautifully patterned in black and white, with magnificent tail plumes and fine scarlet heads. They flew now and screeched, hurling themselves at the high wire. He stood, overawed, and then tried to come up on the side, creeping under the trees. They were not deceived for a moment, and one actually reached the top strand of the wire before falling again. There was nothing for it but to put down the bucket and go back.

Ellen was waiting for him at the door of the kitchen.

'Cockerels, did you say? It's more like a parrot house.'

'Yes, Will, it is really.'

'Well, I haven't fed them. I couldn't get near them.'

'It's only they're frightened. He's fed them all through, they're only used to him.'

'I don't know,' he said, looking up at the window of the bedroom. 'Shall I try again?'

'What I did the last two mornings, Will, was put on his hat and coat and go back. They were quiet then.'

'You mean that really deceives them?'

'Well, I got in anyway, and they took the food. Here, look.' She had the coat over her arm and was carrying the hat. She held the coat, and he pushed his arms in the sleeves and pulled it around him.

'Take the hat, Will. You can put it on when you're in sight.'

'It seems so ridiculous,' he said, but he went back, self-consciously, to the drying green. He stopped and put on the hat, then walked again to the run, picking up the bucket. One bird flew, but the others rushed eagerly to the gate.

'Back now,' he soothed, turning away his face. As he opened the gate, they flew at the bucket. He emptied it quickly, drawing his feet back from under it. Then he went out through the gate and carefully locked it again. Behind him was the tumble of black-and-white feathers, tail- plumes, scarlet heads. He pulled off the hat and coat, and walked slowly back to the house.

It was a quiet morning, and he sat after breakfast and smoked and read. After dinner in the kitchen, he went down to look at the bees and on the way back stopped to talk to Mrs Whistance, who was by her gate. He wanted to ask her if he could see inside the cottage again; he hadn't been in for ten years. But he knew he should not ask, and she did not think to offer. Then it was time to get ready for the bus into Gwenton.

'Is there anything I can get you, Mam?'

'No, we've got everything. Unless Evans gives you those tablets.'

'It's tablets, is it? He didn't say.'

'He said tablets to your Dad.'

He put on his coat and walked down the lane. He had plenty of time; too much time. The balance of feeling was changing, and there was nothing in particular to look at. It was really as if he was living here again; the lane and the mountains seemed ordinary. The bus came, rather late, and in half an hour they were in Gwenton. He got out at the market and walked up the narrow street to the high ground behind the castle. The doctor's house, Powell's house as he still thought of it, stood in a quiet street overlooking the river. It was a low white house, with handsome curved windows and a small black veranda. The hollyhocks along its front had nearly all been cut down by the frost, though two, yellow and pink, still flowered on short stems. The wide door, under its fanlight, was yellow; this was new.

He rang the bell and waited. After some delay the door was opened by a thin, fair girl, wearing a white overall coat. She looked as if she should still be at school.

'I want to see Dr Evans.'

'Surgery's not till five.'

'He asked me to call now.'

'I'll see. What name?'

'Price. Price, Glynmawr.'

'If you'd just wait,' the girl said and left him at the door. He settled to wait; he had chosen to state his call in just these terms. For years now he had watched his friends getting past closed doors and attendants. It was a way of speaking, easy enough to learn, but he had never tried it. It was easier to reduce himself than to assume a right of entry and a special welcome. And then for years, from the other side, he had watched the doors being closed, the attendants briefed. Everyone, it seemed, put himself behind this kind of screen. England seemed a great house with every room partitioned by lath and plaster. Behind every screen, in every cupboard, sat all the great men, everybody. If you wanted to see them, you could see them; that was what they were there for. But you must cool your heels first; a necessary part of decorum. If you went out of your own cupboard, to see a man in another cupboard, still you must wait for the cupboard door to be opened, with proper ceremony, and by a proper attendant. If you didn't respect another man's cupboard, what right had you, really, to expect him to respect yours? Since proper men lived in cupboards, you could hardly insult your host by implying that he did not. Only sometimes, if your approach was right, the cupboard door would be opened with a flourish. If your approach was wrong – it's something you just know about people – then you could wait for a while, looking up at the cupboard door, getting yourself – and why not? – into a proper state of mind.

A door at the end of the passage opened, and Eira came out. For a moment she seemed not to notice Matthew, and then she exclaimed and hurried forward.

'Will, what on earth are you waiting there for?'

'Hullo, Eira.'

'Why didn't you come in? I've been expecting you.'

'I've only just come.'

She looked at him and smiled. Her hair had gone much darker; it was now the full brown that the English call black. She was wearing a brown tweed suit, a brown jersey, brown shoes. She seemed friendly and at ease.

'You just like being awkward, Will. Now don't you?'

'No. Why should I?'

'Go on. Did you see Glynis? I bet you didn't tell her who you were.'

'Certainly I told her who I was.'

'Look, I know you, Matthew Price. People have to recognize you without you saying who you are.'

'No, they don't have to.'

'But to hell with them if they don't. Come in, Will. Don't just stand there.'

He hesitated, looking directly into her face. He saw her cheeks tighten in a momentary uncertainty, as if she were facing a stranger. Then along the passage a side door opened, and Evans came through, pulling off his coat.

'Aye, fine. Glynis told me you were here. I've only just come back.'

'How are you?' Matthew said, putting out his hand. Evans shook hands quickly, and threw down his coat.

'Let's go through and have some tea. Leave your coat here, Price, if you like.'

'You mustn't call him Price,' Eira said. 'It's an English habit he doesn't like.'

'Well, Christ, I'm more Welsh than he is. All right, Matthew is it?'

Matthew had taken off his coat and put it beside Evans's. Eira led the way through, taking over the conversation.

'The trouble with this man is he's got two names. Matthew and Will.'

'Yes, it's a bit confusing. Perhaps that's why I said Price.'

'He's Matthew where he lives, but he's Will to everyone in Glynmawr. I called him Will all the years we grew up together, only then...'

She paused and looked at Matthew, who avoided the look.

'When he went away,' Eira said, 'he called himself Matthew. He expected me to call him Matthew, too.'

'Well, Christ, he can be called what he likes,' Evans said impatiently. Matthew looked at him, relieved, seeing a quality that had not appeared when they first met. He was still very formally dressed, but he had visibly relaxed. He was talking and behaving now like the boy from Llanelly, and Matthew liked him immediately.

'I agree, John. Thanks.'

'Sure. Now let's have some tea. Christ, I'm dry.'

The table was laid for tea, with a silver service and a small kettle on a spirit stove.

'You'll never get enough out of that thing,' John protested. 'Get the big one, girl.'

Eira lifted the lid of the teapot and filled it from the kettle.

'You do the doctoring, mister, I'll do the housekeeping.' John winked at Matthew.

'Sit down, mun. Let her bring it to us.'

'It's laid for sitting at the table,' Eira said.

'Well, I'm here and he's there. So what you going to do?'

'All right, sit like pigs in clover the two of you.'

'Now that, miss, is just where you're wrong. I've been reading it up. Do you read these things, Will?'

'What things?'

'I got a book on wine. It's all right, mind. I'm drinking my way through it. And there's another, she pinched it, about entertaining. Do you know, it's a funny thing? Everything common turns out, in fact, to be correct.'

'Now you're being ridiculous,' Eira said, pouring the tea. 'Do you take cream and sugar, Matthew?'

'Not at all,' John said eagerly. 'The lower orders sit up to table for tea; all right, that's common.'

'You're getting mixed a bit,' Matthew said.

'Aye, I am, but listen. The respectable lower orders sit up to table, but the really common ones just sprawl around.'

'That isn't true, you know,' Matthew said.

'But when you get above the respectable lower orders it's simple – you just sprawl around again. It says so in the book.'

'Not sprawl anyway,' Eira said.

'No,' Matthew said. 'Sit on the edge of your chair.'

'Look, a man who's been busy all day won't sit on the edge of a chair. He'll sprawl.'

Eira smiled. She handed Matthew his cup, and put her husband's on the table behind his head.

'If you lie back far enough, mister, you can drink it by suction.'

'That's an idea,' John said, and lay back. But he did not reach for his tea, and there was a sudden silence in the room. John was lying right back and his eyes were closed. He seemed suddenly desperately tired. At last Eira moved, and brought plates and sandwiches. John sat up with an effort.

'How's your Dad today, Will?'

'A little better, I think. He's been sleeping a lot.'

'Good.'

He took the sandwiches and ate hungrily. Then he reached back for his tea, and drank quickly.

'Got some more?' he asked, holding the cup out to Eira. 'I've got some stuff for your Dad, by the way. Thought I might get out after surgery.'

'I can take it. Tablets, is it?'

'Aye, sleeping tablets. It's a stronger one, that's all.'

'I'll tell him. He likes to know what he's getting.'

'Yes, so I noticed,' John said absently, running his teeth along the edge of his thumb-nail. 'He's an unusual man, Will. Though not in that, mind.'

'Yes.'

'I don't know what it is, but in this game you get to summing a man up. You go into one bedroom after another, bedrooms all much the same, and there you are, in front of you. No, he wasn't what I expected.'

'What did you expect?'

'I don't know. He made me forget it. We live as a rule on about five or six types. We meet somebody and we just try them on quickly for size. Only sometimes you look and the type breaks up and there's a man there. I don't know what it is. I just know it happened, with him.'

'I'm too near, I can't say.'

'That's a father, Will. Have you got some more of those sandwiches, Eira?'

'Yes.'

'My own Dad, now, had this same thing. He died of it.'

'I'm sorry.'

'Well, there it is. We'll do what we can.'

John was palpably nervous now, and the gaiety, like the correctness, had gone, as if both were façades.

'More tea, Matthew?' Eira asked. They both looked up at her suddenly, as if they had forgotten her.

'No, thanks. I must be going soon.'

'No, not yet,' Eira said.

'Stay, mun,' John said. 'You've hardly been here five minutes.'

'I probably ought to get the tablets out quickly.'

'No, no. He won't need any of those until later. About ten, before settling for the night.'

'All right, but still... you're probably busy and tired.'

'Relax,' John said, and managed a quick smile. 'Is Mark coming in?'

'No. I told you. He's at Phyllis's with Adrian.'

'Till when?'

'I said I'd fetch him about six. When I can have the car before you finish surgery.'

'All right.'

They were all silent again. As the talk ebbed, a different reality emerged. Matthew avoided looking at Eira; there would, in any case, be nothing to say.

'This is a nice place, Gwenton,' John said. 'The sort of place I could grow old in. Not that I'm not old, already. Anyhow a bit sweeter than Llanelly.'

'Yes,' Matthew said. 'I feel it, being away.'

'It's your own choice,' Eira said.

'It's my work.'

'I saw Morgan at lunchtime,' John said. 'He was telling me about your work.'

'He's studying Wales,' Eira said, 'and he goes to London to do it.'

'It's not just Wales, girl, like looking at mountains. It's where the records are, is it? London?'

'Yes, most of them.'

'Anyhow, keep on with it, Will. From what I heard, it needs doing.'

'Yes, it needs doing. Only it's getting too big.'

'Don't worry about that, mun. Say your say.'

'If I can,' Matthew said and let the silence edge back. He disliked talking about his work. When a discussion started he always wanted to get out. He saw John, now, observing him carefully. The pale, narrow face was deeply questioning and intent. As they both looked away, the door opened and Glynis came in.

'Sorry,' she said, in her light, unguarded voice. 'Only the doctor's wanted.'

'Oh God, where?'

'Mrs Brown rang. Peter's worse.'

'Yes,' John said, with a sudden gravity that for a moment seemed to darken the room.

'You won't get there before surgery,' Eira said.

'I bloody well will, you know. If I'm late back explain.' He was already moving to the door, and Matthew got up.

'And I'd better go, now.'

John turned on him, with a sudden authority.

'No. Stay. Finish your talk. And get my bag quick,' he shouted to Glynis. 'I'll be starting the car.'

He went out. Matthew watched Glynis close the door behind him, and then turned slowly.

'Sit down, Will,' Eira said. 'Don't be so nervous.'

'I'm not nervous.'

'You look it. As if we'd never been together before.'

'Never mind that. We never have. Forget it.'

'You may be able to. But in any case what are you worrying about? We've each made our own lives. We can meet from that.'

He sat down, and lit a cigarette. It was this he had been afraid of: that had made him reluctant to come. Yet if he watched, as if from a distance, it would settle. Eira sat, easily and correctly, on the other side of the room. She was watching him, and half smiling.

'Poor Will, you do look frightened.'

'Damn you, I am not poor Will.'

'All right, you're poor Matthew.'

He did not answer. He was staring across to where John had been sitting. He could still feel the tension, and now in reaction felt a sudden radical distrust.

'Since I am here, Eira, there's one thing I'll say. I'll pass over the fact that nobody told me John was your husband, or told him who my father was. That, after all, you might all wriggle out of. But there's one thing you can't evade...'

'No, Will, don't say it. There's no need to quarrel.'

'I'll judge the need. The fact is that for years you've been keeping up a completely false relationship with my mother. False on both sides. I'd say you've both kept it up as a sort of lien on me. You don't get anywhere, but it's there, as a perpetual criticism. I can't stand you meeting and talking about me, exchanging your photographs. I find it disgusting.'

Eira did not answer. He saw that her hands were trembling, though her face was unmoved.

'Would anyone else find it disgusting?' she said at last.

'Yes, I think so.'

'Of course they wouldn't. It's your own feeling. I've known your mother since I was a child. We've always been friends. Why on earth, now, shouldn't we go on meeting and writing? Have you really, honestly, any right to try and stop us?'

'Yet you don't tell your husband what Price he's going to. When he's treating a man in the house, the very room, you were born in? A man who's the husband of your friend, as you call her?'

She was silent again, and her hands were still.

'Have you said any of this to your mother?'

'No. Not in these terms.'

'Why not? If you feel it so strongly?'

'It would only lead to a row. I can't quarrel with her as things are.'

'But you can quarrel with me.'

'I can tell you what I think. You haven't a dying husband to look after.'

Again she was silent, and seemed genuinely moved.

'Surely he's not dying, Will. Not necessarily?'

'It's what we're afraid of. Of course we're afraid.'

'But is that the only reason?'

'Why I haven't told her, you mean?'

'Yes, Will. Answer.'

'Of course it's not the only reason. But I'm not being dragged back into all that.'

'All what, exactly?'

'You've no right to ask, Eira. It isn't your business.'

'I think perhaps it is, Will. If you're saying I'm wrong.'

'You just want to get away from the main issue.'

'What issue? That I didn't tell John?'

'Well, that.'

'Suppose I didn't know, Will. I can't possibly know about all his cases.'

'But you knew about this one.'

'Not at first.'

'But later.'

266

'Yes, yes I knew,' she cried suddenly, and got up and walked quickly across the room, wringing her hands. Matthew, quite cold now, watched her carefully.

'Will, do try to understand,' she said at last, turning back. 'When I married John I told him about you, I let it pour out. I had to, don't you see? I couldn't marry him unless I did. And I've talked about you since, so often...'

'That it's getting embarrassing?'

'What's happened to you, Will? What's happened to make you like this?'

'The usual things. I'm not quite so naïve as I was.'

'You're not quite so human either. You seem to have forgotten every ordinary feeling.'

'No, I'm not joining in, Eira. I nearly broke myself once, trying to keep up every kind of relationship, responding too much. I've learned now, anyway, most relationships have to be left unfinished, for it is really that they *are* finished. Then let's accept that. Don't try to make talking a substitute.'

'Is that what we're doing?'

'I wanted to see you. But I shouldn't have come. I came back to be with my father, and for no other reason.'

'I know.'

'But the pressure on all sides is so intense. The real pressure, that I should come back.'

'I'm not dragging you back, Will. Only I've known you so long, I half know what you're thinking. You went away from us, you had to. And we accepted that, though in fact it meant losing you. It's just that it hurts, now, when you come back as a stranger.'

'Not as a stranger.'

'Yes. To yourself even. You're being drawn back, through your father, but can you come, even to him, if you turn from everything else?'

'What should I come back to?'

'To your own world, Will. Bringing your other world with you.'

'It's easy to say.'

'You're making it harder, because you're refusing to give in. You seem frightened of us, really, as if we were trying to involve you.'

'But you are. You say so. And I must find my own way.'

'Very well,' Eira said, and smiled as she moved to the door. 'Between us, in any case, it's quite different. I don't mean that.'

'I was glad to meet John. I like him.'

'Yes. It wasn't easy, Will, but I'm glad you came.'

'All right,' he said, and went past her to the door.

'I didn't want to make it harder, Will,' she said suddenly. He could hear the intensity in her voice.

'It's all right, it's mostly my fault.' He walked on into the hall. Eira followed him, and in the hall walked past him towards the open waiting-room.

'You've heard that Dr Evans may be delayed,' she said, at the door. 'He had an urgent call.'

Matthew watched her as she spoke, and felt suddenly at ease. As she turned back to him, Glynis hurried up with the wrapped package of tablets.

'I thought I heard you come out, Mr Price,' she said, smiling. A middle-aged woman, very pale, with weak red-ringed eyes, looked up from her chair in the waiting-room. She included the three of them, as they stood there, in a resentful stare. 'Yes, you're right,' Matthew said under his breath.

'Well, good-bye then, Matthew,' Eira said easily. 'I do hope we get better news of your father.'

'Yes. Good-bye,' Matthew said and took her hand. Her fingers were very cold as he touched them, and she withdrew them at once. 'And thank you, Glynis.'

'That's all right,' Glynis said, and the light, unguarded voice seemed infinitely pleasant. She went in front of him and held the door open and smiled.

'Thank you,' he said, slipping through. He turned to lift his hand to Eira, but she was already walking back, towards her own part of the house.

2

He did not catch the first bus. He walked round the town till the clocks struck six, and then looked for somewhere to get a drink. Finding a pub was not difficult; they stood at intervals of about twenty yards. But they were not places he was used to drinking in: either small hotels, with commercial saloon bars, or market pubs with dark, bare kitchens. There were difficulties in the way of either, but the hotels might involve him less. He stopped at the door of the largest and prepared to go in, but then turned away. He went quickly across the street and into one of the pubs which was smaller and darker than its neighbours. Several people were sitting around the big fireplace. The bar counter was away in the corner, in the shadows. He ordered cider, and stayed standing by the bar.

'Only he said he'd seen them. He said it in here. He wouldn't say it unless he had seen them.'

The voice came from a woman in her fifties, with a sheepdog lying by the big basket at her feet. All the others in the circle were men.

'I han't thought,' one of the men said, silhouetted against the big fire.

'There's a few, must be. Scattered.'

'Aye, pockets.'

'They was four shillings in the market Tuesday, mind. Poor little things too. Nothing on them.'

'Dealers.'

'Aye, Harris, I saw him. But Harris. He can't make rabbits. They must be somewhere, to be catched.'

'A few, see. Scattered.'

'Well, James said he'd seen them. On his own land. He said it in here. You heard him now, Mr Thomas?'

'Aye.'

'Well there you are then. And if there was only a few, you'd expect them to have something on them. But these, and at four shillings. Poor little things.'

'It's a wicked disease.'

Matthew finished his cider, and walked to the door. A few heads turned to follow him, but with only a casual interest.

'Like a bloody visitor,' he said to himself, in the windy street.

He caught the next bus, and sat in the high-backed seat which seemed to isolate each passenger. He stared from the windows, at the run of light along the banks and hedges. Before the school, he got up and went to the door.

'Not the chapels yet.'

'No, I know.'

'You booked to the chapels.'

'I know. But I'm getting off here.'

'It's a penny less, see, to here.'

'Yes. Thank you.'

He got out and stood back against the hedge as the bus pulled away. Now suddenly the darkness closed round him: the absolute darkness of the country, that he knew and had forgotten. He stood listening, and then walked on down the dark road. The telephone kiosk was just beyond the school. He hurried up to it, feeling the approaching excitement.

Standing awkwardly in the kiosk, he listened to the successive voices of the operators. There were the two Welsh voices, then the London voice, then the steady ringing. He closed his eyes to see the phone in that distant house, his own house, that it seemed so long since he had left.

'Yes?'

'Matthew.'

'Good. I was hoping you'd call.'

He hesitated, gripping the ugly receiver.

'I hardly know myself here. You three all right?'

'We're all right. How is your father?'

'No worse, no better. I think tomorrow I should come back.'

'Well, you'll know.'

'Susan, I can come down again. Only the immediate crisis is over.'

'Is it?'

'It seems so. After the first attack.'

'I can't say. You must decide for yourself.'

'I'll ask the doctor in the morning. If he agrees I'll get the afternoon train.'

There was a pause, and he listened intently.

'Don't, Matthew, if it will hurt you.'

'It will hurt either way. I can't come back here to live.'

'No. Though you sound as if you had. Your voice is quite different already.'

'Is it? Has it changed?'

'Changed back,' Susan said. 'I prefer it.'

'You mean my voice on the phone?'

'You're more excited. But that doesn't matter. Stay with him, Matthew, as long as he needs you.'

'Yes. Only he tells me I must get back to my work.'

'He's thinking about duty. Not about himself.'

'It isn't only duty. It's coming back to my family.'

'Yes. Either way.'

There was a long pause, and he stared into the darkness outside the kiosk.

'Is there much piling up?'

'The usual things. I'm dealing with all I can. I've opened the letters and answered those I could.'

'And the meeting on Friday?'

'Yes, if you can manage it. Edward says it's important.'

'I'll see. I'll ask Evans. I've just been seeing him, actually.'

The time-signal interrupted his voice, and Susan said quickly:

'Good night, darling. Come when you can.'

'Yes. Are you sure you're all right?'

'Fine. Good night, darling.'

'Good night, love.'

He put down the receiver, and went out to the dark road. He stood for a moment, taking the measure of the darkness, and then walked on. The wind was singing, excitingly, in the telephone wires along the road. In the north sky the stars were clear. At the lane, with the sound of the river under the wall, he was in touch again, as if he

271

had walked this road every night. He turned into the lane, into the deeper darkness under the trees, and walked up to the house.

When he got in, Harry asked to see him. He went up, taking the tablets. Harry looked at them and repeated the name, but otherwise did not want to talk. Matthew sat under the yellow light, content to be in the same room.

'I saw Eira and her husband,' he said at last.

'Aye, he's a good chap.'

'I liked him.'

'One of our lads.'

'Ours?'

'Aye, it makes the difference.'

'I see. I'm glad you think so.'

'Of course I think so.'

The silence came again, until much later Matthew said:

'I rang Susan on the way back.'

'Good. How is she?'

'Fine.'

'And the boys?'

'Yes. Fine.'

'I think of them a good bit. But it's no use talking.'

'Yes. I wish you could see them more often.'

'You've got your work. You must be where your work is.'

'You don't mind then?'

'Yes, I mind. Naturally I mind. But it's what I wanted for you.'

'So long as I'm certain of that.'

'Certain? You're working for your boys.'

'Yes, I suppose so.'

Harry rested again, and after a while Ellen came up to give him his tablets. Matthew went back down with her, leaving Harry to sleep. They sat in the kitchen, in front of the big fire.

'Mam, it's a long time and a long way,' Matthew said. 'I feel so far outside. Don't you see it?'

'It is a long way, Will.'

'It seems longer now I've come back.'

'Yes, I suppose it does. But still, it has to be for your work.'

'And for Susan and the children.'

'Well, yes. Though they're where your work is.'

'I don't mean that. I mean that in any case I would have left home.'

'Yes.'

'Only I feel I'm being blamed. Blamed for something that is quite inevitable.'

'Nobody here's blaming you.'

'It isn't what's said. It's a different pressure, the whole atmosphere really.'

'Well now, of course, with your Dad ill.'

'Yes. In any case we won't quarrel about it.'

'Why should we quarrel?'

'We shall, Mam, if we don't get this right.'

Ellen was staring down into the fire. She got up now, quickly, and went to the stove.

'I'll make supper,' she said and began moving about the kitchen. Watching her, he saw how much of her feeling was kept under and controlled by this familiar routine.

They had finished their supper, and Ellen was filling the hot-water bottles at the sink, when a car drew up in the lane, its headlights sweeping for a moment through a gap in the curtains and across the dim ceiling. The side-gate was opened, and there was the expected knock on the door. Matthew was walking to the door when it opened and Morgan came in.

'All at home?'

'Yes, of course. Come in.'

For the next ten minutes, Morgan and Ellen talked, easily, while Matthew stayed on the edge. Then Ellen went to bed, carrying the bottles and a bunch of grapes which Morgan had produced, casually, from his brief-case, just as she was going to the stairs.

'Give him these then, Ellen.'

'Thank you, Morgan. He'll love these.'

'Go on,' Morgan said impatiently, and gestured her away with his hand. She said good night again, and they heard her slow steps up the stairs. Matthew bent and put a log on the fire.

'You needn't go just yet?'

'No, Will, I needn't.'

Matthew sat in Harry's chair, leaning back.

'I didn't know Dr Evans was your son-in-law.'

'See what you miss by being away, Will.'

Morgan was sitting now by the fire, still in his heavy black overcoat, his red face shining.

'I went in today to see them.'

'Yes, I heard they gave you some tea.'

'Tea and talk.'

'You all three know how to do that,' Morgan said, smiling.

'If you mean because we're educated, on the whole you know we slow down.'

'We're all educated, after a fashion. Still, you could tell each other magazine articles you've read. Unless, of course, you read the same magazines.'

'Even then, sometimes. Though mind, when you once get outside this ritual. You know he said and she said and I thought though I didn't say mind...'

'We all know its limits, Will.'

'All right, but then it can all be respected. Ours too.'

'You're assuming a division. As a matter of fact it's in your own minds.'

'If it is, we must live with it. What did you expect us to do?'

'Nothing really. Relax. It's all right.'

'It isn't as simple as that. The division is there, though we're the first to regret it.'

'From your Dad, say?'

'Well there now it's both,' Matthew said slowly. 'The social thing and the other.'

'What other?'

'Well, any father and any son.'

'Yet you get on, you two?'

'Yes. Yes, we do.'

'Look at it this way,' Morgan said after a long pause. 'Have you met now, anywhere you've been, a man that is more of a man, more interesting as a man? I mean, forgetting your categories, that put respect in fact in terms of a job.'

'It's not a real question. He's my father, and there it is. There are no comparisons.'

'You make them though, Will.'

'Not as a father.'

'As what, then?'

'I don't know. We don't understand it. But a part of a whole generation has had this. A personal father, and that is one clear issue. But a father is more than a person, he's in fact a society, the thing you grow up into. For us, perhaps, that is the way to put it. We've been moved and grown into a different society. We keep the relationship, but we don't take over the work. We have, you might say, a personal father but no social father. What they offer us, where we go, we reject.'

Morgan leaned again to the fire, the blood straining in his face.

'This is wrong, Will. I know that it's wrong.'

'Undesirable, you mean? Do you think we don't know that?'

'No, wrong.'

'You tell me then.'

Morgan hesitated.

'Well, I can see you don't like what you're growing into. I don't like it myself.'

'You don't like us, you mean?'

'You're not much yet, Will. Any of you, I mean. You're still growing.'

'But you don't like the way we're growing?'

'I wouldn't say that. You're all still learning. I mean I don't like what you're asked to grow up into, what you say you reject.'

'My senior colleagues, you mean?'

'Your senior colleagues and their colleagues and masters: just that lot, Will. We still think of them as that lot.'

275

'They're not bad. It's just they're like foreigners, when you come where it matters.'

'They're exactly like you, and that's the fact, Will. It's you think you're different, but you're getting more like them. With an occasional kick, you know. A rude noise round the corner when you're sure that they're looking. And please it wasn't me, sir, it was my background.'

'All right, you're writing us off,' Matthew said, with more edge.

'No, not yet, Will. Relax, take your time.'

'But what, really, do you expect us to do?'

'No use asking me.'

'Alright then, leave it to us. We may know what we're doing.'

'I hope so,' Morgan said, and unbuttoned his coat. After a pause he added: 'You tell me what you're doing.'

'My work, you mean?'

'There you are, see.'

'Well, what else? You know about my family.'

'Yes, Harry told me.'

'But not about my work?'

'Well, yes, as he understood it.'

Morgan seemed now so calm and sure of himself that it was an effort to talk back, feeling this pressure.

'I've been on the same thing since the end of the war. But it's kept widening. It's always like that. It started as quite straightforward. Population movements in Wales during the Industrial Revolution. That was difficult, I mean the records were difficult, but at least it was defined.'

'I heard it that far,' Morgan said.

'Well, simply, at a certain stage, the figures got up and walked. That's how I put it, and got laughed at, naturally.'

'Are they not supposed to get up and walk?'

'In theory, yes. But in the tables at least they're solid. When they get up and walk they're not people but ghosts. We don't deal in ghosts.'

'So what did you do?' Morgan asked. He was amused and distant.

'Said I came from a wild place; that I was very superstitious; had thick Celtic blood.'

276

'What did you actually do, I mean?'

'Well, I'd got my general basis. I'd got three mining townships, and the counties and occupations their people came from. That's my Part One. Part Two I'm still doing. It went well at first.'

'Harry said you'd got some diaries and letters. He was very interested, I remember.'

'Some, yes. They're not bad. But by this time, you see, the haunting was perpetual. I wanted, like a fool, to write the history of a whole people being changed.'

'Well? Can't you?'

'I'm an historian, Morgan, an academic historian. One wants to do it, but one wants to do it right.'

'And in fact it's too much?'

'It's beginning to seem so. I've lost heart, I suppose. For I saw suddenly that it wasn't a piece of research, but an emotional pattern. Emotional patterns are all very well, but they're our own business. History is public or nothing.'

'I see. So you won't finish it?'

'Probably not. I shall just be one more of the missing. If I'd stuck where I'd started, I could have had my name on the shelf.'

'Can't you still put that out? You say it's all done.'

'I could but I don't want to. It means nothing, now. It's just so much dead paper.'

'Then you can take your time. See how it comes. Your job's quite safe.'

Matthew looked up, suspecting irony, but Morgan was still quite impassive.

'Yes, the job's quite safe. I can grow grey in it, gather dust, look forward to my annuities.'

'Well, it's no bad thing to be a university lecturer. You've got quite a way.'

The voice was steady, unforced and unemotional. Matthew listened for every shade of motive, but could find none. For a moment, unwarily, he felt safe.

'Oddly enough, Morgan, I'm quite protected from ambition.

Protected, really, by a different pride. I sit absorbed in these patterns, that are a substitute for my world and I know it. But at least they stop me crawling about in the world, looking for dead men's shoes.'

He had gone too far, and realized it at once. But Morgan sat quiet, and the fire had gone low. Slowly he sat forward again, listening to the clock.

'I shouldn't have said that.'

'Why not?'

'It brings up too much. I don't want to get back into that.'

'You're actually afraid of talking, aren't you, Will? About yourself, I mean.'

'I do it often enough.'

'Yes, but to yourself, I expect. You're not among people who accept you, as we accept you.'

Morgan's voice was quiet, but Matthew reacted sharply. This was the challenge he had been expecting.

'I don't know about that. I feel less tension there than here.'

'Tension, yes. But tension's normal, when something's happening. You've forgotten us, really. Forgotten how we live. Here it's got to be in the open, because in the end there's no hiding things, and none of us is going away. What there is we have to absorb, so we have to be straight. It isn't your kind of settlement, that any day might break up.'

'My family won't break up.'

'No, of course. But the rest will decide you.'

'All that may be true, Morgan. What you said about settlement. But I can't feel it, and it's no use pretending. It seems, now, as if everything is breaking up.'

'Not really, Will. Though of course this is a crisis.'

'I'll tell you, Morgan, what I thought yesterday in town. I was looking at people as they went by, looking as if I'd never seen them before. When I saw anyone old, of Dad's age or more, I asked why, by what virtue, are they walking here, and him lying on the edge. It shamed me, of course, but I felt it.'

278

'That's natural, Will. You think it, I expect, when you see me.'

'No.'

'Look, Will, I said be straight. You must be thinking it. I'm thinking it myself. Why do you think I come out here? It's not just to ask about him, or see you. I come because my life is in question. That's what this is.'

'Is it? It seems so for me. All my life I've had one centre, one thing I was sure of: that his life was good. And I suppose I'd believed that the good is somehow preserved. Until now.'

'He'd be glad to hear you say that, Will.'

'He knows it. He knows what I think of him.'

'None of us really know, Will. What you think of him matters, much more than you know. He'd accept it, really, as a verdict. That's what it is, handing your life on to somebody.'

There was a sound upstairs. Ellen had opened the door, and they heard her go along to the bathroom. They heard the water running, and then the steps and the door closing again.

'Every value I have Morgan, and I mean this, comes from him. Comes only from him.'

'I know. That's what your work's about.'

'My work?'

'Yes. The work you've been telling me about. Never mind the actual inquiry. What is it you're really asking? You're asking what change does to people, change from outside them, the big movements. You're asking about him and about yourself.'

'But he's not changed, really. That's the point. I was thinking only this evening. He's done new work, but his centre's been here, with his bees and his garden.'

Morgan did not answer. Looking across at him, Matthew saw open feeling in the ordinarily contained face. He wondered, watching, what this could be.

'You probably know our story, Will. After the strike, between him and me?'

'Yes, I've heard it.'

'We fought that strike hard. We were together then, young, in the box. And when we went down – down, mind, because our leaders got frightened, I insist on that – well, it was never the same for me, after that. I knew I wouldn't live to see any real change. Improvements, yes, but not a change where I could feel it.'

'We're still arguing about that strike,' Matthew said.

He had spoken as if arguing a general question, but Morgan brushed this away.

'Never mind your side of it, Will. I'm telling you what it did to me. What it did, in fact, was to give me a different direction. I gave up the box, and started the business. I did well.'

'Yes. Very well.'

Morgan looked at him suddenly, and laughed.

'You're a boy, Will, still a boy. You talk like you told me once then: if I pass my School Certificate, Mr Rosser, I can get five pounds a week.'

'Well?'

'Harry knows this better than either of us. You know I begged him, for years, as the business got better, to come in on it, take a full share. And it was always the same answer: he didn't see his way. It was the same answer, you remember, for you.'

'I remember. But would it have been better? For him?'

'He'd have more money, Will. A good deal more. And he'd look different. I look different.'

'You think he was wrong then? That he missed his chance?'

'It's what we say, Will. But I know Harry. Better than anyone, really. Because at least I'm persistent, and to argue that out meant getting right through to him, right through to the centre of him.'

'Well?'

'I learned something, Will. Something that in general we all know about, but I learned it from him. He couldn't see life as chances. Everything with him was to settle. He took his own feelings and he built things from them. He lived direct, never by any other standard at all.'

'You built from your own feelings, too.'

'Yes, in a way. At least I tried to. But what were those feelings?

280

What are they now? Just that life wasn't good enough. That others were ahead and why shouldn't I be? Negative feelings, Will, because what I wanted I couldn't have.'

'Can you really say that? What did you want?'

'I wanted a socialist society, Will. Let's sit back and laugh, shall we? When my business got going I went into politics. I'm in a position to laugh.'

'But we're getting it, or at least some improvement. In our own time.'

'No, Will, we're not. We're getting the result of our own denying. We're getting it all except the life.'

'I'm sorry, I don't follow what you're saying. I know a bit what you mean, but what in fact are we to do?'

'Start our businesses, Will, make our careers. What else?'

'You're implying there is something else.'

'What we talk about, Will, he's lived. It all depends on a mind to it, a society or anything else. And the mind we're making isn't the society we want, though we still say we want it. The mind he's got is to the things we say really matter. We say it, and run off in the opposite direction.'

'The values, perhaps, whatever they are. But in fact what we need now is change. Satisfaction is all very well, but change comes from dissatisfaction. We can settle and lose.'

'That's what I say, what I always have said, and why Harry's different. He changes a thing because he wants the new thing, and he settles to it because he wants it right through, not because the rejection is driving him.'

'It comes to the same thing.'

'No, Will, it's coming to a different thing. Take a look.'

Matthew did not answer. He was tired and losing his way in his mind. The bedroom door opened again, and was closed almost at once. He listened for footsteps, but none came.

'Yet in the end,' he said bitterly, 'he's lying up there, on the edge.'

'Yes.'

'If it was right, he'd be right. That's why I get so impatient. All this is sheer sentiment, when you come to it.'

'Because he's ill?'

'Because his heart is failing. Because he can't go on. Because he's used his whole strength up, in this life you say you admire. We all admire it, from a distance. But we take good care not to live like it. We take good care of ourselves.'

'Yes, I agree. It's we who won't change.'

'Would you change places? With him now?'

'You're trying to, Will.'

'Change places?' Matthew said, and then stopped. As he hesitated Morgan got up, buttoning his heavy coat.

'It's late. I'd better be going.'

'With nothing finished?'

'We shan't finish this, Will. It's a lifetime.'

CHAPTER TEN

1

He was sitting above the Kestrel, looking down across the valley. It was strange to be up there alone, with the valley so quiet. The people he had lived with, the voices he had listened to, were all there under his eyes, in the valley. But all he could see from this height were the fields and orchards; the houses white under the sun; the grey farm buildings; the occasional train, very small under its plume of smoke.

He had come up past Parry's farm and the sheepfold, and over the long climbing ridge of Brynllwyd. At first the paths had been wide, through the dense green bracken, past the last cottages and the occasional pool. Then, where the bracken dropped back, the wilder country of heather and whin stretched ahead. The paths became narrower, the air colder, and the mountains around took on different shapes, their moulding clearer. The sheep, in this great open stretch, were few and scattered. He could see the wild mountain ponies, but always in the distance. In the great silence of the mountain the song of the few birds, the strange high sound of the wind, came in a different dimension.

At last he turned back from the open mountain, and crossed above the Kestrel to where he could see the valley again. It was like coming back, after a long journey, to familiar country, yet the valley was still strange: an enclosing feeling had taken and changed it. There was the patch, its houses half-hidden by the enclosing trees. He knew, at recall, every yard of that ground, and of the fields around it, up to the farm and the water-tank. But from here it seemed that a light, a silence, a feeling not ordinarily accessible, had flowed round and enclosed this familiar ground. The patch was not only a place, but people, yet from here it was as if no one lived there, no one had ever lived there, and yet, in its stillness, it was a memory of himself.

There were the two chapels by the river, and the Daveys' cottage. There, up the line of the road, was the school, and the boys' playground, and the green rectangle of the bowl-ing green. It was easy to remember the hours he had played there, the voices and the shouting, but from here it was only a place and a memory. The trains which had sounded so near when he lay at night in his bedroom, or which had been so huge when he stood under the embankment watching them pass, moved now like toys through an imaginary country: like a working needle through cloth, with the thread of the trucks drawing the country behind it in folds, pointed in the direction of the engine and its trail of feathery smoke. The banks and quarries he had scrambled over; the pitches he had freewheeled down on summer nights, with the midges clustering in the warm air; the long line of the old tramroad: all took their place in this moulding of the valley, which could never be seen down there, from within it. It seemed from this height that the whole south of the valley was drawn up from the road towards the peak of the Holy Mountain. Fields that down there were single and isolated were now only chequered pieces of that great movement of the land. The church and the vicarage stood out clearly, with the windows of the vicarage reflecting the sun. The tower that had seemed so high on those cold nights was now only a line, a brief movement, in the wide country. The station was out of sight, hidden in its cutting. Work went on there, in the ordinary routine, but from here it might not have existed, and the trains might have been moving themselves, with everyone gone from the valley.

He sat very still, preoccupied by this strange feeling of quiet. Down over the close turf and the hummocks of bracken the black rock of the Kestrel stood out sharply. The Kestrel, in legend, was the guardian, the silent watcher, over this meeting of the valleys.

Below the Kestrel was Meredith's cottage, and his cattle in the home field. Further below, stretching across to Blakely's, lay the currant fields, their black regular lines very distinct from the wooded meadows around. On the other side of the Kestrel was Trawsfynydd, the steeper, narrower valley, with its dark, ruined abbey. There the Honddu showed clearly in its slow tree-lined course. He could see the detail of oak and elm, in the full hedgerows. There, in an orchard, was an old tedder turned on its side, and the littered straw round a half-eaten potato clamp. He saw the long white wall of a farmhouse, and the end wall, at a curious angle, was crossed by a melting violet shadow. And here, on the high-banked road, was a cart moving, and a dog barked somewhere, insistently, not too far away. This, seen close, was his actual country.

But lift with the line of the Kestrel, and look far out. Now it was not just the valley and the village, but the meeting of valleys, and England blue in the distance. In its history the country took on a different shape. On the high ground to the east the Norman castles stood at intervals of a few miles, facing across the wide valley to the mountains. Glynmawr, below them, was the disputed land, held by neither side, raided by both. And there, to the south, was Gwenton Castle, completing the chain. The little town lay under it, blue in the haze, and the only clear detail was the green cupola of the Town Hall. All that had been learned of the old fighting along this border stood out, suddenly, in the disposition of the castles and the roads. There on the upland had been the power of the Lords of the Marches, Fitz Osbern, Bernard of Newmarch, de Braose. Their towers now were decayed hollow teeth, facing the peaceful valleys into which their power had bitten. All that stayed of that world was the memory, the decayed shape of violence, confused in legend with the rockfall of the Holy Mountain, where the devil's heel had slipped as he strode westward into our mountains.

Or look out, not east, but south and west, and there, visibly, was another history and another border. There was the limestone scarp where the hills were quarried and burrowed. There along the outcrop stood a frontier invisible on the surface, between the rich

285

and the barren rocks. On the near side the valleys were green and wooded, but beyond that line they had blackened with pits and slag-heaps and mean grey terraces. It seemed only an accident of the hidden rocks, but there, visibly, were two different worlds. There along the outcrop had stood the ironmasters, Guest, Crawshay, Bailey, Homfray, and this history had stayed.

He looked out in each direction in turn, his eyes narrowed against the keen wind, his mind excited as it had been when he stood with Pugh on the church tower, looking up at the shapes in the stars. The mountain had this power, to abstract and to clarify, but in the end he could not stay here; he must go back down where he lived.

On the way down the shapes faded and the ordinary identities returned. The voice in his mind faded, and the ordinary voice came back. Like old Blakely asking, digging his stick in the turf. What will you be reading, Will? Books, sir? No, better not. History, sir. History from the Kestrel, where you sit and watch memory move, across the wide valley. That was the sense of it: to watch, to interpret, to try to get clear. Only the wind narrowing your eyes, and so much living in you, deciding what you will see and how you will see it. Never above, watching. You'll find what you're watching is yourself.

The key was in its usual place, on the ledge of the porch. But he stayed in the garden, walking across, as Harry did, to the water-butt under the rose. He rested his arms on the edge of the butt. The water was low, and there was a sour, bitter smell of soaked wood and stagnant water. The sour air seemed to breathe from every pore of the wood. His hair fell loosely forward as he stared down, and he saw its reflection and the blur of his face on the black, faintly iridescent pool at the bottom, where the arc shadow of the rim of the butt spread in a darker third. The butt trembled under his weight, and there were ripples at the edges of the pool. When it went still again, the sheen of the black surface held a pattern of reflection apart from his own: the jointed pipe from the roof, the horizontal rain gutter, the tall, narrow chimney. All these seemed to stir below the surface, and the shapes blurred in the dark slow swell of the water.

September 1938. Was that a time to be going away? Not really that the shouting mattered. You had to shout on your own to feel it as a cause. Not only indignation, but a training to indignation. History omits our particular occasions, as it weaves its spell of a date. Like the meeting last night, in the theatre of Gwenton Town Hall. The protest meeting at which nobody had protested, but only complacently affirmed. This solemn and urgent occasion, with Councillor Morgan Rosser in the chair – councillor on a by-election in the Castle Ward, in the Labour interest. And you might hear, friends, with your inward ear, the bombers droning over this quiet market place, and when should we wake to our danger and our shame? It was all quite right, what they had all said, but what he had said, all he had said, was to Eira, who had been trying to listen. With one thing and another, it may be some time before I see you again. It might be. Do you want to see me again? No, of course not, I shall be glad to be rid of you. That's why you're smiling, I suppose? I'm not, I'm pleased with you. That I'm going away? That you'll come back. But not to see you? Yes, Will, whenever you want.

Being kept in mind then. Only it was like being proud of you. Since the scholarship these words had seemed all people could say. Only why say you're proud of me? So you can feel proud of yourself for saying it? Feel you're doing the right thing? William Evans at it, as hard as with the stick over the harmonium: a great honour for the school. A stick to beat it with. Like a halfpenny and a farthing not a halfpenny and a farthing. Get it right now, the Devil and Willy Price are watching. *Laborare est orare*. And Pugh saying you must go and see for yourself. See what? The end of a pen and the inside of a book: see that from here. And what when they dropped you, like Alun? Well, never ought to have gone, after. Only give him ideas of himself. Aye, certainly gives him ideas. Would you like a sample? Wrap up your pats on the back, take a long look at yourselves. And get on with your own work; leave me to mine.

Still, Mam and Dad going up to Cambridge, on a privilege ticket, and Mrs Howes, at the lodgings, already got a box of honey, and eggs to follow. Don't they feed you up there? Pugh saying about the

287

outpost: starvation rations. Then other times like a guide-book: going to one of the four-star places. When some even said the name, it was like eating cream. Not eating it even, just finished eating it: licking it from round your mouth. They expect you to go up cap in hand perhaps, so they can pat your head. Going to Cambridge: as nice to say really as modern. But honestly, Cambridge, where's that? The only attitude you can take. Go and see.

Go and see, with your clothes in the suitcase Blakely gave you. A good case, green, with the initials on it in black: M.H.P. And that already sounds different. Very good of him to have given the case, wasn't it? Well, he can afford it. Not really though, he hasn't all that money.

One thing at least there's no need to worry about, and that's class. We don't have classes here, sir, except in school. Our place, I suppose, is too poor for that. Or put it the other way round. What it is, see, in Glynmawr, people take themselves seriously. There couldn't, not anywhere, be more important people than them. The men, look, taking themselves seriously. They walk slowly, showing all their layers. Mack open, jacket open, cardigan open, waistcoat open, collar-band open – nothing, you see, to hide. The ruling class. Though, of course, there's accent. Once you cross the river. Still, you can talk as you like: like Pugh certainly; like Billy Devereux if you put your mind to it. Talking's no trouble, not from here. Just leave it to your voice.

Aye, to your voice, but to which voice? The voice on the mountain, a voice waiting to be learned. The voice here, querulous: not the persuasive rhythm, but the unfinished truculence – you're not going to believe what I say. Sour, is it, like this old butt? Well, let it rain and fill up.

There were voices in the lane. Ellen and Mrs Hybart stood by the hedge, talking but also watching Will. The smoke from a bonfire rose thinly across the lane. All right, accept. He took the key from its ledge, and went into the house.

288

2

On the back of an excursion leaflet, in his clear, fine handwriting, Harry had written the times of the trains. Will checked that the paper was there, in his stiff top pocket, as he turned from the lane into the road. The luggage had gone on: Harry had taken the last case that morning. Will had only himself and his bike to get to the station.

As he rode past the school a few early children were standing cold under the wall, by the closed door of the porch. He waved and looked across to the line. He laughed as he saw the down distant signal trembling. This was an old game: originally a sign that he should hurry. He knew he was not late now, but he stood up suddenly on his pedals, and raced to the station. As he pushed his bike down the zigzag path to the platform, where the snapdragons still held a few late flowers, Harry was smiling at the window of the box.

'Taking your time then?'

'Aye, I saw you wagging the distant. What's happened, it stuck?'

'Something of that,' Harry said, and moved back into the box. Will put his bicycle against the parcels office wall, then went up the steps and through the landing. Elwyn, who had gone straight from school to be a platelayer, was sitting on the stool by the high desk.

'All fit then?' Harry asked.

'Aye, I hope so.'

'Look at me, Will,' Elwyn said, grinning. 'I'm practising, see, to be a clerk.'

'Get on, mun, you'd break the pen.'

'Aye, I might at that,' Elwyn said, and got down from the stool. 'Bit too strong in the arm.'

'Which of you two's the biggest?' Harry said. 'Come on, measure up.' Will and Elwyn stood back-to-back by the grid, and Will was just the taller.

'Want to measure us sideways,' Elwyn said, laughing. 'Only when Will turns side-on you can't hardly see him.'

'Have some tea, son,' Harry said, and took a cup from his locker. He put a spoonful of tea in the cup and poured on boiling water from the kettle, stirring it with the handle of the spoon. Will added his own milk from the medicine bottle the milk was always taken in. There was a screw of paper round the cork, that always held the sweet scent of the warm milk. As he drank, he looked across at Elwyn's big platelayer's frail, which lay near the door.

'Shall I make that French toast, Harry?'

'Aye, go on, Elwyn. You want some, Will?'

'No thanks, not for me.'

Elwyn took a bread-and-butter sandwich from a packet on the desk, and stuck it on the long copper-wire toasting fork that Jack Meredith had made years back, even before Harry had come to the box. Elwyn held the sandwich to the fire, bending intently over it, as Will remembered him from years back, when he had stopped on the way to school to show him something he had found.

'There it is,' Harry said, as the train was asked on the bell from Gwenton.

'Aye.'

'You'll write pretty often, mind. Your Mam will look for the letters.'

'Not you?'

'Aye, I expect so.'

'Send me a postcard too, Will,' Elwyn said from the fire. 'Just to see what it's like.'

'Aye, if I can get one.'

Harry went to the grid and pulled off the signals. Will moved to the window, looking down at the dusty megaphone and the two tightly rolled flags, red and green.

'Shall I take these along?' he said, touching the cane handles of the flags. Harry looked across at him, as if the question were serious, and then they both smiled.

'Let's get down then.'

'Aye, better. So long then, Elwyn.'

Elwyn smiled up from his crouch by the fire.

'You'll have to come here, mun, I can't leave this toast.'

Will nodded and walked across. Elwyn took his hand and gripped it tightly.

'Don't forget all I taught you, mind.' He straightened up and followed Harry down the steps. Harry took the bike and wheeled it along the platform to the pile of luggage.

'Will Addis'll put all this in. You just get your place.'

'Being waited on today?'

'Aye, well, it saves time. He knows where it's to go.' Will looked back up at the box, where Elwyn stood now at the window, grinning and eating his curling French toast.

'I'll say good-bye now then, son.'

'Already? All right. Good-bye then.'

They shook hands, and Harry at once turned away. Looking past him, Will saw the distant plume of smoke down the line.

'Only thank you, too.'

Harry heard and looked back. He nodded. Will watched him as he hurried back along the platform and up the steps. Will Addis came out of the office and stood by the pile of luggage.

'You just get in, see, Will. I'm seeing to this.'

'I'll give you a hand.'

'Do as I say, boy.'

Will looked down the line at the high plume of smoke. In shadow, in the box, Harry was pushing back the lever of the distant. Now the train could be heard, and Will waited stiffly. The black engine came noisily to the platform and the carriages drew past. The driver, in washed blue overalls, had shouted up to Harry in the box, and was smiling as he turned back to the brake.

'In by here,' Addis said, and opened one of the doors. Will looked back up at the box, and then got quickly in. He pulled down the window, and watched Addis and the guard loading his luggage in the van.

'Got any change?' the guard was asking.

'What for?'

'Ten bob note.'

'No, I don't think so.'

'Twelve half-crowns'll do.'

'More'n I've got.'

The bike was the last thing to be loaded.

Addis stepped back and held out his arm to the driver. There was a pause, and the train did not move. The guard held out his green flag, and Addis stepped back and looked up the platform.

'I give him the rightaway,' he said to the guard, and held out his arm again. There was a quick whistle from the engine, and the train began to move.

Will looked up at the window of the box. Harry was standing there, alone, with his arms resting on the black bar. The sleeves of the khaki shirt were buttoned at the wrists. The line of the watch-chain came just below the bar. Will lifted his hand, and Harry smiled, broadly, the whole set of his face breaking as he waved back. The train drew away from the platform, and a few seconds later had rounded the curve, leaving the station out of sight.

Alone in the narrow compartment, Will looked out at the steep banks of the cutting. Then, as the banks fell away, he hurried to the far window and looked across at the Holy Mountain. The peak was only slowly clearing from drifting cloud, but the rockfall stood out clearly, and the grey church under it. Hurrying to the other window, he looked up at Darren, and then past the Kestrel into the mouth of Trawsfynydd. The gritted wind came sharply back along the side of the train. The long black ridge of Brynllwyd came into sight, and he crossed the compartment again and looked back across the valley. It seemed, for a moment, that he was seeing it for the first time. He saw the extraordinary richness of colour, too brilliant really to be credible at first: the red earth, the bright green of the grass, the white walls of the houses, the white of shirt sleeves as men bent in their gardens. He saw the movement in it, the sudden steeps and pitches. There, now, was Glynnant pitch, and then the bowling green and the school. The river curved, and there were the chapels, and the patch above them, and Ellen, out on the drying green, waving a paper. Will waved back and then crossed again to look up

292

at Brynllwyd. The ridge was very dark, as dark as the Ship. Under it, white walls and the russet bracken and Parry's barn, low and open-pillared. He stared up until again the train curved away and went in among the woods. Still standing, he saw the river coming back to him, and then suddenly it was under the line, and away on the other side, and the border was crossed.

He sat down, trying to breathe easily. Above him on the compartment wall was the familiar map. Wales, in this drawing, looked more than ever like the head of a pig, with the ears up at Pwllheli, the eye at Aberdovey, and the long snout running out to Fishguard, with Pembroke Dock for a mouth. Pig-headed Wales then, is it? And us at its throat. Stubborn, self-willed, blind, I'm leaving? Not really. Not altogether. Whatever it is, it goes with you and comes back with you. The lines on the map ran out east into England, and he followed them.

In the box Harry looked up at the indicator and saw the train passing his last signal. He crossed, slowly, and pushed back the lever. Five hours to relief, and Will had a journey of seven. Elwyn said something, and picked up his frail and went out. Harry watched him, not really seeing him, as he crossed the line.

When you go out first on your own. When you marry and settle. When your father dies. When your son leaves home.

He looked down at the signal duster he was still holding, and hung it over the clip of the lever. He walked, slowly, to the window, and looked down along the platform. Will Addis was dragging a black basket into the parcels office. Harry watched, and then called down to him.

'Weighing them, Will?'

'Aye, for the safe side.'

The basket of pigeons had come up on the train from Blaenavon, as it had come up every Tuesday for years, as far back as his own coming. Harry watched the basket disappear, and then walked back round the box. Morgan had always been very interested in the pigeons, had talked of getting his own and racing them. What had he not talked of doing? Yet look, still, what he had actually got done. The pigeons were only a game.

'Watch them, Harry?' Will Addis called up, and he walked to the window. Addis was bent over the basket, undoing its leather latches. When they were loose he stepped quickly back, and then suddenly flung open the lid. The pigeons fluttered and flew out.

'Go on, go on, go on,' Addis shouted, kicking at the basket. 'What's the matter? Go on with you. Don't you want to get home?' He put his hand cautiously into the basket, and pushed up the last two pigeons. They fluttered out past his hand and flew up with the others, circling above the bridge.

'That's a game, Harry. All the way here in a basket, then fly back home.'

'It's an interest.'

'Not for them it isn't.'

Harry looked up at the little cloud of birds. They were still circling, high above the station, in wider and wider sweeps. He rested his arms on the bar, watching them slowly space out and draw away from their circling, to fly south and home. From inside the box, a bell rang: the train had reached Pont Dulas. He turned from the window, and answered the bell.

PART TWO

CHAPTER ONE

1

The four train stopped at Glynmawr, and Matthew got out. It was six months since Harry's attack: he had been recovering slowly through the winter, which had been long and hard, with drifted snow deep in the lane. Now the valley was waking in the early spring sunshine, though the mountains were still brown with the old bracken.

Matthew walked down the platform, where the wallflowers were coming into yellow bloom in the beds. Will Addis was talking to the guard as the green flag was lifted and the train drew out. Glynmawr station was being closed in June, as uneconomic: these were its last weeks. Will Addis was going back to work on his sister-in-law's farm. They exchanged a few words before Matthew walked on up the zigzag path to the road. A man was crossing the bridge in front of him, and he overtook him without speaking.

'Stepping it out, Will?'

He turned, and recognized Elwyn. He had missed seeing him on his last visit, and now, after the first recognition, the adjustment was difficult. Elwyn, in his forties, was grey and set, and seemed another person from the wild boy, the confident elder brother, who had been so important and so admirable. As they talked, uneasily, Matthew heard the set, grave rhythms of Elwyn's mature voice, and the settled sadness was unbearably painful.

'You'll find your Dad better, mind. I was over yesterday, the gang was working by the Tump and the chaps was asking.'

'How are you yourself, Elwyn?'

'Oh, well enough. Much as usual, see. Mind, we got a good gang now, we get on all right.'

'I never thanked you for carrying Dad home that day.'

'Don't worry about that, Will. We'd do it for anybody, but now Harry, see, they all say the same mind, they was saying only yesterday in the gang, he's a man everybody likes as worked with him, no trouble with thanking.'

'I'm thanking you all the same, mun.'

'Aye,' Elwyn said, and his eyes flickered.

'After all, you've carried me home a few times, too.'

'That's a long time ago. I was thinking just then when you walked past.'

'I should have known your back.'

'Aye. Still, you look well, boy. Is it all all right up there? All going all right?'

'Yes, I think so.'

Elwyn was watching him very closely, from an affectionate distance. It was the look that is given to a child, a young brother, who still in the freedom of childhood can play, break routine, be indulged. Yet the look was warm, quick, genuine: very moving, suddenly, from this set, grave man who had passed into a different generation.

'No trout where the gang work?' Matthew said, smiling.

'Aye, sometimes,' Elwyn said, with a quick laugh.

'But no rabbits along the banks.'

'Not now. Though there's a few been seen.'

'Come down one evening while I'm here.'

'Aye, I'll do my best, Will.'

'No, come, really.'

'Aye, I'll look in, I'll see how things go.'

There was no more to say, for the time, and they separated. Matthew walked on into the village, feeling himself already altered, so soon after coming back. But the village had altered too, and he saw this more clearly, walking. Before he had got to Cefn more than thirty heavy lorries had passed him, with high, towering loads. For each, after the first, he left the road and pressed into the hedge. He could feel even there the rush of wind as the weight passed. On this narrow road, a slightly widened lane, which the lorries treated as just an odd mile or two on the long haul to the north, there was no separate place to walk, hardly anywhere even to stand, and the few road improvements only added stretches of speed. The houses seemed now to stand in relation to the road, rather than to each other. It was no longer an enclosed village, but a place on the way to somewhere else, as almost everywhere in Britain was coming to be. Many of the trees under which the farms and groups of houses had sheltered were felled, and the walls seemed more open and more naked. The hedges along the road had been clipped short, and in some places replaced by stretches of wire and concrete fence.

Still, as he walked through, a sense of settlement came back. The fields still climbed unevenly into the mountains, and the earth was red in the patches of ploughland. Far up, under the Kestrel, the wall of Meredith's cottage shone white in the sun, and the pattern was still there, over the broad valley, as the names came back: Penydre, Trefedw, Campstone to the east; Glynnant, Cwmhonddu, The Pandy, The Bridge, Panteg to the west. The soft air, as he breasted the hedge and looked down to the curving alder-lined brooks, was still, on his face, the feel of a known country, and still, high up on Brynllwyd, was the ring of the sheep-wall.

Is it all all right up there? All going all right? Elwyn's questions come back suddenly, in their slow rhythm. Going back, in the autumn, standing at the bottom of the lane waiting for the bus, he had stared up at the Kestrel and committed himself again, without conflict, to the work that gave meaning to this moving history. But in practice, in a different atmosphere, moving back necessarily into the long struggle with detail, the emphasis had changed, until the Kestrel was no more than an irrelevant memory. The landscape of childhood never disappears, but the waking environment is adult: the street, the committee, the long, quiet library, the file of revised manuscript, the books shifting under the arm as you run for the crowded bus. The personal meaning is evident in every shape in this country, every sound of the loved voices, but the public meaning is elsewhere, in a different negotiation and in another voice.

The sound of the river came up, curving towards the road. He stopped and looked over the wall where once, in what seemed another existence, he had thrown away the book from the anniversary. A little way up the river, in the white shallows past the Stubs, a boy was dragging out an old tyre, the water in its hollow pouring down his leg. Matthew stared at the boy, caught in his own sense of an ended past.

'Don't slip now, mind,' he shouted down, surprised at the way the words had come. The boy started, and looked up the height of the wall. Under the fringe of hair the face was suspicious and hostile, at this voice from the adult world of 'don't'.

'Is it a good one?' Matthew asked.

'No, it's an old one.'

'Pull it out then.'

'I'm trying to.'

'Can you manage?'

'Aye.'

And he turned his back, pulling the tyre up in front of him, and carrying it, with water still streaming, out of sight to the sand by the Stubs, where you could sit, unseen, among the acrid leaves of the 'wild rhubarb'. Matthew turned away into the lane.

He had heard that the water was coming, at last. Up the centre of the lane was an open ditch, with the red earth heaped along its edge. At the turn by the pitch he came on the diggers: a boy of seventeen in front with a pick, a man in his forties working behind with a shovel. He spoke as he walked past. He knew the man well, though the name would not come. The boy in front was still working, stripped to a red shirt and heavy black trousers. He was obviously enjoying the high swing of the pick; his whole life seemed in it.

'Come to see your Dad, Will?'

'Yes.'

'You remember my boy? Teddy.'

Watkins, Phil Watkins, used to work at Trefedw.

'He's a worker, isn't he?'

'Aye, keeping me at it.'

It came through quite suddenly: a father and son in the same line of work. He spoke to Teddy as he passed, and the boy smiled.

The houses came in sight, and he looked eagerly ahead. Harry was standing by the side gate, in a heavy overcoat, thick woollen muffler and cap.

'Well that's good to see.'

'Aye, a bit better to receive you.'

'Receive me?'

'I reckoned from the train. Only I got out here a bit too soon.'

'I been stopping talking. It's my fault.'

'No fault.'

Harry was thin and pale. The face was different, both drawn and rested, as if there had been more than a physical change.

'This is my first time outside, mind.'

'Aye, well come on in.'

'I'm all right.'

But the eyes were watering, and in the shade the air was cold.

'And still I half turn across home,' Matthew said.

'Aye, well it was your home,' Harry said, staring across the lane at the cottage.

'You're glad you moved though? I mean this is a better house.'

'Yes. When the Watkinses moved I didn't hesitate.'

'Though it's strange to think this used to be Rosser's. And to see someone else across.'

'This is a good house.'

Ellen came to the door of the kitchen, and called them to come in.

'Can you manage, Dad? Shall I give you a hand?'

'No, no. I'll do it myself.'

He moved very slowly, like a child learning to walk.

'I feel inside, Will, like I could walk it and not notice it. Then the actual movement and you find yourself out.'

'Come on,' Ellen said.

'Aye, come to you.'

He smiled, catching his breath, then reached the door and held the post for a moment. Then he walked more firmly across the kitchen to his own chair.

2

On the following afternoon, while Ellen was in Gwenton, Harry and Matthew sat together in the living-room. On the table was a jug of flowering currant, that had been brought in to blossom. The sharp pink of the flowers, and the strange heavy scent, seemed to dominate the room. Matthew sat taking the feel of the room while Harry, in the chair opposite, finished reading the newspaper. With his heavy spectacles on, he looked quite different, in the intentness of his reading. Matthew felt the strangeness as this dimension of his father came back into place. It was years, it seemed, since he had watched him reading. The withdrawn, intent man, who read everything he could lay his hands on, was in some ways more difficult to remember than the first figure, the labouring man forcing his heavy body, as when he had carried the bees down to the road. The difference now, as he folded the paper and looked across over the tops of his glasses, was startling.

'All right, son?'

'Yes. I was just watching you reading.'

'Aye, I still look at it. Though it seems that bit further away.'

'A different world?'

'In some ways. A lot of it's still the same. Disarmament, wages, splits in the Labour Party: it's much of what I grew up through.'

'Will the rail strike come off, do you think?'

'If necessary.'

'Would you like to be back in it?'

'I might. So far as it goes.'

'It still makes sense, you mean?'

'It never did make sense, beyond a certain point. You get hold of change, it's like water. It takes so long to make anything really different.'

Matthew did not answer, for some time, and when he looked up again he saw that Harry was smiling.

'What is it?'

'Nothing. Just John Malton-Davies. I saw his name in the paper.'

'Should I know him?'

'No. I just knew his father to talk to. He was a guard at Resolven.'

'Malton-Davies?'

'Davies. Reg Davies. And the son was John Davies. He went to the County School and to Oxford. Then a major in the war, a good-looking chap. He married one of the Malton daughters, the shipping firm. His experience in shipping, they put it. So on to a Productivity Council.'

'That's the way, isn't it?'

'Aye, to be a kept man.'

Matthew looked away.

'What are you really saying? That he's deserted his class?'

'No. What do class matter? I'm saying what sort of man is he, what sort of living is that?'

'He's probably very able.'

'Able for what? That's what I mean, getting hold of water. It's easy to pick on him, like this putting on a hyphen, mixing up after all that with the owners, Malton and Davies and the hyphen between them. Only it's more than that. I can't say it. It's how real any of it is, how real it's lived through.'

'Is it just growing away, from what used to be real?'

'Growing is easy to say, but there's all kinds of growing.'

'Like I've grown away, though. We both know this.'

'I wanted that, Will. So that you could do what was needed.'

'Needed?'

'I needed it, Will.'

'But I needed it too. And I've gone my own way. I can't be just a delegate, sent out to do a particular job. I've moved into my own life, and that's taken me away. I can't just come back, as if the change was water. I can't come here and pretend I'm Will Price, with nothing altered.'

'Nobody is asking you that. In any case, leave the work aside, you've come back as a man. You saw me and your Gran: we were different. How many, ever, live just like their fathers? None at all like their grandfathers. If they're doing the same work, still they're quite different.'

'Leaving class out of it, you mean?'

'Aye, I hope you leave it out of it.'

'As prejudice, yes. Where it's real, no.'

'Where it's real it's lived through, it has to be in the end. Only finish this difference in kind. You're my kind, Will, and the men you work with are my kind. Yes, the work is changing, but that isn't the heart of it. There's no virtue in the work, but that men should stand as they are.'

'Stand equal?'

'Stand as they are, with nothing bearing them down. For you that was made quick.'

'Part of it was made quick.'

'Only it isn't solved, when it's made quick for you. The rest of us need it, remember.'

Matthew nodded and lay back, staring up at the light from the window. Harry watched him carefully, though his eyes were tired. He had spoken strongly and eagerly, but the effort had left its mark, through his whole body.

'Did you want to say this to me, Dad? Did you think I was getting it wrong?'

'Aye, I wanted to say it.'

'I'm glad we've been able to talk about it. None of it's easy, and I think about it too much on my own.'

'In general don't matter. That's forcing it out, like it gets in the papers.'

'I said on my own.'

'Don't leave it on your own. We're all living with it.'

'I think you've lived with it.'

'I am living with it.'

Matthew looked across and smiled. Harry smiled back, quickly, but his eyes were heavy and closing. He took off his glasses and stretched his hands down over his knees, lying back in his chair.

3

Matthew had to go back, for the start of term. After three days in Glynmawr, he caught the bus to Gwenton, to connect with the London express. While he was eating his breakfast in the back-kitchen, Harry was still asleep. When it was nearly time for the bus, he went up. Harry lay in a deep, quiet sleep, his mouth hanging open.

'I'd better not wake him.'

'He'd never forgive us, Will, if we didn't. He'd want to see you before you go.'

'Are you sure?'

Ellen moved past him and bent over the bed. Gently, she laid her hands on each side of her husband's head, and spoke to him. Matthew watched the hands on the head, the fingers touching the thin hair. The mouth closed, and the eyes opened slowly, still clouded with sleep.

'Will's going now. You want to just say good-bye.'

The eyes moved round, and rested on Matthew. He could see the effort, the tired fight for consciousness. Then the lips smiled, and Harry lifted both hands, taking his son's hand between them.

'Yes, son, have a good journey.'

'Yes, and you rest.'

Matthew felt suddenly afraid, as the words passed between them. At a distance serious illness is dramatic: the wrestle with death, the conflict of strength and pain. But the reality now seemed these long-drawn hours, these gradual days, in which fear was no longer an isolated feeling, but an ordinary element, absorbed and familiar. He had come to see his father recovered, but what he saw now was a harder reality.

'I can't say all that I want, Will.'

'I'll be here again soon, Dad. And I'll write.'

'Aye, good-bye, son.'

Harry closed his eyes. Ellen looked at him carefully, and then turned to Matthew. He could see the strain in her face. She was much more aware of this morning's difference. They went down together, and Matthew stopped by the door.

'Should I go, do you think?'

'Oh yes, you must go, Will.'

'I suppose so. Though I'm sorry we woke him.'

'No,' Ellen said. 'Go on now, or you'll miss it.'

He leaned forward and kissed her cheek. Picking up his bag, he hurried down the lane. The bus was crowded, for it was market-day. He had to stand, and could not look out. But in the warmth of the bus he felt a sudden closeness of contact, that was more than the physical effect of the people crowded around him. He became conscious of it, obliquely, by finding himself thinking again about separation. The bus was carrying him away from his parents, and from the village where so much of his active feeling still lay. But, enclosing this, there was some other feeling, that he could not easily name. 'We went and walked in the market', Harry had said. The words came back now, with a sudden extraordinary force.

In the train from Gwenton, he was alone again, until at Abernant an elderly woman got in and immediately began talking. Her husband was a retired guard, who could no longer get out of the house. She was going to Newport to buy him an overcoat, at the only shop he thought well of, but don't ask her why he wanted an overcoat, when he could no longer so much as walk down the garden. He had given her the money and told her the shop. All his life he'd been a miser, she didn't mind saying. Eight hundred pounds he'd saved, from a guard's wages, and it was all there, in the house, she knew where he kept it, but he was the only one must touch it, and today he had sent her to Newport. He had been a good man to her, though it wasn't the life she'd expected. She was born on a farm; she remembered bringing the lambs in from the snow, and the lambs this season were good, weren't they? She still looked at them, whenever she went on the train. But an overcoat, and she'd have to carry it back. And to say at the shop it was for him. He was on their books; they'd still got his measurements. And it would probably never be worn, though it would come for their son, who'd signed on the full time in the Regular Army but would be finished in the autumn. He'd never wanted him to go into the Army, but he was never happy at home, never settled. And that money always in the house, though they still lived poor, and the Army paid up a pension. When her son came out he was talking of getting a farm; a small place, on the mountain, with a few geese and a few sheep. R. J. Walters it was, the shop; the best value, he said. Just over the bridge from the station.

At Newport, Matthew held open the door, and the woman got out and left him, with as little ceremony as she had begun talking. He walked over the bridge to wait for the London train, but this sudden pattern of another life, half-told, stayed in his mind, unsatisfactory and strange. He could listen, but he could no longer interpret. Not only the barriers, but the categories, were down.

The long platform was crowded, and he moved into one of the few empty spaces. Then he caught what he was doing, and hesitated. It had become a habit, this moving away, a habit no less his own because it was also the habit of this crowded society. The immediate defence prepared itself; that he was country-bred, used to space and aloneness. And this defence was plausible, the need to be alone was real, until the crowded hall, the chapel, the bus, were remembered. He saw how over the years he had been steadily moving away, avoiding contact. The way of thinking which had supported him in this seemed suddenly a dead weight, an immaturity of which he had been conscious since this crisis in his father's life. The sources of denial, the small real denials like this moving away, seemed to flow again in his body, in an overwhelming rush of feeling, and now at last he was in contact with them, had no defences against them. He had to stand where he was and taste this despair, recognizing its elements. Closing his eyes, he saw

Harry's heavy body, and the crowd moved in it, the crowd in its constant pressures. Through his whole body he could hear the deep, strong voice, and the rhythms went out into all the voices around him, until he heard his own voice, differently pitched. For some moments this lasted, the voices rising, until it seemed they would break him. The fear was very deep, and never, until now, had it erupted like this, in this weight of voices. It seemed clearer and closer to him than the actual sounds along the platform. Drawing on all his strength, he took its weight, letting the fear and the anger run through him.

His arm was touched, and he turned quickly.

'Mr Price?'

'Yes.'

'Will Price? From Glynmawr?'

'Yes.'

He stared, not knowing the face. He saw the Inspector's cap, and the pale, narrow features.

'You won't know me, but I know your Dad.'

'Yes?'

'They phoned through from Glynmawr. They said you were catching this train.'

'What is it?'

'Your Dad, Will. Another attack. They want you, if you can, to go back.'

Matthew stared along the crowded platform, hearing only the echo of the tumult of voices.

'I was lucky to find you,' the Inspector said. 'But you're like your Dad, and I took the chance.'

'Yes. Thank you.'

'There's a train in ten minutes. Platform Five, in the bay. I'm glad I found you.'

'All right, thanks. I'll get across. Though I'd better get a ticket.'

'Aye. As you like. Or pay the other end.'

The Inspector was watching him now, strangely. He felt the jerk of habitual resentment, and then his mind cleared.

'Look, thanks,' he said warmly, and put out his hand.

'Go on, boy, I know how it is.'

He hurried and bought his ticket, then crossed the bridge to the other platform. As he went down to the platform the steps were crowded with people, from another train that had just arrived. For a moment, again, he felt the recoil, but it was not shame, now, that arrested it. The pressure which had nearly broken him seemed suddenly cleansing. It was as if the old fear had been burned out of him, though the response that he had learned from it was still there in his body. Yet now, on the steps under the arch, it was no longer a crowd that he saw, but the hurrying, actual people.

He went slowly down the steps, watching the people who passed him. It was as if, for the first time, he was able to know them as himself, and this was like a change in the weight of his body, a deep flowing-back of energy. He was feeling the recovery of a childhood which at the moment of recovery was a child's experience no more, but a living connection between memory and substance. 'We went and walked in the market', he remembered, and the pattern as a whole seemed suddenly clear, as he walked to the train for Glynmawr.

4

Ellen stood in the kitchen, very pale, her lips trembling. Matthew kissed her quickly on the lips.

'Where's Dad?'

'Upstairs, Will. He's been given morphia.'

'I'll go up.'

'Yes. Though don't expect him to know you. With the drug, now, he doesn't know what he's saying.'

'I'll go up.'

The bedroom curtains were drawn, and Harry's breathing was heavy. He stood by the bed, waiting, and suddenly Harry grasped his hand.

'It's all right, Will.'

The lips were very dry, and the tongue came out to moisten them. But the tongue was white-coated, almost scaly, and the deep eyes moved, restlessly, looking round into the corners of the room. Matthew held on to the hand, and the grip tightened again suddenly.

'Sweetheart,' Harry said, turning.

Matthew watched, holding tightly to the hand.

'I get it clear, Will. Then it goes, of a sudden. The clear goes, of a sudden. Only the clear isn't what I started with. You could say the dream isn't real at all. Bringing together things you didn't know they were there.'

'Yes,' Matthew said, holding tightly to the hand. He saw that Harry was surprised by the voice, turning again and looking up into his face.

'Only a small part of your life's your work, Will.'

Matthew nodded. He could not risk speaking again.

'Only one trade to get into,' Harry said urgently, looking out across the room. 'Over there, the top of the wallpaper, the brown line on the top of it. I tell her I keep seeing a man there, a man with a barrow, wheeling along the line. They'd say not to be stupid, but I see him along the line, and I ask where he's wheeling it to. I lie and ask, like the voices coming back. They say not to imagine things. It's only the one trade.'

'You should sleep now.'

'You get these connections,' Harry said urgently. 'Like one way all into filth, and there's filth enough when you're ill. Only one way all into mental filth. Of course not only that.'

'Yes, take it easy.'

'Only the one trade to get into and that's a wife to love you. The only trade, sweetheart. A loving wife. The only trade to get into.'

There was a noise on the stairs.

'That buzzard now. Where's he going? Where's he taking it?' Harry shouted. The door opened, and Ellen came in. She stared at Matthew, her eyes wide and frightened.

'I've brought you some tea,' she said, walking round. 'It's all right. The doctor said you could have it.'

Harry closed his eyes, and pain flushed up through the face.

'Here,' Ellen said, and held out the tray. The cup stood on a white lace mat, which covered the bird on the tray.

'Yes,' Harry said, and opened his eyes. Ellen took the cup, and held it to his lips. The tea spilled as he gulped at it, and he reached down and pushed away the mat.

'There,' Ellen said, leaning over him. 'Don't bother about the mat.'

Harry gulped at the tea again and then smiled.

'Aye, or old Mrs Lucas with her eye on one side will be looking and saying you've wet my mat.'

Ellen's fingers tightened on the cup, until the knuckles were white.

'I was just telling Will what they'd say,' Harry added, smiling.

'Will must go and phone,' Ellen said.

'Phone? Why?'

'We said we'd let the doctor know how you were.'

'Aye, I'm talking a lot of nonsense,' Harry said, lying back.

'No,' Matthew said.

5

John Evans came in the early afternoon. After examining Harry, he phoned for an ambulance and his admission to hospital.

'He needs treatment I can't give him here, Will.'

'All right.'

'I know what you're thinking, boy. There's nothing I can say.'

The house was silent, as they waited for the ambulance. Ellen sat by Harry, who was sleeping. It was the bedroom they had first used when they had come as lodgers with Morgan. The curtains were drawn, except for a gap of a few inches, through which she watched the lane. Across the patch and on the drying green the plums and damsons were already in blossom, and the buds on the apples were white and ready to burst. From the high chimney of the cottage a column of pale blue smoke rose and quickly dispersed. Beyond the line of the roof, the mountains were light.

Towards four the ambulance came, making its way with difficulty past the heaped red earth of the trench for the water. Phil Watkins and Teddy stopped work as it passed them, and Phil spoke to the driver. At the house the ambulance turned and the men came to the back door. Matthew let them in and stood back as they went upstairs. When they had gone into the bedroom, he walked up to the landing. Harry had woken, and was saying something that he could not catch. The stretcher was manoeuvred with difficulty, in the crowded bedroom. Matthew went back downstairs.

Harry was carried slowly down. His eyes were closed again; he seemed not to want to look. The stretcher was carried down the passage, brushing the heavy coats on the wall, and into the kitchen. As they came out Harry opened his eyes and looked quickly but deliberately around. Matthew saw him look over at the cottage as they turned at the gate. Then he smiled up at Matthew, who touched his hand. Ellen came out, pulling on her coat, and carrying a small case. Then the stretcher was lifted in, and she climbed in behind it. The doors were closed and fastened, and the men went round to the cab. Matthew stood with his hand on the gate as the ambulance started and drove away down the lane.

6

On the seven bus, Ellen came back from the hospital. She was very tired and soon went to bed. Matthew went out to phone Susan, who was expecting him home. Then he walked back, and up to the bedroom he had left that morning.

He was woken before it was light, by the bell. It had been fitted to the front door, and was ringing now, very loudly, in short, sharp bursts. He got up confusedly and went out to the landing. Ellen, pulling a coat over her nightdress, was hurrying along the passage below him. He called, but she did not turn. He hurried down after her and saw her opening the front door. He could see only the uniform past her: the policeman's helmet and cape, lightly flecked with rain.

'You've come to fetch me. He's worse,' Ellen said.

The policeman moved and hesitated. Matthew could see his face now. He was new in the village, a stranger. Very young, he was holding himself stiffly. Over Ellen's shoulder, he caught sight of Matthew and seemed relieved.

'What message is it?' Matthew asked.

'I'm sorry to have to tell you Mr Price has died.'

'Yes,' Matthew said, putting his arm round Ellen as she stood by the open door.

'The hospital rang me. It happened just after three o'clock.'

'Come in, Mam. Come away from the cold.'

Ellen turned and looked up into his face. She had prepared her own version of this call and was still bewildered, as if the men were speaking a language she did not understand.

'What is it, Will?'

'Dad has died. You must come and sit by the fire.'

'There isn't a fire, Will.'

'I'm very sorry, Mrs Price, to have brought you such bad news,' the constable said, awkwardly.

'Thank you. That's all right.'

'Very well, sir. Thank you. And allow me to offer my sympathy.'

He watched the door closing, and saw where a few drops of water had fallen, just under the bell. As they stood in the passage, Ellen broke down, suddenly. Without warning, he felt her body violently shaking under his arm, and then the cry came, a terrible unrecognizable cry. Taking the weight of her shoulders, he helped her along to the kitchen, and eased her down into Harry's chair. He turned to the sticks in the oven, and crouched to get a fire going. Taking his coat from the pegs by the door, he wrapped it around her. Then he switched on the kettle, leaning past where she lay in the chair. He did all this mechanically. He was feeling nothing. The dry sleeper sticks began to crackle in the grate, and as he crouched, arranging the coal, he felt their warmth on his eyes. There was nothing to do but to wait, until the fire burned through.

313

CHAPTER TWO

1

The light came as they sat together in the kitchen. They were very conscious of being left alone, but when the day started the news spread quickly, and a process began which was to take over and control all that had happened: a deliberate exertion of strength by this close community, made, as always, for its members who needed help, but made also, it seemed, for the sake of the village, to prevent anything reaching out and disturbing its essential continuity. To Matthew it seemed that Harry was being deliberately forgotten; that the death, already, was pushed firmly into the past. Locked in his own grief, which was only slowly coming to consciousness, he at first resented this pressure. Yet it was not unfeeling. It was a learned reaction, by which the process of restoring the tissue of this common life was at once begun; a reaction as if to danger, requiring this immediate preventive exertion. It was as if the village had accepted death so deeply that it allowed no room for any personal reaction to it. This hard concentration on the living was not easy to bear, as the fact of loss, the slow sense of emptiness, throbbed through the mind. Yet the concentration was so settled, the emotional direction so certain, that it could not in fact be resisted. The shock was overborne and contained by this insistent application of a different energy.

Mrs Hybart came and went straight to Ellen. Matthew went upstairs to dress. When he came back down, Mrs Whistance, from the cottage, was also there. Between them the women were getting Ellen upstairs to dress. Left alone in the kitchen, he felt a sudden physical sickness, and hurried out to the shed to fetch coal, for something to do. When he had filled the bucket and was lifting it back, he saw the block by the door, with its intricate pattern of tiny straight cuts like veins. The hacker was cut into it, its handle pointing upwards, arranged for the hand to take it. Impulsively, he reached for the handle. Its wood had been worn very smooth, and there was an iron ring recently added to it, near the blade. As he touched the handle, the blade moved a little, where it had cut into the block. He did not pull it out, but let his fingers close round the smooth wood, and his hand rested there, finding a strange reassurance. He stood for some time in the shed, which smelt of coal and damp sacking. Then a car came into sight up the pitch, and drew up at the gate. As Morgan got out, Matthew let go of the handle, and carried back the coal.

'Where's Ellen?'

'The women are with her. Upstairs.'

'That's right. Go on, Will, take that coal in, don't let me stop you.'

'Of course. And come in.'

'We'll get some tea on,' Morgan said, as he walked into the kitchen. 'It's a bit sharp, isn't it, this early, still?'

'Yes. I'll put on the kettle.'

'I came out as soon as I heard. Eira rung me just as I was thinking of getting up.'

'Yes.'

'One thing I did stop for, Will. I don't know what you want done, but I just had a word with Harris.'

'Who's Harris?'

'Ted Harris. He's the undertaker. Of course there are others, but we've always known Ted.'

'All right.'

'Ted suggested Monday. You'll have to confirm it. I told him Harry wanted cremation.'

'Did you know that?'

'Yes. From years back. We used to argue about it.'

'Argue?'

315

'Aye, Harry and I were agreed, but some of the other chaps were against it.'

'I shall have to ask Mam. It'll be her decision.'

'She'll know. Anyway, Ted's there, if you want him. It isn't that I want to take things out of your hands, Will. It's just that I know how these things are done.'

'Yes.'

'I don't want to have to argue with you like I argued with Harry.'

'You were friends.'

'More than that, Will.'

The door opened, and Ellen came in. She was wearing a black dress and her hair was tidy and very close to her head. She seemed remarkably controlled, though Mrs Hybart stayed close to her. Then she saw Morgan, who went to her at once. As he put out his hands she broke down immediately, and Mrs Hybart held her as she wept. The kitchen suddenly seemed too warm and crowded.

'No use us talking about it,' Morgan said, at last. 'What you've got to do, see, is rest. Will and I will arrange things.'

'Yes, Morgan. Thank you,' Ellen said, and wiped her eyes. She moved slowly across the kitchen and stood near Matthew by the fire. Morgan and Mrs Hybart began talking. Mrs Whistance stood silently waiting, by the inner door. When the kettle boiled Ellen took over. She made tea and carefully passed it round.

Slowly the morning settled. After a time Morgan went off to phone the various members of the family who had to be told. He seemed to know these details better than Matthew himself: knew where Harry's brothers were, and how they could be reached. When he was sure of his mother, Matthew went over the details of the funeral, and made a list of the things he must arrange. People were still calling, standing for a while in the kitchen. The first question from each caller was, 'Are there to be flowers?' Ellen said yes. Matthew's last question to her was the most difficult: did she want to go to the hospital and see Harry?

'No, Will, I shan't go. I'd rather remember him as he was.'

'I shall go, in any case.'

'Well, that's for you to decide.'

Morgan came back.

'Ready, boy?' he said briskly, as he came into the kitchen. 'I'll take Will in the car, Ellen. We'll get through it quicker.'

They went out together, standing for a moment in the lane and looking out over the patch. On the way down, Phil Watkins stopped them, and put his hand in at the window, reaching across Morgan to take Matthew's hand. He held it very firmly and for much longer than was usual. Morgan became impatient, and with a quick, 'Right, Phil', moved the car on.

'Don't want too much of that sort of thing,' he said as they jolted down the lane. 'Now Harry, see, was quite unsentimental. He wouldn't have wanted a lot of show.'

'I never knew quite what he wanted,' Matthew said. 'I think nobody did.'

'He was a good, practical man. Always sensible.'

'That isn't what I said. Other people worked out what he wanted, but he kept himself clear while he had the strength.'

'We're none of us really strong, Will.'

Their first call, down the pitch into Gwenton, was to register the death. But the office was closed, and a card on the door announced that it would be open on Monday, but closed all Saturday, 'due to weddings'.

'Damn, I forgot that, Will. It's Tax Saturday, isn't it? They're all getting married.'

'Do they have to close? It seems inefficient.'

'No, Will, it's not inefficient. There's only Meredith, see. It's how it has to be done. Only we need a special chit for the cremation, we'll have to get it today.'

'They say, "Closed till Monday".'

'Ah, you give up too easy, mun. You forget what we're like. If Meredith's doing the weddings, we can catch him somewhere. I've got the certificate from the hospital.'

'You didn't tell me that.'

'No. Still. Come on, we'll find him.'

They drove through the narrow streets to the second part of the registry office, where the weddings took place. Morgan led the way in and tapped on the inner door. A girl came out and Morgan explained.

'Well, there's one wedding on now, and another waiting in the waiting-room,' she said. 'And after that he's got to go to the Catholic, then back here for three more.'

'They run it through quick, don't they?'

'Well, not long.'

'Aren't you in the queue now? Where's your young man?'

'He's away in the Army.'

'Well, we can find someone else. Keep the pace up.'

'Yes. You'd better wait in the waiting-room. I'll ask Mr Meredith if he can see you in between.'

'There's a good girl now,' Morgan concluded.

They went to the bare waiting-room. Inside was the wedding-party. The bride, in a lilac suit, stood by the empty grate, with her mother sitting on a bench alongside. The men stood together near the window, all in black suits and with buttonhole flowers. Most of them were young, and the bridegroom could not be distinguished. In their ordinary clothes, Morgan and Matthew seemed out of place. The silence became difficult. After a few moments Morgan was moving impatiently, and at last spoke to the bride's mother.

'You're Mrs Edwards Gwryne, aren't you?'

'That's right, Mr Rosser. I knew you when you come in.'

'Getting married again then?'

'No. Only Ellen here.'

'Well done, Ellen,' Morgan said, as the girl moved and smiled.

'What about you then?' Mrs Edwards asked.

'Me. Well, I'd be in the clink. No, we're here on different business, I'm afraid. Harry Price, did you know, Glynmawr? Died last night in the hospital. This is his son, Will.'

'No, I didn't know him. I'm very sorry to hear it.'

'Thank you,' Matthew said, awkwardly.

318

'Only the other office is closed, see. What with all you young people marrying for the tax man.'

'Aye, it is all today,' Ellen said, looking down at her lilac shoes.

There was movement in the passage outside. The other wedding was evidently over.

'Now we shan't delay you,' Morgan said instantly, 'but we just have to get in to the registrar first.'

Matthew saw Mrs Edwards' annoyance, but Morgan took his arm and hurried him through.

'Here we are, Mr Meredith,' Morgan said confidently, as they stepped from the confetti-strewn passage into the tiny office, where an electric fire threw out a dry glaring heat. The registrar, a small dark man of forty, looked up, obviously annoyed.

'We shan't keep the wedding a minute, but we have to register a death. We must get it done today.'

'Very well. Though I'm late as it is,' the registrar said. He opened a drawer and took out a pile of books and forms then looked nervously around for his pen.

'Sit down,' he said curtly, but the little office was overcrowded, and there was only one available chair, which Morgan offered to Matthew. Matthew sat leaning forward to the desk. He was glad to be in a position to recover any kind of control. It was still, through everything, the emptiest, hardest day he had known, but there was nowhere the least gap for his actual feelings.

'Name of deceased?' the registrar asked, already writing in a slow, formal script.

'Henry John Price.'

'Harry,' Morgan said.

'No. Henry on his birth certificate.'

'Why we have to have it today,' Morgan said, 'it's to be cremation.'

The registrar was writing, but now suddenly looked up.

'Cremation? Well, why didn't you say so? It's a much longer business for cremation. I can't possibly do it now.'

'It's because it's cremation we need the papers today. Ted Harris explained to me on the phone.'

319

'When's the funeral?'

'Monday.'

'Yes,' said the registrar, putting down his pen. 'But still I can't do it now. You saw yourself there's a wedding waiting, and I have to be at the Catholic Church at ten.'

'When could you do it?' Matthew asked.

'If you'll be back here at ten to twelve,' the registrar said, getting up. 'That's the best I can do. I'm sorry.'

'Ten to twelve,' Matthew repeated, getting up.

'It would be much simpler if we could get it over now,' Morgan said. 'This is the dead man's son. It isn't pleasant to keep the thing hanging over him.'

'I'm sorry,' the registrar said. 'Miss Davies, we'll have that wedding in now.'

'All right. Come on, Will.'

They went out past the wedding party lined up in the corridor.

'You should never give in to men like that,' Morgan said.

'Maybe not.'

'What now then, Will?'

'I thought the hospital.'

'No, no. Not yet. Give them time to tidy it all up. What about the flowers?'

'Well yes. Though I must go to the hospital.'

'Tomorrow'll be best for that. I know how they work it. But the flowers, see, there's only today.'

'All right. Where?'

'Go, you're like guiding a stranger round, Will. Roberts, of course. There's only the one.'

'I think I remember it. And as to being a stranger, I was a boy in this town, not a man with this to arrange.'

'You're holding yourself too tight, Will. You're like Harry.'

'I'll hold myself as I am. Roberts, you say?'

'Aye, just at the bottom, Will. And I'll pick you up there, about half past eleven. I must just put in an appearance up the works.'

'Of course.'

'It's different see, now, from when it was my own. I have to write letters, whether I want to or not.'

'What do you mean? Isn't it your own?'

'No. Not since nineteen forty-nine. Though we don't spread that around.'

'What happened?'

'I got a good offer. From Rutherford's. It's happening everywhere, the big people taking over. We're just a depot now, really, labelling the pulp from abroad.'

'Why did you let it go?' Matthew asked.

'It was a good offer. And Rutherford's mean more than I do at the bank. Not that I've suffered. I make more as their manager than I cleared on my own.'

'More money.'

'Yes.'

Matthew looked carefully at Morgan. For the last hour he had been resenting him, but in terms of the old enclosure; judging everything in his own feelings. Now, with this unexpected news, he was conscious of Morgan as a wholly separate life. He looked at the florid, still handsome face, the thickly curling grey hair, the square, heavy overcoat: all the settled presence of the man, but with his history suddenly alive in it, the active composition of a life.

'Harry was one of the few that knew it, see, the way it all went. But a secret was safe with Harry, aside from the fact that I always told him everything.'

'Why have you told me now, Morgan?'

'I don't know. Only I noticed how you reacted to me getting you around. I noticed while I was talking in there. It shows, see.'

'I was glad of your help.'

'Aye, but not how it was given. Still, I know these things. And it's what I told you before, about Harry. You have to say it, at a certain point. Like I said to tell him about what you'd told me. I've remembered that, Will. The whole centre of your life.'

'I said that. But where does it leave me now?'

'Where the rest of us are, Will. That's why I've stayed by you.'

321

'Look, you know I'm grateful,' Matthew said, but Morgan was already turning away, opening the door of the car.

'You get them flowers ordered. Then half past eleven. Back here, it had better be.'

'Right.'

'I ordered mine on the phone, see. I get moving quick when I start.'

'Aye, you don't tell everybody everything either.'

'Not all at once I don't,' Morgan said, and slammed the car door.

Matthew walked down the sloping street to the florist's. But of course it was not the florist's; just a little, low, dark shop – J.J. Roberts, Seedsman. Once he saw it he remembered. A bell jangled as he opened the door, and he was reminded of Mrs Preece's shop in Glynmawr. It seemed a different man he was thinking of, his father pushing the bike and searching the road for the pound that had never been lost. Roberts's smelled of meal, very heavy and sweet. A man in his sixties, older than Harry, came out from a back room.

'Yes?'

'I want to order two wreaths, for a funeral on Monday.'

'Wreaths? No, no.'

'You do wreaths, don't you? Someone directed me here.'

'Yes, we do them, but not on Monday. All the weddings today, I'm right out.'

'No flowers, you mean?'

'None whatever. If you listen to the hymns, spring is the time of flowers, but not really. In the fields yes, but for wreaths, you understand, or for brides to carry, it's very short.'

'Can't you order them, from a market or somewhere? Flowers are available all the year round.'

'Aye, in some places. But there's the train, you see. Not for Monday.'

'You can't help me then?'

'No, I'm sorry.'

'Very well. Thank you. Good morning.'

'No trouble,' Roberts said.

Matthew pushed out through the door. All right, let the place go its own way. There were other ways, after all. He hurried to the library, which he remembered the way to. It was simply a question of getting all the florists' addresses within train distance, then ordering by phone. He waited in a queue at the counter. The librarian had been at school with him, and welcomed him warmly.

'Only the thing is, Matthew, our only trade directory is pre-war. Some of them might be out of business, others the names changed and so on.'

'I'll check with the current phone directory. It won't take long if you can spare me a shelf to work on.'

'Of course. Come with me.'

He walked past the book stacks, at last, after the uncertainties of the morning, feeling competent again. Left with the directories, he worked very fast, but it was still some time before he had a list of twelve numbers. He hurried out of the library, and down towards the post office. As he crossed the street, Morgan pulled up beside him.

'Get in, Will. I've only the one more call.'

'No, I must phone. That fool Roberts is out of flowers.'

'Never?'

'It's the weddings. But it doesn't matter. I've been to the library. I've got this list.'

Morgan took the list, and looked at it.

'You don't want to bother with that, Will,' he said, handing it back. 'You leave it to me.'

'But he's got none.'

'Sit you here, Will. I'll be back.'

Matthew stood impatiently by the car. When Morgan came back, looking down, Matthew assumed the result he had expected. Perhaps at last now he could do things his own way.

'All right then,' Morgan said, getting into the car.

'You mean I should phone?'

'No, no. The flowers are coming.'

323

'But he said there weren't any.'

'Look, Will, you don't do these things our way, so let some-one else do them. If you'd just told Roberts who they were for.'

'I don't see that. Either he has them or not.'

'Of course he has them, but of course, as he told you, he's short. The thing is, he knew about Harry and about the other funerals Monday. He made an estimate for those, and he's not selling beyond that to anybody who happens to walk in.'

'But if they weren't ordered yet?'

'He knew more or less. If you'd just said who you were.' Matthew looked down the narrow street, frowning.

'Yes, Morgan, I've lost the habit of that. It came not to matter. And on the whole I prefer it that way, when it's this sort of preference. But still, if they're ordered. You ordered two?'

'Yes. One for you, one for your Mam. Of course the others are going through, normal.'

'All right,' Matthew said, and crumpled his list into his pocket.

'Now just this call, Will, then we'll clear the rest of it up.'

'Right.'

He managed the rest of the business with only a minimum of attention: everyone else seemed to know exactly what was to be done. Only the death itself remained to be faced.

2

Morgan called on the Sunday morning, soon after eleven, to take him to the hospital. As they drove in they hardly spoke. Morgan was unusually hesitant and withdrawn. He parked the car in front of the hospital, and waited for Matthew to walk round. He looked down at the ground as he waited, and did not move as Matthew prepared to go on.

'Are you coming in, Morgan?'

'Aye, come on.'

'Only come if you want to.'

'It's not myself. It's you, Will.'

'Look, I'm prepared for this.'

'Are you? I doubt it. How often have you actually seen death?'

'I was in the war. I found my grandfather. Every death is different.'

'Only what you must think, Will, it's not Harry we're seeing. The Harry we knew has gone. What's left isn't him.'

'I don't agree. I'm sorry.'

'That's what's been worrying me. I could feel it was like that. And I know, Will, now listen. If you think like that it will break you.'

'No.'

'Look, I'm not trying to preach to you. I'm not trying to tell you this is just his earthly body and his soul is at peace. I hear them say that, and I don't argue, if it comforts them. But it isn't a question of thinking about it, sitting down and thinking about death. You just see it and you know, this is not him. The Harry we knew has gone, no use asking where.'

'Shall we go in?'

'All right, Will. But at least I warned you. And remember this wasn't the gentlest sort of end.'

Matthew did not answer. He was walking ahead to the big door, and pushed it open to enter the wide corridor. It was a small hospital, and there was no place for inquiries. They stood together in the corridor, and saw no one but the occasional nurse hurrying from one of the wards. At the far end a door was open, and they could see men lying in the nearest beds. Music came from a distant wireless.

'Do we just wait?'

'Aye, this is a place for waiting.'

Down the stairs at the end of the corridor came a nurse and an elderly man, supporting a very frail old woman. They were intently concentrated on her stiff, weak movements. The interval between each step seemed intolerably long, and the life that was being supported seemed unbelievably tenuous and fragile.

At last the descent was completed, and then came the long, slow movement down the wide corridor to the front door. Morgan and Matthew stood aside, feeling the stiffness of their overcoats, as the three passed them. The nurse was very young, with a pale, clear, very beautiful skin. From her hair and her eyes the ordinary young life seemed to spring so richly that it could never be used up and worn out. She held herself very stiffly and formally, in the slow progress to the door. Matthew, watching, felt a sudden impulse to go away. This was no place for any personal grief. Individual memory was overridden by a different, undeniable process. The music still played from the distant wireless. At the end of the corridor, the man in the nearest bed turned his head slowly. The front door opened and closed, and again the corridor was empty.

'Well?'

'When she comes back.'

They continued to wait, and at last the front door opened again and the nurse hurried back alone. Morgan stepped forward and spoke to her in an undertone. She nodded and hurried off.

'She's gone for the keys,' Morgan said. 'Then she'll take us.'

The distant music stopped, and was replaced by a voice, so low and muffled that its words could not be made out. They stood with their backs to the high green wall. Then the nurse reappeared. She had put on her long black cape, with its vivid scarlet lining. As she turned, holding the keys, the change to ceremony was distinct and abrupt. They followed her, self-consciously, and the black cape seemed more important every minute, as they went on their winding journey. They turned from the corridor and passed through the back of the hospital, past kitchens and washrooms, along narrowing stone corridors, under smaller windows. Then a small door was opened, and they were out in a narrow paved yard, with a low brick building across it. They crossed the yard in silence, and the door was unlocked.

'Wait here,' the nurse said, leaving them inside the door, in the sudden cold. The floor was of grey concrete, with a tap in the corner, and a length of hose. Where they stood was still slightly damp, and the sunlight from the door fell strangely across it. On the left of the door was a row of cubicles, each with a heavy blue curtain in front of it. The nurse entered several, moving quickly. As she drew the heavy blue curtains the material caught at the swing of her cape. Then she stopped, and went inside the third cubicle from the left. For more than a minute her hands were busy, at the level of her waist. She turned and motioned them forward.

Matthew went up to where she stood. Only a small space was left between the bier and the partition wall. He looked down at Harry's face, and as he did so the nurse put her hands on the head, moving them slowly and gently, in a circular movement, over the temples and the thin hair. This strange movement, a repeated caressing, she continued, looking down. Matthew stared at the face, under the young, moving hands. It was dark and very tight, the mouth very small. He saw the grey set of the flesh; the broadened nostrils, packed with cotton wool; the narrow gleam of the teeth; the moving hands at the temples. Slowly, he leaned forward, and touched the closed eyes and the wisp of hair on the high forehead. The nurse withdrew her hands, as he touched the face. Then Morgan, leaning close behind him, quickly touched the cheeks and the eyes. The nurse took the blanket and covered the face. They backed out of the cubicle, and the heavy blue curtain was drawn again. Without speaking, they walked out into the yard and the sun.

They made their way back, through the stone corridors, the washrooms and the noisy kitchens. In the main corridor, the nurse called them to wait, and at last returned with the case Ellen had carried to the ambulance, and with a grey dressing-gown and Harry's watch. Matthew took the things, and thanked her. She smiled at him, quickly. As she hurried upstairs again, she was already taking off her cape.

3

From early on Sunday afternoon, the house was crowded. Harry's brother Lewis had arrived, and sat in Harry's chair opposite Ellen.

Neighbours and relatives crowded into the living-room and the front room, until every chair was occupied, and some of the younger men were sitting on the floor. The talk was loud and animated. By evening, after the younger women had served tea, the atmosphere was lively and even gay. In the press of people, Matthew felt rested and assured, but when he had to go out, to see Pugh after evensong, this feeling vanished. He walked to the church, and waited for the vicar. Arthur Pugh was now well over seventy, very slow and gentle. There was little to discuss: simply the confirmation of arrangements already made for the funeral. The strain on them both was obvious, as they sat in the darkening drawing-room, where twenty years earlier they had sat so often, on their regular evenings. At last Matthew got up.

'So you went to see?' Pugh said suddenly, from behind him. It was the same slow, sad voice, weakened by age.

'Yes,' Matthew said. 'I was thinking about that.'

Pugh smiled, delighted.

'Were they only the Glynmawr chapels, better built?'

'I don't know. Yes, in many ways. But at times it makes sense, this dialogue of the centuries. As an outpost of that it's important: keeping that conversation alive. And then clarifying, sometimes, where we live ourselves.'

'You told your father about it?'

'Yes. We discussed it.'

'He wanted to know. It was like going himself. And now I'm going away. Giving up. Going back, in July, to my own village.'

'Retiring, sir?'

'Yes, having failed. But not altogether failed. And the village I shall hardly know, but I want to go back there.'

'There isn't success or failure. In those terms.'

'When you go out there is,' the old man said, smiling.

The valley was darkening quickly, as Matthew walked back to the patch. The house was still crowded and the talk fluent. In the living-room Lewis was at the centre of things. The physical resemblance to Harry was marked, but the manner was different. Matthew stood by the door, as Lewis went on with his story.

'"Got your old woman in the bag then?" Dad asked him. Because the fox, see, now, was kicking a bit, and old Davy was clutching it. "Her?" Davy said. "Her han't growed a tail yet." "How d'you know, Davy?" Dad said. "Have you looked lately? Last time I looked..." But old Davy was late, see, and off he goes through the dingle, kneeing the fox in the bag. Harry and I run after him, and Dad let us go. He was staggering, old Davy, and it weren't only the weight. They always said he'd come to his funeral drunk, and breathe it all over the mourners. Anyhow, Harry and I kept by him, till we got to this place in the wood where the let-go was to be. The huntsman would blow, see, as they crossed the road, hundred yards or so down, then Davy was to open the sack and that'd be another quick draw. There was a lot in it, mind. Davy'd been doing it for years. Half a crown, I think, and nothing much to it. Anyhow, Harry and I cooched down by the bag. He stunk, that bloody fox, but old Davy just hung on to him. After a while, of course, up blows the huntsman, and Davy's out with his knife and cutting the string of the bag. He cut the one string but it had twisted somehow, and down he went, cussing away, still cutting at it, see. Well, by now, of course, the hounds was into the wood, and Harry looked at me should we run. We was only seven and nine see, and all the noise of the hunt and that. If Davy'd been sober he'd have done it, but he'd done it before and never been sober, so I don't know. Anyhow Harry and I stood back and Christ was those hounds quick on it. The fox was still in the bag, see, just the one leg out, and old Davy was under them. We just stood back, our backs to the tree, but mind, if we'd known old Davy. Aye, he got bit, but he was on his feet by the time the hounds ripped the sack and tore the fox up. And Harry got the brush. The huntsman give it to him. Only we never went out with old Davy again.'

As everyone laughed, Lewis sat gravely in his chair. Matthew looked across at his mother, who was laughing. Lewis was smaller and darker than Harry, and the features were more composed, the eyes sharper. He sat on, through the laughter, grave and still in his tight black suit and the high formal white collar. It was part of the technique of this story-telling to remain unmoved, to ignore all reaction.

At nine the visitors left, but the house was still crowded. Matthew stood in the kitchen with his cousin Glynis. They had not met since they were children, but they were able to talk about their work and families. Glynis lived in Rhayader, where her husband had a taxi business. She and Matthew found they shared the same reactions to the way the older members of the family were managing this affair.

'I know if it was me, Will, I'd prefer to be left to myself. Not all this endless talk like a party or a wedding.'

'Yes. I thought I was the only odd one out. I've got used to blaming myself, assuming I've gone wrong somehow. Then if I say what I feel I find many of my feelings are common.'

'I guessed that. It's what they said about Uncle. Your Dad.'

'Did they say that?'

'Yes, he was always a bit of a stranger.'

It was a problem where everyone should sleep, but at last it was arranged that Glynis would go across to Mrs Whistance, and Matthew and his uncle would sleep together in the back bedroom. For a moment Matthew wished that he had been sent to the cottage. He walked across the lane with Glynis, glad to be with someone of his own age, and to go even to the door of the cottage.

He waited outside for a while, to let his uncle undress, and then went to the bathroom. As he opened the door he stopped. The bathroom was full of flowers. All the wreaths had been put there. The larger wreaths were in the bath itself, in a shallow layer of water. Over the floor lay the wreaths and sprays, their scent sweet and overpowering in the tiny room.

As he stood looking down at them, the hard strain broke. Alone with these flowers for his father, the weight seemed to shift suddenly. All the words went, and he stood and wept as he had not wept since childhood: beyond the possibility of control. The tears stung his lips as they streamed down his face, but he could not lift his hand to wipe them away, and the bitter taste seemed part of the overpowering scent of the flowers, which he could now hardly see. At last he reached across for a towel, and rubbed his face with a sudden angry roughness. Then he closed the door, and went along to the bedroom.

It was the bedroom where Harry had been through all his illness. It was strange to open this door again, and go in and not find him. There, still, were the familiar pieces of furniture, the photographs on the walls, the flex with its taped join above the bed. Lewis was already in bed, and Matthew hurried to the far corner to undress. Tying his pyjamas, he switched off the light and got in beside his uncle. Lewis kept turned away from him, on the far side of the bed. Matthew lay on his back, staring up into the darkness.

4

It was no use trying to sleep. It was here Harry had been lying, through all the hours when he had come to talk to him. Lying now in the darkness, his eyes still sore from the virgin pain and bitterness of the sudden weeping, there was a loss of identity, that grew steadily more frightening. He wanted to get out and put on the light, to move about, smoke or read: anything to bring the ordinary reality back. But his uncle, very still, lay there beside him, and he was afraid even to move for fear of disturbing him. The driving, emptying darkness continued, establishing a kind of rhythm, a slow, deep pulse of apparent sound, but the sound was the darkness, slowly taking possession of his consciousness: a continuing beat through his body that he could not arrest, though his eyes were wide open and he stared upwards into the dark. Then, very clearly, though the darkness did not change, the dead face he had touched seemed to drive towards him, its eyes tightly closed. It was only the face, with the depth of the head, and he saw it again and again, moving towards him in the now louder beat, though still all around him the darkness was impenetrable. He lay very still, hardly conscious of Lewis beside him, only knowing he must lie there, making no disturbance. The face was grey and clenched tight, as he had seen it that morning. It seemed never to recede yet always to be driving down at him, as if coming from darkness and distance. Fighting for control, he used all the arguments he could draw on, against its reality. For it seemed no longer an image of memory, but actual and beyond him. He argued that he was watching his own mind, under a breaking tension; that the beat of darkness was the pulse of his own body. But his conviction, staring up, was that he was watching the course of death; that it was Harry's death he was experiencing, and the terror beyond it, the drive into darkness, with the mind still active but reduced to this single rhythm. And behind the head a different darkness was forming, and innumerable figures moved through it yet were part of the darkness. The figures streamed past him, moving without movement, and always one face was nearest, in this procession of darkness, streaming across the dark empty pitch. With his eyes wide open, he stared at this driving darkness. The death beat into him, without pity, without meaning, without pause. He could no longer even think of moving, of hurrying to the switch and recovering the familiar world. The terrible mindless rhythm allowed nothing but itself, its own annihilating darkness.

5

It was light in the lane, and there were voices and movement downstairs. Recalled suddenly, Matthew got up and dressed. They were already eating breakfast as he entered the kitchen, but Glynis immediately stood up and made a place for him, going herself to stand by the stove. He protested, but she smiled and shook her head.

'Did you sleep all right, over the way?'

'Aye, not bad, Will.'

'She had your old room,' Ellen said, and as she spoke Matthew turned, for the first time, to look at her directly. She was pale and frightened, but some of this was contained by the fact that, like the others, she was already formally dressed. It was so unusual, at breakfast in the kitchen, to be dressed to go out, that this in itself, while marking the strangeness of the morning, did much to control and formalize it.

'We haven't much time,' Lewis said. 'They always arrive early.'

Quickly, in the crowded kitchen, with the women working at the sink, Matthew shaved at a glass propped on the narrow black mantelpiece. Before he had finished, the bell rang at the front door, and Lewis went to answer it. Matthew wiped his face, and followed him. Edwin and Olwen Parry had arrived, and were putting their wreath down in the front room. Suddenly, within minutes of the breakfast, the house was filling with neighbours and friends. Everyone was asked in to sit down, while Glynis and Gwen carried the earlier flowers downstairs. Matthew stood at the front door, shaking hands with everyone who arrived. This morning nobody went to the back door, and only a few of the younger men stayed outside. Elwyn and Jim Price came together, carrying a large wreath from all at the station. He stood outside with them, in the cold morning air. Arthur Pugh arrived, so heavily wrapped against the cold that he could barely get out of the hired car. He shook hands with Matthew, and then went inside to Ellen. And still, up the lane, came the neighbours and friends, many more than he had expected. Morgan arrived and turned his car.

'I passed them just up the road, Will. Wait here.'

Then, very slowly, under the arch of trees, the hearse came, with Ted Harris sitting by the driver. When Matthew had first seen him Harris had been in old patched overalls, but now he wore a formal black hat and coat, as if he were arriving from a different generation. The hearse was turned, under Morgan's directions, and backed until it was level with the house. Matthew was looking at the coffin when Ted Harris caught his elbow.

'Get the flowers out now? All right?'

'Yes, I'll get them.'

'No, we get them. You stay here.'

The flowers were carried out to the lane, and the family wreaths were put inside, on the coffin, and the others were lifted above, to the roof. When they had all been put up, Harris slung a rope across, and began lacing it along to secure them.

'You get the wind against them,' he said.

'Will,' Morgan said sharply. He turned and Morgan beckoned him in. Along the passage and for some way up the stairs, all the men were lined up facing him, and he saw the line of black suits, and the set of the faces, the long line of men past whom he must walk. In the living-room, Arthur Pugh stood in his surplice and hood. On all the chairs, round the room, the women were sitting, with a place left for Matthew by his mother. On the table stood the vase of pink-flowering currant, its scent sharp as it had been when he had sat here with Harry, only a few days before. The men closed in, and stood in a crowded group at the door.

Opening the Bible, Arthur Pugh stood on the grey rug in the centre of the crowded room. Matthew took Ellen's hand. There was no need for a voice for these words, which were already deep in memory. A time to cast away stone, and a time to gather stones together; a time to embrace, and a time to refrain from embracing; a time to get and a time to lose; a time to keep, and a time to cast away; a time to rend, and a time to sew; a time to keep silence and a time to speak.

The slow voice continued, and Matthew looked round this crowded yet still ordinary room. He looked at the clock and the ornaments on the sideboard; at the cushions; at the pile of papers, in the brass stand; at the coal scuttle, the few books, the writing-desk. Each familiar object remained obstinately itself, and relevant, though it was never for this that this room had been furnished. All go unto one place; all are of the dust, and all turn to dust again. Who knoweth the spirit of man that goeth upward, and the spirit of the beast that goeth downward to the earth? Wherefore I perceive that there is nothing better than that a man should rejoice in his own works, for that is his portion; for who shall bring him to see what shall be after him?

Arthur Pugh looked at Matthew, who turned and helped Ellen up.

The men at the door moved quietly aside, and they walked out to the lane. Morgan held the door of his car open, and they got in. As they left the patch, Matthew felt a sudden wrench in his body, that seemed to come from outside him, as if it were not his own pain.

Briefly closing his eyes, he saw again the black parallel lines of the wheels of the cart. The hearse drove very slowly, immediately in front, and there was nowhere to look but at the coffin and the heaped flowers.

At the road, the procession turned left, and Matthew thought there was a mistake. That way, he remembered Harry saying, but the turn was only to drive through the village before finally to the north. In each house that they passed the curtains had been drawn, and at various places along the road people stood waiting for the cars to go by. As they passed the station, Matthew looked down at the box. The signalman stood at the open window, his arms resting on the bar, looking up at the bridge. Then they were moving along the old road, under the wall of the mountains. Slowly the speed was increased, and the cars strung out. When they crossed the river, the feeling had changed.

The final ceremony was simple. They stood in the chapel of the crematorium, while Pugh read the burial service. At the committal the dark blue curtains drew slowly across, hiding the coffin. There was a low, rolling noise, for no more than a moment, and the service continued to its end. They walked quietly out, into the sun.

They were on a hill, from which they could see over the fields to the valley and the mountains. Matthew stayed with Ellen, but then she went to speak to the bearers, and he was alone for a moment. He looked back at the main building, and at its tall chimney. A pale column of smoke rose quietly into the clear air, and the sunlight caught it before it disappeared.

CHAPTER THREE

1

For thirty miles he had been able to look back at the mountains, at the blue peaks and the long grey ridge, gradually lowering in the sky. Now, when the last contact had gone, he looked out at a different country, flat and open. The spring daylight had a hard bright clarity, which the growth of the land was not yet rich enough to absorb. The hop-fields were desolate, the poles and wires skeletal above the trampled and tyre-marked earth. On the ploughland rainwater lay in the furrows, making regular shallow ditches. The deep red earth of one field gave place to floodwater, over the long, flat meadows. On the occasional higher ground, a waterwheel, a kiln, a timbered church-tower, stood up as landmarks, in a drenched country. Then suddenly in the orchards the trees were in blossom, although the grass under them was still old and faded. Beyond the orchards, the woods closed on the line, and rose above it. Some trees, especially the ashes, were still bare and grey, and the bright green of the leafing trees was still a thin mist, through which the dark branches remained visible. Then suddenly the embankment was yellow with primroses, and the soft rich yellow ran out along the banks, above the fields which were empty and lifeless.

He stared out, knowing this country rich and fertile. Here were the big farms, the country houses, the crowded English villages. It was all very different from the scattered white houses, the small farms straggling to the grey stone walls on the mountains, of his own place. This was the country between the two cathedrals, and beyond the cathedrals was the world he was going back to.

The train filled up through the heart of England. The towns and the villages were larger now, the cars bigger, the country houses more frequent. Slowly, over the long journey, a different world was absorbed. Beyond Oxford the new emphasis was evident: different people, different books, in the compartment; different clothes, different voices; and from the window the by-pass roads, the housing estates, the factories; the sharp primary colours of advertisement hoardings and petrol stations. Glynmawr, now, had gone back to a memory and an image. In the overheat of the train, he felt slightly feverish, but the reality of what he was going back to was clear.

At Paddington he stood with his case, in the crowded corridor. Little time was gained, with this anxious queueing to get out, but still it was right: a conscious entry into a new atmosphere. He could smell the smoke now, through the windows that had been opened for the quick debouch to the platform. Soon he was walking briskly through the luggage-laden crowds, already attuned. Really, perhaps, we are all country people come to London, but none of us look it. There isn't, hurrying through, that much difference between people. Anyway we all seem to know where we're going, and that we haven't much time. What does it matter, now, where we come from? Here the past is very quickly left behind, like the train already taken over by the cleaners and the shunting crew. A gap in the crowd; hurry through.

He made his way to the Underground, and ran for his train as the doors were about to close. The long compartment was crowded, and he was standing facing a boy and girl in their teens. They stood, almost pressed against him, but not quite touching him, except occasionally with elbow or shoe. The touches were not noticed, not acknowledged. Inches from him, they held hands, tightly in their island of the crowd. The girl seemed withdrawn and content, but the boy was tense and self-conscious. After a while they talked, turning their heads to each other and whispering, until at the fourth station they got out. Now, as the train moved on, he stood in relative space.

Alone and self-conscious, he collected the slow looks which he knew from this kind of journey. You do not look often when the other can see you, though sometimes the stare is frank. But you look, with a sharp, temporary attention, this way and that, at this person and that. When you are young you suppose the looks are at you, and you will indeed have been looked at, with apparent care, by most of the others. But you know the habit of your own looking, the restless, intermittent examination, the subdued fever, the taut surface of temporary contacts, until the doors open at your own station.

It was a long way out, and the train emptied. He got a seat at last, and sat with his eyes closed, admitting his tiredness. Then at the station he got up briskly (the mechanical look at each name, and then the sudden impetus) and moved at once into the sharp, hurrying walk. He got out into the street, and walked home in the gathering dusk that was pointed by the lamps.

2

The wooden gate scuffed on the sharp-edged concrete path. The roses along the path to the door were shooting vigorously, in pale bronze curling stalks, although they had not been pruned and there were still blackened hips and yellow sapless wood at the top of the main stems. The roller, on its patch of starved yellow grass, was rusting a little. The sandpit, under the window, had been newly dug over.

As he closed the front door, in the settling silence, the living-room door was thrown open and the boys and the dog rushed out to him. He dropped his case, and bent over the boys, then led them to the living-room where Susan was waiting. She stood quite still, with her back to the fire. Over the shouts of the children they looked at each other, carefully, as always when they had been separated. It seemed a great distance as, still in his coat, and with the boys on each side of him, he walked to the fire. The dog still jumped excitedly around his feet.

The boys stayed up late, because Matthew had come home. They had so much of their own to tell him that there were no gaps for memory or for conscious adjustment. Glynmawr, to them, was a name, a holiday in the country, no part of their ordinary world. They had been told of their grandfather's death, but they seemed hardly conscious of it. They had waited only for their father to come home.

'We've been training Rex, Dad. Only he's slow learning.'

'He's still young.'

'What's in that box?'

'Open it if you like.'

'No, tell me.'

'It's honey. Glynmawr honey.'

'Is that like ordinary honey?'

'Yes. That's just where it comes from.'

Susan brought in a meal from the kitchen: beer, ham, salad, guavas.

'Come on, boys. I'll see you into bed while Matthew eats his food.'

'No,' Jack said. 'Can't we stay?'

'Yes, let them stay,' Matthew said. He was glad to feel them close to him, after so long and lonely a silence. Susan watched them, smiling, though once or twice in the rush of talk he saw her looking carefully at him, with a hint of uncertainty.

'Right then, now bed,' he said, as the meal was finished, and they all went to the bathroom and along to the boys' bedroom. Then Matthew and Susan walked slowly downstairs. They stayed very close to each other, but said little. Back by the fire, he went through the pile of letters that had accumulated. Susan sat opposite him, watching as he read. He made two piles of paper at his feet: one very small, of the papers to be kept; the other of all that had been quickly read and discarded. She smiled, still watching him, as he dropped on his knee by the fire and burned most of the papers.

'This is unusually ruthless.'

'Aye, I suppose.'

'It's as if you're still on the phone, Matthew. It hasn't faded.'

'What?'

'The voice, I meant, but it isn't only the voice.'

'It feels more. Doesn't it?'

Susan did not answer, and for some time they were silent.

'You're tired,' Susan said at last.

'Yes. Though in another way less tired. It really is what Morgan said: putting your own life in question. But in the end it came clear. I can feel it, though I don't understand it.'

'Isn't it just that it forced your love into the open?'

'Yes. Though I check at the word. It wasn't only love, I can see that. He was so very strong that there was bound to be the other. I think he knew that, when he talked to me about his father.'

'Because he was strong he could accept it, even help you with it.'

'It seemed like taking his life, though. For that, in the end, was what I most felt: that I was stronger, as he was dying.'

'He gave you that strength.'

'He gave me my life, but I watched him so often: he didn't want to give up his strength. And this strength that I feel, is it anything to be glad of? They wait in the margin, telling me I am glad my father is dead.'

'No, Matthew.'

'I don't want to believe it. But can we ever be sure?'

'I've seen you together. It was very open between you.'

'That isn't the point. We had to reach some agreement. But have you thought what it means, to replace a father? It can mean so many things.'

'In its deep meaning it is right.'

'What? To take what is his?'

'No, to take what he has given you.'

'I'm looking at it this way,' Matthew said. 'I've always thought he was good. My whole sense of value has been that. And since I left home I've watched other people living, and I've become more certain.'

'You don't have to prove it,' Susan said. 'If you believe it you'll live it.'

He got up, and moved away across the room. Susan watched him carefully. It was true what he had said: that he was evidently stronger, that certain energies were released. There was a difference of physical presence, that she had felt at once before anything was said.

He smiled as he looked back at her. Her face was very open, very young still, under the thick yellow hair. She seemed quite defenceless, in the openness of her face, the retained simplicity of expression, but the strength was there, the certainty of identity, in a way he had only rarely encountered.

'It was as if I stared straight at the sun. A sun that was blinding me, as I was learning to see. I had stared as a child, almost destroying my sight. And I was staring again, at the same centre.'

'Now? In these last days.'

'Yes. In these last days. And Glynmawr station is closing, but I remember when I first left there, and watched the valley from the train. In a way, I've only just finished that journey.'

'It was bound to be a difficult journey.'

'Yes, certainly. Only now it seems like the end of exile. Not going back, but the feeling of exile ending. For the distance is measured, and that is what matters. By measuring the distance, we come home.'

3

He went round the house, seeing to the doors and the fire. As he walked upstairs, he was winding his watch, but his eyes were distant and clouded, as Harry's had been, standing in the living-room in Glynmawr. At the boys' bedroom he hesitated, then went in, switching on the shaded light. The beds were drawn close together, so that they could play across them. Harry's book lay open on his pillow, but his sleep was easy and relaxed. Jack, as always, lay bunched on the pillow, frowning under his mop of hair. Quickly, Matthew bent and kissed them lightly on the smooth fine skin of their temples, but even at this touch they moved a little, in the warmth of their sleep.

Foreword by Dai Smith

Dai Smith holds the Raymond Williams Chair in the Cultural History of Wales at the University of Wales, Swansea. His publications include *Aneurin Bevan and the World of South Wales* (1993) and *Wales: A Question for History* (1998).

Cover image by Charles Burton

Charles Burton was born in the Rhondda in 1929 and painted *Little Train* in 1948. He is one of Wales' foremost artists from a remarkable generation of post-1945 painters, and is collected, by individuals and institutions, internationally.

LIBRARY OF WALES

The Library of Wales is a Welsh Government project designed to ensure that all of the rich and extensive literature of Wales which has been written in English will now be made available to readers in and beyond Wales. Sustaining this wider literary heritage is understood by the Welsh Government to be a key component in creating and disseminating an ongoing sense of modern Welsh culture and history for the future Wales which is now emerging from contemporary society. Through these texts, until now unavailable or out-of-print or merely forgotten, the Library of Wales will bring back into play the voices and actions of the human experience that has made us, in all our complexity, a Welsh people.

The Library of Wales will include prose as well as poetry, essays as well as fiction, anthologies as well as memoirs, drama as well as journalism. It will complement the names and texts that are already in the public domain and seek to include the best of Welsh writing in English, as well as to showcase what has been unjustly neglected. No boundaries will limit the ambition of the Library of Wales to open up the borders that have denied some of our best writers a presence in a future Wales. The Library of Wales has been created with that Wales in mind: a young country not afraid to remember what it might yet become.

Dai Smith

LIBRARY OF WALES
FUNDED BY

CYNGOR LLYFRAU CYMRU
WELSH BOOKS COUNCIL

WWW.THELIBRARYOFWALES.COM